PRAISE FOR

ANGELA JACKSON-BROWN

"This is a harrowing novel about the push and pull of fidelity, family, and faith under the crush of history. Angela Jackson-Brown has written a deeply emotional novel that feels timeless while also speaking to the particularly troubled times in which we live."

—WILEY CASH, *New York Times* bestselling author
of *When Ghosts Come Home*, for *Homeward*

"[*The Light Always Breaks*] skillfully tackles romance, religion, and race relations in a tale that will appeal to readers who enjoyed *The Personal Librarian* (2021), *The Vanishing Half* (2020), and *Black Bottom Saints* (2020)."

—BOOKLIST

"Angela Jackson-Brown's reputation for digging deep and going wide at the same time continues to reward readers. Thoughtfully portrayed characters with deep minds and passionate hearts make *The Light Always Breaks* a memorable story that leaps off the page. You can see it, hear it, and feel it in your marrow. Hard and necessary truths are addressed, and as an avid reader of both historical fiction and historical romance, I found this novel struck a refreshing balance between the two. I highly recommend it."

—RHONDA MCKNIGHT, award-winning
author of *The Thing About Home*

"Jackson-Brown paints a vivid picture of family and community persevering in the pressure cooker of the Deep South. Readers will be drawn to Opal's intelligent and authentic voice, as the book confronts issues of racism, injustice, and white privilege head-on.

This is a powerful Own Voices contribution to the historical fiction genre, joining titles such as Alka Joshi's *The Henna Artist* and Kim Michele Richardson's *The Book Woman of Troublesome Creek* in their unflinching look at the past."

—*LIBRARY JOURNAL*, starred review,
for *When Stars Rain Down*

"*When Stars Rain Down* is a book with religious themes, but if that's not your preference, don't let that stop you. The writing is beautiful, the story compelling, the characters vividly drawn, and religion is a backdrop, not the main story. Opal's voice is pitch-perfect, and the plot has enough surprises to keep you turning pages late into the night. I give this book a whole-hearted thumbs up."

—HISTORICAL NOVEL SOCIETY

"*When Stars Rain Down* is so powerful, timely, and compelling that sometimes I found myself holding my breath while reading it. Rarely have I been so attached to characters and felt so transported to a time and place. This is an important and beautifully written must-read of a novel. Opal is a character I will never forget."

—SILAS HOUSE, author of *Southernmost*

"All in all, *When Stars Rain Down* is worthy of any reader's attention—especially fans of Southern literature. The writing is eloquent, the story is filled with conflict and tension balanced by warmth and charity, the characters are vivid and well-developed, and the impact is profound. This is the kind of book that will resonate long after the last pages are read."

—SOUTHERN LITERARY REVIEW

"Angela Jackson-Brown is a writer to watch . . . Along the way, [Jackson-Brown] deals with a series of issues: racism, teenage love, the death of our elders. These issues are not just talked through. Jackson-Brown the dramatist presents them in a series of carefully crafted scenes, almost one-act plays. Once in a while, one reads a novel and can already see the film to be made from it."

—DON NOBLE, Alabama Public Radio,
for *When Stars Rain Down*

"In this world there are writers and there are artists. Angela Jackson-Brown is both."

—SEAN DIETRICH (SEAN OF THE SOUTH),
author of *The Incredible Winston Browne*

"Angela Jackson-Brown interrogates race, love, and family with empathy and style, making her an author you will want to read again and again. This tale of America's tragic past is both compelling and cinematic as the Pruitt and Ketchum families struggle in the mire of racism in the 1930s. It's a moving novel that boldly illuminates the past but also speaks directly to today's politics and the power of faith. You will fall in love with the book's resilient protagonist, Opal. I certainly did."

—CRYSTAL WILKINSON, author of *The Birds of Opulence*, for *When Stars Rain Down*

HOMEWARD

ALSO BY

ANGELA JACKSON-BROWN

FICTION
The Light Always Breaks
When Stars Rain Down
Drinking from a Bitter Cup

POETRY
House Repairs

HOMEWARD

A Novel

Angela Jackson-Brown

HARPER MUSE

Homeward

Published by Harper Muse, an imprint of HarperCollins Focus LLC.

Scripture quotations are taken from the King James Version. Public domain.

This book is a work of fiction. The characters, incidents, and dialogue are drawn from the author's imagination and are not to be construed as real. Any resemblance to actual events or persons, living or dead, is entirely coincidental.

Any internet addresses (websites, blogs, etc.) in this book are offered as a resource. They are not intended in any way to be or imply an endorsement by HarperCollins Focus LLC, nor does HarperCollins Focus LLC vouch for the content of these sites for the life of this book.

ISBN 978-1-4002-4110-1 (trade paper)
ISBN 978-1-4002-4111-8 (epub)
ISBN 978-1-4002-4112-5 (audio download)

Library of Congress Cataloging-in-Publication Data
Names: Jackson-Brown, Angela, 1968- author.
Title: Homeward: a novel / Angela Jackson-Brown.
Description: [Nashville] : Harper Muse, [2023] | Summary: "Homeward
    follows Rose's path toward self-discovery and growth as she becomes
    involved in the Civil Rights Movement, finally becoming the woman she has
    always dreamed of being"—Provided by publisher.
Identifiers: LCCN 2023021524 (print) | LCCN 2023021525 (ebook) | ISBN
  9781400241101 (trade paper) | ISBN 9781400241118 (epub) | ISBN
  9781400241125 (audio download)
Subjects: LCSH: Self-realization in women--Fiction. | Civil rights
  movements--Fiction. | LCGFT: Novels.
Classification: LCC PS3610.A355526 H66 2023 (print) | LCC PS3610.
  A355526
  (ebook) | DDC 813/.6--dc23/eng/20230508
LC record available at https://lccn.loc.gov/2023021524
LC ebook record available at https://lccn.loc.gov/2023021525

Printed in the United States of America

23 24 25 26 27 LBC 5 4 3 2 1

This book is dedicated to two warriors who never give up, my nephew, R.J. Sanders, and my friend, SE Lowe. The two of you are the definition of courage, and I am honored to know you both.

CHAPTER 1

SITTING ON THE PORCH WITH MY BABY SISTER, ELLENA, WAS ALways the best way for me to clear my mind. When she and I were young girls, we would sit out here and talk about everything. Clothes. Boys. What we wanted to be when we grew up. You name it and we talked about it. Every little thing that ever happened to me in life got resolved on the front porch swing, sitting next to my sister. No matter how big the problem might be, within a few minutes of talking and swinging, the two of us would figure it out. We have an older sister, Katie Bell, and three older brothers—Lawrence and the twins, Micah and Mitchell—but Ellena and I were always "thick as thieves," as Mama would call it. Ellena's spirit spoke to mine, and vice versa. I didn't remember when she was born, but I remembered everybody always saying on the day she took her first breath outside Mama's belly, I pulled her close and said, "Mine."

Ellena was two years younger than me, but she carried a wisdom about her much like Mama's and our daddy's mama, Grandma Perkins. Ellena wanted to be a judge someday, and when we were children, she would hold imaginary court and solve everything from who got the biggest piece of sweet-potato pie to who got to be the pitcher when we would all get together with the cousins and play baseball. But now, I had a problem so big, I wasn't sure whether anybody short of God could fix it. I was twenty-one years old, and right now, it felt like my life was crashing down right in front of me, and there was nothing I could do to stop it. Mainly because I caused the crash.

"What are you going to do, Rose?" Ellena finally asked, interrupting my thoughts. It was a rare thing for Ellena to lead with a question instead of an answer, but after I told her my awful truth, she had no words of wisdom. That scared me. If Ellena didn't have a solution, I didn't know how I would figure this out.

"I don't know." I rubbed my swollen belly. I was pregnant with a baby that didn't belong to my husband, Jasper. Two months ago, Jasper had come home on medical leave after injuring his leg while serving in the Air Force, and he found me like this—pregnant. I was four months when he got home; now I'm six. I had managed to spoil everything that had been right between us over one night. One stupid, dumb night. Jasper had asked if somebody had done this to me against my will. As bad as that was, I could tell he was halfway hoping that I had been taken advantage of instead of willfully committing adultery against him. I shook my head no as tears rolled down my face.

If Jasper had yelled or screamed at me, I would have been better able to respond. Mama always said I had a feisty mouth, so if he had come at me with harsh words, I would have been ready to fight back. He didn't. He just looked at me with sad eyes and started to cry. Every day for two months, that was what he did. Cried and begged me to tell him why I did it. Cried and said he would love this baby no matter what. Finally, I couldn't take it no more. I got on the bus, and I came home to Parsons, Georgia, where I've been for three days. I didn't even tell him I was leaving. I crept out of the house while he was sleeping. I couldn't stay another day longer. I was too ashamed of myself. Up until he came home, I had hidden away in his mama's shack, making sure to stay out of eyesight of everyone as much as possible. As a result, I was able to lie and pretend to myself that this was all just going to go away. Even though it was the middle of the summer, I would wear a jacket to try to hide my shame when I was around Jasper's mother, but she had the same sad eyes as Jasper, so I knew she knew the truth. She never said a mumbling word to me about it though. She just kept hugging me and telling me everything would be all right. But it wasn't going to be all right. Not ever.

When I saw Jasper's eyes after he returned home, I realized how terrible a person I was. All I wanted to do was get out of Hattiesburg, Mississippi, and come to a place where I figured there would be no sad eyes. No hurt. No pain. Just my family. But like everything else, I didn't think it through. I hadn't told anybody that I was expecting, so when I got off that Greyhound bus with my waddle and my big belly, to say Mama and Daddy were stunned was putting it mildly. They weren't dumb. They could count the months. They tried to talk to me about it as soon as we got into the car, but I had cried so hard that they left it alone. Mama had looked at me with hurt and anger in her eyes, and it felt worse than any butt whipping I had ever gotten when I was a girl.

I closed my eyes and leaned my head against Ellena. Despite all the turmoil going on inside my mind, it was nice sitting outside with her again, enjoying the little bit of a breeze that was making its way to the porch where we sat swinging. It was the beginning of August, and the smell of peaches from the orchard was thick in the air. Back when I was a girl, me, Mama, my brothers, sisters, aunties, and cousins would all go down to the orchard and pick peaches for jellies, jams, and pies Mama would bake for Sunday dessert.

I missed those things when I got married to Jasper. There were no peach orchards where we lived. Just endless fields of cotton. Jasper Bourdon and I said "I do" before the peaches got ripe three years ago. At the time he worked on a train as a Pullman Porter. Whenever he had a layover in Parsons, he would come to my daddy's store, where I would be helping out. Daddy never let us out of his eyesight, but he liked Jasper. Said he reminded him of himself, minus the fiery temper Daddy used to have when he was Jasper's age. If Jasper had a long layover in Parsons, he would come over to the house in the evenings and sit on the porch with all of us, laughing and talking until it was time for him to go to Sister Clementine Myrtle's Boarding House, where he would stay when he was in town. She was a church member at Little Bethel where we attended church, and it was the only place in town where Negroes could stay.

If Jasper happened to be around on Sundays, he would walk me to church, like Daddy used to do Mama. We lived in the house that Mama lived in with her grandma Birdie.

With the help of Mama's uncles, Daddy had added several rooms. Mama said it still felt like the home she grew up in, and seeing me and Jasper courting on the same porch that Daddy courted her on did her heart good.

I would feel so proud sitting beside Jasper in the pew of Little Bethel AME while he sang with passion for the Lord, even if slightly off-key. It was all so romantic. I fell hard for Jasper Bourdon, and he did the same. I told him all of my hopes and dreams, including my desire to become a nurse someday. But then we started talking about love, and I let my dream slip away. Jasper didn't ask me to give up on being a nurse, but neither one of us wanted to wait, so I convinced myself that being his wife was all I would ever need.

I never should have married him. I should have gone to nursing school like I had planned. Ellena would be returning to Atlanta soon, where she was a student at Spelman. I should have been going there with her instead of being in this awful mess. Mama and Daddy tried to talk me and Jasper into waiting, but we had one good reason after the other why we should marry as soon as possible. If I could go back in time and undo this mess I made, I would, starting with my saying "I do." I felt a tear roll down my face just as the front door opened and Mama walked outside. I quickly rubbed it away.

"Let me speak to your sister," Mama said. Before I could reach out and grab Ellena's hand, she jumped up with a quick "Yes, ma'am" and hurried inside. My one champion was gone. My sister, the lawyer in training, would not be there to plead my case. Now it was just me and Mama.

Mama sat on the swing beside me. She started rocking

it slowly, then she turned and looked me square in the eye. "You ready to talk now about this baby in your belly, Rose?"

All I wanted right now was to be still and sit here beside Mama. Telling my story to Ellena was one thing, but telling Mama . . . well, I would have rather stood before the Savior himself and confessed my sins than to tell them to Mama. My mama, Opal Pruitt Perkins, was the best person I knew. Her life had not been easy, but she never complained, and she always put everyone else ahead of herself. I wanted to be like Mama, but I had failed in every regard. The last thing I wanted to see in her eyes was disappointment.

"I said, are you ready to talk, Rose?" Mama asked again. This time her tone sounded like it used to when I would do something that made her mad, but she was trying to keep her voice calm so I wouldn't haul off and start crying. Even though I was twenty-one years old and a married, pregnant woman, Mama still could reduce me to tears.

I couldn't never stand for her nor Daddy to be mad at me when I was a girl. Mama used to say I was the worst *water-head* of all her six children. My siblings were all different in their own ways, but the one thing they all had in common was the fact that they coddled me about as much as Mama and Daddy did. And for most of our childhood, my youngest sister, Ellena, would bear the brunt of any punishment that rightfully should have come to me. "*It's easier taking a lickin' than to hear you whine and cry,*" she used to say. Suddenly, I was feeling bad for all the lickins she took on my behalf. I was feeling bad for everything. Grandma Perkins would say I was having a pity party; I suppose she would be right.

"Rose . . ." Mama said in a warning voice. I could tell her patience was near 'bout gone.

"No, ma'am. Can't say that I am ready to talk," I finally said. And I wasn't—ready, I mean, to talk about this baby or how I came to be pregnant with it.

I wanted to stay here close to Mama and not think about anything. I wanted to listen to the cicadas chirping in the trees and inhale the scent of Mama's shasta daisies that were in full bloom. I'd helped her plant them a few weeks before I married Jasper. Hard to believe that was three years ago. Felt like a lifetime had passed.

"Well, like it or not, Rose, we are gonna talk."

I was sure wishing for Daddy to make an appearance. Maybe he could distract Mama, and I could have one more blessed day of not having to talk to them about my shame. Nothing was going like I had planned in my head. I had sat in the back of that pee-smelling Greyhound bus for fifteen hours riding back to Parsons, Georgia, hoping I could bury my head in the sand and pretend like everything was as it should be. I couldn't believe how ignorant I was to everything.

"Rose—"

I shook my head. "Can't we just sit here? I'm tired, and—"

Mama looked at me with waiting eyes.

"I know you don't want to talk, Rose, but it's time. Past time. You are way big in the belly. Bigger than you oughta be with your man just now making his way back home from Vietnam. He's been calling and you ain't been answering. It's time for you to tell us what is going on."

I had begged and pleaded for Jasper not to join the Air Force, but he had gone ahead and done it anyway. A local crop duster had taught him how to fly a plane. He said maybe the Air Force would give him a chance too. I couldn't believe he would volunteer to go and put himself in harm's way and leave me all alone in Hattiesburg, Mississippi, with his mama. Everything that I had heard on the radio about Vietnam told me Jasper didn't have no business hopping up and volunteering. But he had made up his mind, and for the first time since we met, no amount of pleading from me made him change it.

"Rosie, I can't make no living for us on this white man's land," he had said one evening after coming in from a long day's work, his hair full of cotton, making him look like an old, tired, worn-out man. He and I lived in a little shack right beside his mama, Miss Ida Mae. Their living conditions had been a shock to me, considering he had boasted that he was a big-time farmer in Hattiesburg and, if I married him, my way of living wouldn't change one little bit. Daddy and Mama believed Jasper's promises to continue to treat me like a hothouse plant. I believed him too. Our wedding was as whirlwind as our courtship. Before I knew it, I was on the train with Jasper, heading to Hattiesburg. I hadn't even met his mama. We were so eager to say "I do" that we didn't give anyone time to say no or give his mama time to come to the wedding.

When we rode up to his house, he had begged me to forgive him and he had promised me that within a few months' time, he would turn things around. Well, after nearly three years, we were still poor as Job's turkey. I never told my family the truth. I was too ashamed. Whenever they would call, I would make up stories about how good things were, and if they said they wanted to come visit, I'd make up even more lies.

"*Jasper just spoils me so much,*" I would crow to whoever happened to call. "*I'm gonna need another closet for all these pretty frocks he keeps buying me . . . No, it's not a good time to visit right yet. Plus, we'll be home for the holidays. We'll see you then.*"

I knew where Jasper's desperation was stemming from the night he told me he was joining the Air Force. I looked at him that night and I saw the eyes of a man with no other options. A man who would rather stare down the barrel of a gun than to see the disappointment in my eyes anymore or hear me lie to my family one more time about how well we were doing. "*Rosie, what I'll make as a soldier will be more than enough to pay off what we owe Mr. Adler, and then we can move off his land and buy a farm of our own. I can be the man I promised you I would be.*"

I had cried and cried and begged and whined to no avail. "*You brought me all the way down here to Mississippi just to run off and leave me all alone? I ain't got nobody down here to look after me if you leave.*"

Jasper had tried to hug me, but I had pulled away. "*It won't be for long, Rosie. I promise. Just 'til I can see our way out of debt. I know I told you things were better than they were. I just didn't want to lose you. I tried getting back on with the Pullman Porters, but they letting folks go left and right. Just about all the ones left got decades of seniority. This the only way, baby. Plus, you'll have Mama. Y'all can keep each other company 'til I come back. This war*" *won't last long, and with me volunteering and all, I'll get a better position."*

Before I knew what had happened, Jasper had left. Almost as soon as he finished basic training, they sent him over to Vietnam. In his first letter to me, he said he was spraying herbicides in the forests. That didn't sound too bad to me. At least he wasn't taking bullet fire. When Mama and Daddy had called to check on me, I told them Jasper felt convicted by God to join the Air Force. If my parents understood nothing else, I knew that bit about him being "convicted" would be sufficient for them to accept his decision without too much pushback on their part. Both of them had told me to come back home, but I had said I needed to stay and help Jasper's mama with the farm, which was true. Granted, I wasn't a whole lot of help, but I saved her a few steps here and there. I so wish I had listened to Mama and Daddy and come home.

"Mama, I don't—" I stopped, dropped my head, not wanting to meet Mama's eyes. I didn't belong here with my mama, who was a good, wholesome Christian. Mama deserved daughters who brought her sunlight, not awful storm clouds like I was doing.

My tears fell in earnest. Mama watched me as I wiped them away with my handkerchief that had my married name initials "R. B." on them. My sister, Katie Bell, had hurriedly made them for me as a wedding present so I would have something when I went off with my husband on our wedding day.

"It's not Jasper's baby," I finally said. I should have felt relief letting go of this burden. Instead of feeling relief, I felt horrible, even more horrible than before.

Mama's expression didn't change. There was no surprise on her face. "I knew that baby couldn't be Jasper's. It didn't take a genius to figure that out. What happened? Did somebody ... hurt you?" There was that question again. It would have been so easy to say yes when Jasper asked and yes when she asked. But I couldn't add on to my sin with another lie.

"Mama, I ..." Before I could finish, I saw Daddy walking down the street toward home after putting in a long day at the store. If I weren't in the family way, I would have been there helping him. Daddy lost his arm when some horrible white folks from Parsons started shooting at the annual Founder's Day celebration before he and Mama got married. Mama's granny, Grandma Birdie, died that day too. She had raised Mama like she was her own when Mama's mama ran off. Daddy said Mama was never the same after Grandma Birdie died. Daddy and Mama saved enough money for him to take over the grocery store that used to belong to Great-Uncle Myron, Grandma Birdie's oldest son and my favorite of all my great-uncles.

I watched as Daddy tiredly made his way up the stairs to the porch. He had a car, but he usually preferred walking to work on sunny days. He said he was cooped up inside so much, he wanted every chance he could get to be outside. Some afternoons, Mama would walk up to the store so she could walk home with Daddy. He looked over at me and Mama once he was on the porch, and immediately the weariness left his face. Unlike Mama, Daddy was beginning to look his age. Her face was smooth as a baby's bottom; Daddy's face was creased with fine lines. Mama's waist-length hair was black as night; Daddy's hair was now more salt than pepper. But Mama said his spirit was as young as it had been that summer when they fell in love underneath the peach trees down the street.

"There's my girls," he said, smiling. "How y'all doing?"

Mama got up and went over to Daddy and hugged him tight. One thing about my parents, they were still in love even though they were close to their thirtieth wedding anniversary. Daddy looked at me with concern on his face.

"You okay, Pudd'n?" He looked over Mama's shoulder at me. I tried to speak, but the crying only got worse. I put my hand over my mouth to stifle my sobs.

"She's okay," Mama said, turning around so she could look at me sternly. "Pregnant women get that way sometimes. You go on inside and eat. I'll see about Rose. There's some leftover baked chicken, rice, and collard greens on the stove. The corn bread is in the oven. And there might be some of my lemon squares on the counter if you're good."

Daddy kissed Mama on the cheek. "You spoil me, pretty girl," he said, using his pet name for her.

"Long as I'm still your pretty girl, I reckon I'll keep right on spoiling you, Cedric Perkins."

Daddy went toward the door, but then he stopped and turned back around. "It's gonna be all right, Rose. I think your mama cried nine months straight with all of you youngins," he said, looking over at Mama with a grin on his face. "She got right back to being ornery again after she pushed y'all out though. You'll do the same."

"You," Mama said playfully. We both watched as he went inside. For a time, nothing could be heard but me hiccuping through my tears. Finally, Mama spoke again. "I ain't gonna be moved by all these tears, Rose. So you did this? Knowingly?" She came closer, stopping right in front of me.

I hung my head. "Yes, ma'am."

"Don't hang your head now. You weren't hanging your head when you were sleeping with a man who wasn't your husband," Mama whispered. Her voice was calm, but it cut like Daddy's pocketknife. "Get up and go tell your daddy you and me are going for a walk out to the peach orchard. I need to hear this story first. So you dry up them tears. If you old enough to make grown-up decisions, you old enough to deal with the aftermath. I can't believe a daughter of mine would behave in such a way."

I took my handkerchief and wiped my face. Then I got up and went inside to the kitchen where Daddy was fixing his plate.

Daddy looked at me and smiled and I nearly lost it again, but I was determined to do exactly as Mama had said. It was my fault that Mama was feeling disappointment and anger. I didn't have nobody to blame but myself.

Daddy doted on all of us children. He had always used a firm hand with us, but he was always fair. No matter what, Daddy loved us, and he was never ashamed to show it. When we were younger, Mama used to say two things to us when we were on our way to church or school or one of our cousin's homes: *"Don't shame the Lord, and don't shame your daddy."* I looked over at Daddy smiling at me with so much love, I thought my heart would break. *No tears,* I repeated in my head over and over. *No tears.*

"You ready to eat, little girl? I can fix you a plate."

I shook my head and tried my best to smile. "No thank you, Daddy. Mama said to tell you we were going to go for a walk."

"Okay, baby. Y'all be careful. It's hotter out there than it seems. You still a little thing, but you got a big belly. Daddy don't know if he could lift you with his one good arm if you got light-headed out there."

"We ain't going far," I said. "Just out to the peach orchard."

Daddy went to the table and put his plate down, and then he came over to me and hugged me. "I'm glad you home, little girl. Daddy missed you. All of your brothers and sisters are special to me, but you was always my baseball buddy. My shadow. I know your husband wants you with him, but I 'preciate him letting you visit with us for a spell. And I know you say you don't need no money, but if you do, you let me know. I don't care if my girls are married or not. If you ever need your daddy, all you got to do is call."

I nodded. I didn't trust myself to say anything outright. Daddy hugged me again, then went to the table and sat. I stood still as he blessed his food and then opened up the newspaper.

"The Giants are playing the Milwaukee Braves tonight," Daddy said without looking up. "You think Willie Mays is gonna have a good night?"

"Yes, sir, Daddy," I said, trying to sound enthusiastic. Growing up, I was always the one to listen to the baseball game at Daddy's feet, talking stats and players we both loved like Jackie Robinson, Ernie Banks, and Roy Campanella.

Up until the Negro League ended when I was about four or five, Daddy coached the McDonough Brown Thrashers. Daddy said since most of the good Negro players went to play in the white folks' league, there wasn't many folks willing to come see the second- and third-string players play, although Daddy swore they were every bit as good as any of the players in the white league. Daddy tried to get on with one of the white teams, but no one was interested in hiring a Negro man with a missing arm. But that rejection didn't stop Daddy's passion for the game of baseball. If there was a game on the radio, Daddy was always front and center.

"Hurry on back before the game starts."

"Yes, sir." I turned and walked back outside, where Mama stood waiting.

"Walk." She took my arm and led me down the stairs into the street that led toward the peach orchard.

"Mama, I . . ."

Mama stopped and turned toward me. "Not now, Rose. Wait until we are somewhere alone where I can yell at you at the top of my lungs without worrying about being heard."

I dropped my head but quickly lifted it back up. "Yes, ma'am."

She and I walked, waving and speaking to various people who were out and about, but we didn't stop. Mama kept us marching right along like two warriors off to do battle. Normally, I would be happy to take this walk with Mama so I could pick one of those delicious, juicy peaches, but today I felt only dread. Other than Jasper, I was finally going to tell the one whose opinion mattered to me the most. My mama.

CHAPTER 2

MAMA AND ME MADE OUR WAY TO THE BENCH MY TWIN BROTH-
ers had made for us to sit on when we went out to the orchard. The orchard belonged to all the Negro folks who
lived in Little Parsons. It used to be called Colored Town,
but through the years, folks stopped using that word so
much. Little Parsons became the name we all used to identify where the Negro folks lived.

"Tell me what happened, Rose."

"Mama, I don't—" I stopped. I saw the look on her face.
She was not going to allow me to get away with anything
but the truth. So I told her everything. I told her about Jasper
lying to me about his finances and the fine and stately home
he supposedly had waiting for us. I told her about how hard
he struggled to make ends meet and how he finally gave up
on farming and entered the Air Force.

"Why didn't you tell your daddy or me what was going
on, Rose?" Mama demanded. "Why would you lead us to
believe everything was just fine and dandy down there? We
would have helped you children. There was no reason for

16

you to struggle as long as your daddy and me have breath in our bodies."

"I couldn't say anything, Mama," I said, ducking my head. "I was ashamed. You tried to tell me to wait, but I didn't listen."

"Well, that explains part of the story." Mama remained steely. "Tell me the rest."

I continued to look down at the ground for a moment, then I raised my head and looked at Mama, finishing the story I had begun. "After Jasper left, I moved in with his mama. She and I talked, and we decided it didn't make sense for the house Jasper and I shared to stay empty, especially since we needed the money. Neither one of us was up for doing much farmwork, so we rented it out to the Negro schoolteacher, Mr. Bernard LeBlanc."

"A single man?"

"Yes, ma'am."

"Go on with your story." Mama folded her arms across her chest.

"Bernard . . . I mean, Mr. LeBlanc—"

Mama interrupted. "How old was this Mr. LeBlanc?"

"About thirty-five or so." I was just guessing. He never told me his age and I never asked, but somehow, that made everything seem even worse—that I didn't know much of anything about the man I willingly gave so much to in a moment of passion . . . or maybe desperation.

Mama clicked her teeth. "Rose, I . . . Lord have mercy. Girl, just go on and finish what you were saying."

I started again. "Mr. LeBlanc was very kind to me and Miss Ida Mae. He would check on us regularly, and he would bring us things like a mess of fish he caught down by the creek or books from his personal library that he thought I might like to read since we didn't have a television and our radio only worked half the time. Most nights he took his meals with us, making sure he gave us extra on his rent to cover the food. Miss Ida Mae would turn in early, leaving me and Mr. LeBlanc to ourselves." I tried not to let my mind wander back to those moments I shared with Bernard LeBlanc. I just told Mama the truth. All of it. From the kissing to finally, the lovemaking.

"So you started having relations with this man?" Mama snapped.

"Just once," I said hurriedly. "Just once. He and I . . . well . . . we . . . we did that one time and we both were so horrified. We didn't mean for it to happen."

"You said y'all kissed several nights. What did you think that was going to lead to, Rose?" Mama demanded. "Kissing is just the beginning of relations between a man and a woman. You had been married long enough to know that."

I nodded. I couldn't disagree with her. She was right. Everything she said was right.

"Where is this man now? Was he there when your husband returned?" Mama asked in a cold voice. I couldn't stand Mama sounding like that. It was like all feelings for me had left her spirit. I couldn't look at her.

"No, ma'am, he wasn't. The next morning, after we did what we did, Mr. LeBlanc left without leaving a forwarding address or explaining to anyone why he left so suddenly. That Sunday I cried before the altar for my sins, Mama. No one knew why I pled the blood of Jesus so hard that day. I didn't mean to do what I did, Mama. I promise you I didn't. I thought it was all over and done with, but then my monthly didn't show up. One month went by, then two, then three, and . . ." I could barely speak by this point, but Mama just kept looking at me like she was looking at a stranger.

"Jasper came home with an injured leg, and you were carrying another man's baby. What did he say to you? Was it his idea for you to come back home? Did he strike you?"

"No, ma'am." I cried. I couldn't have her thinking badly about Jasper. "He didn't want me to leave. He took the blame for all of this. He said his lies led to my waywardness. He said he didn't blame me. He said I was young, and he forgave me. He said he wanted to raise this child as his own."

"I don't condone the lying he did to get you down there, Rose, but your 'I do' should have sustained you. It should have kept you unsullied while your husband was away," she said. "What do you want to do, Rose?"

"Stay here with you and Daddy." There were a lot of things I didn't know, but this one thing I did. I didn't want to go back down to Hattiesburg, Mississippi. I didn't want to see Jasper's kind, sweet, forgiving face. I didn't want to live one more day in that broken-down shack of a house. I just wanted to stay in Little Parsons with my family and forget all of that ever happened.

"And what about your baby?"

I could see the sweat beading up above Mama's top lip and streaming down the sides of her face. Her headscarf was nearly soaking wet. I didn't know if it was the heat of the day or the heat of her rage that had her sweating so hard. I handed her my handkerchief. She wiped her face and continued to look at me expectantly. She wanted an answer to her question. Finally, I spoke.

"I would like to give it up," I said in a soft voice.

"Give it up," Mama repeated. "Give up your marriage?"

I shook my head. "No, ma'am. The baby. I would like to give up the baby."

Mama stood up from the bench, throwing the handkerchief in the spot she just got up from. "If you don't want to be married to Jasper anymore, that is one thing. But give up this baby? No, ma'am. You will *not* be allowed to shove your child off to some stranger. You will *not* be allowed to pretend like none of this happened. You will *not* give away a member of this family. As sure as the good Lord put this baby in your belly, it will not be tossed away like yesterday's newspaper. Do I make myself clear?"

I started crying again. "Mama, don't make me keep this baby. How can I love this baby knowing what I did to get it?"

"Ain't the baby's fault. The baby didn't do nothing to be punished for," Mama said. "You the sinner. You owe this baby your life if it comes down to it. I know what it's like to have a mama walk away without a second glance, and you will not do that. You will not."

I nearly groaned. I couldn't believe how insensitive I had been with my comment. How, in my selfishness, could I have forgotten Mama's story? Her own mother had left her when she was a baby, and she never heard word from her again. Great-Uncle Myron had done some digging when I was in high school, and he learned that Mama's mama had died in Detroit, Michigan, soon after she left Parsons. The records he found said she died in a knife fight. Mama always said it was good to finally know the truth. I know that pain wore at her like an open sore that would not heal, and here I was adding more pain to her hurt.

"Had you done what you promised the Lord you would do, you wouldn't be in this fix right now," Mama snapped. "You reap what you sow in this life, Rose. You know this. You were raised in the church. This baby is God's way of saying you are forgiven. The dirtiness of what you did will be cleansed by the birth of this child. But you can't run from it. Even if this baby were to end up on the other side of the earth, you would still have to reap what you sowed."

"Are we going to tell Daddy?" I dreaded the idea of seeing the look of hurt on my daddy's face. I would do anything to avoid that moment. I prayed Mama would just tell him herself. I should have known better.

"Oh no, ma'am. *We* are not going to tell Daddy anything," Mama said. "This is your bed, Rose. You are going to have to lay in it all by yourself. Telling your daddy is your responsibility, and I expect for it to happen the second we darken the door of our house. I needed to hear you say the words to me first. Now, you say those words to your daddy."

"Yes, ma'am."

"Come on then."

The walk back home was dreadful. No laughter or teasing. No chatting about the day. Just silence. When we got back to the porch, Daddy and my brother Lawrence were sitting outside talking. Lawrence was married to a sweet girl named Naomi, and they were the parents of six-year-old triplet boys named David, Daniel, and Demetrius. Lawrence was a doting father and an equally doting big brother. I didn't want him to know my shame, although I was sure he and everyone else had figured it out. When he said something the other day, Mama had mumbled that some women carried bigger than others. After that, he started calling me Biggun.

"Hey, Biggun," Lawrence teased as Mama and I walked onto the porch. "Hey, Mama. How you doing?"

Mama looked at me and then at Lawrence. "Fair to middlin', I suppose. Son, let's go inside and try out some of them lemon squares. That is, if your daddy left us any."

Daddy laughed. "Pretty girl, you know better than to leave me alone with your lemon squares, but I think there might be a piece of one left that y'all can share."

Lawrence got up but stopped beside me. "You okay, little sister?"

I nodded. I was trying my best not to cry again. He gave me a quick hug, then went inside with Mama. Daddy was gazing at me intently. Finally, he spoke.

"Come on over here and tell me what's wrong," he said in such a sweet, kind voice that I started crying as hard as I did that Sunday when I went to the altar to lay my sins in front of God. I sat beside Daddy and told him everything, just like I did with Mama. He said nothing throughout the entire story. I was afraid to look at his face when I was done. I didn't want to see the same disappointment and anger I saw on Mama's face. I couldn't believe I had allowed myself to be so selfish and unthoughtful. That lustful time I had spent with Bernard LeBlanc had done so much damage to so many innocent people. Finally, I looked up at Daddy and he was smiling at me. I wondered for a moment if he heard what I said.

"Daddy, did you hear me?" I asked softly.

Daddy took his clean, white handkerchief out of his pocket and handed it to me to wipe my face before he spoke. I did and waited for him to say something. I prayed it wouldn't be "depart from me, I never knew you," like it says in the Bible.

"Before I started dating your mama, I was a hothead. A real rascal," Daddy said, continuing to smile. "Your Grandma Perkins used to love saying she had prayed for the sins she knew I had committed already and the sins I was subject to do in the future. She said God had a book filled with just her prayers for me. So whenever I came to her or my daddy, God rest his soul, she would listen to what I said, and then she would say, 'I talked to God about that a long time ago.' You are forgiven and like the Bible says, 'Go, and sin no more.' Go and sin no more, daughter."

I laid my head on my daddy's shoulder and cried in earnest. Daddy wrapped his good arm around me and rocked me gently.

"Daddy, I am so sorry," I whispered. "I didn't mean for this to happen."

"Course not," he said. "I'm disappointed in the choices you made, Rose. You have always been my little heartbeat, but this was wrong. You did that boy wrong, and you did yourself and your family wrong. You will have to live with that for the rest of your life. For now, we need to figure out what you are going to do moving forward. The sin is never as much about the act itself but how we act after we sin."

"Daddy, I don't want to go back down there." I sat up and looked at him, trying my best not to start crying again. "That place is terrible. I've never seen anybody live like folks live down there. I just want to stay here at home where my family is." I didn't tell him the real reason I didn't want to go back. I didn't want to face the pain I had caused Jasper and his mama. Both of them had loved me the best they could, and I had slapped them in the face with this baby. I just didn't want to see them look at me with their sad eyes anymore. I just didn't think I could bear it.

Daddy looked at me with a serious expression on his face. "Then you are going to need to talk to your husband."

I didn't say anything. I didn't know what to say. My mind was a jumbled-up mess, and I didn't have a clue what to do. And of course, right then the baby started moving. Almost like it wanted to have something to say too.

"Did you hear me, Rose?" Daddy asked.

Before I could respond, Mama and Lawrence walked back outside. Mama sat on one of the porch chairs that faced the swing. Lawrence sat in the opposite chair.

"Daddy, you might as well have eaten them all," Lawrence said, chuckling loudly. "Now Mama is going to need to make a special batch just for me. Ain't that right, Mama?"

Mama and Daddy laughed. Normally I would too, but there was nothing in me that could make me laugh right now. I couldn't ever imagine laughing again.

"You will survive, son," Daddy teased.

"Y'all talked?" Mama asked, looking from me to Daddy.

"We talked," Daddy said.

"I told your brother," Mama said. I groaned.

"I'm not going to judge you," Lawrence said in a serious voice. Of all my siblings, he was the most pious. Everybody just knew Lawrence was going to be a preacher someday. Grandma Perkins had proclaimed as much to everyone: *"Someday he will be a preacher like his Grandpa Perkins."* So far, he hadn't made any movements in that direction, but he still gave some amazing spiritual counsel, whether we wanted it or not. "You should go talk to Grandma Perkins. She has always said she's prayed for every sin we could think to do and when we go to pray about it ourselves, the Lord has already done the labor to forgive us."

" 'It is already done,' " I said softly, repeating one of her favorite expressions.

Daddy and I looked at each other and smiled. We had always been such a tight-knit family that it was not surprising when we all ended up saying pretty much the same thing.

"I just might do that," I said. Grandma Perkins was getting on up in age. She still lived in the old home she once shared with our Grandpa Perkins, who died a couple years after Ellena was born. Everyone said he stayed long enough to see his final grandchild. Grandma Perkins was a stern grandma but also very loving. She also prayed a special prayer for each of her family members when we would come visit. Her prayer for me would always begin with *"God, thank you for this beautiful flower you blessed us with that we have named Rose. She has blossomed into a wonderful woman, and we ask that you nourish her with spiritual water and light so that she can continue to grow."* I tried to imagine what Grandma Perkins would say to me now. I imagined pretty much what Mama and Daddy and Lawrence had all said.

I knew I needed to talk to Jasper. He had called every day that I'd been here.

"I'm going to go inside and call Jasper," I said.

Daddy and Mama looked at me. Mama nodded. She still did not look at me like normal.

"We will be praying for you," Mama finally said.

"Thank you," I said and went into the house. There was a phone in the kitchen, so I went there to place my call. Jasper picked up after two short rings.

"Hello," he said.

"Hi, Jasper. It's me." All I wanted to do was hang up the phone and run away again, but the words Jasper said next nearly broke me in two.

He was quiet for a moment. For a second, I wondered if he had hung up, but then he spoke. "I want to come there where you are. I love you and I want my wife back."

I couldn't believe the words he was saying. Somehow, through it all, he still loved me. I could hear it in his voice even if he hadn't said the words, and it was almost too much to bear.

"I don't think that would be a good idea," I said. "It'll be better for you if I just stay here so you can find yourself a good wife down there. Somebody worthy of your love."

"What about the baby, Rosie?" he asked. "It ain't just about you and me now."

I could imagine his furrowed brow; his thick, calloused hands rubbing through his curly, black hair; his lips, plump and turned down. I could also imagine Miss Ida Mae, his mama, sitting in the corner hunched over in her chair while she chewed tobacco, spitting her juices into a Pepsi bottle. I could see all of it, and worse, I could see my future with him, and it scared me—almost as much as giving birth to this baby. For the first time since turning twenty-one, I didn't feel like an adult. I felt like a little girl trying to make grown-up decisions.

"Jasper, I don't know what to do. Please, just give me some time to figure things out."

"But . . ."

"Goodbye, Jasper," I said and lightly hung up the phone.

After I hung up, I stood there and cried. I had broken the heart of a good man, and I wasn't sure if there was ever going to be a way for me to make things right. I loved Jasper, but I just didn't see how we could fix what I had broken. Him coming here seemed like the absolute worst thing he could do. I knew I was being selfish and thoughtless, but I wanted to stay here at home where things made sense, and I wanted him in Hattiesburg. I guess what I really wanted was my old life back. Unfortunately, there was no way that old life would be mine to have again.

CHAPTER 3

I LOOKED ACROSS THE ROOM WHERE ELLENA NORMALLY SLEPT, but she had gone to spend the night with our sister, Katie Bell, in McDonough, Georgia. Katie Bell had given birth to a baby boy, Luther Jr., three months ago, and he was struggling with sleep, which meant Katie Bell and Luther Sr., her husband, weren't sleeping either. Ellena had offered to go spend the night with them so they could get a good night's rest. I was all alone in our room with my thoughts and emotions. I hadn't eaten a thing tonight. There was a lump in my throat that wouldn't let a morsel pass by. I tried to sit and listen to the ball game with Daddy, but my mind was all over the place and my stomach was in knots, so I just came on in the room and got in the bed.

It was stifling hot though, and it didn't take long for my gown to get soaking wet—partly because of the heat and partly because of my tossing and turning. The baby was moving around a lot too. Seemed like neither one of us could get any peace on this night. I just kept thinking about

Jasper wanting me back. The idea that he would try to love me after what I had done to him was unthinkable to me. My daddy was a godly man and so were my brothers and uncles, but I had never witnessed anything like this. Jasper was showing me what forgiveness looked like, and it made me even more ashamed because I didn't believe I would be that forgiving if he had done the same to me.

When it got to be close to midnight, I finally got up and slid down off the bed onto my knees. Grandma Perkins liked to say, *"If you can't rest, storm heaven with your prayers and God will send you some relief."* I prayed she was right as I pressed my damp forehead against the twisted sheets on my bed.

"God, I'm sorry. I'm sorry for being such a terrible person. I know I asked you to forgive me before, but I wasn't really asking you to forgive me for what I had done. Oh, I said the words, but really, I just wanted to pretend like nothing happened. I did wrong. I did wrong toward you and Jasper and this baby and everybody who loves me, and I am so very sorry." I felt a cry forming in my throat, but I put my hand over my mouth to stifle it and rocked myself until I felt calm again. I continued to pray, trying my best to "cast my burdens upon the Lord." I stayed on my knees until nearly one in the morning. I was so tired.

Finally, I lifted myself off the floor and walked over to open the window, praying a breeze might find its way to me. Then I climbed back into the bed. I had no more tears at that point. I was emotionally drained. I just wanted to go to sleep and escape all the thoughts that were causing my brain to hurt. I pulled back the sheet and light spread.

I touched my belly. Something I seldom did. The little cantaloupe-size belly felt strange since I had always had a flat stomach. "I will try to do right by you," I said to the baby inside. I had never had a kind word for it. I wondered if it could hear me.

The bed felt huge. Jasper and I shared a full-size bed at home, and this was a queen. For the first time in a long time, I wished for my husband. I closed my eyes, tears seeping out of my eyelids. "I'm sorry," I whispered just before I dozed off. My dreams had me restless all night. I kept dreaming that Jasper was trying to get to me, but something kept pushing him farther away. Every time he would call out to me, his voice would be fainter and fainter.

"Rosie," I heard a voice calling me from way off. "Rosie."

"Jasper," I said. "Jasper, I'm here. I'm here." The dream was so real. Hearing his voice was both comforting and distressing because I couldn't get to him. There was thick fog and everywhere I tried to turn felt like I was moving farther away from Jasper.

"Rosie, baby, it's me. Wake up," the voice said again, and this time he didn't sound far off. He sounded like he was right there. I opened my eyes and saw my husband sitting on the bed beside me.

"Jasper." I sat straight up in the bed. He was wearing his Air Force uniform and he had never looked so handsome. I wrapped my arms around him. "Oh, Jasper. I'm so sorry. I'm so sorry."

"You're not mad at me for coming here?" His voice was muffled as he sank his face into my hair, which was all over my head. I hadn't even bothered to tie it up before bed.

"No. I'm not mad at you. I never was mad at you. I was mad at myself, but I took it out on you." I cried. "Please forgive me. Please."

Jasper caressed my cheek. "Rosie, I forgive you. I already forgave you. Do you forgive me? For lying to you? That's how all of this got started. If I had just been honest with you. If I had trusted that you loved me."

I nodded. "I forgive you. I forgive you." I did. None of that mattered. I was just thankful to have Jasper holding me again. Wishing I could rewind the last few months and be his—only his.

He kissed me softly on my lips, and for the first time in a while, I kissed him back. It felt good. Just like I remember it feeling when we first kissed on the day we got married. Jasper had insisted that he didn't want to kiss me until I was his wife. It seemed a bit silly to me at the time, but on our wedding day, it made that moment so special. And to think, I let another man have what was only supposed to be between Jasper and me. I tried not to allow myself to be overwhelmed with shame, but I knew I would feel it until the day I took my last breath.

"What time is it?" I whispered. Jasper didn't answer me. I looked toward the window. Judging from the faint light of the moon, it wasn't quite daybreak. He gently pushed me back down onto the pillow. I watched as he took off his shoes. Then, he stood and removed his uniform and neatly laid it on the chair by the bed. "Where's your mama? Did you bring her with you?" I was confused and maybe still half asleep.

"She's staying with a cousin of hers in Mobile," he said.

"She's going to be there 'til we decide what to do. I didn't want you having to worry about taking care of Mama, you, and . . . and . . . the baby."

"I'm sorry," I said, not knowing what else to say.

"Don't." He slid into the bed beside me, pulled me close, and began stroking my belly. "Don't be sorry. Not no more. This is going to be our baby, Rosie. You hear me? This baby is going to be all ours. Do you understand what I'm saying?"

I didn't understand. I didn't understand at all, but I didn't say anything. I just watched as he bent down and kissed my belly. Then he looked back up at me.

"Will you let me love on you? I mean, let me make love to you so we can make this baby officially ours?" he asked, the words catching in his throat. I touched his face, and it was wet with tears.

"But, Jasper, I . . ."

"If I make love to you right now, in this moment, God will make this baby ours."

"Jasper, I . . ."

"Do you believe in miracles, Rosie?" he asked, his voice so solemn.

"Yes. Of course, but . . ."

Jasper interrupted me, his voice quiet but sure. "If Jesus could change water into wine, feed the five thousand, walk on water, and raise Lazarus from the dead, surely he can make this baby mine and yours. Do you believe that, Rose?"

"Yes," I whispered, my face now wet with tears too. "Yes, Jasper. I believe it."

Our lovemaking was sweeter than anything I had ever experienced. On the night of our wedding, we had been like two carried-away teenagers—groping and petting on each other, calling each other's names so loudly we were afraid somebody would hear us. This night, we took our time. Our lovemaking was calm and gentle and tender. Jasper kissed every part of my body, including my belly. He whispered sweet words of love to the baby that he said would now be ours. Jasper was making this baby his own, and I couldn't thank God enough for giving me another chance at love with my husband.

"Y'all kids better come on out. Breakfast is near 'bout ready," my daddy called from the door. My cheeks got hot. I looked at the clock. It was seven in the morning. I knew Daddy knew we were married, and I knew he knew married people did married people things, but somehow, the idea of him knowing what we might be doing behind closed doors had me feeling embarrassed. Then Jasper went ahead and made it worse.

"We'll be out there just as soon as I finish kissing on my wife, Mr. Perkins," Jasper called back. I heard laughter outside the door. It sounded like Mama and Grandma Perkins. I wanted to fall beneath the floor. Before I could chastise Jasper for being so forward, he reached over and pulled me close, kissing me like he had been doing off and on since he arrived. Suffice it to say, we did not get much, if any, sleep.

"Jasper, we got to stop." I moaned softly. "They gone know."

"They gone know I love myself some Rose Bourdon," he said with a laugh and commenced to kissing on me again. It didn't take long for me to forget everything. Mama. Daddy. Grandma. Everything except my husband. The man I loved and who loved me in spite of my shortcomings. I knew God could answer prayers, but I had no idea he could answer them like this.

Finally, Jasper tore his lips away from mine, nearly gasping for air. "We better get out there before I have my way with you again, wife."

Once again, my cheeks got warm.

"Rose, I need to say something before we go out there."

I looked up at him, afraid of the seriousness of his tone. I worried that he regretted everything, but the look of love in his eyes calmed my fears. Or at least most of them.

"Okay," I said, so soft I wondered if he heard me. He bent down and kissed me, brushing my hair so it fanned across the pillow.

"Last night when we made love, you and me made a baby. You understand what I'm saying? Last night, I put this baby into your belly. Me. Is that clear to you?"

I nodded tearfully.

"Good," he said with a smile, tilting my chin so I was looking him in the eyes. "Then we don't need to mention that other ever again. Not in this world nor the world to come."

"Yes, Jasper."

"Them tears is happy tears, ain't they?"

"Yes," I whispered.

Jasper began rubbing my belly and almost on cue, the baby kicked. He looked at me and grinned. "Was that . . . ?"

"Yes." I laughed for the first time in months, maybe years. I didn't even remember feeling this pure joy before, except on our wedding day. "That was the baby kicking."

"The baby knows I'm her daddy. Say it, Rosie. Say the words. Say, 'Last night, you and me made this baby.'"

"Last night, you and me made this baby," I said, wiping his tears with the back of my hand. This moment was so beautiful that I didn't want it to end. I knew things would still be hard, but we were going to be all right. That's what I told myself. I was going to try my hardest to not allow the dark thoughts to enter my mind again because Jasper and this baby deserved better than that.

Jasper smiled at me, his eyes still shining with tears. "I'm gonna be a daddy. You, this baby, and me is a family. And I only got one more thing to ask you to do for me." He looked at me with so much love in his eyes my heart didn't think it could hold it all.

"What's that?" I whispered, laying my head on his shoulder.

"I want you to give me a pretty little girl who looks just like you," he said with a huge grin. "I don't want no nappy-headed boy. I want our first baby to be a girl. You think you can do that?"

I started laughing. "I don't know. I'll try."

"Well, you try hard." He lifted my head from his shoulder and kissed me softly on my lips. "And every single day, I want you to dress her up in blue dresses. Pretty blue dresses with white lace."

"Blue?" I questioned, still laughing. "Boys wear the blue, Jasper. Girls wear the pink."

Jasper shook his head as he laughed. "Not my baby girl. She gonna wear blue for her daddy because that's my favorite color. Every day, she gone have on a pretty blue dress."

"Oh, Jasper. Yes," I said, smiling through the tears. "I promise you. The prettiest blue dresses you have ever seen. I'll get Mama to help me sew them. I promise."

"Good," he said. "Let's go before they all bust in here on us."

Reluctantly, I got up from the bed and quickly put on a house dress. Jasper put his Air Force uniform back on.

"Why you wearing that, Jasper?" I asked. "Put on some regular clothes."

"I gotta go back, Rosie," he said quietly.

I stopped. I felt like somebody had punched me hard in the stomach. "What you mean you got to go back? Go back where?"

"I got a letter saying I needed a doctor to tell them if my leg had healed or not. Well, I saw the doctor and he said my leg was healed enough for me to return to active duty. Air Force said I gotta report back in three weeks. I'll be going to Wolters Air Force Base in Texas."

"Did you find out all of that before I left?"

He nodded. "I didn't want to worry you. I knew you had a lot on your mind."

"Oh, Jasper." I rushed into his arms.

I felt like crying all over again and begging and pleading him to just ignore the letter, but I knew he needed me to be his wife and not a spoiled little girl. I made myself smile, even though all I wanted to do was cry out to God to fix this so me and Jasper could be together. I didn't though. I had asked enough of God for one night.

"Then we gone make these next three weeks the best ever," I said, reaching up and putting my hands on his cheeks. "I love you, Jasper Bourdon. With all of my heart. Me and your daughter gone be waiting right here when you come back home. Both of us wearing blue. I promise."

Jasper nodded and kissed me once more, then took my hand in his. We walked out to the living room where Mama, Daddy, and Grandma were sitting. They all looked up at us with smiles on their faces.

"There they come," Mama said, reaching over to grab Grandma's hand. They both looked at each other and smiled. I could just imagine the conversations the two of them had this morning.

Daddy looked from me to Jasper and finally he spoke. "Everything good with y'all?"

I looked up at Jasper, and he kissed the top of my head. "Yes, sir. Everything is good. I got a beautiful wife, and I'm 'bout to be a daddy. It can't get no better than that."

Daddy came over and shook hands with Jasper. "That's good, son. That's real good. Congratulations."

When Daddy said that, I knew he understood that me and Jasper had figured things out between us, and he was going to accept things just like Jasper was saying it. Mama got up and came over and hugged Jasper and me. I heard her say down-low, "You are a good man, Jasper. I couldn't want for a better son-in-law."

"Y'all children have made this old woman proud this

morning," Grandma Perkins said as she wiped tears from her eyes.

Daddy cleared his throat. "I got to get to the store soon, so let's go eat breakfast."

We went to the table and Daddy said the blessing, making sure to say how grateful he was for his daughter to be reunited with her husband.

I didn't eat much more today than I did yesterday. I was trying to soak everything in. Things being right between me and Jasper. Jasper having to go back to Vietnam or wherever the Air Force decided to send him. Me trying to wrap my brain around being a mama soon. It was a lot. In less than twenty-four hours, I was madly in love with my husband again, and he was willing to forgive me and love this baby. That was a whole lot, and it took up every space inside me that food would go, or at least that was how it felt.

Once we were done eating, Daddy stood up and looked over at me and Jasper.

"Why don't you young folks drive me to work today and y'all keep the car?" Daddy said. "Maybe go over to Katie Bell's and pick up Ellena. Y'all can go see a movie or eat out. Just be young folks."

I knew Daddy was in a good mood if he was offering us his car to drive. Didn't nobody drive that car but Daddy. It was a 1962 Chevrolet Impala. Daddy had bought it for cash off the showroom floor just a few months ago, and he babied it like it was his seventh child.

"Thank you, Mr. Perkins," Jasper said with a wide grin. "Y'all ready?" he asked, excitement in his voice.

"I got to get dressed, Jasper," I said, laughing. "I can't go out in this old house dress."

"You look fine to me." He looked at me like I was wearing an evening dress and crown on my head like those girls in the Miss America contest.

Everybody laughed. I gave Mama and Grandma Perkins kisses.

"Y'all children come by tonight when you get back. I'll have supper for you," Grandma Perkins said.

"Yes, ma'am." I got up from the kitchen table. "I'll hurry, Daddy."

I went back to the bedroom and looked through my closet for something to wear. My belly didn't make it easy on me. Suddenly, I didn't feel so good about going out. I couldn't embarrass Jasper by looking like somebody thrown away.

"Wear this," I heard a voice from the door say. I turned. It was Mama, and she was holding a beautiful, sleeveless, pleated dress. And it was blue! Jasper's favorite color. "I made it for you. I figured you would need something nice to wear for church."

"Oh, Mama." My eyes filled with tears. Even though Mama had been so angry and disappointed with me, she still was thinking about me enough to make me a dress. "When did you have time to make me a whole dress, Mama?" I held the dress up to me as I looked in the mirror.

"When I can't sleep, I sew. No matter what, you're my baby girl, and I love you." Mama pulled me into an embrace. I could feel the wetness on her cheeks.

"I will make you proud again, Mama," I whispered. "I promise."

Mama cleared her throat. "You and Jasper making up is all I could ask for. Now, let's get you all prettified for your husband."

Mama did my hair for me in a chignon, and then I hurried into the bathroom and washed off. When I put that dress on, I felt like a million dollars. Mama loaned me her Jackie Kennedy pillbox hat that matched the dress. Then she gave me a matching blue purse to carry.

"I feel like a movie star," I said, twirling around in my dress.

"Come on," Daddy called out from outside the door. "Y'all gonna have me late."

I looked at Mama and she nodded with approval. We walked out arm in arm. Jasper was sitting at the table with Daddy and Grandma Perkins, but when he saw us, he stood, a huge grin on his face.

"My oh my," he said, coming over to me, slowly turning me around. "Don't you look mighty fine in this blue dress."

"Thank you," I said. "Mama made it for me."

"You look beautiful, baby," Daddy said, getting up. "Let's go. Time waits for no man. Mama, you want us to ride you by the house?"

"No," Grandma Perkins said, settling back in her chair. "I'll drink another cup of coffee with Opal and get Naomi to take me home. You children go ahead. Be careful though. I was reading in the papers that some mess happened over in Albany. Thirty-nine Negroes got put in jail for doing nothing more than praying. Lord have mercy. What is this world coming to?"

"They were doing more than praying, Mama," Daddy

said in a gruff voice. "They was protesting on private government property. It's that Dr. King and all them young rabble-rousers. They just need to settle down and work with the white folks who want to help us change things. Patience is what they need, not protests."

"I reckon Dr. King and them figure Negroes been patient enough, Mr. Perkins," Jasper said quietly. "Me and the other Negro soldiers serve right along with them white boys, taking the same gunfire they do, and yet, they still have the nerve to hurl ugly names at us. Then when we come home, we still have to sit in the back of the bus. I read about those Freedom Riders and the work they trying to do to integrate the buses and the lunch counters. I don't think that can happen too soon."

Daddy huffed, but he said nothing else about it. "Let's go, y'all." He kissed Mama and Grandma Perkins on the cheek. Jasper and I said our goodbyes and went outside where Daddy was waiting by the car. He handed Jasper the keys. "Go easy on her."

"Thank you, Mr. Perkins," Jasper said with a wide smile. Daddy got in the back seat, and Jasper opened the passenger door for me. Once everyone was settled, Jasper eased the car into the road, and we were on our way to downtown Parsons. "My oh my, this car shore does drive nice, Mr. Perkins. I 'spect I would be driving it around all the time if it was mine."

Daddy laughed. "You wouldn't feel that way if you were buying gas for her at thirty-one cents per gallon. This is a greedy girl, Jasper. A real greedy girl."

Jasper looked over at me and smiled. "When I get back,

I'm going to get us a nice car like this so I can take you and our daughter out in style."

"That would make me mighty proud," I said. "But you don't have to get a fancy car. You just need to come home. That will be a plenty."

"I'm going to do both," he said confidently. I prayed he was right. I didn't want to think about him getting hurt again or worse. But I decided to put all those thoughts behind me and just enjoy spending time with my husband. God had given us more time, and I planned on enjoying every second of it.

CHAPTER 4

"HOW ABOUT RUTH?" JASPER SAID LOUDLY, HIS HEAD RESTING on my lap. The stars were starting to shine bright in the sky as we sat out on the porch swing.

Mama and Daddy had gone to bed, and Ellena was back at school at Spelman, so it was just the two of us. We were trying to come up with baby names. Well, if the truth be told, we were trying to pretend like Jasper didn't have to leave in two days. I had never seen three weeks go by so fast. Jasper and I had taken long walks around Little Parsons. I showed him all of my favorite haunts since child-hood, including the graveyard where I would sit and visit with Grandpa Perkins, my daddy's daddy. I even introduced Jasper to Grandpa, something I failed to do when we first got together.

"This is Jasper," I'd said as we sat down beside Grandpa Perkins's grave. *"Jasper is a good man, and he loves me and this baby so much. You would love him too, Grandpa. I just know you would."*

At first, I wondered if Jasper would think my talking to

Grandpa Perkins was strange, but he jumped right in like it was the most normal thing on earth.

"Pleased to meet you, sir," he said in his most solemn voice. He reached over and tenderly stroked my cheek. *"Your granddaughter and this baby mean the world to me. I am grateful to God that I met her, and I promise I will take care of her as long as I have breath in my body."*

Jasper and I also made several trips over to Katie Bell's house and up to Atlanta to visit with Ellena. But time didn't stop, and before we knew it, it was almost time for Jasper to leave. Seemed like he had just come into my room and made this baby ours, and now we were trying to do everything we could to make time go by as slow as possible.

I wanted to cry, but I refused to let one more tear come from my eyes while Jasper was around. The only time I allowed myself to cry was when I was alone or if Ellena called. She would call me every morning before she went to class. Jasper would be out helping Lawrence with the chores on the farm while she and I talked—or rather, while I cried.

"God will protect Jasper," she would say. *"We're all praying for him. You mustn't worry. Remember when Grandma told Katie Bell to stop worrying or she would have an old-looking baby with a nervous condition?"*

We both laughed at that. Sometimes Grandma and her old wives' tales were spot-on, but other times they were so silly that we grandchildren would bring them up to make each other laugh.

Laughter was the key to everything in our family. If we could find the humor in things, we could find a way to push forward. So I smiled and laughed as Jasper and I discussed baby names.

"They'll call her Baby Ruth, like the candy bar," I said, trying to make a joke. "I don't like that name."

"Okay, how about Clara?"

This time, I couldn't stop the laughter from bubbling up. "You must think our baby is going to be born seventy-two years old, Jasper. That's a grandmama's name."

Jasper laughed too. "Every grandmama was a baby sometime. Clara is a good name." For a time we just sat, lost in our own thoughts. Every now and then he gave the swing a good push. There was a breeze blowing, and the air smelled like summer rain. It wasn't raining yet, but I could tell it was going to start soon. I loved being outside during a rain shower. It was the most relaxing thing ever. We children used to sleep on the porch on nights when it rained, only going inside if the winds got too high or the lightning was striking just a little too close to home. I felt myself almost drifting off to sleep when Jasper spoke again.

"What name do you like then?"

"I already told you," I said, stroking his hair. "I like Coretta, like Mrs. Coretta Scott King, and I like Pearl, like Miss Pearl Bailey."

"Girl," Jasper said, sitting up. "Those names 'bout as old-sounding as Clara."

"Then I guess we'll just call her Baby Girl, since neither one of us can agree on a name."

"I guess so," Jasper said, tickling me until I begged him to stop. He pulled me even closer as we rocked and listened to the sounds of Daddy's coon dogs, King and Jupiter, moving around the yard all restless-like. They would come to the edge of the porch, look up at us, and then make their way back out into the middle of the yard. They used to like to sit up under me before I got married and moved away, but now they just came and sniffed around me and then ran off, looking back at me like I was a stranger to them. They acted like they didn't really know me no more. It kinda hurt my feelings at first, but Mama said some dogs got that way around pregnant women.

"They'll be back to normal soon as you have this baby," she promised me the other morning.

"I'm going to miss you," I said to Jasper, something I had been saying for the entire three weeks. It was taking all that I had inside me to will the tears not to fall. "I am so proud of you, Jasper. You make a dashing soldier."

He laughed. "Hopefully, my dashing good looks will keep me safe."

"I'll be praying for you. So will Mama and Grandma, and their prayers always get up to heaven," I said confidently. My older brother had fallen out of a tree when we were younger, and Grandma had prayed over him. Seconds later, he hopped up, fine and dandy, instead of having a broken arm or leg like everyone feared. Grandma reminded everyone that like it says in the King James Bible, the "prayer of a righteous man availeth much." I reached for Jasper's hands, clasping them tightly, like my life depended on it. "Remember what I said, Jasper," I said, trying to keep the panic out of my voice. "I don't need you to be extra brave. I just need you to get back home to me and . . . and our baby."

Jasper pulled me close so that my back was toward him.

He loved rubbing my belly, so he reached underneath my shirt and began massaging it. He kissed me softly on my neck. "Don't you worry none about me. You just take care of yourself and our baby girl."

I leaned back against him. "And what if this baby is a boy? What then?" I had been thinking about that since we first made this baby ours. Jasper was so unwavering with his belief that the baby would be a girl, I worried how he might react if she was a he.

"Ain't gonna be a boy," he said so decisively you woulda thought he'd already seen the baby for himself. "I already told you what this baby is going to be—a pretty little girl who looks just like you."

At first when he would say that, I wondered did he want a girl because he was afraid if it was a boy it would look like Mr. LeBlanc. I had to confess, that scared me too, so I prayed extra hard every single night that this baby would be a girl who favored me. I didn't want Jasper to have to do no more extra work to love this baby. He had already done enough.

"We should go to bed," I said, even though all I wanted to do was to stay here in Jasper's arms. "Church is tomorrow." And church at Little Bethel was pretty much an all-day affair. We would have Sunday school at 10:00 a.m., morning service at eleven, and afternoon service at three o'clock. Depending on the day, sometimes it was evening before we got home, but nobody minded because church was home and everyone there was family. Usually, my family would come home to eat between services or go to Grandma Perkins's house. Tomorrow there would be dinner on the ground. All the women would bring covered dishes and we would all eat together. Everybody wanted to see Jasper before he left out, so we would stay there and eat together and show Jasper just how much he was loved, especially by my family.

"I know," he said, not stopping his massaging of my hips and belly. Once I told him how that seemed to relax the baby and me, he did it every time we were alone. "Let's stay up just a few more minutes."

"Okay." I sighed, not wanting our time together on the porch to end anytime soon either. Instead, I pointed to the brightest star in the sky. "Do you know what that star is called?"

"My mama said it was the Dog Star." He stroked my hair. "At school they called it Sirius."

"Mama said it's her grandma." I looked up at the sky as each star seemed to twinkle in agreement. "Mama said after her grandma Birdie got killed, she would show up as a star whenever Mama would get to missing her too bad or if she needed a sign to say that everything was going to be all right."

"If anything ever happens to me, I'll . . ."

I sat up, stopping the swing midmotion. "Don't say that, Jasper. Please don't say that."

Jasper leaned in toward me, but I pushed him away.

"You can't go over there planning for the worst. You just can't." I tried to keep my emotions from getting the best of me. It was like every single thing I was feeling was trying to bubble up all at once.

Jasper stroked my face with his index finger. "I plan on

coming back to you and this baby, Rosie, but if we don't talk about the what-ifs, then we are burying our heads in the sand, and I promised I would never do that with you again. Ever. We need to talk about this."

I knew he was right, but the thought of him not coming home hurt, even more than before, because I had seen what it looked like to almost lose Jasper. I didn't want to think about that ever again. But at the same time, I had to honor what he was saying. He and I had to be prepared for anything, including the worst possible outcome. "Okay," I whispered.

"I want you to enroll in nursing school, Rose. Soon as this baby is old enough for you to go. If I make it back home alive, we'll move where there's a school, but if for some reason I don't, I want you to do it still. This is your dream, and I don't want you to let anything keep you from it, especially not me," he said, his voice firm and unwavering. "I should have never let you give up on it before. I was just too afraid of losing you. But you following your dream is not you saying you don't want me in your life. I know that now."

"I don't know what to say," I finally said. The idea of going to school to be a nurse excited me beyond words. All my life I dreamed of taking care of the sick. If any of the animals on the farm got sick, I was always the one sitting with them through the night, nursing them back to health. If one of my siblings injured themselves, I was quick with the bandages and ointments Mama would make. The idea that Jasper wanted me to be a nurse made me happy beyond words.

Jasper put his hands on my shoulders. "I need you to

promise me, Rose. Promise me that no matter what, you'll follow your dreams."

"What about your dreams, Jasper?" I asked, realizing just then that he and I had never had such conversations as this before. We had talked about love, but we hadn't talked honestly about ourselves like we'd done the last few weeks. "What do you want to do when you get back home?"

Jasper went silent for a moment, like he was trying to think up an answer. I found it sad that anyone his age would not be able to see a future for himself. From the time my brothers and sisters and I were small children, Mama and Daddy would always tell us to discover our passion. Mama told us how she enjoyed cooking, cleaning, and sewing for people when she was younger, before we were born. *"There are no bad jobs. If you do an honest day's work, it doesn't matter if you are a lawyer, a doctor, a nurse, or a nanny or a housekeeper. All we want from you children is dedication and pride in what you do."*

I knew Jasper's mama had done the best she could raising him alone after his daddy died. I wished someone could have told him just how amazing he was. Finally, he looked at me with serious eyes. "I don't know, Rosie. Nobody ever asked me that question before. My whole life has been about making ends meet. After Daddy died when I was just a wee baby, it's been just me and Mama. Other than smelling the backside of a mule as I plowed somebody else's land, I never thought about doing anything different. When I got on as a Pullman Porter, that was the greatest job I'd ever done, but I couldn't do that forever. Not with Mama getting older and me being her only child."

I wanted to ask him, *So why did you join the military and take yourself so far away from your mama and me?* but I already knew the answer. He had run out of hope, and when a person didn't have hope, they couldn't see beyond what was right in front of them. That Air Force recruiter came to our little house and filled Jasper's head full of stories of heroism and money. That was all he needed to hear to sign on the dotted line.

"What about flying?" Even though the thought of Jasper flying made me nervous, I had to admit that I had never seen him so excited about anything as when he learned to fly those crop-dusting planes before he went into the Air Force. He didn't make no money doing it. He just liked being up in the clouds. And now he was going to an Air Force base in Texas that trained pilots. Again, I tried to quell my fears and focus on Jasper and what might make him happy. Probably for the first time in my life, I was focused on the happiness of someone other than myself. It felt good.

Jasper laughed. "That ain't a possibility, Rosie. Not really. I mean, the Air Force might let me fly for them eventually, if I stay in long enough, but after I get back home, then what? Ain't no jobs out here for Negro pilots."

I was grateful that we were back to talking about him getting home. "Well, you go and do what you have to do to get back home, and I'll do everything I can over here to fight for you to have the right to fly planes if that's what you want to do."

"What you mean?"

I looked around. Although I knew Mama and Daddy were in bed already, I still talked in a hushed tone. Just to be safe. I knew my words would rile them up something fierce. "Ellena has been working with the Student Nonviolent Coordinating Committee in Atlanta. They call themselves SNCC, like snick. She's been talking to me about things I can do here in Parsons to help our people. I haven't done anything yet, but maybe while you're gone, I can get involved."

"I don't know, Rosie. That doesn't sound safe. How did Ellena get involved with them?" he asked. "I wouldn't peg her as somebody who would raise a ruckus."

I smiled. Jasper didn't know my sister like I did. She had always been the first to fight for what she felt was right. This group of young folks were right up her alley. Plus, if the truth be known, I thought she might have a little crush on John Lewis, one of the founding members of SNCC. Every other word from her seemed to be, *"John said this"* or *"John said that."* She would always deny it when I brought it up, but I knew my sister. She was a bit smitten with the slow-talking man from Alabama. "It seems a lot of the Spelman students and students from other local schools have been volunteering. Ellena started the earlier part of the year and she's still helping them now."

"I'm guessing your folks don't know," he said as a statement, not a question.

"They don't know." I shook my head. "I tried talking her out of it for the longest. But the more she talked about what they do . . . It just feels right, Jasper. Why shouldn't Negroes fight for their rights?"

Jasper pulled me tight. "Just be careful. I don't want anything to happen to the mother of my baby."

I leaned back into his arms. "I will. And you don't let

anything happen to . . . to the father of my baby." It still felt awkward saying those words. I was happy that it was dark outside, and Jasper couldn't see my face. I wished I was as quick to forgive myself as he was. Every day, he reassured me that he loved me and forgave me, but every day I looked into his eyes, trying to find one hint that he wasn't telling me the truth. Every single time, love stared me back in the eye.

"We should get up and go to bed," he said, but he didn't move. While we were talking, a light rain began to fall. We could hear its soft taps on the tin roof. There was no rest like sleeping in a house with a tin roof. The dogs hurried underneath the porch where they normally stayed. He and I sat and rocked and enjoyed each other's company and touch.

"I talked to Mama earlier," he said.

"Why didn't you tell me? I would have loved to have said hello."

"I just needed to talk to her about where she was going to stay." Earlier this week, Jasper and I had talked about moving his mother here if she was willing.

"What did she say?" I was hoping she was open to moving here where both of us could have support.

"She said she is happy in Mobile with her cousin, but when the baby is due, she'll come here and stay for a few weeks."

"Okay." I tried to mask my disappointment. Just like I was able to rebuild my relationship with Jasper, I had hoped to do the same with his mother. She seemed at peace with the baby situation, but I wanted to be the daughter-in-law I had been too selfish to be before. I vowed to myself that I would show Mrs. Bourdon that I was trying to be a better person.

"All right," Jasper said, easing me aside and standing up and stretching. "Time to lay down, Rosie. Morning will be here before you know it."

And then the morning after that, he would be leaving me. I couldn't believe how time had flown so fast. Just as we were getting used to being together again, he had to go. I had so many things I wanted to say to him. Instead, I stood and took his outstretched hand.

"Okay." I tried to quell the fear I had been feeling since I heard he was leaving. I allowed my husband to lead me into the house as the rain fell heavier, almost like God was shedding tears too. I prayed they were not tears of sadness but tears of joy that my husband and I had truly become one for the first time since we said "I do."

CHAPTER 5

"I DON'T WANT YOU TO GO."

I sat on the bed, watching Jasper get dressed in his Air Force uniform. We had made love again when we woke up, and now Jasper was rushing to get ready so he could make it to the Greyhound bus stop on time. It felt so unfair that after all the things we had been through that had kept us apart, now that we were finally being honest with each other and falling in love all over again, he was going away and would be gone for God knew how long.

He walked over and sat beside me. "I don't want to go either, Rosie, but I don't want you to worry about me. I'm going to be careful and before you know it, this war will be over and all of us soldiers will be coming home, big-time war heroes, just like the soldiers during World War Two."

I kissed Jasper firmly on his lips. "I love you, Jasper. I'm just scared."

"I'm coming back to you, Rosie," he whispered, pulling me into his arms. "I will always come back to you now that you are back in my arms again. I promise."

I put my finger to his lips. "Don't promise. Don't make promises like that. Jasper, you don't go over there trying to be no hero. I don't need you to come home with a bunch of medals around your neck. I just need you to come home. You hear me? And if that means you hiding in a hole some-where 'til the danger is gone, then you do that, Jasper. You hide because coming home alive is all that matters to me. You understand?"

Jasper answered with a long, probing kiss. We might have ended up making love again had there not been a knock at the door.

"Yes?" I called out in a shaky voice.

"It's about time to go. Jasper don't need to miss his bus," my daddy called from the door. The other week when he called out to me and Jasper, there were nothing but smiles and giggles. Today we were more somber. God knew I felt like wailing at the top of my lungs but didn't because I didn't want Jasper to see me looking sad. I didn't know how long before we would see each other again, so I wanted to let his last memories of me to be smiles even though my heart was tearing apart. Yesterday after church, the entire family had come over to Grandma Perkins's house to say their good-byes to Jasper. We ate and laughed and played board games and then when everyone left, Jasper and I came back home to Mama and Daddy's house and sat on the porch, talking about our future plans.

"I've been thinking about what you said about me

flying," he said last night. *"Do you really think I could do it, Rosie?"*

"Absolutely," I said firmly. *"Anything you set your mind to do, you can do."*

"Well, when I get to the Air Force base, I'm going to talk to them about getting me into the pilot program. It may take a while to convince them, but the more I think about it, the more I like the idea of flying planes. I sure liked flying that crop duster for Mr. Samuel," he said, and I could tell by his voice that he was already lost somewhere in the clouds, floating around like a bird or something.

Now as I looked at him, all handsome and young, full of hopes and dreams for his and my future, all I wanted to do was get him to hide somewhere—maybe in Daddy's root cellar—until all the bad stuff in the world ended and there was no more need for soldiers. Of course, I knew as long as there were men in power, there would always be a need for soldiers. If women were presidents and leaders, we would never send our sons, husbands, uncles, and brothers off to war. We just wouldn't. But for some reason, men didn't have that same conviction.

Jasper got up from the bed and picked up his duffel bag. He reached for my hand. I was already dressed, wearing that same blue dress Mama made for me. I could tell that I was filling out more. Just a few weeks ago when I first wore the dress, it sort of hung on me. Now, my belly was protruding a bit more—not quite a watermelon but definitely larger than a cantaloupe like when Jasper first got here.

We walked out of the bedroom, hand in hand, and made our way to the kitchen. Mama was busy cooking, the whole house smelling like Thanksgiving or Christmas. She turned to us and smiled just as my brother Lawrence; his wife, Naomi; and their three sons, David, Daniel, and Demetrius, walked in. Directly behind them was Katie Bell, Luther Sr., and their son, L.J., who was being carried by Daddy. Grandma Perkins followed behind them. I missed my twin brothers, Micah and Mitchell, and my baby sister, Ellena, but it was so nice seeing everyone else all come together to say goodbye to Jasper. I looked at Jasper and he had a big grin on his face. He wasn't used to having a large family around him. It was always just him and his mama.

"Don't you go thinking we here for you, Jasper. We here for Mama's good cooking," Lawrence teased as Naomi playfully swatted him on his arm. She was a petite little thing, but she kept Lawrence on his toes.

"Don't you believe that for a minute, Jasper," she said. "Lawrence has been saying how much he is going to miss you. We're all going to miss you."

"That's the truth, son," Grandma Perkins said, coming over and giving both me and Jasper a hug.

"Y'all come on and sit down and eat y'all something," Mama said. "Jasper, since you won't be here with us for Thanksgiving, I figured I would make you my annual Thanksgiving breakfast."

The table was filled with every good breakfast food you could want. There was pumpkin bread; cranberry muffins; sticky buns; ham, tomato, and swiss quiche; pancakes; sausage and bacon; biscuits and gravy casserole; scrambled eggs; horseradish deviled eggs; skillet biscuits with cinnamon honey butter; and homemade grapefruit juice and orange juice. On Thanksgiving, the entire family, including the aunts, uncles, and cousins, would come over to our house for breakfast, and then we would go to Mama's Aunt Shimmy's house later that afternoon for Thanksgiving dinner.

This morning, it was just us. I looked around the table with tears in my eyes. I loved them all so much. Daddy said grace and then everybody started eating, talking, and laughing, trying to pretend like everything was normal. Trying to pretend like we wouldn't be saying goodbye to Jasper soon. Naomi reached over and patted my hand several times, and Katie Bell made sure she shared a smile with me. I knew they were trying to lift my spirits. Before too long, it was time to take Jasper to the bus station. Daddy and Mama were going to go with us. Everybody gathered outside and hugged Jasper before we drove off. He promised to send letters as soon as he got settled. He helped me into the front of Daddy's car and, once again, Daddy let Jasper drive.

I was wishing for the ride to last longer than it did, but it wasn't long before we had made it into the city of Parsons. It had grown a lot in the short time I was gone. There were two new department stores—Woolworth's and Rich's—and two restaurants that did not serve Negro folks—Daniel's Diner and City Café. Right before I moved away, two new family doctors opened up practices as well as a dentist.

We didn't go to many of the downtown stores because of how they treated Negro folks. Woolworth's in Atlanta had started serving Negroes at their lunch counter, but not the one here in Parsons. Grandma said Dr. King and all of them might be able to shut down segregation in other cities, but Parsons was going to have to be drug kicking and screaming. From what I could tell, she was right. Whites and Negroes were cordial with one another, but that was about it. No one challenged the way things were done, and everybody made peace with staying separate.

When Jasper pulled the car into the parking lot of the bus depot, I felt my heart tighten inside my chest. I didn't know what a heart attack felt like, but if it felt anything like what I was feeling, I didn't know how anybody could stand such pain. I could feel the tears threatening to fall, but I didn't want Jasper to have to remember me crying. I wanted him to see me as brave—the kind of woman a good man would fight to come home to. So I put on my brave face. Just as the bus pulled up, he was opening my door, but he didn't let me get out.

"This is good enough." He knelt in front of me. "I don't want you out in this heat."

Daddy had gotten out of the car and was getting Jasper's things out of the trunk. Mama got out too. I know she was trying to give us some privacy.

"I'm going to miss you," I said, trying my best to be brave. "And I am so proud of you, Jasper. I want to thank you for loving me in spite of my flaws. Thank you for forgiving me and giving me another chance to be a good wife. I promise I won't disappoint you."

He leaned in and kissed me. "You don't have to apologize anymore, Rosie. We're past that, remember? It's time for you to forgive yourself. Okay?"

I just nodded. I didn't know that such goodness could exist in one person.

Jasper placed his hands on my belly. "Don't you worry none about me. You just take care of yourself and our baby girl."

"I will."

He leaned in and kissed me hungrily on my lips. For a time, I forgot we were in the middle of Parsons with folks rushing back and forth around us. I just thought about this moment. When Jasper pulled away, I felt like the life had been sucked out of my body.

"I love you, Jasper Bourdon." My throat felt like it was about to close.

"I love you," he said. He got up, but then he knelt back down, his face serious again. "Rosie, if something happens to me, I want you to love again. I don't want you to spend your life grieving for me. Do you hear me?"

I shook my head. "Don't talk that way. Don't—"

"Promise me," he insisted. "I can't do what I need to do if I'm worried that you will give up on living and loving. So promise me. Please."

I couldn't say the words, so I just nodded. That seemed to satisfy him. He kissed me again, and his face looked more relaxed than I had seen it since he arrived in Parsons. I watched as he went behind the car where Mama and Daddy were standing and told them goodbye. Meanwhile, I was still trying to be brave so his last glimpse of me would not be of me being sad. At least not from the outside. On the inside, I felt like I was losing a piece of my soul.

As Daddy and Mama got back into the car, we sat and watched as Jasper went to the bus and gave the man the ticket. He then sat in the back of the bus in a seat facing us.

Because of a recent law, Negroes were allowed to sit where they wanted, but Jasper went straight to the back—out of habit, I reckoned.

It wasn't long before the bus began to leave the depot. Even though Jasper had said he didn't want me to get out of the car, I raised myself out of my seat and stood, waving at him as the bus went by. He caught a glimpse of me and waved back. When the bus was out of sight, I sat back down in the seat. Daddy helped Mama into the back seat and then he climbed in beside me.

"Mama, you want to get up front with Daddy?" I twisted around to face her. I knew I would shed tears later. Probably when I was on the phone with Ellena. But I did my best to keep them at bay for now.

"You stay where you are," Mama said. Then she reached from the back seat and placed her hand on my shoulder. "You are going to be all right, baby. I promise you that."

"She sure is," Daddy said, reaching over and patting my arm with his good hand.

Daddy started the car and was pulling out of the bus depot when I asked him to stop.

"Wait, Daddy," I said. "Do you mind if we stop by Powell's Fabric Store?" It used to be Betty Powell's Dry Goods, but when she died a few years ago, her granddaughter took over and turned it into a fabric store.

"Course not." Daddy made a sharp left turn onto Main Street and stopped the car in front of the fabric store. Mama leaned forward.

"What you need from there?" she asked.

I turned toward her, and this time there were tears

falling down my cheeks. I quickly wiped them away. I was going to occupy myself with sewing dresses for me and my baby in every shade of blue I could find—from periwinkle blue to turquoise to teal. I wasn't as good at sewing as my sister Katie Bell, but I wasn't terrible either, if I took my time; right now, I had nothing but time on my hands. "I need to get some blue fabric so I can make me and this baby some dresses."

Mama smiled. "Then we better get inside and pick you out some pretty cloth."

Daddy got out and opened Mama's door. As always, Daddy was dressed in a three-piece suit. My cousin Jemison was minding Daddy's store today, and Daddy insisted that he dress up too.

"If you want to own a successful business, you got to look like a successful business owner," he would say. He smiled at both me and Mama once he helped me out of the car. Both of us were dressed in Sunday clothes too. I still had on my blue dress, and Mama was wearing a yellow cotton A-line dress with a yellow pillbox hat like Jackie Kennedy wore.

Mama said the Pruitt and Perkins names meant something in this town, so it was our obligation and duty to always be good representatives for the family. I was grateful that my indiscretion would not end up bringing shame to the family. Other than my immediate family, no one knew my secret, and I knew my family would never tell.

"While y'all looking for sewing things, I'm going to drive down to Monk Davis's and fill up this gas guzzler," he said.

"You mean the Standard Oil Company Filling Station?" I said, laughing. I teased Daddy all the time for calling it Monk Davis's even though Mr. Davis died before I was even born. Daddy would say old habits die hard.

"Yes, ma'am." He laughed and opened my door. "Standard Oil Company Filling Station."

"We won't be long." I got out of the car. "I have an idea what I want to get."

"Take your time." After he kissed Mama on the cheek, she and I went into the fabric store. Miss Jainey was standing at the door smiling when we got up close.

"There's two of my favorite customers," she said. "And look at the new mama. How are you doing these days, Rose?"

Miss Jainey was nice. She was unmarried, and she threw everything she had into this store. She even gave sewing lessons twice per week. One evening for white girls and the other for Negro girls. Mama and Daddy would never let us go because they were afraid some of the white folks in the community might start some trouble. So far, if anyone said something to Miss Jainey, she didn't let it affect her none.

Miss Jainey was nothing like her grandmother, who, according to Mama, would make Negroes stand outside while she rang up their purchases. Miss Jainey's store was one of the few stores that allowed Negroes to come inside and feel welcome.

"I'm doing okay, Miss Jainey. Thank you for asking," I said. She had several ceiling fans throughout the store, so once we got inside, a nice, cool breeze was blowing courtesy of those fans.

I went over to the dress patterns first. I had seen a pattern a while back that I thought would make a nice dress for Mama, but now that I was about to be a mama myself, I figured maybe I could pull it off. It was a polyester shift with a high neck and long sleeves. When I found it and showed it to Mama, she shook her head.

"Too old," she said. "You're just in your twenties. It's okay for me to look like Jackie Kennedy, but you need to look young and carefree. What about this?" She picked up a pattern with a flared skirt. The neck dipped down modestly, and the waist was cinched.

I nodded. Mama always did know best when it came to just about everything, but especially fashion. "I like it. What will we do for the baby's dress? Jasper is for certain this baby is going to be a girl."

Mama led me to the other side of the store, and we found a pattern for a sweet infant girl's dress. It had ruffles and delicate lace around the collar and tiny blue flowers. I knew these two dresses would please Jasper. I felt tears welling up, but I quickly brushed them away.

Mama hugged me tight. "You are being so brave. I am so proud of you."

I nodded because I didn't think I could open my mouth without wailing at the top of my lungs. Mama and I took the cloth, patterns, buttons, and lace to the front of the store, and Miss Jainey checked us out.

"Y'all have a good day," Miss Jainey said. "And, Rose, when that baby gets born and is old enough to go out, I want you to bring the little angel by so I can see him or her."

"Yes, ma'am. I will." I reached into my purse for my

wallet. Before Jasper left, he had given me ten dollars in cash and our bank book, which he had meticulously kept and which showed us having seventy-five dollars in savings. He said he had given his mama fifty dollars and paid off everything we owed for the rental of the house and the farmland.

Mama reached for my hand. "Let me get this. It will be a gift from me to you."

"Thank you, Mama," I said as she paid Miss Jainey.

Once we were done, we headed outside where Daddy was waiting by the car. He helped us both in and looked at me with the gentlest smile ever.

"You okay?"

I nodded, trying to smile. "I will be," I said, because I knew that I truly would not be okay until I saw Jasper Bourdon get off the Greyhound and say the words, "Baby, I am home for good."

CHAPTER 6

"MAMA, HOW DOES THIS LOOK?" I HELD UP THE BABY DRESS I had been sewing for the last three weeks since Jasper left. Twice I had to go back to Miss Jainey's store and buy more fabric. I was determined to figure this out, but it was getting costlier and costlier by the moment. Either I would cut something I wasn't supposed to or my stitches would go all zigzaggy. Of all Mama's daughters, I was the worst when it came to things like cooking and sewing. Even Ellena could make a dress from scratch. I was hopeless. At the rate I was going, the baby would be a teenager before I got her one dress made, let alone an entire wardrobe like I had planned. Daddy had offered to take me and Mama shopping in Atlanta for clothes, but I told him I wanted to make the baby's outfits myself since I had promised Jasper that was what I would do. For the rest of our lives together, I wanted my word to mean something.

"Somebody should have paid attention when Mama was teaching us how to sew," Katie Bell teased as she discreetly breastfed her three-month-old son, L.J. He was a fat, sunshiny baby. Now that the colic had passed, the only time I'd hear him cry was when Katie Bell didn't feed him as soon as he wanted. Other than that, he cooed and made noises that sounded like giggles, although Mama said it was just gas. I hoped my baby had just as good of a disposition as L.J. If the way she was behaving now inside my womb was any indication, she was going to be a joy to behold. I seldom, if ever, felt her move, and when she did move, it was ever so gentle, like a butterfly fluttering inside my belly. At first, I was concerned, but Mama said not to worry, that before I knew it, the baby would be letting me know she was there all the time. She said I should enjoy the quiet before the storm.

Mama came over to where I was sewing at the dining room table. "That looks good, baby. Katie Bell, stop teasing your sister. Y'all too old for that."

When Mama turned around and went back toward the kitchen, Katie Bell and I both stuck our tongues out at each other at the same time, causing us both to burst out laughing. Mama turned around and smiled.

"It sure is nice having the sounds of y'all's laughter in this house again. I just wish my Ellena and the twins were nearby," she said with a wistful look on her face. Mama always suffered the most when someone in our family died or moved away. Last summer, Great-Uncle Myron's daughters, Emma and Eveline, came and moved him to Tuskegee, Alabama, where they and their families lived. Every day Mama would call me sounding so sad, like the wind had been taken right out of her. If the truth be told, had I been home, I would have been as sad as Mama. Out of all

Mama's uncles, Great-Uncle Myron and I were the closest. If Mama couldn't find me playing with my brothers and sisters, she knew to go over to Great-Uncle Myron's house, where I would be sitting on the porch with him eating boiled peanuts.

"Everybody will be home for Thanksgiving," Katie Bell said. "We'll be one big, happy, loud family again. And who knows . . . Maybe Jasper will be back home in time for the baby to be born."

"That would be nice to have him home before the baby is born." I let out a huge sigh. Jasper had been gone for three weeks, and so far, I hadn't heard any word from him. Last time he was deployed, I would get a couple of letters per week from him. Daddy said I shouldn't worry, and I truly tried not to, but it wasn't easy. I had already sent him six letters and I hoped that he had at least received some of them. I didn't want him to think for a minute that I had forgotten about him. Mama must have seen my face because she came back over and gave me a big hug.

"Don't you fret," she said, kissing me on top of my head. "You don't want to give birth to a nervous baby."

Katie Bell laughed, putting a cloth over her shoulder and laying L.J. across it to burp him. "Mama, that's an old wives' tale."

"Well, I'm an old wife, so I guess that makes it so," Mama said in a firm voice. "I know you young folks like to pooh-pooh all of our sayings and remedies, but there is some truth to them. They didn't come out of nowhere."

"I'm sorry," Katie Bell said. "I was just teasing. And you are right. There is some truth to that. Any time I got sad or happy, that would affect how much L.J. moved. I know the two things are connected."

I kept quiet. I didn't want to bring up the fact that no matter how much I moved or what emotions I was feeling, this baby of mine did not stir very much. I knew Mama said there was nothing to worry about, but it seemed like a baby who was a whole seven months along would be kicking and bumping around my belly instead of just lying there, barely fluttering. I had a bad feeling, but I kept it to myself. I tried not to think about the worst when it came to Jasper or this baby. But all I could think of was the words of last week's sermon, "Reaping Day Is Upon Us." The pastor preached about reaping what we sow. I prayed that my reaping wouldn't affect Jasper or this baby.

I put down the dress. "Let me hold L.J." I went over to my sister and took my nephew from her. I needed something to take my mind off my own baby and Jasper, and L.J. was a joy to hold. Once I sat down, he snuggled against my neck. Like always, he went hard and fast to sleep.

"Sissy, I need you at the house at night," Katie Bell said with a huge yawn, standing up and stretching. All of us were thin like Mama, and Katie Bell had snapped back to her prepregnancy weight in only a few weeks. I was all belly.

"You know I would be happy to babysit him sometime," I said in a soft voice. I knew the answer before I made my offer.

"He's not ready to be away from me yet." Katie Bell's voice was firm. Mama and I exchanged a knowing smile. Katie Bell didn't even like leaving the baby with one of us so she could take a shower or get dressed. If she went to the bathroom, L.J. went with her in his bassinette. I was surprised she had let me hold him this long. Almost on cue, Katie Bell came over and gently took L.J. from me. She sat down and laid him on a blanket on her lap.

"You need to put that baby in that bassinette over there," Mama scolded. "He is going to be too ruint for anybody to try to help you with him a few months from now when you and that husband of yours are ready for some alone time."

Katie Bell, being Katie Bell, completely ignored Mama's words of caution. "Ain't he the most precious thing you ever saw? Rose, it is going to be so wonderful when your baby is born. L.J. and your baby are going to love each other so much, and L.J. is going to protect his little cousin for the rest of his days."

Before I could stop them, tears trickled down my face. I swiped at them before they took me over. Pregnancy had definitely made me more weepy than usual. Mama and Katie Bell looked the other way. They had become used to my crying at the drop of a hat.

"I hope you're right, Katie Bell. I hope these babies love each other as much as we do." I rubbed my belly, trying to convince my baby to move or do something. I felt a slight flutter, but that was it, and I had to focus hard to even feel that. "Y'all want to watch *As the World Turns*?" I got up to turn on the television.

Katie Bell laughed in a quiet voice so as not to wake up L.J. "I can't believe you like to watch these soap operas. Some days I don't even turn on the television, except every now and then to catch *Queen for a Day*. I just love how that Jack Bailey is all the time helping folks with hearing aids and new washing machines. Last thing I need to see is some white people making moony eyes at each other."

I laughed and turned the television to CBS. *Guiding Light* was just going off. I knew it would be another half hour before *As the World Turns* came on, so I clicked it off and went back to my seat. "It's gonna be a while before it comes on. Girl, Daddy got me hooked watching these soaps."

Mama came into the room with a pan of purple hull peas to shell. "Girl, hush with that. Your daddy don't watch no soap operas."

I laughed. "Mama, he be watching them down at the store in the break room. *As the World Turns* is his favorite. Ask him what he thinks about Penny Hughes and Jeff Baker. He can tell you things about them just like they were members of the family."

Katie Bell laughed. "If anybody would know, it would be Daddy's shadow over there."

Mama shook her head. "I don't think that's my husband y'all are talking about. Cedric has the TV on the baseball games, not no soap operas. That's probably you watching them soaps, and he just be humoring you."

Katie Bell and I looked at each other and laughed. These were the times I had missed so much when I was in Hattiesburg. I had called Jasper's mama the other day and asked her to come up to visit so she would be here when the baby was born. She said she would come at Thanksgiving. I was happy that I would be able to share the holidays with her and show her what it was like to be part of a big family. Also, I wanted to do what I could to earn her trust again.

"Hey, y'all," a voice called from the front door. It was Aunt Lucille and her mother, Aunt Shimmy. The two of them walked into the room smiling. Aunt Lucille was Mama's favorite cousin who was more like her sister, so we all called her Aunt Lucille. Aunt Lucille and Aunt Shimmy were almost like sisters themselves. Where you saw one, the other was close behind.

"What y'all cackling about in here?" Aunt Shimmy said, stopping when she saw L.J. "Come on and give me my baby, Katie Bell, and don't be talking 'bout he's sleeping. Give me my baby."

I grinned. Katie Bell knew better than to argue with Aunt Shimmy. Aunt Shimmy lifted him off Katie Bell's lap and sat at the table with me and Mama.

"Aunt Shimmy, you just scared I'm gonna ask you to help me shell these peas. That's why you grabbed that baby so fast," Mama said. Everybody laughed. "Katie Bell, since your hands is free now, you can come and help me get these peas shelled. Lucille, you can get you a pan too. I'll send y'all some home."

"Lord have mercy, me and Mama come over to see how y'all doing, not get put to work," Aunt Lucille grumbled. But she was also laughing as she went to the kitchen and got two pans for her and Katie Bell.

"Y'all know I don't mind shelling peas by myself, but Uncle Little Bud and Lawrence had a bumper crop. I got two hampers in that kitchen to shell and they talking about bringing another two this afternoon."

"Where is they wives?" Aunt Lucille complained. "They ought to be over here getting their hands all purple too. I know Naomi can't boil water, but she could shell some peas. And where is Cheryl Anne?"

"I see what y'all do when y'all think I ain't around, Aunt Lucille," Naomi said, coming into the house. Everyone broke into laughter. Naomi and I were used to being the butt of everybody's jokes for our lack of cooking skills. "Mama Opal, how you gonna let them talk against me that way?"

"Gal, as soon as they say something untrue, you know I got your back," Mama said with a huge grin, handing Naomi a pan full of peas to shell. "You remember how to shell, baby girl?"

Naomi sat down beside me. "Rose, you all I got. You see how they do us? And Cheryl Anne ain't feeling well. I just spoke to her on the phone."

"Girl, they wouldn't have nothing to talk about if they didn't have us. I'm over here struggling and straining trying to finish this dress before I go into labor. It's not looking good."

L.J. let out a loud cry and Katie Bell nearly upset the table trying to get up, but Aunt Shimmy motioned for her to sit. "Girl, let this baby get used to something other than your tit. Speaking of children, Naomi, where is Triple D?"

I smiled at the nickname my oldest nephews had been given when they were born. Naomi and Lawrence named their sons David, Daniel, and Demetrius—all names from the Bible. They looked so much alike, it was hard telling them apart, so most everybody called them Triple D.

"They at Mama's house getting spoiled rotten, but if

they'd known their little cousin L.J. was here, they would have come with me so they could freak out Katie Bell by breathing on her baby." Everyone but Katie Bell laughed.

"L.J. is only three months old," she said defensively. "I don't want him getting sick."

Mama shook her head as she chuckled. "Aunt Shimmy and Lucille, how y'all 'spect we managed to keep babies alive back in the day when they got taken out to the fields where some of us worked or got left with the oldest sibling while we cooked and cleaned?"

Aunt Lucille clicked her teeth as she shelled peas at a snail's pace compared to Mama. Mama used to be a house-keeper before she married Daddy, so she was far more adept at housework than Aunt Lucille, who was Aunt Shimmy's only daughter and just as spoiled as I was. But Aunt Lucille was a phenomenal cook, and she did beautiful crochet work. She had already made several blankets and sweaters for the baby, all in shades of blue.

"Girl, my Adam and his wife, Tabitha, are the same way with my granddaughter. They'll bring Miriam over for me to keep and will bring me a list a mile long of things I need to do to take care of their little girl," Aunt Lucille said, shaking her head. "I remind them I raised four children of my own, but Tabitha will say all prim-like, 'Those were different times, Mother Lucille.'"

"Somebody go turn on the television," Aunt Shimmy said, reaching into the hamper Mama had brought into the dining room and putting more peas into her bowl to shell. "If I'm going to be shelling peas all afternoon, I need to see what's happening on my stories. Turn to CBS. That's where the good shows are. *As the World Turns* will be on in five minutes."

Mama and Katie Bell let out loud groans, but Naomi and Aunt Lucille chimed in excitedly as Naomi got up and turned on the television. The television faced the dining room, so everyone who wanted to watch could turn their chairs toward the living room.

"Aunt Shimmy, I love *As the World Turns*, but *Love of Life* is my favorite. That Van and Bruce Sterling is some kind of mess," Naomi said. "Can you believe how bad Bruce treats Van?"

"Girl, don't you know it," Aunt Shimmy said. "I ain't studdin' Bruce. He always got his eyes on somebody besides Van."

While everybody was laughing and talking about the show, Daddy came into the house.

"Hey, Daddy." I stood slowly, laughing. "Come tell Mama you like watching the stories too. She wouldn't believe me."

"Rose," he said, then stopped. Daddy looked like he was crying. As I got closer to him, I could see the tears in his eyes. I got scared. Mama went to him and placed her hand on his shoulder.

"What's wrong, Cedric?"

Before he could speak, I saw the letters in his hand.

"Oh, Daddy," I said, laughing again. "Did Jasper's letters finally get here to me? It took long enough. You so sweet. You ain't got to cry though. Everything's fine now that we got word from him. May I see them?"

"Baby," Daddy started, then cleared his throat. "There's

some letters here from Jasper, but there's also a telegram from the War Department."

I felt Katie Bell come up behind me and put her arms around my waist. Aunt Lucille came and put her hand on my back.

"What y'all doing?" I pulled away. "Everything's okay, y'all. Daddy's got letters from Jasper. Look. A whole stack of 'em. Everything's fine."

Daddy shook his head. "It's not fine, baby. He didn't . . . Jasper . . . died. They called it 'friendly fire.' He didn't survive."

"Noooooo!" I wailed. "Noooooo!"

I could feel my legs buckle underneath me. Then I felt Daddy catch me with his good arm as he and Mama pulled me into their embrace.

"Jasper!" I screamed. "Jasper. Jasper. Jasper!"

"It's okay, baby," Daddy kept saying. "It's okay."

I tried to stop my screams. I felt the hands of all the women in the family who were in the room that afternoon touching me, laying hands on me and beseeching God to ease my grief, but I knew there were no words to take away the pain I was feeling in that moment. And even though my daddy kept telling me it was going to be okay, I knew nothing was okay, and nothing would ever be okay again. The words of the preacher kept invading my thoughts.

You reap what you sow. You reap what you sow. You reap what you sow.

CHAPTER 7

I COULD HEAR THE VOICES IN THE FRONT ROOM. I DIDN'T KNOW how long I had been asleep in the bedroom, but it seemed later in the day. I remembered Mama had come in a little while ago to check on me and close the curtains since I was having one of my awful migraines, but other than that, I had done what I used to do when I was a girl: I escaped inside my dreams to a place where nothing could hurt me. In that world, there was no dead husband; there was just quiet. Now, that quiet was being interrupted by all the people I could hear talking on the other side of my door.

It sounded like all of Little Parsons was here. Word of anything—births, deaths, sickness—spread like the fires Uncle Little Bud and Lawrence would set out in the fields they planned on leaving dormant for one or two growing seasons. I heard a knock. I didn't say anything. I didn't want to talk to nobody.

"I'm coming in," I heard Grandma Perkins say.

I wanted to get up, but my head was still pounding. My heart felt like it might break into itty-bitty pieces. I knew Mama had said babies could feel your grief, and God knows I didn't want to cause this baby no more heartache than I had already shown her, but this was more than I could fathom. The notion that Jasper was dead, and I would never see him again, was . . . well, it was too much. So I just kept lying there as the door opened.

Grandma Perkins sat down in the chair by my bed. "Rosebud," she said. I could smell food. I couldn't decide whether I was hungry or about to be sick. My belly felt like it could go either way. "Sweetie, Grandma brought you a plate of food and a glass of that goat's milk you've been craving so much. I even milked that ornery critter myself. You need to sit up and eat and drink a little bit."

"I'm not hungry, Grandma. My head is hurting something terrible," I said, even though I could feel my stomach grumbling.

"You might not be hungry, but that baby of your'n is, and you have to keep up your strength for it. That's probably why your head is hurting, because you haven't eaten properly today."

"She." I sat up slowly, holding my belly until I could find a comfortable position.

"What did you say, Rosebud?" Grandma Perkins stood and put the tray of food on my lap once I got settled. She set the glass of milk on the side table. I could tell by the look and smell of the food that her hands had been the ones to prepare it. Grandma Perkins always put an extra spin to her cooking. The plate held meat loaf with her signature mushroom gravy all over it, rice and stewed tomatoes, roasted green beans with sweet potatoes, and corn bread with little flecks of jalapeño in it—my favorites.

"It's a she," I repeated. "Jasper said he wanted a girl that looked just like me. This baby is a she."

"Well, Rosebud, that is sweet, but . . ." She stopped and smiled at me, sitting back down in the chair by the bed. "You gonna eat a little something for Grandma?"

"Yes, ma'am." I bowed my head as Grandma said grace. I had no words to offer to God at that moment. I wasn't sure how I felt, but I knew talking to God wasn't on my list of things to do right then. So I ate, but tears started rolling down my face, making every bite taste extra salty. Jasper would have loved a meal like this. I never cooked for him— not a single, solitary meal. His mother always took care of the cooking. Now, I thought, I never would get a chance to fix my husband a home-cooked meal. By the time he got home, I had planned on being a good wife like my mama and my grandma had been, but now all I was ever going to be to Jasper was his widow.

Grandma smoothed down my hair. "I know this is hard, Rosebud, and you must be wondering what in the world was God thinking, but you can't allow yourself to go down that road. We have to trust that this happened because it was part of God's master plan."

Normally, Grandma's words would bring me comfort, but this whole argument about Jasper's death being part of God's plan only made me angry. Why would God plan something this awful? Even if God was mad at me, why would he punish Jasper? I had so many questions, but I knew better than to voice them. Grandma would tell me it wasn't right to question God, so I didn't . . . out loud, at least. I quietly ate my food instead. Once I started eating, I realized I was hungrier than I thought I was.

"That's good, baby," Grandma said. "I have a peach cobbler in the kitchen. Just let me know if you want a bowl."

"Yes, ma'am." I ate another bite of the green beans. Then I thought about Jasper's mama, Miss Ida Mae. "Oh no, Grandma Perkins. I need to call Miss Ida Mae. What if she finds out from somebody else?" I put the tray on the other side of the bed and tried to swing my feet over the edge so I could go make the call, but Grandma put her hand on my arm.

"Your daddy has already talked to her. Bless her heart. He offered to fly her up here, but she said she would rather take the bus. She and the cousin she was staying with are going to come up here for the funeral and the burial, so don't worry yourself about that."

"But doesn't she want the . . . the . . ." I couldn't say the word *funeral*. Just thinking about it made me want to wail, but Grandma seemed to know what I was trying to ask.

"Cedric told Miss Ida Mae we would all come down there, but she said she didn't want you trying to travel being so big. And then she said she thought it would bring you peace to have him close by."

Tears fell for real. I didn't deserve her kindness. I hadn't done a single thing to be worthy of it. I held my belly as I cried, praying my baby would stay calm even if I couldn't. Grandma got up and put the tray on the other bedside table.

Then she climbed into the bed with me and pulled me into her arms.

"Why would she be so kind to me, Grandma?" I hiccuped loudly, trying to talk through my tears. "Why? I don't deserve it. I didn't do anything to make her life or Jasper's life better. All I did was make life hard for both of them. Why would she do this?"

Grandma stroked my hair and then started rubbing my temples where the pain was worse. From the time I was a little girl, I would get awful headaches that would send me to bed, and Mama and Grandma were the only ones who could rub them away. "Rosebud, grace doesn't come to us because we earned it. It comes to us because we need it. You have got to turn over this guilt you are feeling to God, sweetheart, and then you must make him a promise that you will do your best to never sin the same way again. That's all we can do, baby. We are all just poor sinners, living off God's grace."

I allowed Grandma's words and her massaging of my head to lull me to sleep again. I could hear her softly singing like she used to do when I was a little girl and was being restless in my sleep.

I'm just a poor wayfaring stranger
Traveling through this world below
There is no sickness, no toil, nor danger
In that bright land to which I go
I'm going there to see my Father
And all my loved ones who've gone on
I'm just going over Jordan
I'm just going over home

When I woke up again, my sister Ellena was sleeping beside me, her back pressed up against mine. I wondered when she got home. Atlanta wasn't that far away, but she had school, so that meant she must have dropped everything and come home sometime last night. That was one thing about me and my siblings. There was nothing so important that we wouldn't be there for each other when possible. My twin brothers were much farther away, at Howard University, but I knew, without even talking to them, that they would be home in the next few days to see about me.

I looked at the clock on the table beside the bed and saw that it was nearly five in the morning. I got up gently so as not to awaken Ellena. She moved around a little in the bed, but she didn't wake. My bladder was full, so I put on my robe and hurried down the hallway to the bathroom. Once I was done, I went to the kitchen where Mama was starting a pot of coffee.

"Morning, Mama."

She jumped, putting her hand to her heart. "Lord, chile. I didn't hear you come in."

"I'm sorry, Mama." I gave her a hug, letting my head rest on her shoulder for a bit.

"That's okay." She kissed me on top of my head. "I'm not used to anybody being up this early except me, the roosters, and God. How are you feeling? Is that headache gone?"

I sat down at the kitchen table. "Yes, ma'am. It's better. When did Ellena get home?"

"Cousin Hiram drove her home last night." She went to the refrigerator and took out the bottle of goat's milk. It had a big label on it that read "Goat." I was the only one who liked it. No one wanted to accidentally use it thinking it was cow's milk. She poured a glass and put it in front of me. "Drink up. You only picked at your food yesterday."

"Yes, ma'am." I took long sips of the tangy milk. I had never liked goat's milk before, and Mama said once my pregnancy was over with, I probably wouldn't care for it again. She said pregnant women craved all sorts of strange things. She had a hankering to eat Georgia clay when she was pregnant with the boys, but Aunt Shimmy, who delivered all of us, warned her against it. "Have you heard from Micah and Mitchell?"

Mama nodded as she went to the cupboard and took out flour, baking powder, and sugar for biscuits, something she made every morning since they were Daddy's favorite. "They have exams today and tomorrow, but after that, they'll be flying home, so they will make it in time for the funeral."

As soon as Mama said the word *funeral*, I felt my eyes well up with tears. "I can't believe he's gone, Mama. It just doesn't seem possible."

"I know, baby," she said. "I'm so sorry. Jasper was a good man."

"Is there something I need to do . . . for the . . . funeral?" I was overwhelmed at the thought, but I wanted to make sure that I at least did right by Jasper in his death.

Mama started mixing up her biscuit dough. "Your daddy spoke to someone at the military base in Texas, and they said that Jasper would arrive here by next Tuesday and he would be given a full military funeral. Cedric spoke to Connelly's Funeral Home, and they will work with the military to take care of all those details. So right now, there aren't any decisions you need to make."

I didn't know what a military funeral was. Mama explained that military people would be on hand to play "Taps," fire off a three-gun salute, and give me the American flag that was going to be draped over Jasper's casket.

"I want his mama to get his flag," I said as I wiped away tears. "She ought to get it instead of me. And anyway, I'll have Jasper. The least I can do is let her have the flag."

Mama looked at me and smiled. "I think that is a good decision on your part, sweetie."

I heard footsteps behind me and turned. It was Daddy. He came to where I was sitting and kissed my cheek.

"How are you feeling today, Pudd'n?" he asked. Daddy still had on his robe, which was unusual since he was usually already dressed and ready to go to work by now.

"I'm okay." I knew I would be answering that question a lot in the upcoming days, and I didn't mind because it just meant I was surrounded by people who loved me. "Mama told me about the military funeral."

"There's still some things to be worked out, but I thought I would get with you and his mama when she gets here day after tomorrow. She had some things to take care of before she headed this way, and since Jasper's remains won't get here 'til next week, I told her not to rush. We already have the church for next Wednesday. I figured that would give us time to make sure he was dressed properly and looked presentable."

I nodded. I was feeling sick to my stomach and my headache was coming back.

"I think I'm going to go lay back down for a while." I held on to the table to steady myself because along with feeling nauseous and headachy, I was also feeling a tad bit dizzy.

"You feeling sick?" Mama asked, looking at me closely.

"Yes, ma'am."

"Well, you go relax and when breakfast is ready, I'll come get you and your sister."

"Yes, ma'am."

Daddy must have noticed I did not look all that steady, so he came over and offered me his arm. I gladly took it, and he led me back to the bedroom where Ellena was still sleeping. I tried to get into the bed without making any noise, but getting up into our bed took more effort than normal. By the time I got settled, Ellena had awakened. She propped herself on her elbow and began rubbing my back, as if she knew I was sick. Katie Bell was like a second mama, but Ellena was always my best friend.

"How are you holding up?" she asked me softly. "I didn't want to wake you up when I got home. I'm so sorry, Rose."

I knew if I tried to answer her, I would start crying again. Instead, I took her arm and pulled her close, so she ended up lying behind me with her hand draped across my belly. This is where we stayed until we both fell asleep.

I awakened later that morning with a start, sitting straight up in the bed. I had been dreaming about Jasper. He was trying to tell me something, but it was like water was running and I couldn't hear him. I would call out to him to speak louder, but the water sounds were getting louder and louder. Once I sat up, I realized the sounds I had been hearing in my dream came from the rain outside. I could hear it beating hard against the metal roof.

Ellena was gone. I heard laughter on the other side of the door. For a moment, the sound of their happiness made me angry, but I realized laughter was a part of who we were. The last funeral I remembered attending was when Mama's first cousin and Daddy's best friend, M.J., died in a farming accident. It was such a sad funeral, but by the time it ended, everyone was telling stories about Cousin M.J. and laughing until the tears fell—but this time as a release instead of from the pain they had just felt at the funeral. That was just how we mourned the dead.

I got up, feeling like something was sticky between my legs. I turned on the light so I could see what it was, and immediately my eyes went to the bed. My white sheets were bright red with blood.

"Mama!" I started screaming. "Mama! Mama! Mama!" I kept screaming until finally she rushed into the room.

"What is it, chile?" she cried, but then her eyes went to my nightgown that I just now realized was red with blood too. She hurried over to me and helped me back to the bed, where she got me to sit.

"What's happening, Mama?"

Before she could answer me, Ellena rushed in. "What's wrong? What . . ."

"Ellena, go call your daddy," Mama said, hurrying over to the closet and coming back with sanitary pads and a belt. "Tell him we got to take your sister to the hospital. Right now."

"Yes, ma'am." Ellena took off running.

"What's happening, Mama?" I begged again. I didn't know whether this was normal. I hadn't paid too much attention when the women around me got pregnant. I was seven months, and all I knew was, when it was time for me to have the baby, I was going to get a tightening of the belly and a rush of water was going to flow from my privates. Nobody told me there would be blood.

"Probably nothing," Mama said calmly. "Let's get you into some fresh clothes and underwear. You just stay still and let me do the work."

Mama raced out of the room and came back with a pan of warm water and a bath cloth. Then she hurried to the closet and took out a housedress. She reached into the dresser drawer and pulled out a pair of underwear. She came back, cleaned me up, and helped me into my clean clothes.

"Better?"

I nodded. "Yes, ma'am." I was trying not to get upset. I worried that all the crying I had done had made my baby sick. I was determined not to do any more damage, so I sat still and waited.

Minutes later, Ellena came back into the room. Aunt Shimmy was with her. Aunt Shimmy was wearing a robe and had rollers in her hair. She looked at the bed and then at me.

"We need to take her to the hospital," Mama said to Aunt Shimmy, still sounding calm. Then she turned back toward me. "Just to get you checked out, sweet pea."

"That ride on them rough roads might not be for the best," Aunt Shimmy said, sounding just as calm as Mama. The way they were talking, it was like they were discussing the weather, which was good. I figured if things were really bad, they would be crying and taking on. So I relaxed—a little. "Ellena, go call that new doctor working out of old Doc Henry's office . . . Dr. Russell, I think his name is. Tell him we need him to come check your sister."

"Yes, ma'am." Ellena hurried out of the room again.

Seeing a doctor wasn't something women did for childbirth in my family. Aunt Shimmy was a midwife, and she delivered most of the babies. Once again, I felt like I was failing in some way.

"Niece, I know you are concerned, but let's make sure we have something to be concerned about," Aunt Shimmy said. "Let's get this bed cleaned up and get Rosebud back into it. I think for now, us not panicking is the best decision."

"Yes, ma'am," Mama said. I looked up at her face. She nodded and patted my cheek. "We are going to listen to Aunt Shimmy."

"Yessum." I leaned back into the chair as Mama and Aunt Shimmy cleaned up the bed and put clean sheets on it. Just as they were about to help me into the bed, Daddy and Ellena rushed into the room.

"What's going on? What's wrong with Pudd'n?" he demanded, looking from my aunt to my mama. He was wearing a pair of overalls, so I knew he must have been close by, probably helping Uncle Little Bud and Lawrence in the fields just down the road. I wondered if Aunt Lucille's son, Jemison, was minding the store or if Daddy had closed it for today. "Little girl, you all right?"

"I'm okay, Daddy," I said, although my voice sounded

weak even to my ears. I just wanted to sleep. It felt like the entire room was spinning.

"She had a bit of bleeding this morning, so we gone have Doc Russell come check her out," Mama said.

"Don't worry, Cedric," Aunt Shimmy said. "We'll keep a close watch on her, and if we need to go to Atlanta to the hospital, then that's what we'll do. Ellena, go across the street to the house and get me a change of clothes."

"Yes, ma'am," Ellena said, leaving the room again.

"Okay, baby girl," Aunt Shimmy said. "Let's get you in that bed."

"Yessum." I tried to remain conscious even though I felt like it would take nothing for me to fade away into darkness. Aunt Shimmy must have figured out I was feeling weak.

"Rose, honey," she said, her voice sounding farther and farther away. "Rose . . ."

That was the last thing I remembered hearing. After that, everything went dark.

CHAPTER 8

WHEN I CAME TO, I WAS LYING IN THE BED, MY BELLY WAS TIGHT-ening something awful, and the bed was soaking wet. A white man about Mama and Daddy's age was looking down at me. I was terrified.

"Mama!" I called. "Aunt Shimmy!"

"I'm right here, baby," Mama said just over the shoulder of the white man. "I'm right here, and Aunt Shimmy is right beside me. This is Doc Russell. He's going to take care of you and the baby."

"Mama, I'm all wet." I worried it was more blood.

"It's okay," Mama said. "Your water broke. You are okay."

"Hello, Rose," Doc Russell said. His eyes looked kind. "It looks like this baby of your'n wants to be born today."

I shook my head. "No. That's not right. It's not sup-posed to come until eight more weeks. Ain't that right, Aunt Shimmy?" I looked around wildly until she came and stood on the other side of the bed. I knew Aunt Shimmy would talk some sense into this man. She was the family birthing woman. She would tell him I couldn't have this baby until November.

"Yes, Rose, you're right. The baby isn't supposed to be born 'til November, but babies have minds of their own," she said. "Your labor has started, and your water just broke. So like or not, we are going to have a baby sometime today or tomorrow."

I started crying, but before I could give in to the tears, my stomach contracted again. I had never felt such excruciating pain in my life. I thought my insides were going to be squished in two. I started gasping and panting.

"Rose, do you mind if I examine you?" he asked.

I was panting so hard I couldn't get any words out. Once the pain ebbed a bit, I nodded.

"Yes, sir—I mean, no, sir, I don't mind."

"Good. Now I want you to lie back and relax as best you can."

I did as I was told, and although the examination was painful, I just kept taking deep breaths like Mama and Aunt Shimmy had told me to do when we discussed what it was like to give birth to a baby.

Once he was done, he looked at Mama and Aunt Shimmy. "I need one of y'all to boil me some water and bring me some clean towels and a blanket." Then he turned to me. "Rose, I wish there was time for you to prepare, but there isn't. You are fully dilated. The next time you feel a contraction, it will be time to push."

Aunt Shimmy rushed out of the room to get the things Doc Russell had asked for. Mama came and took my hand in hers.

"You squeeze whenever you need to, baby," she said. "Mama is right here."

"Yes, ma'am," I said just as another contraction ripped through my body, causing me to cry out. "Ohhhh. Ohhhh." I tried not to scream. I didn't want to scare nobody, but I felt like I was about to split wide-open. "Can . . . I . . . push?"

"Yes, Rose," he said. "You can push."

As soon as he gave me the go-ahead, I bore down, pushing with all my might. I was ready to get this baby out of me and stop this awful pain. I didn't have to push long. After three more contractions and three more big pushes, I pushed out a baby. The room was silent. The baby didn't make a sound. Doc Russell rushed over to the other side of the room with it and Mama went with him.

"Is the baby all right?" I called out. "Mama, is the baby all right?"

She didn't say anything. Just then, Aunt Shimmy hurried back in the room. She went over to Mama and Doc Russell, and then I saw her shoulders slump. She came over to the bed and took my hand in hers. Tears were streaming down her face.

"Aunt Shimmy." A lump formed in my throat so big I was surprised I could get any words out. "Is it a girl? Is it a girl like Jasper said?"

"Yes, sweetie," she said, choking on the words. "You had a baby girl."

"What are they doing to her?"

"They're cleaning her up." Aunt Shimmy stroked my hand. I wanted to rip my hand away, but I was trying to be patient even though no one was telling me anything. The baby was being so quiet, just like she was in my belly. It was like she didn't want to bother nobody by moving or now crying, but I wanted her to cry. I *needed* her to cry.

I watched as Doc Russell handed the baby to Mama. She walked toward me with my baby in her arms, wrapped up in one of the blankets Aunt Lucille had made for her.

"Let me have the baby," I said. Panic rose in my chest, almost taking my breath. If I wasn't so weak, I would have gotten up and snatched my baby from Mama.

Mama stopped in front of the bed, and I saw she was crying too. "Sweetheart, she didn't . . . she . . ."

"Give me my baby!" I screamed. Mama placed my silent baby into my arms. I looked down at her. She looked like she was sleeping, but it was plain to see she was gone. My baby girl was dead. She was the most perfect-looking baby I had ever seen. She had a head full of dark, curly hair and her skin was flawless like a baby doll. I kept thinking if I just held her long enough, God would give her back to me. What had Mama said? *"The baby didn't do nothing to be punished for"*? So I just knew if I kept looking at her and loving on her, eventually God would realize he was wrong to take her, and he would give her back to me. He had to know I didn't mean what I'd said about giving her away. I was just scared.

"Rose, let Aunt Shimmy have the baby while we clean you up," she said. I was already shaking my head no.

"I'm going to keep her right here where I can see after her," I said, not taking my eyes off her peaceful little face.

"Rose," Mama said. "We need to clean you up."

I was about to say no again when my stomach con-tracted like before. "Ohhhhhh," I cried. "My belly is hurt-ing again."

Mama gently took the baby from my arms while I pushed out the afterbirth. When I was done, Aunt Shimmy brought in some warm, soapy water and started washing me from head to toe. I kept my eyes on Mama and my baby. Mama stood right where I could see her. She was rocking the baby like she was trying to get her to sleep, but tears were streaming down Mama's face.

No tears had come from me yet. I was still waiting on my miracle. I hadn't given up that God was going to give her back to me. He would realize he had punished me enough by taking Jasper. But as the minutes went by as Aunt Shimmy gently cleaned me, I realized she wasn't coming back. Once Aunt Shimmy finished washing me, she changed the sheets with me still in the bed, and then she pulled them over me.

"Let me have her," I said when Aunt Shimmy was done.

Mama placed her in my arms, then lay down with me and the baby on the other side of the bed.

"Ain't she pretty, Mama?" I asked, never taking my eyes off my tiny angel. I wondered how much she weighed. Prob-ably no more than two or three pounds, if that, I figured.

"She is beautiful." Mama put her arm around my shoul-ders as we both gazed at the baby.

"Miss Shimmy," the doctor called out from the corner of the room. I had forgotten he was still there. I didn't even pay attention to what Aunt Shimmy said or did. I just kept staring at my baby.

After a few minutes, Aunt Shimmy came to the bed and

put her hand on my arm. "Rose, I'm going to walk the doctor out and tell everybody . . . well . . . I'm going to go tell them about the baby. I won't be gone for long."

Mama said something, but I was trying to memorize every part of my baby girl's features. I wanted to be able to call her up to my memory no matter how many weeks, months, or years went by. There was a knock at the door, and Mama looked at me. I could tell she was worried about me. It was like my heart was so full of love for this baby I would never hear cry, I was speechless.

"Do you want anybody to come in?" Mama asked. "I can tell them now isn't a good time."

"No, they can come in," I said in a hoarse whisper. "I want them to see her."

Mama eased out of the bed and went to the door. Daddy, Grandma, Katie Bell, and Ellena were standing there. I watched as they all drew closer to the bed. Daddy had his good arm around Ellena, who was crying. The room was quiet except for her sobs. I didn't want to hear my sister in so much pain.

"Come here, Ellena," I said, surprising myself with the strength in my voice. Daddy guided her over to the bed and she got in beside me, laying her head on my shoulder like she used to do when she was a little girl. "Look at her, Ellena. Ain't she the prettiest baby you ever seen?"

"Yes." Ellena sobbed, lightly touching the baby's face and then mine. "She's beautiful. Oh, Rose, I'm so sorry."

"I know." I stroked the baby's hair. It was so soft. I wanted to make sure I cut a little lock of it to keep after . . . well, to keep. I wasn't ready to think about what was going to happen soon. I didn't want to think about them taking her from my arms forever. I pushed that thought away for now.

I looked up at Daddy, Katie Bell, and Grandma. Grandma and Katie Bell were holding hands and wiping tears. Daddy sat in the chair beside me. His eyes looked like he had been crying too. He reached over and lightly touched the baby's head. Then he stroked my cheek.

"You okay, little girl?" His voice was thick with emotion.

I nodded. I didn't know why I wasn't crying. God knows I was hurt and angry, but it was like the tears wouldn't come. It was like something was keeping me from feeling the entire grief that a mother should be feeling right now. Especially a mother who just lost her husband too. "I'm okay, Daddy. Hey, Grandma. Hey, Katie Bell. Y'all want to see her?"

Grandma inched closer and bent down and kissed my baby's head. I heard her whisper a prayer and then she stood.

"See, Katie Bell," I said. "She is just as pretty as we thought she would be."

"Yes, she is," Katie Bell said, and then she started to cry. Grandma put her arms around Katie Bell. Grandma was so strong. She always made sure she took care of us over herself.

"Y'all don't have to worry about me," I said firmly. "I'm okay. She's going to be with Jasper. He'll take care of her."

"That's right," Grandma said, with a watery smile, as she patted Katie Bell on her back. "Jasper said from the start she was a girl. Well, Jasper got his little girl, and he will take care of her until we all see each other in the by-and-by. And don't forget Grandpa Perkins. I'm sure he's already cuddling her and saying she is the prettiest thing he has ever seen."

That's when the tears started. One tear at first. Then another. Then several more. And before I knew it, I was making sounds I had never heard come out of me before. It was like they were coming from my soul. I couldn't stop myself and my wails and sobs got louder and louder. Grandma came over and Mama and Katie Bell, and they all put their hands on me and the baby. Nobody tried to tell me to stop. They just let me cry. It was too much for Daddy. He left out of the room sobbing himself. But my sisters, my grandmother, and my mama kept their hands on me, crying with me, like we were a chorus of weeping women. I heard the door open, and I felt more hands. All the women in my family were there. It was like I was birthing a baby all over again, but this time, the baby was grief, and they were my midwives. They weren't here to stop my pain; they were here to bear witness to it.

Much later in the day, once the others had left out, it was just me, the baby, Ellena, and my sister-in-law, Naomi. After a long spell of quietness, Ellena asked me what I was going to name her.

"You don't want 'Baby Girl Bourdon' on the headstone," Ellena said decisively. "She needs a name."

"I don't know what to call her. I sent letters to Jasper asking him what he wanted her name to be, but—" I stopped. I didn't want to say he died before I could get an answer.

"Wait," Naomi said. "Didn't Mama Opal say Jasper sent you some letters? Did you open them yet?"

I shook my head. "No. I couldn't. I don't know if I can now."

"What if he put a name in the letter that you might like?" Naomi asked. "I can look. If you give me permission."

"Okay," I said hesitantly. I wasn't sure if this was the right thing. I didn't want to start crying all over again. I hurt from the pain of giving birth and from the pain that, at some point, they were going to come take my baby away. I touched her little face that was now cool to the touch. The warmth was gone. Pretty soon, she would be gone from my arms.

"You don't have to let her do this if you don't want to," Ellena whispered in my ear.

"I know, but if we don't look now and I find out later that Jasper did have a name that he felt strongly about, I'll feel awful." I pointed toward my drawer across the room. "Go look in the top drawer, Naomi. Mama put them there inside a satin bag."

Naomi went over and after looking for a few seconds, she came back and sat in the chair beside the bed.

"You want to look or you want me or Ellena to look?"

"You can look." I knew there were four letters. I watched as Naomi opened the first letter and skimmed through it. She said nothing, and her face didn't change. She opened the second letter, did the same thing, and then she opened the third one. I watched as her face softened and a tear slid down. She brushed it away and looked at me with a sad smile on her face.

"He had a name. Do you want to read the letter, or do you want me or Ellena to read it to you? Or do you just want me to tell you the name?"

I paused for a moment, but then I made my decision. "I don't think I can listen to Jasper's words right now. Just tell me the name." He and I had discussed so many possible names, but I knew without knowing that whatever name was in that letter was the name I would give this sweet little baby girl. Jasper had earned the right to give her the name I would always remember her by.

Ellena put her arm around me and her hand on the baby.

"He said he wanted you to name her Olivia Rose." She brushed away another tear.

I felt the tears rolling down my face too.

"Olivia Rose," I said softly. I pulled her up closer, so her little cheek was near my face. "Your daddy says your name is Olivia Rose. What you think about that?"

There was a knock at the door, and I felt my heart drop. Mama, Daddy, Katie Bell, and Lawrence came in. Naomi had said he was too broken up to come in earlier. Lawrence came straight to me and knelt on the floor and cried. I put my hand on his head.

"It's okay, Lawrence," I said. Naomi knelt down beside him and wrapped her arms around his waist. Katie Bell came up behind them both and placed her hands on their backs.

Daddy cleared his throat and Mama put her arms around him. "Pudd'n, we need to, uh . . . we need to . . . uh." Daddy shook his head and then started again. "Mr. Connelly from the funeral home is here to get . . . uh . . ."

"He's here to pick up the baby, Rose," Mama finished. She came over to the bed and put the blue dress I had been sewing on my lap. She also laid a little blue sweater on top of it. "She can wear this dress that you started, and I finished. Your aunt Lucille made the sweater."

"Thank you," I said, pushing back the tears. "Everybody, Naomi looked through the letters from Jasper, and he said he wanted her name to be Olivia Rose, so that's what we're gonna call her. Olivia Rose. Daddy, can you make sure they put that on the headstone?"

"Of course, Pudd'n." Daddy nodded and wiped away tears with his handkerchief. "We'll do whatever you want, and baby, that is a beautiful name. It fits her. She looks like an Olivia Rose."

I smiled. "Thank you. And I was wondering, would it be okay if we buried her with Jasper?" I wasn't sure if that was something that could be done. I had seen mamas get buried with the babies when they both died during childbirth, but I had never seen a baby get buried with its daddy. I didn't want to do anything disrespectful, but it would sure make me feel better knowing she was resting in Jasper's arms.

Lawrence leaned over and kissed Olivia Rose on her head. "We will do whatever you want, little sister."

Everybody stood around the bed as I began dressing Olivia Rose. The dress was big on her, but she looked so precious in it. Ellena got up and found some little ribbons. She lightly finger-combed Olivia Rose's hair and put two blue ribbons on her curls on each side of her head. Finally, I put on her sweater.

"Do you want me to go get the camera?" Daddy asked. It was strange hearing him sound so unsure. I thought about it for a minute. A part of me didn't want the photo because it felt like it would hurt too much to look at it, but then I thought I never wanted to forget a single thing about her, and a photo would help.

"Yes, sir." Lawrence took Olivia Rose from my arms while Katie Bell and Ellena helped me sit up and get presentable. Katie Bell combed my hair and put it in a French braid like she used to do when I was a girl, and Ellena straightened my gown and the bedsheets so that when Lawrence put the baby back into my arms, we both were ready for our first and only mother-daughter photograph. I had dreamed about taking that first picture. I knew Jasper probably wouldn't make it home in time to witness her birth, so I had planned on getting Daddy to take a bunch of pictures to send. I couldn't believe how quickly my dreams turned into a terrible nightmare.

I tilted her so her little face would show. Daddy took a picture of me and her, and then he had me lay her on my lap. He pulled back the blanket and took several more pictures. Once he was done, we knew it was time.

Everybody held hands, and I held Olivia Rose against my face. Although I hadn't meant to cry anymore, the finality of what was about to happen hit me and the tears fell. Daddy started the prayer, but he couldn't finish. Lawrence picked up where Daddy left off, but he couldn't finish either. It was my little sister, Ellena, who said the last of the prayer.

"Dear Lord, receive unto you our little Olivia Rose. Make sure you tell her often that she was greatly loved and when we get to see her again, we will not let her go," she prayed.

Together, we all said, "Amen."

CHAPTER 9

I COULDN'T STAY AWAY FROM THEIR GRAVE. IT WAS GETTING later in the day, and the heat was just beginning to give in to the coolness of the evening. The funeral had ended hours ago, and although all my family was back at the house, I didn't want to be there with them. I didn't want to sit around and listen to them talk about how handsome Jasper looked in his Air Force uniform or how sweet Olivia Rose looked in her blue ruffled dress. And I didn't want to listen to my cousins and brothers talking about whether or not the Pittsburgh Pirates were going to make it to the World Series. And as much as I loved them both, I definitely didn't want to see Katie Bell rocking L.J. in her arms while my arms remained empty.

So, even though I knew Mama and Aunt Shimmy wouldn't want me out walking so soon after losing my baby girl, I had to go back to the graveyard. I was drawn to it like lightning bugs were to the gas lanterns Daddy had hanging outside on the walkway leading up to the house. I wanted to be where Jasper and Olivia Rose were, even though I understood on a spiritual level that they had already left this earth for a much better place. When I got there, the undertakers had finished covering up their grave. I looked around at this place that was filled with so many of my kin. Most of them I didn't even know, but somehow I felt better knowing they were there surrounding my Jasper and Olivia Rose with their love and protection.

There was just a mound of dirt covering Jasper and the baby's grave, but in a few weeks, the funeral home would bring the headstone that would have Jasper's and Olivia Rose's names on it.

I had changed into a loose-fitting, sleeveless dress Mama had made for me. My belly had shrunk a lot since I gave birth to the baby, but I still appreciated the roominess the dress gave me. I eased myself down on the ground and put my hand on the dirt. It felt warm to the touch. I tried not to think about the cold bodies that lay underneath it.

"I know y'all ain't here," I whispered as one tear after another fell from my face onto the soil, "but it shore feels like you are."

I closed my eyes and imagined them both alive. Instead of us being in a graveyard, we would be sitting out on a blanket having a picnic in the peach orchard. Jasper would be laughing with the baby in his arms instead of lying inside a coffin in his dress uniform with Olivia Rose's head pressed against his.

The funeral had been nice, befitting of someone as special as Jasper. It was just the kind of service he would have liked. Reverend Shipman, our pastor at Little Bethel AME, preached about Abraham and his faithfulness. He had asked me who in the Bible Jasper reminded me of the most, and I immediately thought about Abraham. I asked his mama what she thought, and she smiled through her tears. "He would like that, Rose."

Because I wanted her to feel included in all decisions, I asked her to pick the songs for the choir to sing. She chose "Amazing Grace," "Just Over in the Glory Land," and "Jesus Promised Me a Home." All three were songs I remembered Jasper singing at the little country church near his mama's house in Mississippi. He didn't have the best singing voice, but he always made up for it with his passion and enthusiasm for the Lord. His voice would rise above everyone else's—almost like he was trying to sing loud enough for the angels to hear him. I knew he would be happy with everything she and I had selected.

I had never been to a military funeral before, so I didn't really know what to expect. A lot of things about it were new to me, like the three-gun salute, the playing of "Taps," and the folding of the flag. His mama teared up when I told her I wanted them to give her the flag. She and I both wore blue today instead of black since that was Jasper's favorite color, and Mama and Daddy made sure the church was filled with blue flower arrangements—hydrangeas, carnations, and roses. Mama ordered them from the same Negro florist in Atlanta who decorated the church for my wedding to Jasper.

"You would have really loved today," I said softly, patting the dirt with my hand.

"Rose?" I heard a voice calling out to me. "Rose?" It was Mama.

"I'm over here," I called back, brushing away the tears.

Jasper and Olivia Rose's grave was on the other side of a chinaberry tree near where Grandpa Perkins and his mama and daddy, Great-Grandpa Preacher and Great-Grandma Apple, were all buried. There was a space beside Grandpa Perkins for Grandma Perkins when her time came. I always tried to ignore that empty space. It always filled me with sadness. Now, I was thinking about the space next to Jasper. I finally understood what Grandma Perkins meant when she said her happiest day would be when we laid her to rest beside Grandpa and she could gaze upon Jesus' face. I would ask her how could she bear leaving all of us. Now I understood. I would give everything to be right here beside Jasper and our baby. The pull to be with them was stronger than the pull for me to stay.

Mama came up behind me and placed her hand on my shoulder. "Why didn't you tell somebody you were coming back to the gravesite? One of us could have come with you." She eased down on the ground beside me, smoothing out her dress so that her legs were covered. A lot of women had started wearing pants, but Mama still believed in wearing dresses. So far, all of us girls still wore them too, although knowing Ellena, she probably snuck and wore pants every now and then at college. The only time Mama let me wear pants growing up was when I played ball with the boys or went hunting with Daddy.

I pressed my head against her shoulder. For a time, we just sat there being quiet. Finally, Mama broke the silence.

"When my granny died, I was just like you," she said. "I didn't want to leave her grave. Felt like if I stayed by her grave, I could somehow stay close to her."

I nodded in agreement. "It's like I can feel Jasper and the baby's spirit here," I said hoarsely, thankful that Mama understood. She wrapped her arms around my shoulders.

"I know that's how it feels, but listen to me, Rose. You can't let this become a habit. One thing I know for sure about Jasper is he would not want your life to end here at this grave with him and Olivia Rose. Your Grandpa Perkins pretty much said the same words to me about Granny, and he was right. Mourn their passing, but honor their lives by doing the hard job of living a full life yourself."

"I wish I would have died too," I said softly. "I don't want to live without Jasper and my baby."

As soon as I said the words, I waited for Mama to scold me and tell me I was being blasphemous and ungrateful, but she just stroked my hair as we continued to sit and the sun began to hang low behind the pecan trees in the distance. After a little while, she spoke again.

"I understand the desire to be with the people you love the most, Rose. It's hard when they leave you behind. But you have to believe that there is a purpose for your life that is greater than even you can imagine right now. God wouldn't have left you behind if he didn't have a reason."

"How do you know that?" I tried to keep the despair out of my voice, but the pain I was feeling was coming in such rapid succession, it reminded me of the time Daddy and Mama took us to Tybee Island and we got to swim in the Atlantic Ocean. I was always a strong swimmer, but that tide was like nothing I had ever experienced in the lakes and ponds I was used to swimming in. That was how my emotions were feeling right now. Just one huge wave after another.

"Did I ever tell you about Miss Lovenia Manu?"

I wracked my brain and finally I thought I recalled Mama talking about somebody by that name, but I couldn't remember anything specific about her other than she lived to be over a hundred.

"I think so. She was real old when she died. Right?"

"Yes," Mama said. "Miss Lovenia was a root woman."

"Hoodoo?" I couldn't believe my devout Christian mother was sitting with me talking about a hoodoo woman. I shivered at the thought, but to my surprise, Mama kept talking. She told me this incredible story of the time Great-Grandma Birdie, her grandmother, was killed and Daddy lost his arm, and this root woman gave Mama a magic bag that supposedly protected Daddy from dying that day.

"Mama, you can't seriously believe that." I pulled away and looked at her intently, trying to discern something on my mama's face that would let me know she didn't believe the words she was speaking. But Mama's face was as serious as the day is long.

"I'm sure when the children of Israel put blood on their doorposts, there were those who didn't believe or understand it," Mama said, her voice soft and soothing. "Rose, I don't understand the logic behind that little bag Miss Lovenia gave me, but I needed to tell you that part of the story so you would understand the next part."

I was almost afraid to know what the "next part" was, but I waited for Mama to continue speaking.

"A week or so before you were born, one of Miss Lovenia's twin sons came to the door of the house and said Miss Lovenia wanted to see me."

"What did she want?" I asked, pulled into the story in spite of myself.

"I asked the twin, Mars, I think it was, and he said, 'Just come.'" Mama stood and reached for my hand, which I reluctantly put into hers. I knew it was getting late, and if we wanted to make it home by dark, we needed to get to walking. I didn't want to leave. Not yet. But Mama's hand was persistent, so I allowed her to gently pull me to a standing position. "Rose, I went to Miss Lovenia's home, a place I had not visited since before Grandma Birdie died, but she looked the same and the house looked and smelled the same. Lavender. It was like the entire house was filled with lavender. She said she needed to tell me what she saw for you before she left this place."

"Me? What do you mean, me?" I didn't understand what Mama was trying to tell me. How did this woman have something to tell Mama about me and I wasn't even born yet?

Mama guided me out of the cemetery toward the dirt road that would eventually connect to the main road. "Miss Lovenia took me to the room where she would see her customers and give out potions and healing tonics, and she said, 'This daughter you are carrying is going to suffer great losses, but if she stays strong, she will regain all that she lost tenfold.'"

"Oh, Mama," I said with a sigh. "That's just some made-up stuff."

Mama stopped walking and turned toward me. "Maybe. That's what I told myself through the years about the little bag she gave me and this prophecy. But what if she wasn't making things up? All through the Bible we see examples of prophets and wise men and women. Who's to say God didn't send her that message to give to me before she died and before you were born? I don't know. And at the end of the day, I don't think it matters, Rose. What matters is the message. God can use anybody to be his messenger, and I believe the message for you is to not give up. Today was awful, but you're still standing, and God wants you to know that better days are waiting for you. You just got to keep moving toward it."

We didn't say no more to each other, and that was all right. Sometimes a situation didn't call for words. My family loved to talk through situations, but sometimes I just wanted the silence. I was grateful Mama figured that out and didn't keep pushing. I thought about Mama's words and the words she said Miss Lovenia Manu said about me. What if she had been telling Mama the truth? What if God had sent her a message that, like Job, I was going to lose everything, but eventually God would bless me to be happy again? I couldn't imagine that day coming, but I had to admit, it helped to think about it, pray about it, and wish for it.

As we walked toward home, I could hear the familiar sounds of our little community. The older folks still called it Colored Town. It didn't matter what you called it, because at the end of the day, it was home. I heard the mournful sounds of the harmonica. I knew it was my brother Lawrence playing. Mr. Tote, one of the old-timers who used to live next to our house, taught Lawrence how to play before he died. I also heard a guitar, which meant Great-Uncle

Little Bud was on the front porch too. By the time we turned the corner, we could see a crowd on the porch and in the front yard. Mama squeezed my hand.

"Don't run from them, Rose," Mama said. "They just want to help you through your pain. Let them help you the best way they know how."

I knew what she was saying was true. Everybody sitting out on that front porch and in the yard loved me. I didn't want to hurt their feelings, but all I wanted to do was go to my bedroom and cry.

"Thank you, Mama." I gripped her hand like the lifeline it was. Mama and me sometimes butted heads, but she had been a blessing to me since I came back home. Yes, she was stern with me when it came to how I treated Jasper, but she was also the most loving and caring mama a girl could want after I got my heart broken twice in just a few days. When we got to the porch, everyone stopped singing and talking and looked toward me and Mama. Finally, Great-Uncle Myron, who had come back from Tuskegee for the funeral, cleared his throat.

"You come sit here by your old Uncle Myron, Rose. I ain't had the chance to look at you good since I got back home," he said.

Ellena stood up and pulled me into a hug. I wanted to say something to her—to everyone who was on that porch for me—but I didn't have the words, and anyway, I knew they knew I loved and appreciated them. Ellena released me from her arms, and my twin brothers came to me next.

"We can stay," Micah and Mitchell said in unison, something they frequently did. If they weren't finishing each other's sentences, they were speaking the same words at the same time. Mama used to call them Parrot 1 and Parrot 2.

I shook my head and kissed them both on their cheeks. I found my words. "You both need to be in school. I will be all right. I love you both for wanting to stay with me though."

They were scheduled to fly out the next day and I didn't want them getting behind in their studies. I continued to make my way to Great-Uncle Myron. Various people reached out and touched my hand as I walked by—like they were offering me some of their strength. I sat down on the swing by Great-Uncle Myron, and he wrapped his arm around me, pulling me close. Even in his seventies, Uncle Myron still exuded the same strength that I remembered from when I was a child.

"I know folks say, 'God don't put more on a body than they can bear,' but this is a lot," he said as he leaned his head against mine, his voice choked with tears. "Yes, this was a whole lot, my Rose, and you got a right to feel what you feel. Don't let nobody tell you different, and if they do, tell them to come talk to me. I still miss my Josephine like her dying was yesterday, and it's been over thirty years now. You own that pain you are feeling. God will take some of it away in due time. In his time."

I nodded as the tears trickled down my face. Uncle Myron slowly pushed the swing, causing us to sway back and forth. My tears turned to sobs, and for a time, the only sound that could be heard on the porch was me crying.

"Sing something, Uncle Little Bud," Mama said, her voice choked. I watched as Daddy came over and put his arm around her waist. She leaned her head against him. In that moment, I couldn't watch. It was like if I looked too closely at someone else's happiness, it caused my grief to spill over like water in a pitcher that had been filled up too much.

"Gonna sing Mama's song," Great-Uncle Little Bud said, wiping away a tear. He waited for a moment, and then he began strumming a song that was familiar to all of us. Lawrence joined in on the harmonica. Even though none of us children had met Great-Grandma Birdie, we all knew her song. It got sung whenever we celebrated her birthday every year or at Thanksgiving or Christmas when we all gathered together. No matter the occasion, almost without fail, someone would begin humming the song, and before we knew it, everyone would join in singing.

So when Great-Uncle Little Bud said he was going to sing Great-Grandma Birdie's song, every person from the oldest to Lawrence's sons could tell you it was "Keep on the Sunny Side." Mama said Great-Grandma Birdie used to listen to the radio every day waiting for that song to come on. Great-Uncle Little Bud started singing first, but it wasn't long until the entire porch and front yard was singing right along with him.

There's a dark and a troubled side of life
There's a bright and a sunny side too
Though we meet with the darkness and strife
The sunny side we also may view
Keep on the sunny side, always on the sunny side
Keep on the sunny side of life

It will help us every day, it will brighten all the way
If we'll keep on the sunny side of life

I couldn't sing along. Every single word was stuck in my throat, but I did listen, and I did start to feel calmer and less like I wanted to take off running back to the cemetery. Their voices were like a balm coating my soul. The pain was still there, but not as raw. I couldn't imagine the pain ever healing completely, like Great-Uncle Myron had said, but I prayed for moments of respite—moments where I could breathe and not feel as if I would choke on the memories of Jasper and Olivia Rose lying motionless inside that casket.

I leaned back and continued to sit beside Great-Uncle Myron until he leaned over and kissed my cheek.

"I'm going to head on home, baby. Uncle Myron can't sit up late like I used to. I'll be by tomorrow to check on you."

"Yes, sir," I said. "Thank you."

"You don't ever have to thank me for loving you. That's what family does. Love each other through the happy and through the sorrow."

He rose from the swing and said good night to everyone. Ellena took Great-Uncle Myron's seat, and I laid my head against her shoulder. I was tired, but I didn't want to go to bed. Now that the funeral was over, I was afraid that my pain would magnify and my dreams would be filled with death and loss.

It wasn't long before others started getting up to leave too. Tomorrow was a workday for most everybody, and with half of the people being farmers and farmers' wives, their days started earlier than most. Within a manner of minutes, everyone was gone except for my siblings, Mama, and Daddy. Naomi had taken the triplets home before it got dark, and Luther Sr. was inside with L.J. He and Katie Bell were going to spend the night so we all could have breakfast together before the twins had to fly back to Washington, DC.

"Well, Mama, you ready to head in and leave these children to themselves?" Daddy asked.

"Yes." Mama came over and kissed my forehead. "Don't stay up too late, Rose. Your body still has some healing to do."

"Yes, ma'am."

"Good night, my angels," Mama said, something she used to say when we were younger.

"Good night, Mama. Good night, Daddy," everyone said as they went back into the house. Katie Bell came and sat on the other side of me on the swing, and Micah and Mitchell sat down beside each other on the porch. One thing about the twins, they were never far apart from each other. They were so joined at the hip that when they were little boys, if one went to the bathroom, the other one would be standing by the door waiting for him to come out. Daddy said once they went to college, they would grow out of it, but it didn't seem to be the case. They seemed as close if not closer than they were when they lived at home.

"How is school treating you boys?" Katie Bell asked.

"Fine," they said in unison, causing everyone to laugh. Grandma Perkins used to say the twins did talking duets.

"Them boys is speaking a duet again," she would say.

We learned that if we wanted a singular answer, we had

to address the question to a specific twin, and even then, they still might speak together. To be honest, I was happy the attention was moving away from me. I just couldn't handle talking about how beautiful the funeral was with another soul. Not even with my siblings.

"Micah, is that teacher, Dr. . . . Dr. . . . Dr. whatever his name is still giving you fits?" Lawrence asked.

Micah laughed. "Dr. Vernon Michaels? Lord, yes. He is the toughest teacher we have ever had in our lives. Don't get me wrong, every doctor at Howard is difficult, but Dr. Michaels is a special kind of difficult."

"He quotes the medical book, *Gray's Anatomy*, like Grandmother Perkins quotes scriptures from the King James Bible, and he expects us all to do the same," Mitchell said, laughing along with his brother. "But I think we're growing on him. Don't you think so, Micah?"

"Absolutely," Micah said. "He told us that Negro doctors owe an allegiance to the places that they come from."

"He's right," I said, standing up, the exhaustion finally hitting me. "Little Parsons needs you. The white doctor is a good doctor, but no one will take care of our people like one of our own—like both of you. Everyone, I'm going to bed. Thank you for today. I . . . I . . . I couldn't have made it through this day and the last week without you." I felt my voice begin to crack, and before anyone could say anything, I hurried inside. My sister's husband, Luther, and L.J. were asleep on the couch. I quietly made my way to my bedroom at the back of the house. I quickly undressed and put on my gown. I knelt beside the bed to say my prayers, but no words came to me. I didn't know what to say. I was angry with God. Even with all the explanations people had given me about God only "taking the best" or "God never makes mistakes," I was still confused and totally bereft. So I said the only thing I knew to say in that moment.

"God, why?" I beseeched, so full of anger and grief at all that had happened in such a short period of time. I tried to force my mind back to the words my mother had spoken earlier—words that the old root woman had spoken to her. *"If she stays strong, she will regain all that she lost tenfold."* I wanted to believe those words, needed to believe them. But in this moment, I could not imagine being strong ever again. At this moment, I couldn't imagine getting through today, let alone a lifetime, with no Jasper and no Olivia Rose.

CHAPTER 10

GETTING ON THE OTHER SIDE OF THE HOLIDAYS WAS TRULY THE blessing I didn't know I had been looking for. At first, I thought Thanksgiving, Christmas, and New Year's would be a welcomed respite from all the sadness I was carrying, but I quickly saw that it wasn't. Even though the house was filled with all my kin, I had never felt more alone. Perhaps the only other person feeling the type of grief I was feeling was Jasper's mama, but she had left a few days after the funeral. I didn't even have her to commiserate with over our loss. I tried calling her a time or two, but she seemed so distant. I realized I was probably a painful reminder to her of all that she had lost, so after a while, I let her be.

So there I was, trying to be normal at a time when normal was impossible. My normal lay dead in Little Bethel AME Church's cemetery. Although Mama had said I shouldn't be a fixture at their grave, I found myself walking up there every other day or so. At first, I said I wanted to make sure the headstone was the way I had ordered it. Then I said I wanted to make sure the grave stayed free of weeds. After that, I didn't say anything. I just went. Even if I only stayed a half hour or so, I needed to be close to them. Someway. Yes, the holidays nearly leveled me to the ground, in spite of all of the joy and goodwill that surrounded me.

All I could think about at Thanksgiving was *I'm supposed to be having my baby around now.* So seeing my nephews, L.J., David, Daniel, and Demetrius, brought me both joy and pain. Sometimes their laughter would make me laugh right along with them, but other times it would send me to my bedroom where I would go and quietly cry to myself, wishing I could hear Olivia Rose's cries filling the house. Then came Christmas, and I was thinking, *This is supposed to be Olivia Rose's first Christmas.* The tree, like always, was surrounded with gifts for everyone in the family, but none of them bore the name of Olivia Rose or Jasper. My little family had been wiped out like trees during a tornado. One minute they were there, within my reach, and the next minute, gone—blown clear away to Glory. And when New Year's Eve came, I was thinking about the kiss from Jasper I would never get. I watched the married couples and the courting couples share sweet kisses and promises for the new year while I sat alone, wishing desperately for one more night with my husband.

So when we got to January 2, I was relieved. Relieved that all the tinsel and ornaments were being taken down and the holiday visits were coming to an end. Yes, I was going to miss everyone, especially Great-Uncle Myron, who had stayed on through the holidays but went back home to Tuskegee the day after Christmas, but I needed the quiet again. I needed to be able to go somewhere alone and process all that had occurred.

The day after New Year's Day was cold and windy, the temperature never rising much above thirty degrees. I knew if I went to the graveyard, I would have to sneak out because Mama would not want me to risk getting sick. Growing up, when everyone else would catch a cold, I would get bronchitis or pneumonia. I didn't know how I would get out past her searching eyes, but I was determined to go spend some time with my family, cold or no cold, flu or no flu.

Ellena had just left that morning to return to Spelman. After she left, I went to the bedroom and slept until it was time for my stories to come on. Around one o'clock, I got up and popped myself some popcorn, about the only thing I felt like eating, and then I went to the living room and began watching *As the World Turns*. The soap operas had become my way to escape. The lives of Penny Hughes and Jeff Baker, two characters on the soap, became the center of my world. Their triumphs were my triumphs, and their sadness, my sadness. But just as Penny and Jeff began arguing over something or another, Mama walked into the room and turned off the television.

"Mama," I said angrily, sitting up and pulling my robe tighter. Now that company was gone, I didn't even bother getting dressed. It wasn't like I had anywhere to go or anyone to see beyond my family. "I was watching that."

"No more," Mama said quietly. "No more."

"No more what?" I didn't know what she was talking about.

"I'm not losing you, too, Rose." To my surprise, tears were falling down her face. "I know you're hurting, but you can't keep laying around here moping and pining for your husband and your baby. They ain't coming back."

"I know that, Mama. It's just—"

"It ain't healthy," Mama interrupted. "Rose, I've seen folks die from the Melancholy. Uncle Myron almost died from it after Aunt Josephine passed away. I almost succumbed to it after Granny died. I won't let that happen to you. I just won't. This family has already lost enough folks before their time. I will not lose you. I couldn't bear it. I just couldn't."

I sat up from my slumped-down position on the couch and put the bowl of popcorn on the coffee table. I touched my head that was filled with the rollers my little sister had put in last night. Normally, the first thing I would have done in the morning was get dressed and take out the rollers and comb my hair. If Grandmother Perkins could see me, she would scold me something awful. She said a lady always starts her day with prayers and good hygiene. Since losing Jasper and the baby, I hadn't acted little like her definition of a lady.

I didn't get dressed mainly because my clothes no longer fit. All of my prepregnancy clothes were sagging on me because I hardly ate. Even with all the delicious holiday food that had been on the table these last few weeks, my appetite just didn't make an appearance. I guess, if the truth be known, I was willing myself to die. Mama sat down beside me and reached for my hand.

"Lord knows I don't know what it's like to lose a husband or a baby, Rose, so I don't want you to think for a moment that I'm making light of your pain, 'cause I'm not.

But baby, pain will eat you up inside and leave you bitter. Don't let that happen. I can't lose my Rose. And maybe I'm being selfish, but I want you to stay. For me. I want you to fight to survive this awful pain you are feeling. For me. Please."

I nodded slowly. "I'll try." I wasn't sure how I was going to pull myself out of this dark space, but I knew one thing: I didn't want to cause Mama to grieve over me. Somehow, someway, I was going to try to fight to stay present. To accept the love Mama and so many others were offering me.

"Good. Now let's get you up and get you clean and looking like Rose. Then I want you to come back out here so we can talk about something your daddy and I discussed."

"But, Mama," I started. "I don't want to . . ."

"I know," Mama said, pulling me up from the corner of the couch. "I know you don't want to talk. I know you want to sit here and watch this television, but that ain't an option. Not no more. So hurry up and fix yourself up, and come on so we can have this conversation."

"Yes, ma'am." I went to the bathroom, took a quick shower and changed into one of Ellena's dresses from when she was in high school. It was big on me but not as big as my clothes had gotten. Plus, it was blue. Jasper's favorite color. I took the rollers out of my hair, but I didn't comb out the curls because I planned on putting the rollers back in just as soon as it got dark. When I walked out of the bedroom, Mama was waiting in the living room. She smiled.

"You look good, baby," she said. "Come sit here." She patted the seat beside her on the couch. Once I was seated, she took my hand. "You need to go away for a spell, Rose."

I looked at her, confused. "What do you mean, Mama? Go where?"

"Away from here," she said firmly. "At least for a while. It's not healthy for you to be here right now. Everything is reminding you of what you lost. You need a change of scenery."

"But this is my home." Tears rolled down my face. "You and Daddy don't want me here no more?"

Mama took a handkerchief from her pocket and wiped my tears away. "That's not what I'm saying. I'm saying you need to go somewhere other than here for a little while. Just a little while. A change of scenery can be good for a body."

"Where would I go?" My voice quivered. I felt like I was being thrown to the wolves, and the idea of Jasper and Olivia Rose not being a stone's throw away nearly caused me to go into a panic. Mama must have seen it in my eyes because she pulled me tightly to her.

"It's okay, baby," she said soothingly, rubbing my back in gentle circles. "Just to Atlanta where your sister is at Cousin Hiram's and Cousin Florence's house. Ellena will be right there with you."

I felt better knowing they wanted to send me where Ellena was, but I still didn't want to leave.

"I'll do better, Mama." I still felt like I was being punished. "I'll get up every day and get dressed, and I'll help around the house. I can even go back to helping Daddy at the store. Please, just don't send me away."

Mama kissed my wet cheeks. "I'm sorry, baby. This is how it has to be. For now."

I knew that tone of voice. I knew Mama wasn't going

to waver, which was why I didn't bring it up again until after we had come back home from Wednesday night Bible class. I couldn't tell you a single thing that was discussed. It took everything in me not to run out of the church into the cemetery and throw myself on Jasper and Olivia Rose's grave. The only thing I remembered was the church all standing together at the end of service and singing "Swing Low, Sweet Chariot" and me wishing that chariot would dip down low and swoop me up into the clouds.

When we got home, Daddy went to the living room to watch *Mister Ed*. I sat beside him. Mama was in the bedroom rolling up her hair, and I figured this was my best chance to try to soften Daddy's heart about sending me away. I knew I wouldn't be able to change Mama's mind, but I thought maybe, just maybe, I could get Daddy on my side.

"Daddy." I lay my head on his shoulder.

"Hmm?" he said, distracted. *Mister Ed* was getting all of his attention.

"Daddy, please don't make me leave home." I was trying to sound calm, but even to my ears my voice sounded desperate.

"Go turn that television off," Daddy said in a quiet voice.

I got up and turned it off and came back to sit next to him. He took both of my hands in his hand.

"Your mama and me is worried about you, Pudd'n. That's all. We don't want you to go away, but we truly believe this is for the best."

"I'll be good," I said, sounding like a little girl, but I couldn't help it. "I'll do whatever y'all want. I just don't want to leave. I . . . I don't want to leave them." There. I said it. And I knew as soon as the words came out of my mouth that there was not to be any convincing Daddy or Mama to let me stay.

Daddy didn't say anything else. He just pulled me close with his good arm. The tears came, but he didn't allow himself to be moved by them. He just rocked me and told me everything was going to be all right.

The next morning, Daddy and Mama loaded me into the car, took me by Grandma Perkins's house to tell her goodbye, and then hurried me off to Atlanta before I had time to protest again. Once there, we stopped at Rich's Department Store, where Mama picked out some new dresses for me to wear. There was a time when I would have been excited to get a new wardrobe, but now I just nodded at whatever Mama selected. She asked me if I wanted to eat lunch in the Magnolia Room, but I said no. It had been only in the last few years that Negroes could eat there. Dr. Martin Luther King Jr. and several students from my sister's school, Spelman, and other surrounding schools had all staged sit-ins until stores like Rich's changed their rules concerning segregation.

"I'm not hungry, Mama." So instead of getting food, we went on out to the car, where Daddy was sitting reading his newspaper. As soon as he saw us coming, he got out and put the bags in the trunk. He opened the door for Mama and then me. Once we were all in the car, he shifted around and looked at me.

"You find what you needed?"

"Yes, sir. Thank you, Mama and Daddy, for the new clothes. I appreciate it."

"You don't have to thank us," he said gruffly. "Anything you, your brothers, and your sisters need, it's already yours. I don't care how grown y'all get. Your mama and me just want you to find your way again, Rose. I know this feels like we are pushing you away, and maybe we are a little, but not because we don't love you and not because we don't want to have you underfoot. We just want you to be all right, Pudd'n. That's all."

"I know, Daddy."

"Before you know it, you'll be coming home."

I could tell he was trying to make me feel better and maybe even make himself feel better, so even though I was feeling miserable, I forced a small smile on my face.

"Yes, sir."

"Well, let me get you over to Hiram and Florence's place," he said. "I know your sister been sitting there at the window watching for us all day."

That part did make me smile for real. Even though I was apprehensive about being so far away from home, I was excited about spending more time with Ellena. I knew if anybody could get me out of the doldrums, she could.

Just like Daddy had predicted, as soon as we drove up to Cousin Hiram and Cousin Florence's house, Ellena bounded out of the front door, waving and jumping like she used to do when we were children. You would have thought it had been months since we had last seen each other instead of just a couple of days. As soon as Daddy stopped the car, I hopped out and ran into her arms. A sob escaped me before I could stop it.

"Oh, Sissy," she said soothingly. "It's going to be okay.

It's going to be okay." She kept saying the words over and over in my ear.

I tried to speak, but the words wouldn't come. I was so worn out from everything. I just wanted to go somewhere and curl up into a ball, but I knew that wasn't what Mama and Daddy wanted. They wanted me to use this time away to regroup and figure out what I wanted to do next with my life. That all sounded well and good except I was at a loss for how to move forward.

Cousin Florence came out behind Ellena. She was a little bit older than Mama, but she didn't look it. Her jet-black hair was done up in an elaborate updo, and she was dressed like she was about to go somewhere. She and Cousin Hiram lived alone now that their children were grown and living in their own homes, and they spoiled Ellena rotten from what she had told me.

"We are so happy you are coming to spend some time with us, Rose," Cousin Florence said, putting her arms around me and Ellena. "We love having your sister here with us, and you are just going to be the icing on the cake."

Mama and Daddy got out of the car, and while Daddy took my luggage and packages to the room I would be sharing with Ellena, we all sat in the family room and visited with Cousin Florence. She had plates filled with cookies and ham-and-turkey sandwiches. There was also a large carafe of lemonade. Mama and Ellena were helping themselves, but I still had no appetite. I was grateful that no one said anything about it. When Daddy came back into the room, Cousin Florence looked up at him with an apologetic smile.

"Hiram is so sorry he is going to miss seeing you," she

said. "The basketball team he coaches has a game this afternoon. Cedric, I can tell you how to get to the school if you want to go up there and watch the game and let me visit with Opal before y'all have to go back home."

Daddy came over and put his hand on Mama's shoulder. "No thank you, Florence. Opal and I need to make our way back home. I want to get us there before dark."

I felt the panic rise in my chest. I didn't want them to leave. I had to fight hard to keep myself from screaming, "Please don't leave me! Please don't leave me!" But I didn't do any of that. I plastered a half smile on my face, and I kept it there until Mama and Daddy said their goodbyes. Before they walked outside to the car, Mama put her arm around my waist and pulled me close.

"You will be all right," she said, her voice sounding so sure and confident that I did my best to believe her words. "God will take care of you, Rose."

"Yes, ma'am."

Daddy came over and kissed my cheek. I could tell he was working hard not to get choked up himself.

"If you need anything, you call me," he said. Before we left home, he had given me an envelope filled with cash. "I don't care how large or how small, Rose. I don't want my girls up here wanting for anything. And I know what your mama and me said, but if things get too hard for you, and you need to come back home, you call me, and I'll come get you."

"I'll be all right," I said, reassured by Daddy's promise. It felt good to know Daddy was only a phone call away if I needed him and Mama. Mama said she wanted me to stay until Ellena got done with spring classes. That seemed like an awful long time, but I was going to try my best to do what she and Daddy wanted.

"I'll take care of her," Ellena said as she put her arms around my shoulders. Mama and Daddy kissed and hugged Ellena, and Cousin Florence promised them both that she and Cousin Hiram would take care of us.

"They won't want for a thing," she said. "Don't worry. I'll love on them just like I do my own children and grandchildren."

We all waved as Mama and Daddy finally drove off.

Cousin Florence took my hand in hers. "Come on, sweetie. Let's get you settled." Ellena took my other hand and the three of us made our way inside. I thought back to the words Mama had said. *"God will take care of you."* I prayed she was right. Oh, how I prayed she was right.

CHAPTER 11

"COME ON AND GO WITH ME TO THE SNCC OFFICE, SISSY," ELLENA said, smoothing down her new pixie cut that resembled Audrey Hepburn's, her favorite actress. She cut it herself right before she came back to school. Mama was scandalized at first, referencing every Bible verse there was about hair, both in the Old and New Testament. But Daddy and I calmed her down, telling her how perfect the style looked on Ellena, and it did. It fit her personality. I couldn't imagine cutting my shoulder-length hair, but I wasn't a risk-taker like Ellena. She always enjoyed shocking folks.

I sighed as she came and sat down beside me on the twin bed I slept on. Her bed was on the other side of the room. Cousin Florence had offered us separate bedrooms, but we both insisted we wanted to sleep in the same room together. I was grateful for that, because some nights, Ellena would squeeze into the bed with me and hold me as I cried bitter tears, tears I tried to suppress when I was around other people.

"It's time for you to get out of this house," Ellena said

firmly. "You've been here two months now and you haven't hardly left the house at all, Rose, except to go to church. You might as well have stayed at home."

It was a little after lunchtime on a Thursday, and the only thing I planned on doing that afternoon was paint my toenails and study my Bible lesson for the week. I had done my hair earlier, but I was wearing a simple skirt and sweater. The idea of freshening up and changing clothes overwhelmed me.

"There hasn't been anywhere I wanted to go," I said simply. Except back home to Mama and Daddy, but I didn't say that out loud. I didn't want to hurt Ellena's feelings. I loved being with my little sister, but I missed going to the graveyard and visiting with Jasper and Olivia Rose each day. I felt like a spider who had lost some of her legs. Oh, I could still get around all right, but it wasn't the same. "You go on, Ellena. Just be careful." I understood, to a degree, Ellena's passion for activism and why SNCC would be appealing to her. I just worried about her. The thought of losing her, on top of my other losses, made my heart quicken.

"I'm not taking no for an answer this time, Rose, and anyway, I want you to meet my friends at SNCC." Ellena lowered her voice even though we were in the bedroom alone. She didn't want to take the chance of Cousin Florence or Cousin Hiram walking into the room unannounced and hearing her invitation to me. They had warned her several times to stay away from those "young troublemakers," as they called them.

"All they are going to do is bring more death and destruction to good law-abiding Negroes," Cousin Hiram had

said at the dinner table one night after reading in the news-paper about John Lewis and other members of the organiza-tion going to Selma, Alabama, to help register Black people to vote. Ellena had told me she was going to go with them until I had begged her almost hysterically not to. She had finally agreed not to go, reluctantly, but I knew she was not going to listen to anyone, not even Cousin Hiram, speak badly about her good friend John Lewis and the other young people involved with SNCC. I cut my eyes at her and shook my head as Cousin Hiram continued speaking. *"Between that hothead Lewis and that troublemaking King, some-thing awful is going to happen. You mark my words. The whites are bombing Birmingham left and right and be-fore you know it, they'll be bombing Atlanta too. I mean, it wasn't that long ago that those racist crackers bombed that Jewish temple, and that was white folks bombing other white folks. What y'all think they'll do to a bunch of rabble-rousing Negroes?"*

"But, Cousin Hiram," Ellena had interjected, her pas-sion for SNCC written all over her face. *"John Lewis and the others are simply trying to demand that white people give us our due. Don't we deserve to vote? Don't we deserve to live wherever we choose and eat at whatever lunch coun-ters we want? And don't we deserve to not have to fear for our lives just because we don't agree with white people?"*

"Oh, honey," Cousin Florence said, clicking her teeth. *"We have everything we need. There is no reason for us to bother our pretty heads over some white folks' mess. Let them have their Woolworth's lunch counters and their political elections. I wouldn't vote for one of those stinkers if*

I had to. And as far as fearing for our lives, well, as long as we do what the Good Book says to do, God will protect us."

I reached over and touched my sister's hand. I knew she was about to get wound up. Whenever anyone made statements like that, she was quick to bring up the fact that our great-grandmother was a praying woman who believed in the Good Book, and yet, that didn't stop her from being killed by white racists, or those same racists robbing our father of his pitching arm. She looked at me, her eyes firing like shooting stars, but she gave me a curt nod and said no more that night about civil rights or SNCC. But now, once again, she was fired up about that organization and equally fired up about me going to a meeting with her.

"Ellena, I don't want to go sit and hear a bunch of speeches and such," I said with a groan. I just wasn't political like my little sister. I didn't care about any of the things she was so fired up about. Oh, I agreed with her that the way white people treated us wasn't fair, and for a time, I thought maybe she was right. Maybe we should fight back. But now, having lost so much, I just couldn't imagine getting into a battle that we would surely lose.

"No one is going to be speaking today. Today we are just getting together to talk and brainstorm about planning sit-ins around Georgia, especially in rural communities like back home," she said, looking at me with a glint in her eye. I didn't know whether she was pulling my leg or not, but I knew I had to try to talk some sense into her stubborn head.

"Don't you even think about it, Ellena Ashley Perkins," I said, trying to adopt a stern voice like Mama's. "Don't you try to bring your politickin back to Parsons. Daddy and Mama would have your hide."

I watched as Ellena went to the closet and took out a green fit and flare dress Mama had made and sent to me. It was short-sleeved and had a Peter Pan neckline. I had looked at it briefly but ended up disinterestedly flinging it onto the bed, where it remained until Ellena had hung it up. She walked back over to my bed and laid the dress over my lap. "Then you must get out of this bed and go stop me from doing something foolish. Left on my own volition, who knows what kind of devilment I might get into? If you don't want Mama and Daddy to 'have my hide,' then get up and be the big sister and watch out for me."

"You are awful, Ellena," I said with a loud groan, but I got up and began dressing. "So what are you going to tell Cousin Florence and Cousin Hiram when they ask where we are going?"

Ellena laughed, grabbing her purse from the bed, putting on a pair of oversize sunglasses like Audrey Hepburn wore in *Breakfast at Tiffany's*. "They are going to be so excited that you are up and about and going out that they won't ask a single question. You watch."

And she was right. Cousin Hiram was at the school coaching a basketball game, but when Ellena told Cousin Florence she was taking me out to see the city, Cousin Florence's face nearly split with happiness, to the point that I almost felt guilty we weren't exactly telling her the truth.

"You girls have a good time," she said, handing Ellena the keys to her Buick. I still didn't know how to drive, but Ellena was as good as any of the boys in our family. She even knew how to drive a tractor and would sometimes help Lawrence during harvest season. "And, Rose, you look so pretty in that dress, and you, too, Ellena. Y'all's mama should be selling her clothes in some downtown boutique here in Atlanta. Y'all stay there for a minute and let me take a picture so I can send it to Opal. She will love seeing y'all all dressed up."

Ellena was wearing a yellow skirt and a matching yellow short-sleeved sweater. We posed for a few pictures and then headed out to the car. Once we were in the car, Ellena looked at me with a huge grin. "I told you. Grown folks are always missing what is just underneath their noses." She navigated the large car onto the street and made a quick trip to the SNCC office located on Auburn Avenue. After parking in front of the building, she looked at me with excitement. "You are going to love everyone just like I did. These young people are change-makers, and they aren't scared like so many of the elders. The work SNCC is doing is invaluable, far more progressive than what the SNLC is doing, I think," she said, referring to the Southern Negro Leaders Conference. "Dr. King is doing great work, but I worry he will get reined in too much by all of these conservative Negroes, like Cousin Hiram and Daddy."

"Don't be disrespectful, Ellena," I cautioned. "Daddy has been through a lot, and he and Cousin Hiram have seen more death and destruction by the hands of white folks than we can imagine. Marching around singing Freedom Songs might seem romantic to you, but it's not. People are dying, and although I understand the desire to be free, is it worth you losing your life over?"

"Second Timothy 1:7," she muttered.

Of course, I knew the scripture. *"For God hath not given us the spirit of fear; but of power, and of love, and of a sound mind."*

I reached over and took her hand. "Psalm 110:1. 'Sit thou at my right hand, until I make thine enemies thy footstool.'"

Ellena glared at me but then burst into laughter. "You always were the best at remembering scripture. Okay, Sissy. I won't go toe to toe with you over this, mainly because I would lose this particular verbal exercise. I promise not to do anything reckless. I just want to introduce you to some of my friends."

Ellena got out of the car before I could answer her and was opening my door. She tucked my arm into the crook of hers, and we entered the building where the SNCC office was located. Once we were inside, I was amazed by the number of young people crammed into the space and the level of activity going on. People were talking animatedly on the phone while others were busy typing away on one of the many typewriters throughout the room, and still others were huddled together talking in small groups. But as we entered the room, everyone seemed excited to see my sister as they waved and called out greetings to her. She waved and answered back with her own hellos, then she led me to the back of the room where a young Negro man was talking rapidly, gesturing with his hands like he was simultaneously talking in sign language. I noticed he had something strange-looking on his head. It seemed familiar to me, but I couldn't place it.

"What is that on his head?" I whispered to Ellena.

"It's called a yarmulke. That's Isaac Weinberg. He's Jewish," she whispered back.

"A Black Jewish person?" I questioned in a hushed voice. "I didn't know there were any Black Jewish people."

"You would be surprised to know that most Jewish people aren't pale-faced, Sissy," she said with a smile. "But Isaac wasn't born Jewish. He was adopted and raised by a white Jewish family in New York. He's down here attending college at Morehouse, or he was, at least. I think he's here at the office or out in the field working more than he's attending school. Of course, that's true for just about everybody."

"In the fields?" I said incredulously. "He's a farmer too?" I couldn't imagine the thin young man out in some field planting tobacco or peanuts. Carrying schoolbooks was about all he looked capable of doing.

Ellena laughed. "No, silly. People who go out into the various communities and help register Negro voters and disseminate information to them are referred to as field staff workers or field secretaries. Here, let me introduce you to everyone." She guided me to the group where Isaac was still talking. "Excuse me, Brother Isaac," she said with great flourish. I was a bit embarrassed to suddenly have all eyes on us. "I apologize for the interruption, but I wanted to introduce all of you to my sister, Rose."

Everyone but Isaac smiled and greeted me, telling me their names and welcoming me to the group. Clearly, he was not pleased at being interrupted. Once Ellena and I sat down, he resumed talking.

"Our fight for equality should not supersede our efforts to educate our people about their history," Isaac said passionately. "We can integrate white schools all day long, but do we honestly believe they will teach our children their history? We know better. They will call it integration, but what it will actually be is assimilation. The slow and steady genocide of all that makes us unique. In less than a generation our children will be hated and ignorant, two states of being that will lead only to the further demise of the Negro race. Don't be fooled by the antics of liberal whites. Trust me when I say this. I grew up around them, so I know first-hand how they can give you the old bait and switch. They reel you in and then they cut off your head."

I was shocked by his words for a number of reasons. First, because of what Ellena shared about him being raised by white people, but second, because a number of the young people sitting in the circle around him were white. I scanned their faces to see if they were angered by his words, but most of them were just nodding as if in agreement with him. It was all quite peculiar. Before I could whisper my questions to Ellena, she jumped into the conversation.

"Then what do you propose, Brother Isaac? Do we continue being separate and unequal?" Ellena asked. "Brown versus the Board of Education was not flawless, but it was a start. So what do you expect us to do? Pull away from the union and form our own state? We all understand that there will be pitfalls with integration, but the alternative doesn't seem to prove any more beneficial for our people. So again, I ask, what do we do?"

I was so proud of her strong voice, challenging this young Negro man who seemed so confident and sure of himself to the point of sounding arrogant. One thing was for sure: Our parents did not raise us to be shrinking violets even though we were girls. Our voices were always welcomed in conversations, whether it be with other children or the adults in our lives, as long as we showed respect. Now, Ellena was always more vocal than me or even Katie Bell, but none of us felt like what we thought didn't matter in our home growing up.

"Sister Ellena, I appreciate your questions, and they are valid," he said with a smile. "My main point is this: We must not see integration as the end goal but, instead, the halfway point to the true freedom and equality we seek. If we stop our efforts when all of our children are forced to attend white schools where they will be hated and despised by the students, the teachers, and the administrators, then we will find that we are going backward, not forward. Remember the Little Rock Nine and how they were treated? Every day when I go out in the field and encourage Negroes to put their lives on the line by registering to vote and participating in sit-ins, I ask myself: Am I doing the work of the Almighty or The Movement? The two are not necessarily synonymous."

"It's clear the work we are doing is God's work," said another young Negro who had introduced himself as Julian Bond, the communications director of SNCC. "If you can't see that, Isaac, then that is your lack of vision, not SNCC's."

I held my breath, wondering how Isaac would react, but he laughed loudly. "Touché," he said. "I am always ready and willing to stand corrected. Of the things I just stated, I pray I do eat those words someday. Now, I bet there are some letters that need to be stuffed across the room. I will leave you all to your conversation."

"Oh stop, Isaac," one of the young women said with a laugh, calling out to him as he walked away. "Can't we play nice? Last I checked we were all on the same team."

Isaac just waved his hand and kept walking. The young woman turned to me and grinned. I thought she said her name was Judy Richardson. "Well, Sister Rose, welcome to SNCC. In spite of what you just witnessed, we do get along. More or less. Julian and Isaac have a water and oil kind of relationship. Isn't that right, Brother Bond?"

"More or less," he said with a smile as he placed his hand on the leg of a young woman I would later learn was his wife, Alice. "I don't believe we have seen you around here before, Rose. Your sister is a constant fixture, but your face isn't familiar. Are you from out of town?"

I nodded. "Yes. I'm visiting my sister and some of our family who live here in Atlanta." I didn't feel like telling everyone the circumstances that brought me here. I was still dealing with my grief in my own way. These young people, in spite of the heavy work they were doing with SNCC, seemed so carefree and young. I didn't want to have to explain how I, at such a young age, had both a dead husband and a dead baby.

"Well, welcome to SNCC," Julian Bond said. "I'm sure if you hang around, there will be plenty of things for you to busy yourself with. Would you concur, ladies?"

Judy snorted. "Of course, Brother Bond. We women-folk are here to serve you men and The Movement. Maybe we could run and make you all a sandwich or bake you an apple pie."

The other women laughed. I joined in with them,

although I wasn't exactly sure why. He just shook his head and walked toward Isaac, who was deep in conversation with a group of men on the other side of the room. Ellena stood.

"Well, I brought my sister to meet everyone and get some work done. I'll show her the ropes and we will get busy stuffing the envelopes Brother Isaac mentioned, although it doesn't look like he made it all the way over to the workspace."

"That's no surprise," Judy said with a shake of her head. "They are highly skilled at pontification, not so much with labor of the secretarial nature. They leave that to the womenfolk."

"Be that as it may, the work needs to be done," Ellena said primly and then led me to the other side of the room. The table had flyers about how to register to vote. "I refuse to allow myself to get caught up in the bashing of our menfolk. The white folks do enough of it. We don't have to add fuel to the fire. Of course they are going to be the leaders in the group. Something as big as the civil rights movement is going to have to be led by a man. That's just how it is."

"You all are so . . . mature," I said, searching for the right word. They were all so sophisticated and different. Ellena had always been smart and well-read, but I never remembered her to be quite so grown-up acting. I had missed out on a lot by marrying Jasper and moving away. My sister had grown up on me and I hadn't even noticed.

"So these flyers are going to go to as many pastors as we can reach throughout the South," she said. "I worked on getting the list together. Every Negro church from Tupelo, Mississippi, to the far reaches of Kentucky is getting mailers from us. Black people might not be unified Monday through Saturday, but on Sunday, we are often on one accord, so we want to try to persuade the clergy that supporting our efforts is truly the work of God."

"I just don't know about all of this," I said, sitting down at the worktable, putting flyers inside the envelopes that already had addresses on them. "I don't understand the rush."

"If not now, then when, Sister Rose?" a voice said from behind. I turned around and saw Isaac making his way to the table. He sat down beside me and started stuffing envelopes too. "Negroes have been waiting for freedom since 1619. I wouldn't call what we are doing rushing."

I felt a bit out of my league talking to someone as educated as Isaac. I wasn't like my sister Ellena. I didn't have quick comebacks, so I just went silent and focused on stuffing envelopes.

"I'm sorry," he said after a moment's pause. "I get pretty wound up about all of this. The last thing I want to do is to insult a beautiful woman."

I felt the sides of my cheeks get warm. I almost placed my hands on them, but I just kept stuffing envelopes. "You don't have to apologize. I just hate to see anyone die from this."

"They've been killing us from the start, Sister Rose," he said. "Whether we fight racism or not, Negroes will die."

"That's the truth," Ellena said, standing up. I was relieved. I hoped this meant we were going back to the house. I started to rise, too, but she placed her hand on mine. "Don't get up, Sissy. I'm just going down the street to get a couple of sodas. I'm absolutely parched, and there's never anything cold to drink here. Would you like a soda, Brother Isaac?"

"No thank you." He continued to push flyers into envelopes.

Before I could say anything, she was heading toward the door.

"Your sister is one of the strongest volunteers here at SNCC," Isaac said. "I know your family must be very proud of the work she does."

"They don't know," I said softly. "This isn't something she can share with the elders in our family."

"I can't imagine not having my family's support," he said, shaking his head. "That's sad that your family doesn't understand the importance of the work we all are doing."

His words made me angry. He didn't have a clue about my family and what hardships they had endured. But I didn't say anything.

He looked at me and sighed. "I'm sorry, Sister Rose. I didn't mean to sound so arrogant. I'm sure your family is quite supportive of Sister Ellena. Otherwise, she wouldn't be attending school here in Atlanta. I just get so passionate about the work we do. I sometimes forget that all Negroes aren't on the same page when it comes to this, and generally for very good reason."

For some reason, I couldn't make myself look him in the face. I had never felt so shy around a man before. I thought about Jasper and how forward acting I had been with him. Maybe I was comfortable around him because we were intellectual equals. He and I were simple folks. We'd both graduated from high school, but that was all. I know he and I had discussed me going to nursing school someday, but the idea of being around people like Isaac and these other young folks made me nervous. This SNCC crowd just seemed like they were from another world, especially this Isaac. He reminded me of Dr. King. So smart and quick with his words—so sure of himself. I looked around, hoping someone else would come over to the table, but everyone seemed busy and deep in their conversations or work.

"What do you think about SNCC?" he asked. "I know you said maybe we were all moving too fast, but do you think the work, in and of itself, is wrong?"

I shrugged. I wasn't sure how best to answer that question. I didn't really know what all SNCC was doing. Oh, Ellena talked about it, but to be honest, my mind hadn't been too focused on what she said because my mind and heart still belonged to Jasper and the baby. But as I finally glanced up at Isaac, he did seem to care what I thought, so I tried to answer as best I could. "I sort of worry that if we fight so hard to be everywhere white folks are, we'll forget what it means to be with each other. I fear we'll stop wanting to be with each other. I love my family and my community, and I don't want that to change."

Isaac nodded as if he was pondering what I was saying. "I agree, Sister Rose. You actually explained what I was trying to say earlier, just more eloquently. We do have to walk a fine line. We deserve equality, but we must also strive to hold on to what makes us Negroes. You are very insightful."

I turned away, embarrassed.

"What does your husband think about all of this?" Isaac asked. "Does he share your thoughts?"

For a moment I wondered how he knew I was married . . . had been married, but then I realized I still wore my wedding band. I touched it lightly.

"My husband was killed during training in the Air Force. Friendly fire," I said, grimacing at the awful term. "But I imagine he would think Negroes have the right to want whatever it is we want. At least that's what I think he would believe." I felt sad that Jasper and I had so little time to get to know each other. I wish I could have one more conversation with him where he shared with me all his thoughts and feelings about everything.

"I'm sorry, Sister Rose," Isaac said. "I didn't know. I didn't mean to bring up painful thoughts for you."

"Of course you didn't," I said softly. "There's no reason for you to feel bad. You just asked a question."

He reached out and patted my hand. I pulled it away. I didn't want to be getting my mind mixed up over any more men. I was Jasper's wife until . . . well, until forever. Before we could say anything else, Ellena came walking toward us. I stood up.

"I'm ready to go home," I said. She looked from me to Isaac and back to me.

"Okay," she said without argument. Ellena could read my face better than anyone, so I know she picked up on the fact that I was not feeling comfortable here anymore. "Let's go. Isaac, you take care."

Ellena took me by the arm and quickly guided me out of the SNCC office before Isaac had a chance to say anything. "Are you okay? He didn't say something to hurt you, did he? I swear, I'll—"

I shook my head. "No. He didn't do anything wrong. I'm just a bit tired and overwhelmed."

"Okay then. Let's go. By now, Cousin Hiram is probably home, and he'll be worried about us."

I didn't say anything. I just let Ellena guide me to the car. As she drove off, I looked back toward the building and saw Isaac standing outside watching us leave. I leaned my head back against the seat, closed my eyes, and willed my mind to go into its deepest recesses where I would find the spirit of my husband, Jasper, waiting patiently for me.

CHAPTER 12

"WHAT IS THE NAME OF THIS THING WE'RE GOING TO AGAIN?" I asked Ellena for what seemed like the hundredth time, but I just couldn't seem to wrap my tongue around the name. I knew it started with "Sha." I had a really good memory, but for some reason that strange-sounding name just didn't stick. I knew it was a holiday that Jewish people celebrated each week, and I knew it was something Ellena had gone to before, but besides that, I was a bit unsure about what it was we were attending. For the last three weeks, I allowed Ellena to drag me to more SNCC meetings, events on the Spelman campus, and a church social. I knew she was doing her best to get me out of the house so that I wouldn't constantly be thinking about my losses. But what she didn't know was that even when I was smiling and talking to people, my mind was still floating away to a place where my husband and daughter were alive. I couldn't move past my grief. My loneliness. If I closed my eyes I could feel Jasper's touch, and if I really concentrated, I could smell the newborn smell of my baby girl. I knew everyone would tell me what I was doing wasn't healthy, so I tried to do things that would calm their concerns. But my heart remained broken, and I had no idea how to fix it.

Ellena had told Cousin Florence that we were going to a Bible study at a professor's house. She reassured her that other students would be there, and we wouldn't be late getting back home. I had cringed for every falsehood or stretching of the truth she had told, but I didn't try to stop her or correct her in front of our cousin. I knew that once Ellena made up her mind to do something, it was practically a done deal, so the best I could do was just go and be there with her and not add or detract from her explanation of what we would be doing.

"It's called Shabbat," she said as she navigated the Buick through the streets of Atlanta, heading toward the home of the professor and his wife who were hosting this gathering. I had asked Ellena if they were Black and Jewish, like Isaac. She said no; they were white. I felt strange going to the home of white people. I had never been around them that way before. Back home, we stayed close to our family and the people at our church. We would smile and speak to the white people in Parsons if we ran into them downtown, but other than that, we didn't try to interact with them, and they didn't try to interact with us. I was shocked at how comfortable Ellena was with the idea of eating dinner with white folks. She was still my baby sister, but so much about her was different. I guess, if the truth be known, so much was different about both of us. I prayed our differences would never create a wedge between us.

Ellena said this professor whose home we were going to was her history professor, and his wife taught in the English department. She also said they were supporters of SNCC, often donating money to the cause and attending some of its meetings. Of course, I knew that if they were involved with SNCC, that was all Ellena needed to know about them. I listened as she continued to tell me about Shabbat. "From Friday sundown to Saturday sundown, Jewish people rest from all duties and celebrate togetherness. They light candles, have a huge meal, sing hymns and pray, and read from the Talmud—a book similar to our Christian Bible. This is my second time going to Shabbat at Professor Edelman's home. It's nothing to be worried about. We will still be Methodist when it is all over."

I knew she was poking fun at me. I had told her I didn't think Mama or Daddy would like us going to a Jewish celebration, but she said this professor never made non-Jews feel out of place. I told her I would go, but the second things felt weird or strange, I was leaving, with or without her. She agreed, but she also knew I would never leave her.

When we pulled up to the house, several people were walking toward the door, including Isaac. I had seen him only once since our first encounter, and it had been brief. We spoke, inquired about each other's health, and that was it. Tonight, like before, he was dressed in a dark suit with the Jewish hat on his head. Once again, the name of it escaped me. I watched as he walked over to us.

"Shabbat Shalom, Sister Ellena, Sister Rose," he said with a deep bow.

"Shabbat Shalom," Ellena quickly responded. "Nice

seeing you, Brother Isaac. I trust your week has been a good one."

"It's going well. I am planning to join James Forman, our executive secretary at SNCC, and some of the others in Greenwood, Mississippi, next week. They are already down there helping to register voters. Things are heating up, and they need all the help they can get," Isaac said. Excitement was visible on his face. I wondered what would make a person with no connection to our part of the world want to put themselves in harm's way. I knew Daddy and some of the others in the family called them "rabble-rousers," but I knew it had to be something more than that. It made me think about the verse in Deuteronomy where God's people are said to be "peculiar." I would definitely call Isaac and the rest of the SNCC members peculiar. They seemed driven by some force of nature that I just couldn't put my finger on.

"I sure wish I could help," Ellena said. I could hear the wistfulness in her voice. My sister never met a battle she didn't want to jump into. As much as I wanted to be back in Parsons, I was thankful that I was here to maybe talk some sense into my sister before she did something she might later regret.

"There is much work to be done right here, Sister Ellena," Isaac said, lightly patting her on the back. "Everyone can't be on the front lines and there is no shame in that."

"This all sounds very dangerous," I said. Having lived in Hattiesburg, Mississippi, I was quite familiar with Leflore County, where Greenwood was situated. That place was known for its lynchings and other acts of violence toward Negroes. I prayed again that my sister would not get caught up in the excitement of doing this work. "Perhaps there is another way," I said softly.

"If you figure out what that way is, please, let us all know," he said. "Until then, we pray for the Almighty's protection, but we don't shy away from doing what is right. Ladies." He motioned for us to continue toward the door, where a smiling white man and woman were standing. Just like Isaac, the man was dressed somberly, also wearing that same hat on his head. The woman was dressed in a long black dress with her blonde hair pulled back into a chignon. I was happy that Ellena had counseled me on what was appropriate attire. She and I both had on gray dresses with dolman sleeves Mama made for us.

"Shabbat Shalom," Professor Edelman said, reaching out and patting Isaac on the back. "Good to see you, Isaac. Good to see you, Ellena. And who is this with you?"

"This is my sister, Rose," she said, shaking hands with her professor. "She is staying with me here in Atlanta until the school term ends."

"Good evening, sir. Ma'am." I tried not to sound as nervous as I was as I shook their outstretched hands.

"Good to meet you. So are you thinking about enrolling at Spelman too?" he asked. "You couldn't ask for a better school."

"I'm not sure," I said. I still had thoughts of becoming a nurse, but that all seemed so overwhelming. I couldn't imagine focusing my mind on studies right now. Every bit of extra thought I had seemed to go to the baby and Jasper. I wasn't sure what my future was going to look like.

"Well, the fall will be here before you know it," he said

in such a firm voice it made me feel a bit awkward. Almost as if I had no choice but to enroll in school.

"Stop grilling the child," his wife said, stepping forward and putting her arm around my shoulder. "You must excuse my husband. He truly believes Spelman is the answer for all things that are wrong in the world."

"That would be an affirmative," he said with a smile. "I apologize, Rose. But just know, you haven't heard the last of my spiel."

We all laughed as his wife continued with the introductions. "My name is Professor Bella Edelman and I teach Shakespearean literature. Since Hosea and I are both professors," she said, motioning to her husband, "most people call him Professor H and they call me Professor B. Thank you all so much for coming to our home to celebrate Shabbat. The other young people are gathering inside. Isaac and Ellena, show Rose where everyone is."

We thanked them again and followed the voices inside to the back of the house, where a huge table was filled with food, most of which I had never seen before.

"Mother never knows how to fix a simple meal," a young woman about my age said, walking up to us. She was almost a carbon copy of her mother, from her long blonde hair to her statuesque height. "Shabbat Shalom. Welcome to our home."

"Sissy, this is Esther Edelman," Ellena said, giving the girl a quick hug, just as someone called out to Ellena.

"Go say hello to your friends," Esther said. "I'll keep your sister company. Hello, Isaac."

"Hello, Esther," he said awkwardly before hurrying off.

I watched as Esther rolled her eyes. She must have noticed the curious look on my face because she laughed slightly. "I fancied myself attracted to Isaac, but the feelings were not reciprocated. Seems the idea of dating a white girl was more than he could stomach."

I think my mouth must have been gaping open because she laughed and shrugged. "I figured if Sammy Davis Jr., a Negro Jewish man, could love a white woman, why not Isaac, but he is not interested in anyone but Negro women. I can't even be mad at him for it."

I didn't know what to say. This girl was like none I had ever met before. She gave me a quick hug, which was even more startling.

"Darling, you must ignore me completely," she said. "I'm just a typical Jewish girl from the Lower East Side trying to fit in at Spelman with all of these amazing young Negro ladies."

I didn't think I could get any more shocked than when she mentioned being interested in Isaac. I finally found my voice. "You go to Spelman?"

"Yes, I do. I'm an exchange student there this year."

"What does it mean to be an exchange student?"

"I actually attend Sarah Lawrence College," she said, guiding me over to two chairs by a bay window overlooking the backyard. "But Daddy's friend, Dr. Zinn, who is the chair of the history and social sciences department at Spelman, came up with this brilliant idea for Black students from Spelman to attend northern universities and vice versa. I think I'm sort of their guinea pig. But I must say, I have enjoyed my time here this year, and I will be sad to leave. So much good humanitarian work is going on at Spelman and around town. I hope to do what I can when I get back to New York to keep this movement going."

"That sounds interesting," I said, not sure what else to say. She reminded me of Holly Golightly in *Breakfast at Tiffany's*. I could just imagine her holding court with a bunch of hipsters like the ones in the movie.

I looked over at Ellena and Isaac, who had joined the group of young people on the other side of the room. All in all, there were about ten of them, both Negro and white. Ellena looked over at me and waved, and I waved back.

"Are you and your sister close?" Esther asked.

I nodded. "Very. She's my best friend."

"I have always wished for a sibling, but it's just me," she said with a wry smile. "Fortunately, I make friends easily and I adopt people as my brothers and sisters, so be careful, or you might be next."

Before I could respond, her parents came into the room and announced that they were about to get started.

"We would like to welcome you all to our home to help us celebrate Shabbat," Professor Hosea said, putting his arm around his wife's waist. "Just to give the new folks a sense of what happens during Shabbat, first, there is the lighting of the candles that you see on the table. My wife lit them about twenty minutes before sunset and she said a prayer. Now, we will sing 'Shalom Aleikhem,' which means 'Peace to you.' After that, I will say the blessing over our daughter, Esther, as well as blessings over the wine, the washing of our hands, and the Challah bread. Then we will eat this delicious meal my wife has prepared. Honey, would you tell them what is on the table?"

The table looked beautiful. The china looked very old and delicate. This table reminded me of how Mama and Grandma Perkins set their tables for Thanksgiving, Christmas, and Easter. I had hoped the day would come when I would set such a table for my family. I felt a tear slide down my face. I swiped at it, but not before Esther saw it. She reached over and took my hand in hers.

"Are you okay?" she whispered.

I nodded. I didn't have the words to explain why I would be overcome with emotion right now.

"This can be a bit overwhelming," she said with a smile. "You won't have to do anything but just relax and let the Jews take the lead."

I smiled at her. I had never had this type of conversation with a white girl before, but she was nice and I found myself relaxing. We both listened as her mother explained what all was on the table—dishes I had never heard of before like gefilte fish and baba ghanoush, which she said was similar to hummus, which didn't help me at all since I didn't know what that was. But there were other things that were familiar—like roast beef with mushroom sauce, baked chicken, and a soup made from sweet potatoes. For dessert she said there was green-tea cheesecake and chocolate mousse.

Esther squeezed my hand, then went to stand by her parents as they and the other Jewish people in the room sang. Ellena came over and stood by me, putting her arm around my waist.

"Are you okay?" she asked.

"Yes, I'm okay."

I watched as Professor H placed his hands on the head of his daughter. "Y'simeich Elohim k'Sarah, k'Rivkah, k'Rachel, ooch'Leah."

Even though I didn't know what the words meant, they sounded beautiful. Coming here, I didn't know what to expect at Shabbat, but so far, everything seemed both different and familiar at the same time. Not Christian, but not foreign feeling either. I watched the others in the room who were Jewish, and they seemed as reverent as we all were when we did things like take the Lord's Supper or recite the Lord's Prayer. Once the blessings were done, we all sat at the long table. I found myself between Ellena and Isaac.

"What do you think about Shabbat?" Isaac asked, passing me the platter of roast beef. I was very careful reaching for the platter. The last thing I wanted to do was break any of this china. It looked irreplaceable.

"I've enjoyed it." I put a sliver of beef on my plate and passed it to Ellena, who was deep in conversation with the person to her left. "I didn't understand what Shabbat was before arriving here, but so far, it has been a pleasant surprise. It feels very . . . ancient, which I suppose it is. I'm not saying it right. I guess what I'm trying to say is I felt a connection to what happened tonight and I don't know why."

Isaac smiled. "You're saying it exactly right. A lot of people feel that way the first time they experience Shabbat."

I was relieved that I didn't sound stupid. I was gradually feeling a little less awkward around Ellena's friends from SNCC. They were still a bit intimidating, but they all had such good hearts and they wanted to be of service to people in our community. I had to admire them for that.

"Are you nervous about going to Mississippi?" I asked. "I lived there for a while. It's nothing like Atlanta."

"I know," he said in a voice so solemn that I could tell he had thought about this for a while. "Yes, I am nervous, but I am happy that I can use my education and knowledge for good. I don't just want to be a lawyer like my father. I want to be on the ground doing work that changes the day-to-day lives of my people."

"Your parents are okay with that?" I couldn't imagine them wanting him to be involved with such dangerous work. I know Mama and Daddy would be beside themselves if they knew Ellena and I were doing the little bit that we were doing in the SNCC office.

Isaac laughed. "My parents are the reason I'm doing this work. Once Father learned about SNCC, he said, 'You have the rest of your life to be an attorney, but you have only this moment to be part of the historic work SNCC is doing.' Mother was a bit concerned, but she is as proud of my work as Father. They said when my biological mama was dying of cancer, she made them promise not to raise me to be spoiled and entitled."

"Do you remember her?" I asked.

He shook his head as he put more roast beef on his plate. "Not really. I was only four years old when she died. I have vague memories of her, but mostly I just know the stories Mother and Father shared. She was their housekeeper, but she and Mother were as close as sisters—or at least that is what Mother says."

His description of his two mothers reminded me of what Mama used to say about her Grandma Birdie and the white woman they both worked for up until Great-Grandma Birdie died. Mama said they were as close as a Negro and a white person could be. I had never witnessed anything like that, so it was interesting hearing this young, Jewish Negro man say the same about his white mother and his Black mama.

I found it easy talking to Isaac. He reminded me of my brother Lawrence. So serious and so thoughtful about everything he said. I felt comfortable talking to him, which was why I shared a bit of what I was feeling about the loss of my family.

"I don't know how to start the healing that everybody keeps telling me about," I confided, pushing the tears away. "I miss them so much. I never got to know my baby girl, but I miss her like I had been her mama for a lifetime."

"I'm so sorry, Rose," he said, putting down his knife and fork. "Last year, my father's mother, Bubbe, died suddenly. I was close to her and losing her felt like a huge part of me died. Jewish people do something called 'sitting shiva.' It's basically seven days of mourning to honor the departed. The thing about it that brought me such comfort was we got to talk about Bubbe for seven days straight, and the ongoing joke was Bubbe would have given anything to be there to hear us talk about her for that long."

In spite of myself, I had to smile about that. His bubbe sounded a lot like Grandma Perkins. She'd already told me exactly how she wanted her funeral to be, from the dress she would wear to the hymns that would be sung to the scriptures she wanted read. "We do some things similar," I said. "But we definitely don't take seven days. I think that might be helpful. After the funeral, it's as if everyone just wants you to pick up and carry on as usual. They forget that the pain isn't left at the grave. If anything, the pain begins there."

He nodded. "I understand. But Rose, you must do the things that help you. Don't allow anyone to tell you when you should be healed from the pain. I don't think there is any such healing. I think the pain scabs over and you just learn to deal with it."

I nodded. This time a tear did fall. I dabbed it away with my napkin. "Thank you, Isaac. You are very easy to talk to."

"Thank you," he said. "You are as well. And as such, I have one more bit of advice. Find your passion, Rose. Whatever that is. Life is too short to be in everlasting pain. That was something the rabbi said to us after Bubbe died. That's sort of why I do what I do. The only way I have been able to live with my own losses is to be in service to others. Do that, and although it won't cure your pain, it will make it more tolerable. I promise."

"Thank you." It was so strange hearing someone so young offering such sage advice. Later that night, after we had made it back home, I stayed on my knees longer than normal, asking God to show me what my path was and to give me help getting to it.

CHAPTER 13

THE LAST FEW WEEKS WENT BY IN A HURRY, AND I WAS GRATE-
ful for that. Otherwise, I would have been staring at the
calendar, waiting for Mama and Daddy to come and get us
once Ellena was done with classes. Instead of sitting around
moping, I tried to stay busy volunteering in the SNCC office
with Ellena when she wasn't in class. I let her make up whatever excuse came to mind with Cousin Florence and Cousin
Hiram, although to be honest, they didn't really question us
too deeply about where we were going. They trusted us and
were happy that I was finally getting out of the house. I felt
a bit guilty about their trustfulness, but at this point, I was
just happy to be out doing something that felt useful.

The more I learned about SNCC and the young people
who ran it, the more I appreciated the work the organiza-
tion was doing. Charles "Chuck" McDew, the chairman of
SNCC, was only twenty-four or twenty-five, but he seemed
so much older. All of them did. Like Isaac, Chuck was also
Black and Jewish, and he frequently reminded us of the
words spoken by Jewish scholar Hillel the Elder, who died in

the first century: "If I am not for myself, who will be for me? And being for myself, what am I? And if not now, when?" Chuck would say this whenever it seemed like people were forgetting why we were working so hard.

When Ellena and I would go to the SNCC office, I would do whatever was needed of me, whether that was stuff envelopes or help with coordination of the legal team to the various communities where the field staff workers were working. Soon after Shabbat at Ellena's professor's house, Isaac left for Greenwood, Mississippi, to help with voter registration. Before Isaac left, he asked whether he could write to me. I didn't think that would do any harm, and actually, once the letters started arriving, I looked forward to them. They were never inappropriate, just informative. By his third or fourth letter, I noticed a change in his tone. He went from sounding excited to being overwhelmed by all that he saw down in Mississippi.

Dear Rose,

I pray this letter finds you doing well. I wish that I had happy news to share, but unfortunately, things here are bad. Worse even than we were told. I have never seen people suffering from such abject poverty and disparity in my life. I knew I had been sheltered all of my life, and I also knew that most Negroes did not have the advantages I have had, but I was not prepared for what I have seen here in Greenwood. Negroes are living in homes with no electricity or indoor plumbing, and while we are trying to convince them that voting is what they need, the majority of them just want the basic comforts in life that I have taken for granted. And then, on top of that, the hatred from the whites is brutal, Rose. Their hatred for us pierces like a dagger. I am trying very hard to be brave, but it isn't easy. I know you and I come from different religions and backgrounds, but I say without any hesitation, pray for us, Rose. We are facing our potential killers every single day and it is nearly debilitating to me. All I want to do is tuck tail and run back to Atlanta, but the work here is so important. I ask that you pray for the strength I so desperately need to do this most important work.

Sincerely,
Isaac

Every night when I said my prayers, I asked God to bless all the field workers and people in Mississippi and elsewhere trying to do what was right—trying to fight against what I was beginning to see truly was oppressive, something Ellena had been trying to tell me for the longest. But I also spoke directly to God about Isaac, my friend. "Please, calm his fears and help him to continue to be brave," I prayed. Unfortunately, things continued to spiral downward in Greenwood. Toward the end of March, Isaac and ten other field workers, including the executive secretary of SNCC, James Forman, were arrested. According to the report, they had "incited a riot" and had "refused to move on" after the police turned a dog loose on them.

Everyone at the SNCC office was in an uproar over the news. I found myself busy taking dictation from Chuck and others and then quickly typing letters that would go to the United States Department of Justice, the Civil Rights Commission, and the Federal Bureau of Investigation. I was thankful for the distraction of the work because the thought of Isaac and the others being in jail was terrifying. It seemed the phone calls and the letter writing worked. Attorney General Robert F. Kennedy, the president's brother, got involved and immediately everyone was released.

That night, Ellena and I were so excited, we sat up talking into the wee hours. We started off rehashing everything that had happened in Greenwood, but Ellena soon turned her attention to her constant desire to integrate Parsons.

"We need this kind of work to be happening back home, Rose," she said as she put pin curlers in her hair, the passion in her voice almost brimming over. "I've been talking to Brother Chuck and the others, and they are willing to send some field workers to help us after school is over. Sissy, we can have the same kind of change we're seeing happen all over the South right in our own backyard."

I shook my head, putting down the copy of *Ebony* magazine I had been flipping through. "Daddy and the others wouldn't stand for it. It's taken too long for whites and Negroes to live in some semblance of peace. We can't bring this to Parsons."

"So the rest of the world fights for freedom and we just sit back and sip on sweet tea and eat Mama's lemon squares?" she asked, raising her voice.

"Not so loud," I whispered. "You'll wake Cousin Hiram and Cousin Florence."

"They need to wake up," she insisted. "And Mama and Daddy need to wake up too. The fight is happening right up underneath our noses. I'm not going to let this go, Rose. It means too much to me."

I knew she was telling the truth when she said she wouldn't let this go. One thing about Ellena—once her mind was made up about something, that was it. Over the next few weeks, I tried to talk some sense into her, and she seemed to calm herself down. So when Mama and Daddy came to pick us up, I figured it was all over and done with. Plus, I was so happy to see them, I didn't think about nothing else.

"Mama!" I cried as I ran into her arms the second she entered the house, her tears matching mine. We clung to each other like we were each other's lifeline. Mama and Daddy hadn't been to see us while we were gone. We had talked on the phone, but that had been all.

"My baby," she said over and over. "My sweet baby, I have missed you so much."

Daddy came up behind us and stroked my hair. "We missed you, baby girl. Every day, your mama asked me if we were doing the right thing and whether we should bring you back home."

I looked up at them both with surprise. Neither of them had said anything like that when we talked on the phone. Quite the opposite actually. They would say I needed to stay and continue to heal. As much as it pained me to be away, I now knew they were right. I needed time away from Parsons. I needed time to figure out what I was going to do for the rest of my life. I wasn't sure what that something was going to be, but I knew I wanted to somehow be in service to others. I thought about Chuck McDew's words of inspiration again: "If I'm only for myself, what am I?"

For the first few days after we got home, I stayed close to Mama. I planned on going back to the store and helping Daddy, but I had missed her so much that I just wanted to be where she was. Ellena got a job helping out at Powell's Fabric Store, so it left me and Mama at home. I decided to talk to her about my future. She and I were sitting on the porch waiting for Daddy and Ellena to come home. Supper was ready and we wanted to be outside where it was cool.

"Mama," I said, pushing the swing slowly with my left foot. Daddy's coon dogs, King and Jupiter, were back to being my shadows and were both positioned underneath the swing. It was nice having them close by again. Earlier that day, they had walked with me to the graveyard. I had promised Mama I wouldn't become a fixture out there, but I wanted to visit with Jasper and Olivia Rose. I didn't stay long, and when I came back inside the house, Mama had smiled, the relief clear on her face. Now she looked at me expectantly.

"What is it, sweetheart?" She was sewing a baby outfit. While I was away, Katie Bell announced she was pregnant again, so Mama was doing what she always did when somebody in the family got in the family way.

"I think I want to go to nursing school," I said, finally putting my thoughts to words. "Before Jasper died, he told me he wanted me to go to school like I had wanted to do before he and I met. What do you think about that?"

Mama put down her sewing and smiled. "I think that is wonderful. I'm so proud of you, baby. You've come a long way in a few months. Your daddy and I will do whatever we need to do to help you."

"Thank you," I said just as Daddy and Ellena drove into the yard. Daddy parked his car in the shade underneath a pecan tree. Ellena hopped out of the car and began making her way toward the house.

"Hey, y'all." She plopped down on the steps. "I am exhausted."

"You look tired," I said. "Miss Jainey kept you busy today?" Ellena was working at Miss Jainey's fabric store this summer to make a bit of spending money for when she went back to school.

Ellena put her hand to her forehead dramatically. "Lord, yes. I think every white woman in Parsons, Georgia, was looking for fabric for new summer dresses, or should I say their 'girls' were looking for fabric."

Daddy walked toward the porch, and King and Jupiter raced to him. They knew Daddy had a treat for them. He gave each dog a bone and they scurried underneath the porch.

"Hey, baby," he said, coming over and kissing Mama on her forehead. "I don't know which one of us is more tired—me or Ellena, to hear her tell it."

"Oh, Daddy," Ellena said.

"Did one of y'all bring me my paper?" Mama asked.

Daddy nodded and handed it to her. "I sure did. I know you like to keep up with what these white folks are up to in Parsons."

The Parsons Gazette was printed three times per week, mostly covering stories about local farmers, bridal showers, and news about the white schools. On rare occasions, there would be an article about someone in the Negro community. Those articles typically focused on achievements the Negro students were making at school or in the military. When the twins went away to Howard Medical School, there was a huge spread about them—in the back of the newspaper, of course. Even the news was segregated.

"Daddy, do you want me to go get you a plate so you can eat out here?" I asked, getting up. Even though it wasn't summer yet, it was hot. Inside, it was even hotter.

"No, I'm not hungry yet." He sat on the porch beside Ellena.

"Dr. King is coming to town," Mama said.

"What?" Daddy, Ellena, and I said in unison.

"It says"—Mama read slowly—"'Dr. Martin Luther King Jr. will be speaking at St. Luke's Missionary Baptist Church on Sunday, May 5, at 2:00 p.m. The pastor of the church, Reverend Clinton Hamilton, says the church is dedicated to supporting the work of Dr. King, as well as any initiatives that promote equality and justice for all people, regardless of their race, color, or creed.'"

Daddy jumped up from his seat like he had suddenly been scalded with hot water. "I knew that Reverend Hamilton was not going to be good for this community. He slinked into town and started spiriting away the members of Little Bethel with his fancy talk and his shiny suits. Bringing that Dr. King to Parsons is just going to get these white folks riled up," he said. "Excuse me but I need to go inside and call the leadership of the church. Maybe we can talk some sense into Hamilton before he turns Parsons into Birmingham."

Daddy was referring to the march that had taken place last Friday in Birmingham. It had been horrible to watch on the news. Walter Cronkite had sounded so solemn as he shared images of young Black children getting assaulted with water hoses, attack dogs, and billy clubs. Mama had become so upset, Daddy had turned off the television, but we couldn't stop seeing the horror of it all in our minds.

As Daddy walked away, I looked at Ellena, who was nearly bouncing in her seat.

"It's happening," she said, sounding totally giddy. "It's happening. I just knew it. I just knew it."

"Knew what?" Mama asked, looking at her suspiciously.

I gave Ellena a knowing look and she seemed to catch herself.

"Oh, just that Parsons is finally going to be on the map for something besides peaches," she said quickly. "But, Mama, aren't you excited that Dr. King is coming to town?"

We both looked at Mama and waited. Finally, her face broke into a slight smile. "Yes. I guess I am. He is a mighty fine speaker."

Almost as quickly as Ellena got happy, her face fell. "Daddy won't let us go," she said solemnly. "He can't stand Dr. King or for him to be at a Baptist church at that."

"We will go hear King," Mama said in a firm voice.

"Ma'am?" I questioned, not sure I had heard what I thought I heard.

"We will go to St. Luke's and hear Dr. King speak," she said resolutely. "We cannot continue to be afraid. What we saw on the television—those babies getting brutalized by the police—must never happen again. Must never happen here."

"Oh, Mama," Ellena said and came to where we were sitting. She took Mama's hands. "Do you mean it?"

"What about Daddy?" I didn't want to dampen either of their spirits, but I didn't see how anyone, including Mama, would be able to change Daddy's mind. "I don't think he'll let us go."

Mama laid her hand on top of mine. "Cedric and I have lived our lives cautiously ever since . . . ever since what happened that day to his arm and Grandma Birdie. The only problem with living one's life that way is you end up settling for the crumbs. No more crumbs."

"Yes, ma'am," I said softly. "But what if something bad happens? What if . . ."

Mama smiled. "'Blessed are the dead which die in the Lord.' Don't be afraid, daughter. There is nothing that the enemy can do to the flesh that God can't undo on the other side."

For a time, we all three sat in silence with our own thoughts. I was comforted by Mama's words but still worried about what might happen if Dr. King did come to our little town. Things weren't perfect in Parsons, Georgia—not by any stretch of the imagination—but somehow we all had figured out how to coexist without rubbing one another the wrong way. Every now and then, there might be a skirmish or two between Negroes and whites, but they were usually diffused fairly quickly. This thing the St. Luke's pastor was doing—inviting Dr. King to their church—was sure to stir up things that we all had tried hard to tamp down. I realized how much of a hypocrite I was. I had volunteered at SNCC, helping field workers like Isaac to go and stir up hornets' nests in other communities, and yet, here I was, terrified at the thought of them coming here. I felt ashamed.

"Mama, I . . ."

Daddy walked back onto the porch. "The elders of the church are going to meet tonight. We're going to come up with a plan to convince that preacher at St. Luke's that having King come and speak isn't the right decision for us. They don't get to make a blanket decision for all Negroes in Parsons. We're all in this thing together."

"Rose and Ellena, let me and your daddy talk," Mama said.

"Yes, ma'am," Ellena and I said in unison. Ellena got up from the porch and we walked inside, allowing the screen door to shut behind us. I didn't know what Mama was going to say to Daddy, but I prayed that he be receptive to her words.

"Do you think Daddy will change his mind?" Ellena asked.

"I don't know. I just don't know."

She and I sat in the living room and waited for Mama and Daddy to come inside, but their conversation went long. Every so often we heard one of their voices grow loud, something we never witnessed them do with each other. Ellena reached for my hand, and together we sat as the evening sun began to set. I prayed that whatever decision they made wouldn't tear our family apart.

CHAPTER 14

IT TOOK MORE THAN ONE CONVERSATION TO CHANGE DADDY'S mind about us going to hear Dr. King speak. It would be late in the evening and he and Mama would still be up debating the wisdom of us attending. Actually, it took more than Mama to change Daddy's mind. It wasn't until Grandma Perkins got involved that Daddy finally agreed for us to go. Mama, Daddy, Grandma Perkins, and I were all sitting in the living room as Daddy explained, yet again, why he did not support us going to St. Luke's.

"Every day we live our lives as Colored—I mean Negroes, we are in jeopardy," Grandma Perkins had said, listening to us go back and forth over whether it was a good idea to go to St. Luke's on Sunday. "The Lord doesn't mean for us to be fearful. Dr. King is a man of God who is trying to make the world better for all of us. Of course we should go to St. Luke's and support his ministry."

"Mama, I don't want to go against you or Opal, but I'm the head of the family, and I need you all to respect that fact," Daddy had said more forcefully than I had ever heard him talk before. It startled me a bit. Daddy was always easygoing—especially with his mama. I knew he loved all of us children, but I also knew Grandma and Mama were his hearts. If they said they wanted the stars, he would go get all the constellations and the moon for good measure. That was just the way he was. So hearing him argue with the two of them was a bit off-putting.

"Cedric, no one is challenging your role as head of the family," Grandma Perkins said in her usual quiet voice. "But, son, sometimes the head has to listen to the tail. Change is coming to this nation, and that includes Parsons. We all must do our part and we mustn't let fear be our guide."

I could see every emotion known to mankind play out on Daddy's face, but after a minute or two, he sighed. "Well, if this is the consensus of the family, I won't be the one to say no. I can't fight all of you. But if I hear tell of there being even a hint of trouble, we will not be attending. Understood?"

"Understood," Mama said and patted Daddy on his leg. He looked at her solemnly, but eventually he leaned over and kissed her on the cheek. I knew the two of them would have more conversations between now and Sunday, but the matter at this time was settled. We would be going to St. Luke's this Sunday as a family to hear the Reverend Dr. Martin Luther King Jr. speak.

Later that afternoon when Ellena came home, I pulled her into the bedroom and told her what all had happened.

"I can't believe Mama *and* Grandma Perkins want to see Dr. King," she said as she got out of her work clothes and changed to a housedress. "I just never pictured either one of them as being anything other than a Moderate Negro like Daddy."

"There ain't nothing wrong with being cautious," I said, trying not to get angry at her.

Ellena sighed heavily. "It's about having choices. That's all."

"Well, I can understand us wanting the right to vote. That shouldn't be taken from anybody. But as for the rest . . . well, I choose to stay around people I love and who love me right back," I said decisively.

"What about going to the movies?" Ellena asked. "Wouldn't you like, just once, to sit on the floor where the best seats are instead of having to sit up there in that drafty old balcony?"

"Who says those seats on the floor are the best?" I insisted. "I love sitting in the balcony. Just last Saturday me and Aunt Lucille went to see *The Courtship of Eddie's Father* and we weren't bothered about sitting in the balcony. Not one little bit. And then afterward, we went over to Brother and Sister Talbot's restaurant. They treated us nicer than anybody at that Woolworth's counter would have treated us."

Although the Woolworth's in places like Atlanta had integrated due to the marches and sit-ins orchestrated by SNCC, Dr. King, and so many others in The Movement, in smaller places like Parsons, Georgia, the counter was still a forbidden place for Negroes. But like I said, I didn't care. I didn't want to eat their bland food anyway. I much preferred the down-home food Sister Talbot made at her and Brother Talbot's restaurant. You could give me fried fish, collard greens, and potato salad over a toasted ham-and-cheese sandwich any day.

"Well, I can see you are as stubborn as Daddy about this," Ellena said. "I thought the work we did with SNCC had changed your mind."

"Not all of it." Ellena was smart and wise beyond her years, but she didn't understand things the way us other kids did when it came to this family's legacy. She would pooh-pooh anyone trying to "relive the past," as she would call it, but the past didn't seem so far-off to me.

That next morning, I was up early hanging the wash on the line when Naomi and the triplets came walking across the street. I heard the hullabaloo the triplets were causing with their playing and teasing of each other. Naomi didn't say a word to them. She just herded them like she was a sheep handler and they were her flock.

"Hey, girl," I called out. "What you know good?"

"Hey, girl," she called back to me. "Nothing much. I was getting ready to go over and let the triplets see their grandma. They've been talking about her nonstop today in that triplet gibberish they do. I didn't recognize half of what they were saying, but every so often, I would hear them say 'Gan.'"

Somehow, Mama had become "Gan" and Grandma Perkins was "Gan Gan." The boys toddled toward me, all three of them with their hands out. I knelt and hugged each one.

"Hey, David. Hey, Daniel. Hey, Demetrius." They giggled and smiled. As usual, Naomi had the boys dressed like they were about to go to church instead of across the street to visit with Mama. They were wearing sailor suits and matching hats.

"Ti-Ti!" they all exclaimed. I had to admit, the boys were a blessed relief from my ongoing sadness, as well as a constant reminder that my sweet baby girl would never run up to me and give me hugs and kisses. Not on this side of life, at least.

"Let's go see if Mama is awake," I said, forcing myself not to get in a bad state of mind. "You know she is going to say something about how they are dressed."

Naomi laughed. "I just like for my boys to look decent when they go out of the house. That's all. Hey. Lawrence said we were all going to go hear Dr. King speak on Sunday. What you think about that?"

"I don't know." I grabbed Demetrius's hand before he took off running. Naomi took David by his hand and reached down and picked up Daniel, her little shadow. "Dr. King is a mighty good speaker, but so many bad things have been happening. He keeps getting arrested, and the violence . . . well, it's scary. I just don't want to see that happen here in Parsons."

"Well, I figure the Lord will take care of us one way or another," Naomi said as we walked across the street to the house. When we got inside, Mama was sitting in the living room with her Bible open on her lap.

"Gan," the triplets called out as she embraced each of them.

"Hey, my babies," she said. "Y'all dressed up like it's Easter Sunday. Naomi, you need to let these boys be boys and stop putting them in Sunday clothes on a Friday."

Naomi laughed. "Mama Opal, these boys play hard, and they get dirty. I just want them to look good when they come to see you."

"They at home when they over here too," Mama said. "Ain't gotta dress them fancy to come see Gan. Ain't that right, boys?"

They laughed and yelled together in clearer English than I had heard them speak that day, "Yes, ma'am!"

I took the boys to the kitchen and got them each a sugar cookie I had made the previous day. Then I took them to a little play table Daddy had set up for them to use when they came over. They had their own space to eat, draw, or play with the toy cars Daddy kept in a box for them. It didn't take long for them to get occupied playing, which gave me, Mama, and Naomi time to talk.

I went back over to where Mama and Naomi were sitting. Before I could say something, Aunt Lucille and her mother, Aunt Shimmy, walked inside the house.

"Hey, my babies," Aunt Shimmy said, greeting us and giving Mama, me, and Naomi kisses. "Y'all looking like new money up in here."

We all laughed as they took their seats.

"I'm just happy to come visit and not have Opal give me something to peel or shell," Aunt Lucille said as she leaned against Mama. Mama pinched her lightly on her hip, causing Aunt Lucille to play hurt. The two of them always seemed more like little girls than adults when they were together. They reminded me of me and my sisters. I hoped that when we were their age, we would still be carrying on just the same as them.

Aunt Lucille put her hands on her hips. "What is this I hear that you want to go listen to that Dr. King speak at the Baptist church?"

"It is the right thing," Mama said in a firm voice. "Time for change."

"Yes, but does it have to be with that man?" Aunt Lucille said, sitting on the other side of Mama on the couch. I sat in Daddy's chair, while Naomi sat in the chair Mama normally did.

"What do you have against Dr. King?" Naomi asked. "I'll admit that I am a bit nervous about what these white folks around here might do, but as far as King goes, he seems to be a good person."

"I just don't like how he keeps putting his wife and kids in harm's way," Aunt Lucille said decisively. "Ain't no man ought to put his family's needs second to any movement."

"I agree," Aunt Shimmy said. "I believe we need to keep striving for change, but that doesn't mean we get reckless about it. Him, Abernathy, Lowery, and Shuttlesworth aren't going to be happy until somebody else gets hurt. It wasn't that many years ago that somebody bombed King's house and Shuttleworth's house too. If they want to put their lives in danger that's one thing, but women and children, that's too much."

"Mama is right," I finally said, surprising myself with my words. But after hearing how much my family was against going to hear Dr. King preach, I realized, or at least

I was starting to realize, the truth in what Mama and Ellena were trying to say to us. It was wrong of me to want to see everybody else fight for change while I did nothing but sit back and reap the benefits. "Dr. King isn't the problem. The white people who won't give us our rights are the wrong ones, and maybe Dr. King is just what the Negro people need to urge us to push back."

Mama looked over at me with a huge smile on her face as she nodded in agreement. "There were more people who hated Jesus than followed him," she said.

"King is not Jesus," Aunt Shimmy said decisively. "But, having said all that, we are a family, and if one of us goes, we all go. I might not trust King's judgment, but I trust my niece's all day, every single day." Aunt Shimmy leaned over and pulled Mama into an embrace.

For the next two days, various family members came to the house to try to change our minds, or really, they came to change Mama's. They figured if she suddenly decided going to hear King wasn't the right decision, then everybody else would back away from going. I could have told them Mama's mind was made up. No matter who tried to convince her not to go, whether it was one of the uncles, aunts, or cousins, Mama stayed unmovable, and when Sunday came, Daddy asked her one more time if she really wanted to do this. We were sitting at the table eating breakfast and Daddy had just finished the blessing.

"We ain't got to do this, Opal," he had said soon after he said *"Amen."*

"It's the right thing to do, Cedric."

So we went to morning service at Little Bethel AME, our family's church, and then, that afternoon, we all made our way to St. Luke's Missionary Baptist Church. When my family and I entered the sanctuary, the church was rocking, as my Grandma Perkins would say. All of us together took up nearly three rows, and once we got settled, I looked over at Grandma Perkins; she was standing and waving her hand, singing along with the choir as they belted out a rousing rendition of "Precious Lord, Take My Hand." I had never heard it sung that way before, but I recognized the organist just from the sound alone. It was Sister Antoinette Spencer. Nobody played the organ like Sister Antoinette. Daddy used to say she was a whole choir all by herself. She used to be the organist at our church until she became a member at St. Luke's. Our organ hadn't sounded the same since she left. I thought about Jasper as she played. Every time I heard good gospel music, I thought about my husband and how much he loved good singing.

The choir was singing and clapping, and Dr. King was standing up in the pulpit clapping along with them. Our pastor, Reverend Shipman, was sitting with a solemn look on his face, but he was nodding along with the music. Dr. King's wife, Coretta, wasn't there because, according to Ellena, Mrs. King had just had their fourth child, a girl they named Bernice. Yesterday Ellena had said to me down-low when we were all sitting outside on the front porch, *"Watch and see. The ladies will be all over Dr. King tomorrow. Just like white on rice."*

I hoped that wasn't the case. I hoped the Negro women of Parsons would behave themselves. I knew firsthand the dangers of noticing a man who wasn't my husband. I peered over at Mama and Daddy. Daddy had his good arm around Mama's shoulders, patting it slightly, and Mama had a smile on her face.

Being here made me nervous, what with all the violence that had happened over Dr. King and his nonviolent civil disobedience. I was trying to stay "prayed up" as Grandma Perkins called it, and then no matter what evil came our way, we would be covered by Jesus' blood. But then I wondered, *Does that mean the ones who did die at the hands of white folks weren't "prayed up"? Weren't covered by Jesus' blood?* I tried not to think about such things, but it wasn't easy. I believed in God, but sometimes I wondered what his decisions meant.

I had been in St. Luke's only a handful of times—mostly for funerals. It was a beautiful sanctuary. It was twice the size of our church, and from what I could tell, Negroes came from far and wide to the services here. Daddy said there was nothing wrong with Baptists because we all believed in the Father, the Son, and the Holy Ghost, but there were enough differences that they should worship their way in their church, and we should do the same in ours. So until now, visiting each other had been out of the question.

I watched as Reverend Hamilton, the pastor at St. Luke's, walked up to the podium as the choir finished their selection. Just like Dr. King, Reverend Hamilton wasn't an old man. He was in his late twenties or early thirties, and that was another reason so many of the older folks didn't like him. They thought he was too green, too flashy and showy, and not grounded in the Word.

But you wouldn't know anyone felt that way if you judged it by the number of people present and the number of pastors sitting up in the pulpit from every denomination one could imagine. Some of them I recognized, like Rev. Fred Shuttlesworth and Rev. Joseph Lowery. I had seen them on television with Dr. King, and the Negro newspapers wrote about all of them on a regular basis. Others were familiar faces from nearby churches in places like McDonough, Locust Grove, and Hampton. The church was filling up fast, and the ushers were steady bringing out more chairs. Ellena leaned over and whispered, "This happens every time Dr. King preaches."

I nodded and smiled. Ellena was a wealth of knowledge when it came to anything related to Dr. King and SNCC.

"Praise the Lord, saints," Reverend Hamilton said loudly into the microphone, causing it to crackle slightly.

"Praise the Lord," everyone repeated back to him.

"Let me begin by giving honor to God, who made today possible. And second, let me recognize Sister Hamilton, because she is the one I am returning home to this evening. So I want her to know I see and acknowledge her good works, and I thank her for her continued service to our family and this church. Stand up, Sister Hamilton, and let the church give you a handclap."

A modestly dressed young woman in white, from her dress to her head wrap, stood and waved at everyone as two young children, a boy and a girl, pressed themselves against her. She took her seat and pulled her children close.

"I want to say thank you to everyone for coming out today and supporting us with this program," Reverend Hamilton said, continuing with his introductions and acknowledgments. "It's especially nice to see our sisters and brothers from Little Bethel here today. Thank you to their leader, Reverend Shipman, and the deacons and elders there for joining us in welcoming Dr. King and these other fine dignitaries to our community. It just goes to show that when it is all said and done, we are all one with Christ who strengthens us. Amen?"

"Amen," everyone repeated.

Then he recognized the other pastors and congregations that were present. Finally, he got to the introduction that everyone was waiting for—Dr. King's.

"Today, brothers and sisters, we are honored to welcome none other than Dr. Martin Luther King Jr. to our church and our community."

Folks clapped and stomped as if Sidney Poitier or Harry Belafonte had just walked into the church. I had never seen anyone carry on for a man the way folks were carrying on today. Grown men were standing, waving their hands in the air like they had just heard the most powerful word instead of just being told Dr. King would be speaking soon.

Reverend Hamilton raised his hand to quiet everyone while he finished the rest of his introductory remarks. Once he had stated all of Dr. King's accomplishments, he asked everyone to stand—although most people were already standing—hold hands, and sing, "It Is Well with My Soul."

I reached for my sister Ellena's hand and Aunt Shimmy's, who was sitting on my right. We all joined in and sang with the rest of the people in the church.

When peace like a river attendeth my way.
When sorrows like sea billows roll;
Whatever my lot Thou hast taught me to say,
"It is well, it is well with my soul!"

Dr. King walked over to the pulpit and gave Reverend Hamilton a hug. Then he turned and looked over the crowd of singing people. He closed his eyes and waited until the singing was done, and then he began to speak.

CHAPTER 15

"'WHEN PEACE LIKE A RIVER ATTENDETH MY WAY,'" HE SAID,
slowly repeating the words of the song. "When I was a wee
boy, I asked my daddy what did those words mean, and he
said, 'Son, that's the kind of peace that rushes over you like
a great rushing water.' Today, saints, I will speak to you on
the subject of peace," he said, his voice booming throughout
the sanctuary, which was surprising considering he was such
a small man in stature.

I had always imagined that Dr. King was at least six or
seven feet tall; he wasn't. He was a tiny man, but his presence was larger than life. One could quickly forget that he
almost appeared delicate, easy to break. But it was clear by
his words that he wasn't fragile. He was a giant of a man,
and I felt honored to be in his presence. Right at that moment, I was grateful to Mama and Grandma Perkins for
insisting we all come to hear him preach. I looked down at
Mama, and she had tears streaming down her face. I leaned
forward in my seat so that I would not miss a single word
Dr. King uttered. Somehow, I knew this moment would have

greater meaning as time went on. I didn't know how I knew, but I remembered the older people constantly talking about waiting on "the one." Sort of like how the children of Israel were waiting on Jesus. Negroes were waiting, believing that God would send us a leader who would lead us out of bondage. I never knew what they meant by that until now. I truly believed that Dr. King was "the one" the old people used to hope and pray for. I wondered if they recognized it too.

"We have been taught as a people that peace is synonymous with allowing our white brothers and sisters to walk all over us," he said loudly and firmly. "They are continuously and without impunity denying us our basic rights as human beings. We should be saying to them, 'No, sir. We will not stand by and swallow your disrespect in great gulps as if we were thirsting for it.' But instead of doing that, we hang our heads in shame as we slink away, talking about 'we must keep the peace.'"

"Preach, Doc," somebody called out.

"Teach us, teacher," another person yelled among the chorus of "Amens." I looked over at Daddy, and he was sitting quietly, not making a sound, but my brother Lawrence was nodding his head and yelling "Amen!" right along with the crowd. I felt a stirring inside my chest, but I just continued to listen.

"I don't know about y'all's Bibles here in Parsons, Georgia, but mine teaches that Jesus came to declare war on evil. Do y'all's Bible teach you that?"

"Yes, sir!" most everyone yelled back. "It shore does."

"Well, then let me tell y'all a story from that Good Book we all have in common. That book tells me that when Jesus decided that peace was not going to work among those leaders in the temple, Jesus had to move. That's what happens when our lives are guided by the Holy Spirit. No matter what, when it says 'move,' we have no choice but to comply. Now what did our Lord and Savior Jesus Christ do up in that temple, Reverend Hamilton?" Dr. King asked, turning around to look at the other preacher.

"He tore that place up, Doc," Reverend Hamilton said, standing up, his hands behind his back as he swayed back and forth, as if he were in a rocking chair.

"That's right," Dr. King said and turned back around to face the crowd that was nearly at a fever pitch. "Jesus was not talking about keeping the peace with those folks who were disrespecting his Father's house. No, sir. He tore that temple up. John 2:15–16 says, 'And when he had made a scourge of small cords, he drove them all out of the temple, and the sheep, and the oxen; and poured out the changers' money, and overthrew the tables; and said unto them that sold doves, Take these things hence; make not my Father's house an house of merchandise.' It's time, brothers and sisters. It's time for us to tear down the temple."

"Tear it down, Doc," Reverend Shuttlesworth echoed, standing up beside Reverend Hamilton. "Tear that temple down."

The talking back and forth was like a theatrical performance. Dr. King would call, and they would respond, as if they had rehearsed it. In some ways, they probably had. I imagined this was how most of his sermons went. He would throw it out there; they would catch it and then throw it back to Dr. King, similar to how we children used to play catch with one another. I watched as every preacher, including Reverend Shipman, stood in solidarity with Dr. King. Even if they didn't agree with everything he said, through that one gesture they showed everyone that as men of God, they were in step with one another.

"That's right, Shuttlesworth," Dr. King said in agreement. "If we are to be about our Father's business . . . if we are to create a future for our children and grandchildren that is better than the present we are all living in, then we must disturb the peace, not keep it. We do not have to kill and maim to fight against injustice, but we must be prepared to revolt against the commonly held belief many of us are carrying about peace. True peace begins only when the Negro has equal and fair access to all of the rights and privileges that our white brothers and sisters possess. Until that happens, my good brothers and my good sisters, there will be no peace."

The entire church erupted into applause and shouts of appreciation as Dr. King shook hands with the clergy in the pulpit and made his way back to his seat. An usher brought him a glass of water. I found myself standing right along with everyone, tears pouring down my face. This was what SNCC and all these leaders had been working for—putting their lives in danger for. It hit me like no flyer or letter I had typed had done so far. This message by this man reminded me that the work I had been a part of was right and good. I watched as even Daddy stood. He had a grim look on his face, but he stood, and it made me so proud. I knew what it took for him to stand up when he still carried the fear of what happened all those years ago.

I couldn't believe what we had just witnessed. Dr. King had spoken an incredible word. Women were getting caught up in the Spirit, shouting and praising God, and many of the men weren't far behind them. It was as if Dr. King's message was what everyone had been waiting on. Sister Antoinette began playing the organ and the congregation raised its voices as one as we sang "We Are Climbing Jacob's Ladder." This went on for a good while until finally, Sister Antoinette moved into playing "Precious Lord, Take My Hand" so softly it was almost like the organ was whispering to us to settle down and let God be God. After a moment went by, and everyone began to grow calm and listen as Sister Antoinette made that organ moan, Reverend Hamilton made his way back to the pulpit.

"Did y'all's souls get fed today?" Reverend Hamilton asked, his voice reverberating with emotion.

"Yes, sir!" the majority yelled back.

"Then I want you to listen to the next speaker. His name is John Lewis, and he is the new chairman of the Student Nonviolent Coordinating Committee. He is here to share with you some details concerning how the Negro community here in Parsons, Georgia, can get involved with The Movement that is happening all over this country, but especially right here in the South."

I was curious to hear what John Lewis had to say. I looked over at my sister. She was gazing up at him like he was the moon and the stars. John just recently became chairman of SNCC and she couldn't be more excited.

"Chuck was an amazing chairman," she had said after she got off the phone with one of her friends from SNCC

who called her with the news. *"But John will lead the organization to places we've only dreamed about. Just you wait and see."*

Unfortunately, the reception for John today was not the same as for Dr. King. There were a few scattered handclaps, but mostly there were grumbling sounds. I felt sorry for John Lewis having to speak after Dr. King. He was a hard act to follow—especially when the people were already uneasy about the message they anticipated John was going to deliver. King's message was one of hope; John's message would be one of action.

John came up to the pulpit. Like Dr. King, he was a small man in stature but big on personality. I thought it might have been better if he had spoken first, but John gave it his all. "Thank you, Reverend Hamilton, for the invitation to your church, and thank you to the man of God who just delivered that soul-stirring sermon. And finally, thank you to all of the esteemed leaders in this great town and beyond."

Again, there were a few scattered handclaps, but mostly people looked and remained subdued, as if they were bracing themselves for what he would say next.

"We want to thank you for your hospitality, but we come as more than your guests for this one day," he said, raising his voice so that it boomed throughout the sanctuary. "We come with a sense of urgency to see change begin to happen right here in your fair city. Reverend Hamilton and the members of St. Luke's Missionary Baptist Church have asked the Student Nonviolent Coordinating Committee to come down here and help with voter registration and the integration of local businesses, like y'all's Woolworth's. We have graciously accepted the invitation."

This was when the murmuring began to increase. This was when the good feelings that erupted after Dr. King's sermon drifted away like fine mist. The peace that washed over one like water receded so far into the distance that it was like it had never existed.

"I knew it," Daddy muttered. "I knew that Dr. King wasn't just coming here to preach a sermon."

Mama patted Daddy's arm, but Reverend Shipman, the pastor from our church, stood up and made his way to the pulpit, very gently moving John Lewis aside. He didn't push him, but he didn't give him the space to continue with his speech either.

"I am not going to speak for everybody in this church today. That would be presumptuous of me, but I will say this: One church does not get to seal the fate for all of us," Reverend Shipman said, and many in the audience shouted in agreement. "Our kind of peace might not be appealing to some of you young folks, but many of us are content to let justice happen at a more natural pace."

By the time Reverend Shipman got those words out, pandemonium erupted throughout the place. Everybody had something to say about what John Lewis and Reverend Shipman had just said, and no one was listening to one another.

"We were worrying about the white folks coming here and starting trouble," Ellena said, shaking her head, "and here these Negroes are fighting among themselves."

"Shhh," I said, pressing my fingers to my lips, just as Mama looked down at us and cut a stare that let me know she didn't care that we were both adult women. In her eyes, we were still little girls who needed to be reminded of how to behave in church. Daddy stood up and I figured he was about to usher us all out of the church. Instead, he made his way to the front of the sanctuary. When he held up his good arm, everyone stopped talking. One thing was for sure: People respected my daddy, and that made me so very proud. But I was nervous about what he was going to say.

"My name is Brother Cedric Perkins, and I'm a deacon at Little Bethel A.M.E. I also run the general store across town. Let me begin by saying this: I stand before you with one good arm. My wife over there sits without her Grandma Birdie. Why? For no other reason than we are Negro. White folks took my arm and killed my wife's grandmother," he said, wiping the tears from his eyes. "That happened here in Parsons a little over twenty-five years ago, and I know some of you are too young to remember that awful day, but those of us who experienced it will never be the same. We are not interested in stirring up no mess with these white folks again," Daddy said. "Change is gonna come. It always does. We just have to be patient."

"Three hundred and forty-nine years, sir," a voice from the back said. I turned around and tried to see who it was, but there were too many people. Still, the voice sounded vaguely familiar.

"Say what?" Daddy asked.

As the speaker grew closer, I was shocked to see it was Isaac walking toward the front of the building. The last time he had written to me, he was on his way to visit his parents in New York.

I need some time away to catch my breath again. There are a lot of powerful things in the making, but right now, I just can't wrap my brain around any of it. Mississippi nearly took me out, and I'm not even exaggerating. Maybe I'm not cut out for this work. Maybe I have been deluding myself this entire time.

I had written back something that I hoped was encouraging, but I never received a response. And now, here he was in my hometown.

He made his way around the people who were seated in the aisle until he arrived at the front where Daddy was standing.

"Sir, Negroes have been waiting for 349 years to get what is due to us. How much longer do we have to wait, sir?" Isaac asked. "How much longer are we going to let them dictate what our happiness looks like? Negro soldiers have fought in every major war this country has been involved in, and now it looks like we'll be heading into another one. They don't mind us shedding our blood for their causes, but they have a problem with us demanding our basic human rights. That's not fair, and all we want to do, sir, is to make sure that if we end up dying, that our death is for a worthy endeavor—that it leads to all of our people being free, truly free."

Many of the people in the room began clapping, including John Lewis. One thing I had noticed about John was he never worried about getting the limelight. He was always about the business of serving others. That wasn't always true with the men of SNCC.

I thought Daddy was going to say more, but he just shook his head and walked back to his seat and sat down beside Mama. She put her hand on his leg and he brushed her cheek with the back of his hand. I watched Isaac take a seat in the front of the church as John Lewis continued talking.

"Everyone, we are not here to cause any trouble. If there is trouble, it will be caused by the white folks of this community. We simply want to educate the people about their basic civil rights," John Lewis said. Dr. King got up and put his arm around John Lewis.

"We thank the young people in SNCC for their courage and their tenacity," Dr. King said. "I think it wise for the men to meet after this service is done and try to come to a general understanding, if that is all right with everyone." Once he got a smattering of support, Dr. King said the benediction and the prayer, and suddenly service was over, and people were talking in loud voices all over the building. I wondered whether any of this would get resolved today.

"It's not all right with me that we womenfolk are suddenly dismissed from this conversation," Ellena grumbled in a low voice. "Every single time, these Negro men try to push us to the side as if we aren't out there marching and protesting right along with them. It just burns me up."

I shushed her again, but as I looked around the sanctuary, I could see that Ellena was not alone in her feelings. A number of the women, particularly the younger women, didn't seem to like the fact that they were being excluded from the conversation.

I didn't feel slighted like them and Ellena. I liked the idea of Daddy and my uncles and Lawrence figuring out complex issues like this. I didn't have any answers, so I would rather they decide for me. But I was beginning to understand why that kind of thinking was probably as outdated as Negroes waiting for white folks to do the right thing by us. I supposed if we women wanted the men to treat us like equals, we had to be willing to act like equals and not always let them make decisions on our behalf.

"I'm going to go talk to the men from Little Bethel," Daddy said. "We all need to be on one accord with this mess. That Dr. King and those folks from the Student Nonviolent Coordinating Committee are going to start a bloodbath here in Parsons if they aren't careful. And that Baptist preacher at this church is the instigator of it all."

"Try to stay calm, honey," Mama said. "The girls and I will ride on home with Aunt Shimmy and Cousin Lucille."

"I'm going to go say hi to John and Isaac," Ellena said in my ear. "Do you want to go with me?"

I shook my head. "You go. Just make sure you don't linger. Daddy is already hot as fish grease as it is."

"I won't be long." She hurried to the front of the church. I watched as John and then Isaac gave her hugs. Isaac looked toward me and raised his hand in greeting. I waved back and quickly turned toward Mama.

"You okay?" Mama asked.

"Yes, ma'am," I said quickly. "I'm fine."

It was a bit startling seeing Isaac after so many weeks of writing letters. When I got ready to leave Atlanta when Ellena's school term ended, I had asked him not to put his address on the front of the envelope. It's not that we were saying anything wrong to each other. It's just that I didn't want to have to explain to Mama or Daddy why I was getting letters from a strange man. We weren't saying anything out of the way, but I didn't want to cause them to worry again.

I motioned for Ellena to come on and watched as she said her goodbyes to John and Isaac and then hurried back to where we were inching out of the door. There were so many people that it wasn't easy getting out, but once we did, we followed Aunt Shimmy to her recently purchased Dodge Phoenix. Aunt Shimmy's husband, Uncle Lem, had gotten it for her for her birthday. Mama got into the front seat with Aunt Shimmy, and Aunt Lucille, Ellena, and I got in the back.

"You okay?" Ellena whispered in my ear.

I nodded and squeezed her hand, keeping my eyes straight ahead. I prayed that everything would be okay for all of us, but sadly, my heart told me that things were going to get way worse before they got better.

CHAPTER 16

IT WAS NEARLY THREE WEEKS AFTER DR. KING SPOKE AT ST. Luke's Missionary Baptist Church when Isaac and two other SNCC members arrived in Parsons. He and I didn't speak while he was in town the last time, and we hadn't shared any more letters either. I didn't know what to say, and I figured he was miffed about what Daddy said and at me for not coming up to speak to him after church.

When they drove up, I was rearranging the canned goods on the shelves at Daddy's store. I watched as Isaac and another young man and woman hurried out of their car, just as a sheriff's cruiser drove up behind them and parked across the road. The officer didn't get out or say anything to them; he just sat there, watching. I immediately began to sweat. Daddy had taken Mama to Atlanta for the day, and my cousin Jemison, who normally helped out at the store, was home sick with the flu. Normally I wouldn't mind being at the store alone, but this made me nervous. I had never had an interaction with the police before, and after everything I had seen on the news, I didn't want to start now.

Every Negro alive knew about the dangers of the police. Just a little over two years ago, the Klan had attacked Freedom Riders all over the South in places like Anniston and Birmingham, Alabama, as well as Jackson, Mississippi. All I could think was that now it was about to happen here in a place I had loved and called home my entire life.

"It's okay," Isaac said, reassuring the other two as they entered the store. "He's just trying to spook us. No need to be worried." Then he turned to me. "Hello, Rose."

"Hello, Isaac," I said, trying to keep the fear out of my voice. He had a serious look on his face and clearly, whether he admitted it or not, the policeman had spooked him too. "Are y'all in trouble?"

He shook his head, but before he could speak, the woman who was with him spoke up with a harsh laugh. "There's nowhere in this white world that a Negro can go and not be in trouble."

"I apologize for bringing this mess to your doorstep," Isaac said. "But we were running low on gas, and this is the only Negro store in town that sells gasoline."

"Are you all okay?" I asked, looking outside just in time to see the sheriff drive off. "He's leaving," I said, steadying myself by grabbing the counter. I didn't realize just how rattled I was until I saw the sheriff drive away. I thanked God that Daddy wasn't here. He would have been furious at them for stopping.

"Lord help us all," the young woman said, taking a handkerchief out of her purse and dabbing at her forehead. She walked over to the cooler and pulled out three Coca-Colas. She came back and placed fifteen cents on the counter, then handed the other two sodas to Isaac and the other young man. "He started following us not long after we got on the outskirts of Atlanta. Someone must have let it slip that we would be coming to your town today. God, do I need a cigarette right about now."

I tried to hide the shock from my face, but she looked at me and laughed. "Girl, yes. I smoke. You do this type of work and you find something to get you through the night. Most of the menfolk look for warm bodies. I look for Winstons."

I didn't know what to say. I had never heard a woman speak in such a manner.

"Just ignore Deirdre," Isaac said. "She's rough around the edges, but she would take a bullet for any of us."

"And I would fire one off too." She patted her purse, shrugging. "It's all a part of what we do. And I apologize for being rude. My name is Deirdre Sparks. I'm a junior at Spelman and a member of SNCC. I spent the school term working in various parts of Mississippi doing voter-registration training, so I didn't get a chance to meet you when you were in town." She thrust her hand out and once I gripped it, she firmly shook my hand. Deirdre was someone to behold, for sure. She was tall and lanky. She wore a blue pantsuit with a peach-colored shirt. She even had a matching fedora perched on her head. If she didn't have such long hair hanging down her shoulders, she might have passed for a man. I tried to imagine what Mama would say if one of us girls showed up dressed like that.

"I'm Clifford Anthony Miner," the other young man said, extending his hand, which I shook. I noticed that his grip wasn't nearly as strong as Deirdre's. "I'm a freshman at Morehouse. Nice to meet you." Like Isaac and Deirdre, Clifford was wearing a suit too. They all looked so professional. I wondered how local people were going to take these official-looking Negroes.

"Everybody's been talking about y'all coming to town," I said. "There was even a write-up about it in the papers." I slid the paper across the counter, and Deirdre picked it up and began reading.

"'It was just a matter of time before Negro agitators made their way to our fair city,'" she read and then stopped, looking from one of her companions to the other. "These white folks sure know how to turn a phrase, don't they?" She clicked her teeth and then continued reading. "'Clearly, these rabble-rousers won't be content until they see this entire country erupt into a civil war—Coloreds against whites. It would behoove them to remember that the law is on our side and so is the firepower of this nation's military. Our sincere hope is that the Negro leaders here in Parsons will fight the urge to join forces with these puppets of Dr. King and instead join forces with local white leaders to keep our city the peaceful refuge that it is for all concerned.'"

"We knew there would be no ticker-tape parade welcoming us into town," Isaac said. "This is why we train so hard—for moments like this."

"I don't know how y'all do this," I said. "Just having that sheriff car follow me would have left me terrified."

I was still debating whether or not it was a good thing for these SNCC workers to be here. Ever since Dr. King left, the entire Negro community of Parsons, Georgia, had been at odds with one another. Half of the people wanted the young folks from SNCC to come and help organize the vote here locally, and the other half wanted them to stay far, far away. Just last Sunday, a group of men from the church had come over to talk to Daddy about it. It was the talk of the town, and from what Daddy was saying, a lot of the white folks were showing their concern too. Miss Jainey, from the fabric store, had even stopped by to beg Mama and Daddy to do something.

"*Y'all are leaders in this town,*" she had said, sitting in our front room. I stood just outside the room where I could listen and not be seen. "*I've been hearing some things that have me worried, Opal and Cedric. Y'all must talk to the other Negroes who are pushing for these civil rights. Tell them now is not the right time.*"

"*When will be the right time, Miss Jainey?*" Mama had asked. "*When should we expect for good white folks to do right by us?*"

Miss Jainey had said something about "waiting" and "God's time," but at the end of the day, she never said she thought what was being done to us was wrong. I knew Miss Jainey was a good woman. She treated Negroes better than any white store owner in town, but the Bible says good deeds alone will not save you. We were surrounded by "good white folks." They would speak to you if they met you on the street, and if you needed to get a lift to town because your car broke down, they would pick you up. But they didn't think their children should have to go to school with our children, and they didn't believe we had the right to vote or run for office. I still didn't much want to sit next to them at the movies or at church, but voting? That seemed like the very least thing they could give to us. Mama said something when Miss Jainey was at the house that stuck with me. She said, *"White folks don't mind taking our money at these stores or for taxes. Don't make sense y'all won't extend to us the right to vote."* I was trying to be braver and see the good in the fight, but that sheriff had spooked me.

"Where are you all staying?" I asked, focusing my eyes on Deirdre. If Isaac was angry with me, I didn't want to see it in his eyes. I valued his friendship, but the other Sunday was too much. The last thing I wanted to have to do was explain Isaac to my parents. I doubted they had ever seen a Black Jewish person either. If I had to explain that he was my friend . . . well, I just wasn't ready for all of that. Maybe I was a coward, but I didn't want to see disappointment on their faces again.

"Deirdre will be staying with Reverend Hamilton and his family," Isaac said. "Clifford and I will be staying just outside of town at Brother and Sister Talbot's house. Do you know them?"

"Yes." I knew the Talbots. An older couple who used to be faithful members at Little Bethel. Like so many, they had decided to make their way over to the Baptist church. "Well, I hope your stay here is . . . productive," I said, struggling to find the right words.

Isaac stepped forward and offered his hand. I tentatively placed my hand in his, still not meeting his eyes. "Thank you, Rose. We know our presence here isn't welcomed by all, but we hope that as time goes by, more people will begin to see that this work we are trying to do is necessary."

"Maybe," I said, although I was doubtful. If my daddy was any indication, hades would become a frozen place before he and the other naysayers would admit the work these young people were trying to do was a good thing. I wished I was brave enough to tell him what I had seen when Ellena and I were in Atlanta. I wished I could convince Daddy and the others that these young folks were willing to die to make things better for the rest of us.

"Sister Rose, do you mind if I go outside and fill the car with gas?" Clifford asked. "I want us all to get to our respective places sooner rather than later."

I gently pulled my hand away from Isaac's. "I don't mind if you pump the gas. That will actually be a blessing to me. Daddy has shown me how to fill up a car and check the oil a number of times, but I'm afraid I'm not very good at it."

"No reason for you to be good at it as long as there are folks around you who do know how to pump gas," Clifford said with a smile. He turned to Deirdre. "Maybe you could keep me company?"

Deirdre looked from me to Isaac, and then she smiled. "Absolutely, Brother Clifford. I will make sure you put the petrol in properly. Excuse us," she said and took Clifford by the arm as they walked outside. Neither seemed concerned that maybe the sheriff was still lurking about. I peered out after them, but I didn't see anybody. For a moment, Isaac and I stood awkwardly, not saying anything. Then we spoke at the same time.

"I missed receiving letters from you, Rose," he said quietly.

"I'm sorry," I said. I didn't know what else to say. I

missed his letters and friendship, too, but that Sunday was a lot. I didn't want to risk going against Daddy. I also didn't want it to even appear as though anything inappropriate was going on between Isaac and me. He was my friend, and that was all, but I knew other people might see it differently, especially after my behavior when I was down in Mississippi.

"I hope you will join us at one of our meetings," Isaac finally said. "We could use your help. You know what SNCC is all about, and having you reassure people in the community would be a blessing to us."

I shook my head and laughed. "I'm sure my sister Ellena will be a fixture at your meetings. Probably my twin brothers, Micah and Mitchell too. I'm better at stuffing envelopes and typing."

"I don't agree. The Movement needs everyone. We all must work together if we want change to happen. This community needs a leader. Why not you?"

I laughed nervously. "Y'all are all college students and graduates. I barely made it out of high school. People around here won't listen to me."

"Although it is good to have people with specialized knowledge, it isn't a necessity for being part of this movement. We just need dedicated people. Think about it. You know people around here better than we do. You would be surprised at how willing folks are to listen to their neighbors, relatives, and friends over us."

"I don't know." I shook my head. I didn't want the wrath of Daddy coming down on me, and that was exactly what would happen if he thought any of us were helping these radicals, as he called them.

"Think about it," Isaac said with a smile. "Just think about it."

After a moment of silence, I did have a question. "I wondered if . . . well . . . if it makes you uncomfortable being around so many Christians."

"Hmm," he said. "No one has ever asked me that question before."

I felt my cheeks grow warm. "I'm sorry. I didn't mean to be . . . insulting. Just forget—"

"It's okay, Rose." He smiled. "I don't mind the question. I haven't ever thought about it much. When my parents adopted me, I was young. My biological mother died from cancer, and since she didn't have any family to speak of and she never mentioned who my father was, the Weinbergs took me in. Their religion was just part of the package deal."

"I'm so sorry," I said, feeling awful that I had made him relive bad memories. "You don't have to say any more."

"I don't mind." He paused and then continued his story. "My mother and father raised me in the Jewish faith, but they allowed me to have free will to explore other religions. So far, I'm still Jewish," he said with a laugh. "But more importantly, they taught me that I had a moral obligation to help my people. Dad used to say, 'I can write checks all day long, but your people need men and women like you who have an education and a desire to serve.' So that's what I've been doing, and it doesn't matter if I'm working with a Jew, a Christian, a Muslim, or an atheist as long as they are fighting for freedom. That is all that matters."

Before I could say anything in response, Lawrence rushed into the store. He was still wearing his bib overalls and work boots, so I knew he had hurried here from the fields. "What's going on?" he asked, looking from me to Isaac. "Miss Jainey called the house and said she saw the sheriff parked out front when she was on her way to town. Who is this?"

Isaac held out his hand to shake Lawrence's, but Lawrence didn't move. I couldn't believe he was being so rude. I knew he was just worried, but we were raised better than this.

"Lawrence," I said softly, chidingly. "This is Brother Isaac Weinberg. He's here to help with the voting. Don't you remember seeing him at the Baptist church the other Sunday?"

"You and your friends need to be on your way," Lawrence said coldly, not even acknowledging my words. "My sister does not have anything to do with what you all are involved with, and your being here is putting her in danger. So with all due respect, you need to move on down the road."

"Lawrence!" I said, unable to keep the shock out of my voice. "Apologize to Brother Weinberg." I didn't want him to act this way, although, if it had been Daddy, it probably would have been much worse. A whole lot worse. I knew my family was divided when it came to the SNCC people coming to Parsons. I mean, if the truth be known, the entire Negro community was divided. I didn't see a way for this to work out peacefully. The sheriff was already showing these visitors to Parsons that they were not welcome by the white community either. I feared for them. I feared for all of us. But being ugly was not the answer. That much I knew.

Isaac turned to me and smiled. "Don't worry, Sister Rose. I understand your brother's concern." He laid six dollars on the counter for the gas. I tried to hand him change but he shook his head. "Take care," he said and walked back outside. I watched as he and his friends got into the car and drove away.

"You should have called me the second those people drove up," Lawrence scolded. "You could have been killed. That sheriff could have come in here and . . ."

I watched as Lawrence gripped the counter. I could see the fear all over his face. I didn't want to worry my brother. Lawrence was tenderhearted when it came to his family. I felt terrible for causing him an ounce of concern.

"No one got hurt, Lawrence," I said softly, putting my hand on his arm. "The sheriff didn't even come inside or say anything to anyone. Maybe he was just riding by. And anyway, I thought you supported their work."

"I don't support anything that could get you or any member of my family hurt," he said gruffly. "Daddy would be furious with you if he knew you waited on those people without one of us around to protect you."

"What was I supposed to do, Lawrence? Lock the door? They needed gas. And like I said, the sheriff didn't even get out of his car. He just stopped for a minute, and then he drove on his way. No one got hurt. This is Parsons. Ain't nobody gonna do anything to anybody." I tried to believe those words because I needed them to be true. I needed to believe that Parsons, Georgia, was different, even though everything inside me knew I was telling myself a lie. There was hatred for Negroes throughout this country, and

Parsons was no exception. I knew this, but I needed to tell myself otherwise because if I didn't, the fear would grip me like a vise.

"No one got hurt *this* time," Lawrence said, wiping the sweat from his forehead. "You stay away from those people. Go get your things. We're closing early today."

"Lawrence, why do we have to—"

"Go get your things," Lawrence said, raising his voice. "I'm not telling you twice."

Normally, I would have said something like "You're not my daddy," but I realized Lawrence was not playing or joking with me, so I began to cash out the register. Then I went to the back and started turning off the lights as Lawrence turned off the lights in the front. I went back to the counter and retrieved my purse from underneath. I remembered the television was on in the little break room in the back, so I went there and switched it off.

"Do you think Daddy will be mad at me?" I asked.

"What do you think?" he asked as he led me out of the store and out to his truck.

Two hours later, when Mama and Daddy returned home from Atlanta, I got my answer.

When Lawrence and I got back home, he told me to make sure I told Daddy what happened. Ellena had argued on my behalf, saying there was no reason to upset Daddy over this, but Lawrence had been firm that either I tell him or he would. When Daddy and Mama got home, I quickly filled them in on what had happened. I had never seen Daddy look so afraid and angry, all at the same time.

"Rose, I cannot believe you let those people come into the store," Daddy said gruffly. "You could have been killed. You could have all been killed."

"Don't be cross with the girl," Mama said, reaching over and patting my hand as I sat desperately trying to choke back the tears.

"I expected better from you, Rose," Daddy said. "I left you in charge of the store because I thought I could trust you to do the right thing."

"Daddy, she waited on paying customers," Ellena insisted. "What is wrong with that? You're just being contrary because you loathe the work SNCC is doing."

"Don't you stick your nose in this conversation, Ellena," Daddy snapped. "This ain't about you or your college friends. This is about my family keeping their noses out of this whole civil rights business. We're simple folks. We mind the law, and we stay out of white folks' business. Don't let those city ways you have taken on get us all killed."

"Daddy, I know you are worried, but maybe you could take some time and just hear what the young people from SNCC have to say," I said softly. I didn't want Daddy mad at me, but I felt like I had to say something.

I looked at Daddy hopefully, but his face became stone.

"I've said the last I'm going to say about this matter." He stood up and walked toward the door leading outside, but he stopped and turned back toward us. "You children better remember who the parents are in this house. My word is still law. Now, y'all have chores you can be doing, so I suggest you go and do them. How long before supper will be on the table?" He looked from me to Ellena.

"It's almost done," Ellena said and headed toward the kitchen. Before I could follow behind her, Daddy motioned for me to follow him outside. I went onto the front porch and sat with him on the swing. For a moment, neither of us said anything. We just swung back and forth, enjoying the light breeze. Finally, Daddy spoke.

"I love you, Rose, and the thought of losing you or any of your brothers and sisters tears me up inside," he said as he pulled me into an embrace.

I reached up and kissed Daddy on his cheek. "I know, Daddy. I'm sorry. I never want to worry you about anything."

"That's all part of being a parent," he said. "I'm depending on you to be a good example for your siblings, especially Ellena. She can be stubborn, but she will listen to you before she will listen to me or y'all's mama."

"I'll talk to Ellena," I said, trying to make Daddy feel better, but as he and I continued to swing, I didn't think there was much chance of me convincing Ellena of anything. She was bound and determined to work with the SNCC group. I wasn't far away from wanting to get involved too. The best I could do was try to urge her to be careful and try to keep Daddy from jumping down both of our throats.

CHAPTER 17

COUSIN JEMISON WAS HELPING LAWRENCE ON THE FARM SINCE Uncle Little Bud was down in his back and not able to get around like he used to. Daddy needed me at the store to run the register and help him with things he couldn't do with one arm, which surprisingly wasn't much. I didn't mind. I liked being at the store and I liked being with Daddy.

The store was pretty much the same as when Uncle Myron ran it. The main thing that changed was the name. Before, it was Pruitt's General Store and now it was called Pruitt & Perkins General Store.

We carried everything from food staples like milk, bread, and fresh fruits and vegetables to various hardware and electrical supplies. There was a Piggly Wiggly in town, but most of the Negroes shopped at our store because, well, everybody knew us, and we allowed folks to buy on credit. This white man from some part of Louisiana named Alfred Chennault opened up a grocery store near the edge of town, but he was so mean to Negroes—calling folks names and trying to cheat them by charging too much—no one I knew went there to shop.

Out of all the things I could be doing, like cooking and cleaning, I liked working at the store the most—mainly because Daddy didn't mind letting me try out things to help the store sell more stuff. Just last night, after we closed up and were walking home, I asked Daddy what he thought about us putting some of the harder-to-sell items near the register so people would see them just as they entered the store. Daddy had told me to try it out. Judging from the sales we had so far today, my idea was working. Woman after woman came in and practically stripped the displays clean. I had put all sorts of things up front that I knew women would want to buy, and I tried to arrange them in an appealing way—from Ponds Cold Cream to Thayers Witch Hazel Toner to Posner's Bergamot hair conditioner. I made sure the display was the first thing they saw when they walked into the store, and I pointed them toward it if they acted like they didn't see it. It didn't take long for Daddy to declare my idea a success.

"Some of these things have been on the shelves since Uncle Myron ran the place. I did a smart thing bringing you in here," Daddy said, causing me to smile. "You sure you want to try nursing? This store can be yours someday. None of your other siblings seem interested."

I didn't want to hurt Daddy's feelings, but nursing was still on my mind. I had missed the deadline to apply this year, but come next year, I planned on enrolling if I was picked. The nursing program was selective about who they admitted, but when my twin brothers arrived home the other day, they gave me some of their medical books to study.

"*You can't go wrong with* Gray's Anatomy *textbook,*" Mitchell had said. Micah agreed.

"*It's the foundation for everything in medical studies,*" Micah said decisively. "*You study this book and get familiar with certain terms, and you'll be ready for more than nursing school.*"

So every day I brought it to work with me. In the afternoons when I visited Jasper and Olivia Rose's grave, I sat and pored through the pages, trying to commit as much as possible to memory.

"Thanks, Daddy. You hungry?" I asked, trying to change the subject.

"Well, I got my answer to that question."

"Oh, Daddy, I'm sorry. It's just that . . ."

"It's just that you want to be a nurse," he said. "It's okay. And yes, I could stand to eat a little something." He raked his fingers through his hair. "Why don't you cut us a few slices of that salami and cheddar cheese. I got a box of crackers underneath the register. Unless you want some sardines," he said in a teasing voice.

I scrunched up my nose in disgust. "I'd rather not eat if sardines are our only choice." Daddy loved a can of sardines, day or night, but he stopped eating them around me when I was pregnant. Back then, I could see an unopened can of sardines and feel weak in the stomach.

I went to the cooling case, took out the salami, and sliced several pieces. I did the same with the cheese and wrapped them both in paper. By the time I got back to the counter,

Daddy had two paper plates for us to put our food on. I divided up the food, giving him most of it. I was drinking water, but Daddy had opened himself an RC Cola. I was just about to dig in when I heard the police sirens. First one car went flying by and then a second and a third. I looked at Daddy. I saw the same fear in his eyes that I was feeling. The local police seldom turned on their sirens. In fact, I couldn't remember the last time I'd heard them go by with their sirens blaring. I was just about to say something when the phone rang. Daddy picked it up before I could, and I watched as a look of horror crossed his face.

"She did what?" Daddy yelled into the receiver. "No, no, no. Why in the name . . . after I told y'all . . . Never mind. I'll go down there now. Don't . . . Listen, don't tell your mama. I'll meet you down at the station."

"What's wrong?" I asked once Daddy hung up the phone, panicked by his words and demeanor.

"I've got to go," he said, reaching under the counter for the jacket to his suit. He hurried from around the counter to the front door. "Lock up and head home," he ordered, but then he stopped and turned back toward me. "No. I don't want you out by yourself. Come on with me."

By this time, I was terrified. What had happened and who was he talking to and talking about?

"Daddy, please tell me what's going on." I hastily shut things off, similar to how I had done the other week when Lawrence had made me close up early, but somehow, this felt worse. Something inside me said this was not good—at all.

"Your sister got arrested," he barked. "Now come on."

I didn't have to guess which sister he was talking about.

Ellena. I started silently praying. I knew better than to ask any more questions. I took off behind Daddy, only stopping to lock the door. By the time I had everything locked up, Daddy had pulled his car in front of the store.

"Get in," he ordered. I hopped into the passenger side. We sped down the road toward town. I thought Daddy would fill me in on what he learned from the mysterious caller I assumed was Lawrence. I wondered how he found out. All of this was confusing, and I desperately wanted answers, but I wasn't going to make Daddy any more anxious than he already was by asking a whole bunch of questions. So we rode in silence.

When we got to the police station, Daddy turned toward me. "I want you to lock them doors and don't open them unless you know the person trying to get inside, and by that I mean family or somebody you know from the community." I knew Daddy meant the Negro community.

"Yes, sir." I watched as he made his way up the steps that led into the police department. I immediately resumed my praying. I was terrified of what might have happened to my sister and now what might happen to Daddy. Everybody knew the Parsons Police Department was made up of a bunch of racist white men. They would pull a Negro over for going too fast or too slow. Every Negro knew to stay out of their way. I couldn't imagine what Ellena had done, but I knew without a doubt that it had something to do with SNCC.

It seemed like hours had gone by, but really it was only a few minutes before Daddy walked back to the car—alone. Lawrence drove up in his pickup truck with our great-uncles—Uncle Little Bud, Uncle Michael, and Uncle Lem—all sitting in the back. They all still had on their work clothes, and Lawrence's blue jeans were painted red from the Georgia clay. The uncles were all getting on up in age, but once Lawrence stopped the truck, they got down out of the back of it like they were all still in the prime of their lives. I got out too.

"Where's Ellena?" Lawrence nearly yelled. "Where's my sister?"

"Pipe down," Daddy cautioned.

By this time, I was in tears. Daddy placed his hand on my back, rubbing it as he talked. "The sheriff's got her and about five more young folks. They took them to the jail in McDonough."

"What are they saying she did?" Uncle Little Bud asked.

"She and some of them outside Negroes went to the Woolworth's counter and tried to order off the menu. They called the sheriff on them. I got to go to McDonough and see if they'll let me get her out."

"It's that Dr. King and those Snack children," Uncle Lem said. "We was doing fine before they came to town."

Any other time, I would have laughed at Uncle Lem for calling them *Snack* instead of *SNCC*, but there was nothing to laugh about. Things were as bad as they could be.

"That old police chief, Tommy Burnett, said he doubted they would let anybody loose today," Daddy said, his face like a storm cloud about to burst open. Daddy was particular about his daughters. He loved his sons, but we girls were truly his heart. I couldn't imagine him leaving Ellena locked up without a fight. Sure enough, he looked at all of us, a glint in his eye. "I'm going to go get Ellena. Y'all go on back home."

"Ain't gonna let you do this alone, Cedric," Uncle Little Bud said, resting against the truck. I could tell his back was bothering him, but his resolve was strong as ever. "She's our niece and we ain't going back home to worry like a bunch of nervous hens. So let's stop wasting time and get on up the road to McDonough before it gets to be night."

"Let's go then," Daddy said and turned to get in the car. "Get in, Rose," he said to me. I tried to catch Lawrence's eye, but he was busy helping the uncles into the back of his truck. I got into the car, but before Daddy cranked it up, he turned to me. "Did you know about this?"

"About what, Daddy?" I asked.

"This sitting-in thing your sister and the rest of them did," he snapped. "Did you know she was mixed up in all of this?"

I shook my head. "No, Daddy. I didn't know about a sit-in and I surely didn't know Ellena was involved. I promise. If I had known she was doing this, I would have said something to you."

Daddy nodded and started the car. I waited for him to say something else, but he pulled the car out into the road and took off toward McDonough without another word. It seemed like the drive to McDonough would never end, but in less than twenty minutes, we were pulling up to the county jail.

Before Daddy stopped the car, I made my case for going in with him. "They might let me see her, if . . . if they decide not to let her go. Please let me go in. I won't say anything."

Daddy looked tired. I could tell he had no energy to argue with me. "Come on then," he said, and we both got out of the car.

The uncles and Lawrence got out, too, but Daddy stopped them. "Y'all let me and Rose go in. If they see more than a couple of us, they'll swear we trying to start a riot."

"We'll be right here," Uncle Lem said. "But you let them peckerwoods know she ain't alone in this world, and we will fight with everything we got in us to get her out of this place."

"Ain't no sense of them bringing her to this jail with all these hardened criminals," Uncle Michael said, the anger rising in his voice. "Don't make no sense at all."

Daddy patted him on his back. "It's going to be okay. We'll fix this," Daddy said and turned to me. "You ready?"

"Yes, sir," I said even though I was terrified. Daddy took my hand and we walked toward the entrance. I wasn't used to being around a whole bunch of white folks, but especially white folks with guns on their bodies and sticks to beat us with if they didn't like what we said or did. I didn't understand how Ellena could have been brave enough to go sit at that Woolworth's counter. I didn't think I could ever do something like that.

Just as we were about to go in, three officers walked out, laughing like they didn't have a care in the world. They stopped when they saw us and blocked the entrance to the jail.

"What you people congregating out here for? Y'all trying to start some trouble?" one of the men asked, putting his hand on his holster. The other two did the same.

I caught my breath, and Daddy pushed me behind him so that he was standing between me and the police. "We here to see about my daughter, Ellena Perkins—Ellena Ashley Perkins."

"Never heard that name," one of the officers said, spitting out a wad of chewing tobacco near Daddy's shoes. "And I've been processing niggers all afternoon," he said and laughed. The others joined in. "Maybe y'all should come back next week. She's bound to show up by then."

"I think we'll go inside, sir," Daddy said. I hung my head, trying to stop the shaking of my body. I had never felt fear like I was feeling right at that moment.

That awful man spit again. This time, it landed on Daddy's shoes. "Suit yourself," he said and laughed again. "Come on, boys. Good luck, nigger." They walked off and I watched as Lawrence and the uncles looked our way. Daddy waved to signal everything was all right, but it wasn't all right. Nothing was all right as long as my sister was in there with these awful men. I shuddered to think of her being alone and scared. I watched as Daddy bent down and wiped the tobacco juice off his Sunday shoes.

"You want to go back with your uncles and brother?" Daddy asked.

"No, sir," I said, making sure my voice sounded strong and brave. "Let's go get Ellena."

Daddy looked down at me and gave me a tight hug. Then he took my hand, and we walked inside. The place was filled with armed officers and there was a long line of Negro men and women standing against a wall. Some of them looked terrified, mostly the women, but others had their heads raised defiantly, like they weren't afraid of anything or anyone. I wondered how many of them were here because they had actually done something wrong. I scanned the line for Ellena or someone else I might know, but I didn't recognize any of them.

"Let's go see what they can tell us," Daddy said.

We walked up to the desk and stood as the man sitting behind it kept talking into the phone. After a while, he hung up, but he didn't address us at all. Instead, he leaned back in his seat and picked up a newspaper and started reading.

"Excuse me, sir," Daddy said, clearing his throat. The red-faced white man didn't utter one word. He just kept looking at his paper, slowly flipping the pages. Finally, Daddy spoke again. "Sir, I need your assistance, please."

The white officer folded his newspaper and placed it on the desk. Then he looked up at Daddy with such hatred, it was hard to stand there, but we did. I gripped Daddy's hand tightly, and he squeezed mine like he was telling me things would be okay. I silently started praying, asking God to show up and soften the hearts of these awful men.

"What you want, boy?" the officer asked. Hearing him call my daddy "boy" ate at me something fierce. How dare he? I wanted to say something, but Daddy squeezed my hand and I remained quiet. However, I knew if Ellena would have been the one standing here, she would have insisted that the red-faced man show our daddy some respect.

"I'm here to get my daughter, sir. I was told by Police Chief Tommy Burnett over in Parsons that y'all brought her here. I want to take her home to her mama," Daddy said. "I can pay the bond."

"Well, wasn't that a nice speech," the white man said with a slow drawl. "What's your daughter's name?"

Daddy told him and he began flipping through a book. Slowly. Painstakingly slowly. After a minute or two, he looked at us again. "Don't see her name. Try back tomorrow."

"Sir, I beg you to look again," Daddy said. I could hear the near panic in his voice. I was feeling it too. I just wanted to run to the back and go get my sister. Somehow I just knew she was here. Daddy continued to try to convince this man to help us. "Police Chief Burnett said she was here, and I don't want her to have to stay in this jail overnight. I can pay."

"What did she do?" Something about the officer's demeanor made it seem like he knew more than he was making out.

"She . . . she went to Woolworth's to get something to eat," Daddy said. I could tell he was choosing his words carefully.

"Ain't no crime in that," he said. "If she got arrested, she must have done more than that."

"Sir, my daughter is a good girl," Daddy said. "Please check your papers one more time."

The man laughed. "Well, since you being such a good Niggra, I'll check my books once more." He slowly turned the pages until he finally stopped. "What you say her name is again?"

"Ellena. Ellena Ashley Perkins."

"Oh. That girl. Oh, she ain't going nowhere today. She's got to see the judge first, and that won't happen until Monday or Tuesday of next week. Come back then," he said and slammed the book shut.

"Noooooo," Daddy cried. "She can't stay here that long. She's a little girl, sir. She don't know nothing about this."

"She knew enough to disturb the peace and break laws that every Niggra ought to know. Parsons, Georgia, ain't Atlanta. Evidently, she never got any home training to speak of," the policeman said. I felt Daddy move toward the desk, and I pulled him back. He looked at me and I shook my head.

"Sir," I said, my voice quivering. "Sir, I'm her sister. Do you think you could just let me go see her? Not for long or nothing. Just make sure she's okay?"

"Why wouldn't she be okay?" the man asked. "We take care of our prisoners. She's fine. Y'all come on back next week and the judge will figure this all out and let y'all take her home. But for now, jail is where she is, and jail is where she is going to stay. Now y'all have a good day." He picked up the paper and commenced to reading it again, clearly dismissing us. Daddy kept talking.

"Sir, today is Thursday. Please don't make her stay all weekend," Daddy said. "I'll pay whatever needs to be paid, and I will guarantee to get her back here to see the judge on whatever date y'all set. Just . . . please . . . Her mama . . . This will hurt her beyond measure."

"Your daughter wasn't thinking about her mama when she broke the law, now was she?" he asked. "Y'all niggers go on." He leaned back in his chair and flicked the paper one more time, dismissing us with the motion.

"Come on," Daddy said, taking me by the arm. I looked at his face, and tears were streaming down. They matched mine. It was all I could do to keep from screaming and running in search of my sister, but I knew it would only make things worse. I walked toward the door with Daddy but placed my hand on his arm to stop him from going outside.

"What are we going to do, Daddy?"

"Get your sister out of here," he said. "Them Negroes from Atlanta got her into this mess. They gone have to help get her out of it."

"Yes, sir." I worried that nothing was going to speed up this process, and no matter what anyone tried to do, Ellena might have no choice but to stay in this place until next week. I continued to pray silently. At this point, I wasn't sure if anyone was listening.

CHAPTER 18

AFTER WE LEFT THE COUNTY JAIL IN MCDONOUGH, WE WENT back to the police station in Parsons. Lawrence and the uncles followed behind us again and stayed outside while Daddy and I went inside. Daddy and I went up to the desk where the police chief was sitting, just like when we were in McDonough. Daddy explained to him what happened, but he didn't seem very interested in helping us. Just like the officer in McDonough had said to us, he also said, "Try back later."

When we got back outside, it was close to dinnertime. Daddy told everyone else to go home and when he knew something, he would let them know. He told me to go with them, but I wasn't about to leave Daddy by himself. Although he wasn't happy about it, he let me tag along with him. Our next stop was to go see Reverend Hamilton. He met us at his door. He tried to invite us in, but Daddy refused.

"Brother Perkins, I am so sorry this happened," he said, stepping outside onto his front porch. I could hear the sounds of children playing in the background. "I just got off the phone with Vernon Jordan. He's the field director for the

NAACP, and he promised me they would get some lawyers down here by tomorrow."

"Tomorrow ain't soon enough to get my daughter out of that jail," Daddy nearly yelled. To Reverend Hamilton's credit, he took Daddy's anger in stride.

"I understand, Brother Perkins," he said. "I would be feeling the same way you are if it were one of my children. But your daughter knew what she was getting herself into. They all did."

"No the hell she didn't!" Daddy yelled. I hadn't heard him ever talk this strongly. I put my hand on his arm. He looked at me and nodded. "I'm sorry. Pardon my language, but I can't let my daughter sit up in that jail all night. It would kill her mother. So somebody's got to help me."

"I'll keep making calls," Reverend Hamilton said, but I could tell by his posture that he didn't really believe he could do any more than he was already doing. "And again, sir, I am sorry. I was visiting with a dying member; otherwise, I would have been at the sit-in myself."

"I am sorry about your dying member, but my daughter . . . my children . . . are all my wife and I have in this world that means anything to us." I could see tears forming in his eyes again. "I will move heaven and earth for them. If you can't help me, then I will continue to go door to door until somebody, white or Negro, decides to do something. This ain't right. Come on, Rose."

Daddy turned to leave, and I nodded goodbye to Reverend Hamilton. I was too choked up myself to say anything. I hurried to keep up with Daddy. He didn't say anything either as we went back to the car. By now, it was starting to get dark. There was still a bit of light, but evening was fast approaching. I couldn't imagine what Mama must be thinking. I prayed Lawrence went over to see about her and make sure she wasn't worrying too much. Daddy opened the car door for me and helped me inside. Once he got back to the driver's side, he fell into the seat like every drop of energy had seeped out of his body.

"What are you going to do, Daddy?"

Daddy just sat there and gripped the steering wheel. Then he let out a long, deep sigh. "There ain't no worse feeling for a man than knowing he ain't got the power to protect his own family."

"Daddy, you . . ."

He kept talking as if I didn't say anything. "I felt this same way on the day your Great-Grandma Birdie got shot to death. I tried to protect her from those bullets, but I couldn't. I lost my arm, but I would have given my life if I could have saved your mama's granny."

I didn't know what to say, but I knew we needed to go home to Mama. I knew that she would be worried to death by now. "Daddy, let's go home. You'll figure something out. I just know you will."

Daddy reached over and patted my chin. "I reckon you right. We better go home. I just didn't want to go without your sister." Daddy cleared his voice and then eased the car onto the road. I held my breath the entire way. I was terrified that one of the white policemen would get behind us, but it was all quiet—that is, until we got home. The yard was full of cars—so many cars we couldn't even park near the house. It looked like somebody had died.

"Daddy, you don't think—"

"Oh, Jesus," Daddy said, cutting me off. "Your mama knows. Got to get to Opal," he cried out, slamming the car into Park and running toward the house. I took off after him. When we got to the porch, it was hard to get around people. Daddy pushed through, and I followed in the path he created. When we made it into the living room, Reverend Shipman, our pastor, was speaking to Mama, who was sitting in a rocker. She looked calm. I was thankful for that. Daddy rushed over to her and pulled her into his good arm. I watched as she rubbed his head, holding him like she used to do us children. Before I could move toward Mama, my siblings all crowded around me.

"What is everybody doing here?" I whispered, looking from one to the other.

"They all heard Daddy had gone to talk to the sheriff, so they thought maybe he would have some news about the others," Lawrence said. "I tried to tell them we didn't know anything, but they wouldn't leave."

"Know anything about what?" I asked.

"It wasn't just Ellena and them SNCC young folks who got arrested," my brother Micah said. "Bobby Snell and Ronald Davis got arrested too." Bobby and Ronald lived near McDonough, but I remembered them from high school.

"We should have been there too," my other twin brother, Mitchell, said. "We didn't know she was going to do this. She promised she wouldn't."

"Y'all should have told me. I could have talked her out of it," I said, trying to keep my voice down, but I was angry.

"What is Daddy going to do next?" Katie Bell whispered,

shifting L.J. to her other hip. He was nearly a year old and way too big for my sister to carry, especially now that she was big with another baby. Her husband, Luther, came over and took him from her and went back and sat next to Grandma Perkins, who was rocking with her Bible, her eyes tightly closed. I knew she was deep in prayer. I prayed God heard her prayers because mine didn't seem to go anywhere.

"I don't know," I said. "He just wanted to come and make sure Mama was okay."

I watched as everyone began to leave once they realized Daddy didn't have any new information. After a while it was just us. Mama and Daddy continued to talk in hushed tones until finally Daddy startled us all with a loud outburst.

"Absolutely not!" I heard Daddy say loudly. "We will not contact that man."

Almost in unison, we all went toward Mama and Daddy. Daddy didn't ever raise his voice at Mama, so for him to be doing it now, we knew whatever Mama had said was serious.

"What's wrong?" Lawrence asked. I could tell he didn't like Daddy talking loud at Mama. But Mama didn't seem bothered at all. Despite Daddy raising his voice, Mama's face looked completely calm. Daddy looked like he was ready to spit fire. I couldn't imagine what Mama could have said to rile him up so much.

"I told your daddy we should contact Jimmy Earl Ketchums. He can help us," she said simply, her hands folded in her lap.

"The senator?" I asked. I remembered Mama telling stories about how she and Great-Grandma Birdie used to work for Senator Ketchums's family before she and Daddy got married and before Great-Grandma Birdie was murdered, but I didn't know much else about him. I didn't follow politics very much, but I'd seen him on television talking about getting better benefits for local farmers. I never heard him mention anything about helping Negroes, though. But if Mama thought he might help us, I didn't understand why Daddy would be so against it.

"Daddy, why don't you want Senator Ketchums to help? Maybe he can get Ellena out of jail tonight." I tried to put my hand on Daddy's shoulder, but he moved away quickly.

"I would rather she stay in jail than have a Ketchums putting their nose in my family's business. Ellena is my daughter," he said angrily. "I'll see that she gets out of jail myself."

Without another word, Daddy stormed out of the room. I looked back at Mama, and she had a determined look on her face.

"Why is Daddy so angry about you calling the senator?" I asked. I just couldn't understand why Daddy wouldn't want to use any resource we might have—especially a white senator from this community. His word alone might get Ellena free tonight. Nothing was making any sense to me.

Mama pursed her lips. "Your daddy has a forgiveness problem when it comes to Jimmy Earl and his family."

"Why is that, Mama?" Katie Bell asked, sitting in the chair beside Mama and putting her hand on Mama's.

Mama patted Katie Bell's arm and then looked at each of us. "There are things you children don't know. Things we just didn't talk about because . . . well, for a number of reasons."

"What, Mama?" I was suddenly feeling scared of what she might say.

"We never talk about it, but it was Jimmy Earl's father who shot my granny and shot off your daddy's arm," Mama finally said.

I was stunned. I had never heard this story before. All I ever knew was it was some poor white trash. That's what Mama, Daddy, and all the uncles and aunts would say if we children ever brought it up. Nobody ever said any names in front of me. I just sort of figured they were white folks from somewhere else.

"Mama, Daddy's right," Lawrence said. For him, that was a big jump because he always took Mama's side. "We don't need those people helping us."

"If Jimmy Earl can get my baby out of that jail, then so be it. Short of Satan himself, I don't care who gets her out of jail as long as she gets returned to us, safe and sound. Now, reach over there and get me the telephone," she said firmly, looking directly at me.

I wasn't about to argue with Mama, so I handed her the phone that was just out of her reach. She put it on her lap and began to dial the operator. I listened as she asked the operator to connect her with Senator Jimmy Earl Ketchums in Washington, DC. We all held our breaths as we waited— or at least I know I held mine. I agreed with Mama. I didn't care who got my baby sister home. I just wanted her back with us where she would be safe—or at least safer than she was in that jail.

It wasn't long before Mama said, "Hello, Jimmy Earl. This is Opal Perkins from back home." They exchanged niceties and then Mama told him what was going on. She ended with a plea. "Jimmy Earl, I need my child home tonight. I've never asked you for anything, but I need my Ellena back home with me and her family. Please do whatever you can." She was quiet for a few more minutes before saying her goodbyes. She gently placed the phone back on the receiver. Mama looked up at us with a watery smile, but she didn't shed a single tear. As always, Mama was the strongest person I knew, even though she was ripped up inside about Ellena. "Jimmy Earl said he would make a call. So now we wait. Twins, y'all go check on your daddy. Tell him I need him to come back out here with us."

"Yes, ma'am," they said in unison, like always, and lumbered out of the room toward Mama and Daddy's bedroom. Katie Bell's husband had gone out to the porch with little L.J. while Mama was on the phone, so I went over and sat beside Grandma Perkins. She looked up at me and patted my cheek.

"You okay, Rosebud?" she asked. "I know Ellena is your other heartbeat."

"I'm all right, Grandma Perkins. Are you all right?" Grandma Perkins wasn't a big woman. She was just a few steps away from being frail. And she suffered with the gout so often I worried that a night like this might set her back. She smiled and patted her Bible.

"No matter what happens, the Word will always stand," she said. "No weapons formed against my family will prosper. God has got your sister and all of those other young folks."

I laid my head against Grandma Perkins's shoulder. No

matter how thin she got, her shoulders were always as strong as the Rock of Gibraltar. She put her arm around me, and we sat there, both waiting for the phone to ring. Mama held that phone in her lap like it was a baby. She didn't say anything; she just stared down at it. A few minutes later, Daddy walked back into the living room. I watched as he and Mama had a silent conversation with nothing but their eyes. He finally went to her and stroked her cheek.

"Praise the Lord," Grandma Perkins whispered. "The storm is over."

I looked up at her and smiled, whispering for her ears only, "They just like us kids. They can't stay mad at each other for long."

The phone rang and I jumped. We all looked at Mama. She closed her eyes and whispered words that only she and God could hear. Then she picked up the receiver.

"Hello," she said. I tried to guess what she was hearing but she didn't say anything. Then she thanked the caller and hung up. We waited for her to say something, but she just sat there with the phone in her lap.

"Well," Daddy finally said. "What did you find out?"

Mama cleared her throat. "Jimmy Earl said he called the sheriff and spoke to him personally. He said he asked the sheriff that the young people be released to their families or on their own volition depending on their ages. He said the sheriff told them he would let them go without waiting to see the judge if they would sign paperwork agreeing not to go back into the Woolworth's again."

"Well, all right then. That's that. Let's go get Ellena," Lawrence said excitedly, standing up. "Daddy, I'll ride with—"

"Wait," Mama said, standing and handing the phone to Katie Bell. "Wait."

"Wait for what?" Daddy asked, walking toward the door. "Come on, Lawrence, if you coming. It's getting late. If we leave now, we—"

"She wouldn't sign the paper," Mama said hurriedly. "None of them would."

"What you mean she wouldn't sign the paper?" Daddy asked. "That sheriff is lying. He just don't want to let them children go."

"Jimmy Earl said no," Mama said wearily. "He said the sheriff swore he gave them the option to leave, but they wouldn't agree to his terms."

"I'm going back to that jailhouse and after I get through with her, she'll sign whatever that white man tells her to sign," Daddy said, starting to walk out the door.

"Stop, Cedric," Grandma Perkins said, raising her voice.

"Mama, I got to go and see about—"

"Stop," Grandma Perkins repeated. She got up from her seat and walked over to Daddy. "She done made her decision, and she is as hardheaded as you was at that age. Ain't nothing gonna get done tonight, so be still and let God be God."

"I'm her daddy," he snapped. "She'll listen to me."

Grandma Perkins smiled and patted Daddy's cheek. "No, she won't. Come take me home, Cedric. I need to lay these bones down. Ellena will be all right. I talked to God."

"What does that mean? You don't think all the other Negroes who got drowned or hung by these white folks didn't talk to God or didn't have family who prayed until their knees got raw from kneeling?" Daddy demanded, his voice louder than I ever remembered it being before. "Every Negro I know has talked to God, and what good has it done? We still dying out here, Mama, and you just want me to leave my baby at that jailhouse all alone and defenseless? She don't know what they capable of doing to her."

I was startled by Daddy's words. This didn't sound like my daddy. My daddy was a praying man whose faith knew no bounds. I had heard him say passionate prayers in church that caused other grown men to weep. This person sounded like his faith was weak or maybe nonexistent. This person scared me because my faith was wrapped up in Daddy's and Mama's faith. If their faith got weak, I didn't know what would become of mine.

"You said a lot, son," Grandma Perkins said, her hands on her hips. I was surprised that she didn't raise her voice with anger, but she talked to him like she used to talk to us when we were young and would have tantrums. Her voice was the voice of patience and godly love. "But let me start with the first thing you said. Just so you know and everybody in this room knows—God always answers our prayers, son."

"How you gonna say that, Mama?" Daddy snapped. "Look at my arm. Is this what you prayed for? 'Cause I know it wasn't what I prayed for."

Daddy seldom talked about his arm and what happened to it. He always seemed to take it in stride, but now, looking at the hurt on his face, I could see that he had not healed from the pain of losing it. Not the physical pain, but more than that, not the emotional pain. It was more than a little overwhelming to see my big, strong daddy so sad and hurting. I wanted to go to him and try to hug his pain away, but I looked at Mama and she didn't move, so I didn't move either.

"I meant what I said," Grandma Perkins said. "God always answers our prayers. Just not always the way we think he should. You might pray for God to give you a car so you can drive to work, but instead, God sends you a new pair of shoes because he knows a car would do you more harm than you getting out there and walking. I don't question God's answers to my prayers, and neither should you. This situation will be worked out and it will be according to God's will. Not your will. Not Opal's will. Not any of our wills."

"You children leave me to talk to your daddy," Mama said. "Lawrence, you take your grandma Perkins home."

I decided to go with Grandma Perkins. That way Katie Bell, Luther, and L.J. could sleep in my and Ellena's room. I didn't want to stay there without her anyway. I kissed Mama's cheek and then Daddy's. I watched as Mama took Daddy by the hand and led him out of the room toward their bedroom. I hurried to my room and packed an overnight bag, then rushed back out so I could meet Grandma Perkins and Lawrence out at his car. Once we were in the car, I asked Grandma Perkins if she thought Daddy would be all right.

"Your daddy is fighting a lot of old demons," she said, her voice sounding tired for the first time that night. "But I meant what I said before. No weapons formed against this family will prosper. I believe that, Rosebud. I hope you kids believe that too."

"Yes, ma'am," Lawrence and I both said in unison. But as we drove out of the yard, I couldn't help but hear the doubt Daddy had expressed ringing in my ears. At the end of the day, I just wanted my sister back. I prayed God was in agreement.

CHAPTER 19

THE NEXT MORNING, I WOKE UP AT FIVE. I COULDN'T GET BACK to sleep, so I decided to walk home. Mama was an early riser, so I knew she would be awake by the time I got there. I left Grandma Perkins a note so she wouldn't worry, then I took off walking down the street. It was still dark outside, but I wasn't afraid. I had walked these roads my entire childhood—sometimes with my siblings, but more times than not by myself. Many a night I would wake up at Grandma Perkins's house after having spent the night and decide I wanted to go back home.

The graveyard was on the way to the house, so I stopped to visit with Jasper and Olivia Rose. Just before I got to their grave, I saw a patch of daisies growing. I bent down and picked a bouquet. When I finally made it to their spot, I was surprised to see a bench. I immediately knew it had been Lawrence. First, I could recognize his handiwork; second, this was just the kind of brother Lawrence was— always thinking about his younger siblings and their needs. As much as I know Mama and Daddy were worried about

Ellena, I knew Lawrence was equally worried. I doubted he slept a wink last night.

I sat down on the bench and laid the flowers on their grave. It was perfectly manicured. Again, I knew that was Lawrence's doing. He pretty much took care of the entire graveyard—pulling weeds, cleaning headstones. He said making sure all of our dead's place of rest was clean and inviting for family and friends to visit was his ministry. I felt a rush of peace just being back where my little family lay. It's funny—I never much liked going out to the graveyard when I was a girl. Not even to visit the graves of close family members. They always felt so far away. Now, with my own close, personal family lying here, I needed to be in their presence, especially now with all that was going on with Ellena.

"Hi, Jasper. Hi, Olivia Rose," I said softly. It was so quiet in the cemetery. It just felt like everybody was taking a long, restful nap. I knew better than that, of course. I also knew they couldn't hear me, but it sure made me feel better to talk to them like they could. "I don't know if you know about what happened with Ellena. She got herself arrested. Part of me admires her for being so brave, and another part of me wonders how she could do something so thoughtless. She could have gotten killed."

I placed my hand on the headstone, rubbing the imprint of their names. Daddy had bought them a gorgeous marble headstone that had a chiseled-out image of a man holding a baby. I cried so hard when I first saw it. It touched me as much as anything Daddy had ever done for me.

"Jasper, I don't know if you're a guardian angel yet, or even if that's something you want to be. If it is, would you look out for all of us, but especially my sister? I just don't think I could live through losing anybody else."

For a time, I just sat there, listening to the night sounds becoming morning sounds. A few crickets were chirping here and there, and the sky was beginning to turn all sorts of colors, marking the dawn of morning. I knew I needed to get up and head toward home. I didn't want Grandma Perkins to wake up, see my note, and call for me at the house and I not be there, so I reluctantly rose from my seat. I placed my hand on the headstone once more. "I'll check on y'all soon. I promise I won't be so long with my next visit. I love you, Jasper. I love you, Olivia Rose."

I bent down and kissed the top of the headstone, then started down the road again. I still couldn't see very well, but I knew these back roads like I knew the back of my hand. White pines, dogwoods, and ash trees were all around, creating a cocoon effect. It was like the trees were hugging the road leading to home. I felt at peace in these wooded areas where people and buildings had not started to overwhelm nature. Out here truly felt like God's country.

As I continued to walk, I saw a light on the horizon. It looked like car headlights. It wasn't unusual for someone to be out this time of the morning, so I didn't pay it much mind until I made my way up the hill. Evidently, the person in the car saw me, too, because they immediately turned on the swirling overhead lights of a police car. It was parked on the side of the road. The light from it was so bright it was difficult for me to see. I shaded my eyes, trying to make out a person in the car, but it was too dark. Instantly I got scared. I was still about a mile away from home, so it was just me and who I assumed was a man alone in the road. I wasn't sure what to do. I almost turned back around, but I knew that no matter if I went forward or backward, I couldn't get away from this policeman if I wanted to. All I could do was pray he stayed in his car and left me alone.

I tried to keep walking in a natural way, but I was near 'bout running when he got out of his car and walked to the center of the road.

I stopped. My feet felt planted like a tree. There was nothing I could do at this point but wait and see what it was he wanted.

"Please watch over me, Jasper. Please, God, send me a protective angel," I whispered. I hoped that angel would be Jasper, but at this point, I didn't care. I needed something or somebody. I looked around again, trying to see if there was somewhere I could run to without getting caught; once again, I acknowledged that I was trapped. There was nowhere to hide. All I could do was pray for mercy.

"Where you going to this early in the morning, gal?" he yelled, walking toward me.

Again, I wanted to turn around and run, but I knew it wouldn't take much for him to catch me, especially with my legs as wobbly as they were.

"I'm going home, sir," I called back. "I just left the graveyard. My husband and daughter are buried there." I hoped that somewhere inside him there was a merciful heart. I prayed he had some semblance of goodness in him. I prayed silently to God to help me out of this situation.

"Come here so I can take a look at you," he called out.

I heard his command, but I couldn't move. And then,

to add insult to injury, I felt urine trickling down my legs and tears in my eyes. I struggled hard to keep from letting out a wail. I was humiliated. My fear was so great, I stayed rooted in my spot. I couldn't have moved if I had wanted to.

"I said come here, gal," he repeated, his voice sounding ominous.

I opened my mouth, but no words came out. It was like my words were trapped somewhere deep inside me, and I couldn't let them out even to save my life. I didn't know what to do as I stood there, wet, embarrassed, and terrified. I felt my lips tremble, like the words wanted to exit my throat, but nothing escaped from my mouth, not even a whisper. My vocal cords were failing me, and I feared I wouldn't get out of this situation alive.

"God dang it, I said come here," he barked and then made his way toward me. When he got to where I was standing, he grabbed my arm—hard. I screamed with pain and shock. "Ain't you ever been taught how to act in front of an officer of the law?"

I just shook my head. I had given up on words.

"What's that smell?" he demanded.

"I . . . I . . ." Before I could stop it, more pee trickled down my leg. This had happened to me only once before, when I was a little girl and the twins tied me to a tree in the woods and left me there—or at least that was what I thought. They had been only just out of my eyesight. I had gotten so scared, I peed on myself. I couldn't believe I was a fully grown woman, and this was happening to me now.

"God dang it!" He slapped me hard several times across

my face, causing me to fall to the ground. "You pissed on me, you stupid nigger."

I could feel blood streaming from my nose. I prayed I didn't get blood on him too. I just lay there on the ground with my hand on my face, trying to brace myself for what might come next.

"I ought to just . . ." he started and then, almost like God himself spoke, a voice on the officer's radio interrupted his tirade. He took his handkerchief out of his pocket and wiped my pee off his shoe. Before he went to his car, he threw the handkerchief on my face. I pulled it away and watched as he spoke to someone on the radio.

It wasn't long before he slammed his car door closed and drove off without another word to me. I could feel my lips swelling. Blood was still trickling from my nose. I had been wearing a white summer dress Mama had made for me a few summers ago. It was covered with Georgia clay, blood, and urine. I was so embarrassed. I didn't want to go home looking like this, but I didn't want anyone to find me in the road looking this way either, so I slowly got up from the ground. I brushed off as much of the dirt as I could, but I was a filthy mess. I ached, but I didn't think I broke anything from my fall. Ordinarily, I could get home walking from the cemetery in about fifteen minutes, but today, because of the pain in my body and the fear that still had me in a tight noose, I barely made it home in thirty. When I did enter the yard, Mama was outside hanging up clothes on the clothesline. Daddy had bought her a brand-new Maytag dryer for Christmas two years ago, but she still insisted on hanging up clothes outside to dry if the weather permitted. Today was looking to be a nice, warm summer day even though I felt like I had a huge rain cloud over my head.

"Mama," I called out. For a second, I almost didn't recognize my own voice. It sounded foreign to me. Distant. I tried to keep moving, but I found that my body wouldn't go any farther. I sank to the ground. The smell of my own urine almost made me sick. I choked back my gagging and called out to Mama a little louder. I watched as she turned and looked around the yard until finally her eyes landed on me. I knew I must have been a sight because Mama dropped the pair of pants she was about to hang up and took off running toward me as she screamed for Daddy. "Cedric! Cedric, come quick!"

I wanted to get up off that ground, but I just couldn't. All of my strength had been used up getting me home. Instead, I started wailing. I wanted to be quiet because I didn't want to scare Mama any more than she already was, but I couldn't stop myself. The wails came from such a deep place inside me that quieting them was impossible at this point. Instead, I stuffed my fist inside my mouth to try to muffle the sound, but my lips were so raw from being hit, I had to place my hand over my mouth instead.

"What's wrong?" Daddy yelled, rushing out of the house with his pants on and his shirt undone. Lawrence must have been inside, too, because I heard him calling out to me. He made it to me before Mama or Daddy.

"What happened?" he yelled hoarsely, sitting on the ground and pulling me into his arms, shaking me as I continued to cry out. "What happened to you, Rose?"

Daddy and Mama both got to me and knelt down on the ground too.

"Let me have her," Daddy commanded, pulling me into his embrace with his one good arm. I immediately felt safe. My cries soon became hiccups. "You're okay. You're okay now." Daddy rocked me as Mama stroked my head. After a while, I felt calm enough to speak.

"I-I was walking h-home from Grandma Perkins," I managed to stammer. "Policeman was in the road. Couldn't run nowhere. He hit me in the face over and over. I peed on myself," I cried, the wailing threatening to overwhelm me again, but Daddy continued to rock me in his arms.

"You're okay now. You're okay now," he kept repeating.

"I'll kill him," Lawrence said, getting up from the ground. "I will find the bastard and I will kill him for putting his hands on my sister."

Mama stood and grabbed Lawrence by the arm. "Be still. Don't you run off and do something half-cocked. Let's get your sister in the house. Then we'll figure out what our next steps are."

"I'll take her," Lawrence said gruffly. I could tell Daddy didn't hardly want to let me go, but he moved aside so Lawrence could carefully lift me up from the ground into his arms. I felt embarrassed that Lawrence was picking me up like this, but I just couldn't imagine standing up and walking on my own yet. I had no more energy to do much of anything. "You okay now," he muttered, repeating Daddy's words. I could see the tears flowing down his face. I buried my head into his chest, trying to make the whole world disappear.

"I'm getting you wet," I moaned. 'I'm so sorry."

"Shhh. Don't matter. Don't worry about that. Let's just get you inside and get you cleaned up. You all right now."

"Take her to the bathroom, Lawrence," Mama said, walking closely beside Lawrence and me. "Mama will get you cleaned up in no time, baby. Don't you worry about nothing."

Before he could get me into the house, I heard voices. I yelped from fear.

"It's okay. It's Aunt Shimmy and Aunt Lucille," Lawrence reassured me, tightening his grip as if he was shielding me from everything and everyone. I wrapped my arms around his neck and kept my face buried in his chest even though the roughness of his shirt made my face sting. I didn't want to talk to anybody just yet. I just wanted to get inside and be where I knew it would be safe. Out here I felt too exposed.

"Lord have mercy," I heard Aunt Shimmy say. "What's going on? Me and Lucille were having coffee and we heard the yelling and screaming. Is Rose okay?"

Mama pushed us inside. I didn't hear what Daddy said to them. Once we were in the bathroom, Mama told Lawrence to sit me on the toilet. "I got her from here," Mama said. Lawrence kissed me on the top of my head and then made his way out of the bathroom, leaving just me and Mama. "I'm gone run you a bath and use some of those bath salts you like that your daddy got me for my birthday. Okay?"

"Yes, ma'am," I said, barely above a whisper, but Mama must have heard me because she started running the water in the tub. At first, I closed my eyes and tried to relax. All I could see was that awful red-faced white man slapping me over and over. I forced my eyes to stay open, even though my left eye was a bit swollen from one of the slaps that landed a bit off the mark of my nose and mouth. I couldn't believe a grown man would do a woman that way. It only made me worry more about Ellena. If he would do that to me in the middle of the road, what in the world would they do to her in that jailhouse?

Pretty soon, the bathroom started smelling like lavender and I felt myself begin to relax. Silently, Mama helped me out of my clothes and into the bathtub. I couldn't help but sigh when I sank into that warm water. Mama started washing me like she used to when I was a little girl. Then she started singing real softly a song I remembered hearing the Clara Ward Singers sing on the radio just the other morning—"I Open My Mouth to the Lord." Mama's voice was soothing. More soothing even than the bath. As she washed my body and sang, I allowed peace to move from the top of my head to the bottom of my feet. Finally, I closed my eyes and listened to Mama sing.

I open my mouth to the Lord,
And I won't turn back.
I will go!
I shall go!
To see what the end's gonna be.

Mama shampooed my hair and conditioned it. Once she was done, she stood and offered her hands to me to help me out of the tub. Mama enveloped me in a towel and held me close. I laid my head on her shoulder, but she pushed me back just a little so we were looking at each other eye to eye. "I won't ask you to say any more about this than you need to, but Mama needs to know. Did that man do anything to you besides hit you?"

The tears began to lap underneath my chin, but I shook my head vigorously. She dried the tears with the edge of the towel, then pulled me close again. "You don't have to say anything more to me about that. I have been where you are, and I know all you want to do is sink into the earth. You are not alone."

I looked at Mama curiously. "Someone did this to you?"

So much about Mama's past was a mystery to me—to all of us kids. Lawrence knew more than most of us because he was the oldest, but even he didn't know a great deal about Mama's past. Daddy talked a little more about his childhood, but Mama never said a whole lot. We children would ask her stories about when she was young, and more times than not, she would just say, *"The Lord didn't bring me out of the past for me to keep looking back at it."* She would say that after we asked her about her mother, who left her when she was a little wee baby, or details about her grandma Birdie. Mama never seemed sad about the past; she just never seemed to want to discuss it. So it was shocking to me, to put it mildly, that Mama was revealing even this much.

She stroked my face softly and kissed my cheeks. "A long time ago a twisted young man tried to hurt me, but just like God intervened for you today, he intervened for me too. Let me go get you some clothes," she said as I sat down on the toilet seat.

I reached for the Jergens lotion and began slathering it all over. By the time I was done, Mama had come back with a clean summer dress for me to put on. Once I was dressed, I started feeling a bit shy about going out where everyone was waiting for me to come and tell them what happened. I didn't want to talk about any of this. I just wanted to go to my and Ellena's room and find her there and get in the bed with her and cry until all the hurt I was feeling was out of my spirit.

"It's just your daddy, Lawrence, Aunt Shimmy, and Cousin Lucille. They want to know you're okay," Mama said, taking my hand. I followed her out of the bathroom, my eyes on the floor. We went to the living room where everyone was sitting. I couldn't make myself look them in the eyes. I felt so responsible for their concern. I shouldn't have left out in the dark. I should have realized that times had changed. I should have realized that anything could happen to me and the men in the family would take it as a personal attack and feel obligated to do something about it. It pained me to no measure that I may have done something to put my daddy, brothers, and uncles in harm's way. Suddenly, I noticed the twins weren't around. In fact, I hadn't seen them at all.

"Where's Micah and Mitchell?" I asked hurriedly, trying not to let the hysteria that was threatening to bubble up to overcome me.

"They out in the country helping Doc Russell," Daddy said. "Don't worry about your brothers. Are you okay, baby?"

"She's okay," Mama said, pulling me close. "Just a little rattled right now, but she's okay."

"Did he . . ." Daddy started but then stopped. I could tell he had been crying. Daddy didn't shed tears often, but when he did, it nearly broke my heart. Like now. I was so sorry that I did anything that would make him cry for me. He was already full of tears for Ellena and now, I was adding to his sadness.

"He hit her, Cedric. Nothing else," Mama said, her voice reassuring, sounding like she does when she talks to the grandboys.

"'Nothing else,'" Lawrence said, his voice filled with rage. "Ain't that enough? He could have killed . . . We should be out looking for him. Not sitting here wringing our hands like a bunch of ninnies."

"Hush up, Lawrence," Mama said with a warning voice.

Daddy came to me and pulled me into a hug. "I'm so sorry, baby girl. I am so sorry."

Daddy led me to the couch where he and Lawrence were sitting. Mama sat on the other side of Daddy. Lawrence took my hand and looked at me with searching eyes, just like he used to when we were younger. It was his way of asking me if I was okay. I nodded to let him know I was all right.

"I understand we need to be thoughtful and prayerful about how we handle this, but we need a plan of action," Daddy said to all of us, but I could tell he was talking to Mama. There wasn't much that Daddy did that he didn't consult with Mama first. He'd say for the biggest decision or the smallest, "*What you think, Opal?*"

Mama leaned forward and looked at me. "Did you see him good, Rose? Could you identify his face again?"

I knew without a doubt I could pick his face out of a crowd of red-faced white men, but the thought of seeing him again made my chest hurt. I did something I felt terrible about later. It was all I knew to do at that moment to preserve my mind. I told my mama a lie.

"It was too dark. I didn't see his face."

Mama looked at me long and hard, as if she was trying to study the truth out of my face. After a moment she turned back to Daddy. "Then that settles it. If she can't picture his face, there ain't nothing we can do."

"Rose, you have to remember something," Lawrence insisted. "We can't just let this go."

"Think on it a bit, sugar," Aunt Shimmy said. "I know this is hard, but if you can, just try to come up with one thing that will help us identify him."

"Yes, baby," Aunt Lucille said in the same soothing voice as Aunt Shimmy. Both of them were still dressed in housecoats with their pin curlers in their hair. I knew they had to be worried about me to leave home like that. "Any little detail will help. Just think on it for a spell."

Before I could say anything, Lawrence jumped up excitedly. "His car. The police will know what cars were out in these parts. Maybe a lawyer can make them tell."

"They aren't going to help us," I said, standing up from my seat. "Why would they help us when they hate us so? I'm not going to report this to anybody. I just want to be left alone." I rushed out of the room. I tried to keep the tears from flowing, but they were already streaming down my face. I threw myself on my bed, groaning as my bruised face hit the pillow. I just wanted my sister. I just wanted Ellena.

That was all. I lay there crying into the pillow until I heard Mama's voice.

"It's gonna be all right, Rose." Mama sat beside me on the bed. She stroked my hair and I felt some of the stress flow out of my mind and body. Mama's touch was like having the hand of God touch you. "Your daddy and brother are about to be on their way to see about Ellena. I just want you to rest and don't think about any of this. We will figure this out. As a family. Okay?"

"Yes, ma'am," I said as I closed my eyes, praying that I didn't see the face of that evil red-faced man again. I remembered my prayer and plea to Jasper and God to send me a guardian angel. I wondered if they did or if they left me to fend for myself. I guess I would never know, but right now, I felt more alone than I had felt in a very long time.

CHAPTER 20

"WAKE UP, SISSY. WAKE UP." I HEARD A FAMILIAR VOICE CALLING out to me. I sat straight up in the bed. To my delight, Ellena was sitting there beside me, but the look on her face caused me to turn away. I knew my bruises must have looked awful. I could feel the tightness in my face from the swelling and my eyes were almost slits. It hurt to smile, but I tried to turn up the corners of my mouth to reassure her I was okay as she tilted my chin until we were looking at each other once more. Tears were sliding down her face. "Oh, Sissy. What did he do to you?"

"I'm okay," I whispered. I reached for Ellena and held her like I was never going to let her go again. I felt a small tear fall down my face as well. I lightly brushed it away. I wasn't about to allow myself to get wound up again. I was safe and Ellena was back home—that's all that mattered. "I was so scared they would hurt you too," I said. I leaned back and looked at her as best I could, putting my hands on her face. "They didn't hurt you, did they?"

Ellena shook her head, dabbing her eyes with a handker-chief. "No. They tossed us around a bit when they were arresting us, but other than that, we suffered no injuries . . . at least none one can see with the naked eye," she said with a bitterness I had never heard in her voice before. "They didn't even bring us food to eat, although I probably wouldn't have wanted their nasty food anyway." She let out a slight laugh that didn't reach her eyes. "But they didn't hurt me. They were nothing like that bastard who put his hands on you."

I shook my head. "Don't talk like that," I said. "I'm all right."

"I know you are all right," she said, standing up and pacing the room. "Thank God. I just don't know about all of this nonviolence rhetoric that John Lewis and his mentor, Dr. King, are spouting. Where is it getting us? I had hot soup thrown on me yesterday and a white man spit in Isaac Weinberg's face, and guess what? We are no closer to getting served at the counter in Woolworth's than we were before we marched in there. They know violence. That is the language the white man speaks. Maybe we should speak the same language back to them."

I didn't know exactly what to say. Right then, I knew my sister would never rest until she saw change begin to happen, and if it didn't happen at the rate she wanted it to, I knew she was willing to die for it. That fact scared me more than any beating I could receive.

"I just want to forget about all of this," I said. I prayed all of those SNCC folks would go back to Atlanta so we wouldn't have to worry about these white folks in Parsons getting angry at us and hurting us worse than they had already. *Maybe if SNCC left, Ellena would settle down some*, I thought, although I knew it was wishful thinking on my part.

"I'm afraid we can't just forget about what happened, Rose," Ellena said. "Everybody is outside waiting for you and me."

"What do you mean 'everybody'?" I could hear the sounds of voices outside the door. It sounded like it did on the holidays when all the family came together here at Great-Grandma Birdie's old place, but their voices did not sound happy and joyful. There was no laughter, no loud joke telling. Just a low rumbling.

"Daddy called a family meeting." She stood, running her fingers through her short, cropped hair. "I'm sure he and everybody else will give long lectures on us being good, faithful Negroes who accept everything these ofays dish out."

This wasn't my sister. I had never seen her express this level of anger and frustration toward anyone. Yes, she was passionate, but not so angry. I worried for her life. I worried for her mind most of all. I could tell that no matter what anybody said during the meeting, she was going to continue her work with SNCC, and if they left Parsons, she would work alone if need be.

"Ellena," I said, trying not to get emotional again. "Listen to Daddy and the others. They just want to keep us safe. That's all."

"But we aren't safe." Her voice was full of exasperation as she came back to the bed and sat down beside me. She lightly touched my face and I winced. "Look at you. Look at what that awful man did to you, and the law is on his side because he *is* the law."

"It could have been worse," I whispered.

"That's the measuring stick we Negroes always use when it comes to the tyranny of white people. They lynch one of us and we say, 'It could have been worse.' They steal our property and refuse us the right to vote and run for office and again we say, 'It could have been worse.' Aren't you tired of the crumbs they offer us? Aren't you tired of it all?" she asked, sounding like someone twice her age.

Finally I nodded. "Yes. I guess I am. But I don't want to die, and I don't want any of my kin to die, because having the right to vote or eat at the Woolworth's counter doesn't mean more to me than my family."

Before she could say anything else, Mama came to the door. "You girls come on out. Everybody's here."

I felt shy about going out with my face looking the way it did. I didn't want anybody saying anything about it. Ellena went marching out of the room like she was going to battle, but I hung back. Mama came over and pulled me close.

"It's okay, baby. Everybody knows what happened. They won't make a big thing about it," Mama said. "Let's go and get this talk out of the way."

"Yes, ma'am." I allowed myself to be led out of the bedroom and into the living room, where most of the family was congregated. The twins came over to me, and Micah lightly touched the side of my face. "Mama called Doc Russell's office and told the receptionist what happened. We brought something home to put on your face. It will heal it right up. Won't even leave a scar."

I gave him a hug and let him guide me to the couch, where I sat between them. Lawrence and Naomi's triplets came and sat by my legs. I reached down and petted on each of them. Everyone was here except for Uncle Myron and his family, who, of course, were in Atlanta and Tuskegee. I hoped no one called Uncle Myron and told him what had happened. I looked over at Katie Bell and Naomi. Naomi gave me the thumbs-up, and Katie Bell tried to smile, but I could see that she was shedding tears. She was holding L.J., who was sleeping. I tried to smile back at her, but my face hurt.

Grandma Perkins got up from her seat and came over to me. Micah stood and gave her his seat. She sat beside me and pulled me into her embrace. It took everything inside me to keep from crying. I expected Daddy to get up and speak, but instead Uncle Michael got up. He was the second oldest of the great-uncles, and he seldom said much. I watched as he walked into the middle of the room. He was dressed in a pair of overalls, and his curly white hair was slicked back. He looked good for his age. All of Mama's uncles did. It was surprising to see Uncle Michael stand first, because it was usually either Uncle Myron or Uncle Little Bud who did the talking during family gatherings. Sometimes their other brother, Uncle Lem, would say a word or two, but today, they all sat as Uncle Michael took the lead.

For a moment, he didn't say anything. He just stood before us with his head down and his hands clasped like he was silently praying. The room got quiet, and then, as the silence continued, almost like during church, various ones began to cry out—mostly the women, although I saw Lawrence wipe a tear or two. It was like we were all going through the emotions together. Grief. Anger. Bewilderment. Finally, Uncle Michael cleared his throat and said a short prayer. Once he was done and we all said "Amen," he spoke.

"This isn't the first time this family has had to come together in Mama's old house over some evil done to us by white folks," he said, his voice hoarse with emotion. "Probably won't be the last, but this time, I think we have to listen to the young folks. I think we have to fight back. Not with guns or knives but with conviction. What was done to Ellena and what was done to Rose this morning cannot be allowed to go on anymore."

"Finally," Ellena nearly yelled, standing up from her chair on the other side of the room. Mama cut her eyes at her and she slowly sat back down. No matter how old we get to be, and no matter how many children we gave birth to, a look from Mama cut just as deep as when we were little children.

"Uncle Michael," Daddy said, although he looked around the room at each of us. "We don't need to get mixed up in any of this fight to vote or fight to eat at some food counter. It's not worth it. And Rose doesn't remember who hurt her. It would be a fool's mission for us to try to fight these white people. Y'all realize this is life or death, don't you? This ain't no game."

"Yesterday, I would have agreed with you, Cedric," Uncle Michael said, shifting his weight so he was resting on his walking cane. "But today, after all that we've been through, I believe we have to let these white people in Parsons, Georgia, know we are not troublemakers, but we will not lay down like a bunch of house pets when trouble is brought to our doorsteps."

The talking in the room got loud as various ones began making their points to each other. It was becoming chaotic. All I wanted to do was go back to my bedroom and hide from all of this, but I watched as Ellena went up to Uncle Michael and took his hand. She didn't say anything. She just stood there, gripping his hand tightly. He smiled at her and kissed her cheek. Then, almost like on the last night of revival meeting, others stood. Lawrence and Naomi went up and joined hands with Uncle Myron and Ellena. The boys hopped up and ran to their parents. I watched as Lawrence lifted David and Daniel into his arms while Naomi lifted up Demetrius. Then, one by one, my family joined Uncle Michael, all clustered together and holding hands.

"Come on, baby," Grandma Perkins said as she slowly stood, grasping my hand in hers. I didn't want to get up. I didn't know what all of this meant. I wasn't ready to fight. I didn't feel strong enough to fight anyone. It was only a few hours ago that I was covered in pee. I wasn't a fighter. But Grandma didn't let go of my hand. "It's okay. You won't be standing alone," she said, and as I looked at everyone standing in a semicircle—save me, Grandma Perkins, Mama, and Daddy—I knew she was right. But I didn't want to go against my parents. I looked at them, and Mama smiled at me and nodded. Then she turned to Daddy.

"Cedric, you and I have lived in fear long enough," she said, her voice strong and loud. "When I fell in love with you, you were a young hothead. I prayed to God to take that fire away from you. I stand here now in front of our family and God, and I ask that he give that same fire back to you today. Alone in our fear, we cannot do anything. But with our family and God on our side, we are stronger than an army of ten thousand."

Everyone remained quiet. Waiting. Even though the uncles were older, they usually looked toward Daddy in moments like this. I knew that if Daddy refused to be part of whatever it was they were proposing we do, the others would back down. Grandma Perkins guided me over to Daddy and Mama. She placed my hand in Mama's hand, and then she placed her hand on what was left of Daddy's left arm. Daddy called it his stump. I knew it embarrassed him sometimes to not have a whole left arm, but I wished I could let him know that with or without an arm, he was the greatest and strongest man in the world to me. We all listened as Grandma Perkins began to speak. "Son, it wasn't just Opal who prayed for God to take away your fire. I prayed that prayer too. So did your daddy. But I'm on the side of Opal and everyone else. It's time for us to stand up for ourselves and our community."

"Are you saying it's wrong to turn the other cheek?" Daddy asked. "Are you saying we shouldn't wait on God? My whole life you've preached that message to me. What has changed?"

"'Behold, I give you the authority to trample on serpents and scorpions, and over all the power of the enemy, and nothing shall by any means hurt you,'" Grandma Perkins said, quoting Luke 10, verse 19. "In our fear, we sometimes forget those words of promise from God. It's time we let God show us, once again, that he is on our side."

"Amen," several of our relatives said behind us, but I didn't look at them. I just looked at Daddy. I could tell, even with Mama's words of encouragement and Grandma Perkins's scripture, he still wasn't convinced.

"Over twenty years ago, those white folks took my arm. And Opal," he said, looking at Mama with pleading eyes, "they murdered your Grandma Birdie. Yesterday, white folks arrested my baby girl, Ellena, and this morning, a police officer, a man of the so-called law, beat up my Rose." Daddy looked from one of us to the other. "I understand y'all want to fight, but look around this room and tell me, who are you willing to lose next? Who among us are you at peace to bury in that cemetery? Because that is what will happen. This ain't about singing gospel hymns and marching. Y'all say you are willing to die for your freedom. Well, these white folks here in Parsons, Georgia, are willing to help you into your early graves."

The talking in the room started up again. Everybody was talking over one another, and no one was listening. I thought about everything everyone had said, and I decided it was past time for me to use my voice.

"I want to fight," I said. My voice sounded weak to my ears. No one paid me any attention. I decided if I was ever going to be unafraid again, I had to speak up in front of the people I loved the most—the people who were saying they were willing to go to battle for me, themselves, and every other Negro in Parsons, Georgia. If they were willing to do that, then I needed to be brave with them. I repeated my words. "I said I want to fight." This time I raised my voice loud enough for everyone to hear. The room went quiet. I knew they were as shocked by my words as I was for saying them, but I did not mean to back away from my newfound convictions. This morning I asked Jasper to be my and my family's guardian angel. Now it was time for me to trust that he would be.

"Say your piece, baby," Grandma Perkins said. I looked at her and she looked proud—like she used to when we children would recite our Christmas or Easter speeches perfectly. Her encouragement gave me the strength to continue, even though I wondered if she would be proud after I said what I had to say.

"This morning, I wasn't honest," I said, making sure my voice carried throughout the room. "I told everyone that I didn't see the face of the man who attacked me, but I did. I was just scared, but I'm not scared now, or at least I'm not as scared as I was. I don't know if I can be as brave as Ellena and all of you, but I promise I'll do what I can, starting with going down to that police station and telling them what happened, even if they don't do anything about it."

"Absolutely not!" Daddy roared. "I forbid it."

I almost shrank back behind Grandma Perkins, but I stayed still, and I hoped the resolve remained on my face. I didn't feel brave enough to contradict Daddy verbally, but I wasn't going to move away from his glare. If I couldn't face my own daddy's anger, how could I stand firm against those white policemen?

"We will go with her, and we will take a lawyer," Mama said firmly. "It's the right thing to do, Cedric. Remember when that Ketchums boy beat me up and I begged you to not do anything?"

"Of course I remember. I . . ."

"I shouldn't have stopped you." Mama moved closer to Daddy and placed her hand on his cheek. The love that transpired between the two of them was so deep and personal, it almost hurt to watch because I didn't know if anyone would ever look at me that way again. I tried to focus instead on Mama's words: "I should have trusted you to do what was needed to be done to protect me, my love. This child, in spite of her fears, is willing to face those awful people. We must face them with her, Cedric. Otherwise, what's the use? If we don't fight back, then they've won."

"Listen to your wife, son," Grandma Perkins said, pleading with Daddy like someone pleading the blood of Jesus over a fallen sinner. "Listen to your daughter. It's time for that old Cedric to come back. We never should have asked you to give up that part of yourself that made you brave."

We watched as every emotion crossed Daddy's face. Then it softened, and he reached for me and pulled me tight.

"It's been a long time since your old daddy was fearless. But if you are willing to fight, then I'll fight right along with you. Even with just one good arm."

"Oh, Daddy." The tears began to fall as we hugged each other tight. I felt Mama's and Grandma Perkins's hands on my back. Right then, I had everything I needed. I prayed I would feel that way later. Everyone stayed until after lunch, discussing what was the best course of action. Daddy said he would call the NAACP and see whether they could recommend a lawyer to help us. Ellena told everyone there was going to be a meeting later tonight at the Baptist church that had become the headquarters for the local Movement. I was scared but I was resolved to do everything I could to help, even if it meant facing my worst fear again—that awful white police officer.

Soon after everyone left and it was just Mama, Daddy, me, and Ellena, there was a knock at the door. We all looked at one another as Daddy rose from his seat and went to see who it was. It wasn't long before Daddy led Isaac Weinberg, an unfamiliar Negro man, and two white men into the room. One of the men I recognized as Senator Jimmy Earl Ketchums. I had never seen him up close, but I recognized his face from the newspapers and the television. He was a tall, thin man with a large potbelly. His head was completely bald, and he wore big, thick glasses. The Negro man and the other white man I didn't know, but they looked official with their briefcases and business suits. Daddy's face looked tight, but he led them over to us. We all stood.

"Everyone, this is Attorney Joel Shannon; he's from the NAACP," Daddy said, introducing everyone to us. "This here is Senator Jimmy Earl Ketchums, and these other two are Isaac Weinberg and his father, Attorney Tobias Weinberg. They've come to talk to us about some of the legal things going on pertaining to the arrest of Ellena and the others."

"It's a pleasure to meet you ladies," Attorney Weinberg said. "When I got the call yesterday about my son, Isaac, and the others, I hopped on a plane, and I reached out to the senator and Attorney Shannon. I met both men a few years ago, and I knew what we were facing was going to take

Attorney Shannon's legal prowess and the senator's community connections. We've visited the other families who had young people involved, and we wanted to come see if there was anything you needed or if there were any questions you needed answering."

Everyone greeted one another and Daddy offered them seats. Mama and Ellena went into the kitchen to get refreshments. I continued to sit. I glanced over at Isaac, and he was staring at me. I lightly touched my face; I had completely forgotten about the bruises and swelling. I turned away, not wanting to see the questions in his eyes.

Mama and Ellena soon walked back into the room with a pot of coffee and some sugar cookies they had baked earlier. They poured everyone coffee and put the cookies within reach, but everyone was focused on what was being said by Attorney Shannon. He was an older man with salt-and-pepper hair and a cleft lip.

"They haven't a leg to stand on when it comes to the sit-in yesterday," Attorney Shannon said, his voice booming loudly throughout the room. "The young people did exactly what they were trained to do. They went in and sat and were respectful, and when the police came to arrest them, they did not offer any resistance. Monday we will go in front of the magistrate and settle this situation once and for all."

Everyone seemed satisfied with his words, but Senator Ketchums's mouth was twisted slightly. Clearly, he didn't agree with what was being said.

"As I mentioned to Opal last night, the police will arrest them again if they try to do any more demonstrations,"

Senator Ketchums said slowly, his Southern drawl thick like Mama's peach preserves. "I understand their passion, but this could get ugly."

"*Could* get ugly, Senator?" Attorney Weinberg said with a wry voice. "It has already gotten ugly. Young lady, excuse my prying, but what happened to your face? Were you part of the demonstration?"

I felt myself shrink into the chair. I looked from Mama to Daddy and then down toward the floor. Mercifully, Daddy spoke on my behalf.

"This morning when my daughter was walking home from her grandmother's house, a police officer attacked her. She wasn't messing with nobody, but he beat on her like she was some outlaw."

Even though I didn't have any reason to be ashamed, I still hung my head. I wished over and over I could redo the morning and just wait at Grandma Perkins's house until the sun came up and Daddy or Lawrence could have come for me.

"Did you all report this?" Senator Ketchums asked in a loud voice. I glanced up and saw a look of dismay on his face. It was strange having somebody like him sounding bothered by what happened to me. "This is atrocious. I will call Chief Burnett and get to the bottom of this. May I use your phone?" He stood up, but Attorney Shannon stopped him.

"I understand your desire to help, Senator," Attorney Shannon said. "But this might not be the hill you want to die on. Because the girl didn't file charges as soon as it occurred, they will likely brush it off. Doesn't matter that it was a few hours ago. They will still have something to say about her delaying her complaint. And since there were no other witnesses, I foresee this only causing trouble for this family. Justice will not be meted out."

"This is ridiculous," Senator Ketchums said.

"Excuse me," I said. I got up and hurried to the kitchen. I didn't want to hear any more. All of this was making me anxious. "You were so stupid," I muttered to myself as I started putting the dishes that were in the drain in their proper place. I wasn't a coffee drinker, but I poured myself a cup. When I did drink it, I always drank it black, like Daddy.

"Are you okay?" a voice said.

I turned around quickly. It was Isaac. I didn't hear him enter the kitchen. I wondered if anyone else noticed. I didn't want anyone to think there was something inappropriate between Isaac and me or between me and any man.

"Yes," I said nervously. "I'm okay. Do you need something?"

Isaac was tall and his skin was like polished onyx. He was a very handsome young man. I wished I didn't notice such things. Mama used to call me boy crazy. I didn't want to be that. I wanted to be a good widow who only focused on my dead husband and baby girl.

"No, I don't need anything," he said. "I feel responsible for what happened to you. Maybe if we hadn't come here, you wouldn't have been attacked."

"You can't know that," I said, my voice barely audible. "The evil that man did was all his fault, not anyone else's. He could have just left me alone."

Before he could respond, Ellena walked into the room.

She walked over to me and wrapped her arm around my waist.

"You okay?" she whispered in my ear. I nodded yes, but I was sure happy to have her in the room. She turned to Isaac. "Brother Isaac, your father and Attorney Shannon are leaving now," she said. Then she turned to me. "We aren't going to call the police. But we are going to have a meeting tonight to discuss our next steps, and that includes voter registration. Even though a lot of Negroes are ambivalent about eating at the Woolworth's, most are clear that we should have the right to vote and run for office. So we will meet people where they are."

I couldn't help but breathe a sigh of relief. I was committed to standing by my promise to go to the police, but it did terrify me—the thought of seeing that officer face-to-face again.

"That sounds good," Isaac said. "I hope to see you both tonight." He turned and walked back toward the living room.

Ellena looked at me with concern. "Are you sure you're okay? I know this day has been terrible, but we will get through all of this together. Don't worry."

"I'll try," I said. "I think I'll go take a nap."

"Okay, Sissy." She kissed me on my cheek. As I walked to my bedroom, I prayed that my dreams would be filled with Jasper's sweet words of love and devotion and not the horrors of this morning. I needed desperately to drift away to a safe place where I would be protected from everything that had happened over the last few days.

"Please, God," I whispered. "Take away these bad

thoughts in my head and replace them with my sweet husband and baby."

Once I got settled in the bed, I found myself drifting off to a familiar place, where Jasper was waiting for me with open arms.

CHAPTER 21

"STARTING TONIGHT, WE WILL BEGIN TO PREPARE YOU FOR THE arduous task of getting those of you over the age of eighteen registered to vote here in Henry County," Isaac said from the front of the main sanctuary of St. Luke's Missionary Baptist Church. It was strange seeing a Jewish man standing at the front of a Christian church. I guessed when it was all said and done, racism didn't care what your religion was. I was beginning to understand this more and more as time went by. When that policeman attacked me the way he did, he didn't care what God I served or if I served any God at all. He looked at me and saw nothing—but especially not a child of God.

I looked around the room. There was a large crowd of about seventy-five or eighty people. I knew some of their faces but not all of them. Some of the people were still dressed in their work clothes and you could see the tiredness on their faces, but you could also see the resolve to make change happen in our community on their faces too. These folks weren't allowing fear to overtake them. They were willing to take a chance on freedom. It was funny. All this time, I thought I was free. I thought because I didn't want to go to their schools or shop at their stores or vote in their elections, that it meant I was exercising my free will not to be around them either. I believed it was mutually agreed upon on both sides, but I was realizing it wasn't. The more I thought about all of this, the more I knew this for sure—until we were all free to choose, none us were free.

I smoothed out the wrinkles in my skirt. Mama had insisted that we dress like we were going to church, so I was wearing an ankle-length blue skirt and a high-collared, blue ruffled blouse with short sleeves. I tried to wear Jasper's favorite color as often as I could. It reminded me of him, and I needed that. Ellena had put makeup on my face to camouflage some of the bruises. The swelling around my eyes had gone down, and I felt halfway presentable.

"I'll turn the program over to Sister Deirdre Sparks," he said, stepping aside so she could move toward the front. They were all dressed in suits and dresses, too, and everyone looked official and fearless. I sat up to hear what Deirdre Sparks had to say. I noticed that a lot of the other girls and women in the room did the same thing. It was nice seeing a young Negro woman take charge of this meeting. It was a reminder that we all had a part to play in The Movement.

"The registrar's office is not going to make this process easy, as many of you already know," she said. "The registrar's office has changed their hours of operation—open only from 9:00 a.m. until 10:30 a.m. during the week. They chose those hours because they know for many of you it will be impossible to take off work and register. They know that—"

An older man in the audience stood up and interrupted her. "I'm here tonight because I want to do what I can, but my boss, Mr. Bingham, said if any of his hired hands registered to vote, he would fire us on the spot. I fought in World War II at the age of forty-three. They threw a ticker-tape parade when we got home, but we quickly figured out the parade wasn't for us. The white boys went on to get good-paying jobs, money to go to school, help buying a home, and us Colored soldiers went back to the cotton fields. I want better for my grands and great-grands. So whatever I have to do, job or no job, I'll do it."

He sat back down as everyone began to clap. I didn't know that man, but he made me proud to be a Negro. He made me want to do better. Ellena reached over and squeezed my hand. I looked at her and she had tears in her eyes.

"We thank you for your service, sir," Isaac said once the clapping slowed down. "We are not here to make your lives worse. But we would be remiss if we didn't acknowledge that things will get ugly before they get better, and we will not fault a single person for deciding this is too much. At the end of the day, when we return to our homes, you still have to live here. So please, if anyone feels like the burden to fight segregation is too much, it is okay if you leave, and no one here will think less of you."

Isaac stopped talking and we all waited in silence, wondering who would leave first. As the seconds ticked by, no one did. Everyone remained seated in their chairs. The biggest smile went across Isaac's face.

"Thank you. We promise that we will do our best to make sure you are prepared and protected," Deirdre said, a huge smile on her face too. "We will split you into three groups, and we'll go over with you the steps necessary to become registered voters. As I stated before, it won't be easy, but what in life that is worth having comes easy?"

She and Isaac divided us into groups. The older men were put into a group, and so were the older women. The third group was made up of us younger folks from eighteen to thirty. Deirdre taught our group, and she was even more candid than she had been in the main auditorium. It was about twenty of us in one of the back rooms that was used for Sunday school for the teenagers, and as Daddy often said, she didn't pull any punches.

"I am not going to sugarcoat any of this," she said, looking around the room as she moved stealthily from one side to the other, making sure she was making good eye contact. "Teaching you how to prepare for the test is the easy part. Preparing you for the hate and the possible violence will be the hard part. But for now, let's discuss this so-called literacy test." She held out the papers. Ellena and one other young person jumped up to pass them around. Once everyone had a copy, she told us to look it over.

"Are they for real?" Hayward Shipman, the pastor's son at our church, exclaimed. "How are we supposed to learn all of this?"

"If you want to vote, you will learn it and even more," Deirdre said. "They expect you to have that attitude. They expect you to give up, but we are not going to give them reasons to say no to your voter applications. We will only give them reasons to say yes."

I flipped through the pages. Although I didn't say

anything, I wasn't too far away from what Hayward was feeling. I didn't see how I could learn all of this information. The more pages I turned, the more discouraged I got. *Who is the solicitor general of your state judicial circuit and who are the presiding judges? What are the names of the federal district judges in Georgia? How may a new state be admitted to the Union? List the fifty-six signers of the Declaration of Independence.* The questions left me breathless. I could feel my brain doing flip-flops just like it used to do before a test when I was in school. I wasn't like Ellena and the twins. I had struggled throughout school and counted it a blessing that I even graduated. My saving grace was that I excelled at memorizing things. But the things I memorized in school were nothing like this. I felt defeated before we even got started.

"We'll take it step by step," Ellena said in my ear. "We'll study together, and by the end of the summer, you'll be ready to register to vote right along with me and whoever else sticks with it. I promise."

I just nodded. I didn't believe I would ever be ready for the test, but I didn't want to discourage Ellena. Deirdre kept talking about the steps we would take to ready ourselves for the tests and the abuse we would surely experience.

"They might spit in your face. They might put their hands on you," she said as calmly as if she were saying they might shake your hand and give you a hug. "They will do anything and everything they can do to dissuade you from registering to vote, but the tactic we must employ is nonviolence. We must stand firm, but we must not fight back."

"And why is that?" my brother Lawrence asked, standing

up and looking around the room at all of us. "Negroes have lived a long time not fighting back, and as time goes on, I wonder, what has that done for us? How has turning the other cheek time and time again won us any victories? We do nothing and our women and children get abused."

He looked at me when he said that. I turned away. I knew he didn't blame me for what happened, but I did. Seeing the hurt and anger on his face only made it worse. Ellena reached over and squeezed my hand.

Several of the young men nodded and grunted their agreement. My family had always lived by the Bible verse "'Vengeance is mine; I will repay,' sayeth the Lord." But like Lawrence, I wondered, did God really mean for us always to be the takers and the white folks always the ones to dish out pain and suffering? I wondered when our day would come. When would we no longer be the doormats?

Before Deirdre could respond, Isaac entered the room. "I apologize for interrupting, Sister Deirdre; I was hoping you might have some extra handouts. We have a few more new students interested in preparing for the test. However, I would love to respond to the brother, if you don't mind."

"Please," she said, smiling. It was clear that they had a good working relationship with each other. I watched as she stood aside as Isaac stood in front of the teacher's desk.

"Brother . . ."

"Lawrence. Lawrence Perkins," he said, his voice gruff with emotion. We had been through a lot these last several months, and I knew Lawrence was operating from a space of being overwhelmed with grief and anger. He felt his own pain and he felt all of ours. He always had been that way.

Lawrence took his role as the eldest seriously, and anything we felt, he felt double. To now take on this new battle . . . well, it was a lot. I hoped Isaac would take it easy on him.

"Brother Lawrence," he said. "I understand your frustration—"

"Do you?" Lawrence interrupted. "In the last two days, my baby sister has been arrested and one of my other sisters has been beaten up by the police. Two days. And you want us to sign up for more pain and degradation, but on top of that, we can't fight back? At all? You all ask a lot. More than you can even imagine."

I looked down at the floor as others in the room looked at me. I wished Lawrence hadn't referenced what happened to me. I knew most everybody in the room knew what happened; I just didn't want to have all eyes on me. I didn't get angry with him though. He was hurting and I was thankful to have a brother who cared so deeply. I wondered what Isaac would say in return. He didn't seem in a rush to speak. It was like he was weighing each word before speaking. Finally, after what seemed like forever, he spoke.

"Rev. George Lee. Brother Lamar Smith. Brother Herbert Lee. Brother William Lewis Moore." Isaac's voice was full of emotion. "Each one of them died for the cause of ending segregation. I can't tell you if they were filled with anger at the end of their lives. I can't tell you if in their heart of hearts they wanted to strike back. What I can tell you is this: They realized this movement was bigger than their individual lives. That isn't an easy conclusion to come to, Brother Lawrence. Like I said before, we understand this fight isn't for everyone. But if you do want to work peacefully for justice, we will teach you the strategies we know will work in the long term."

I wondered if Lawrence would respond, but Naomi reached for his arm, and he silently sat back down beside her. Naomi had a calming effect on Lawrence, similar to Mama's on Daddy.

"Again, I apologize for interrupting, Sister Deirdre." Isaac took the handouts and quietly exited the room. The rest of the meeting went by smoothly. She gave us study tips and encouraged us to make flash cards that we could use to quiz each other. She said we would meet twice per week, and there would also be training for those who wanted to help spread the word throughout Parsons—particularly among the people in our community who didn't attend today's meeting.

"The majority of our energy and resources will go to teaching and supporting you all as you journey toward becoming registered voters," she said. "But we would also like your help reaching out to those who didn't come to the meeting but are of an age that they can register. If you are interested in learning how to teach others what we are teaching you, make sure you sign your name on the list up front before you leave."

She dismissed everyone, and I watched as the twins and Ellena rushed to put their names on the list. I was nervous to sign up but willing to push past my fears. I made my way to the front of the room, and after my sister finished signing her name, I did the same. She looked at me with surprise.

"Are you sure?"

"I'm not sure, but I'm going to do it anyway. That is if Daddy and Mama say it's okay."

She pulled me into an embrace. "We'll be careful. We won't do anything foolish."

If the truth be known, it felt like everything we were doing would be seen as foolish to others who didn't understand it. I didn't know if I completely did, but I was willing to try. I went back to my chair. I opened the study materials we had been given and found myself getting lost in the information. It was a lot, but the advice we had been given was sound. Dierdre had said we should make sure we understood the material first. Memorizing without understanding was a sure way to fail. She said we should arm ourselves with dictionaries and thesauruses so we could look up anything we didn't understand. I became so engrossed in the material that I didn't notice everyone had left the room. I got up to leave and Isaac entered. He went to the desk and picked up the volunteer sheet, looked at me, and smiled.

"I see you signed up to help get the word out," he said, walking toward me. "Thank you. It will go a long way in getting your friends, family, and neighbors to register to vote. Sister Deirdre says there are roughly 250 eligible Negro voters here in Parsons and the surrounding areas. If we could just get half of them to register, what a difference we could make in your local government alone."

I watched as the excitement played across his face. It was clear he loved the work he was doing. Somehow, he blocked out the danger of it all and just focused on the good his work would do for everyone. I hoped I would be able to do the same.

"I don't know how much help I'll actually be, but I will do my best," I said.

"I'm sorry you got hurt." He looked at me with kind eyes. "I understand why your brother is angry. We all have a right to be angry, but we have to figure out how to leverage those feelings into positive outcomes. It took me a while to believe the teachings of Gandhi, but when it finally sank in, I couldn't imagine any other approach that would work besides nonviolence."

I looked at him with puzzlement. "You mean Dr. King, don't you? He's the one that came up with the nonviolent movement, didn't he?"

"Dr. King has definitely put his stamp on the nonviolent movement, but he wasn't the originator." Isaac sat in the chair beside me. "He has patterned our movement after the teachings and activism of Mohandas K. Gandhi, a Hindu man who fought for India's independence from British rule."

I knew I should be making my way back out into the main sanctuary where my family was probably waiting, but I didn't think it would hurt to just talk with Isaac. We were in the church, after all. I couldn't imagine anything bad happening here, but more than that, I couldn't imagine Dr. King, a Baptist minister, getting all of his ideas from a non-Christian. I felt guilty for thinking that. So many of the SNCC members were Jewish, and look at all the good work they had been doing. It was strange how all these bad things were bringing together so many people from so many different communities. Maybe this was all in God's plan after all.

"Why do you do this, Isaac?"

"Why do I do what?" He smiled at me, causing his whole face to light up. "You mean this work? It's the right thing to do."

"But you don't know anyone here. There aren't even any Jewish . . . What do you call where you worship?"

"Temple," he said with a smile. "Rose, when I got involved in The Movement, it was because I was seeing black and brown faces like mine on the television and in the newspapers getting slaughtered and having their rights stripped away from them in the most violent of ways. I knew I couldn't sit back and watch. Plus, my parents raised me to fight for the underdog. Always."

"But you could die. We all could die doing this." I tried to keep the fear out of my voice, but it was impossible. I was shaken by the thought of dying at the hands of men like the policeman who jumped on me just hours ago. I never wanted to go through that again, and I couldn't imagine how Isaac, Ellena, or the others could be so calm about it. This was all very scary, and it felt as if things were going to get worse before they got better . . . if they ever got better.

Isaac put his hand on mine. I almost pulled away, but I remained still. I didn't want to appear rude, and anyway, he was just being nice.

"You know how I wrote you a while ago saying I was going home to get my mind right again?" Isaac asked.

"I remember. You sounded very overwhelmed."

He nodded. "I was. I wasn't sure if I could do this anymore. I felt like for every good thing we did, something terrible would happen that almost seemed to cancel it out. When I got home, I went to visit Rabbi Levovitz, who used to be the rabbi at the temple I grew up in. Now he is in a nursing home. His body is frail, but his mind is just as sharp as always. I told him about my fears, and he said something to me I will never forget. He said, 'A man who lives his whole life in service to himself is a man who has not lived a life worth speaking of.'"

Before I could respond, Ellena walked into the room. "Mama and Daddy are ready to go," she said, looking from me to Isaac, then back at me. "You two are awful serious."

"These are serious times," he said. "It feels like the time for us to be young and carefree has passed us all by. Take care, you two. See you at the next meeting." He left the room.

"Are you okay?" she asked.

"Yes, I'm fine," I said, linking my arm with hers. "Let's go home." The two of us walked out of the room, and even though I carried on small talk with Ellena, my mind kept returning to what Isaac's rabbi said. I prayed that I could find the gumption to live the kind of life that would bring honor to my family, both alive and deceased. That was my fervent prayer.

CHAPTER 22

THE WEEKEND WAS PRETTY UNEVENTFUL, BUT ALL OF US WERE nervous about Monday when Ellena would have to appear before the judge. She and I were awake most of the night, going over and over what might happen the next day.

"I don't want to go back to jail," she said tearfully. I had wondered when my strong sister would finally crack under the pressure. Sometime around midnight, her fear kicked in. For once, I was the one who comforted her. I climbed in her bed and pulled her close.

"Isaac's daddy won't let that happen. He's a good lawyer."

"It doesn't matter," she said, wiping the tears from her eyes. "These horrible people don't care about the law. If they did, they wouldn't have arrested us in the first place. We weren't doing anything wrong. Negroes get lynched every day for doing nothing but trying to survive."

I didn't know what to say to her. The pain in my face was still there from me walking down the road doing nothing. Ellena was right. No matter how good our lawyer might be, we were still at the mercy of people who hated us just because we were Negroes.

I pulled her close and we stayed that way until it was time to get up and get dressed. Neither one of us slept very much. I couldn't imagine my life without Ellena around. She was my best friend, and the thought of her being in some nasty jailhouse for an extended period of time had me terrified.

Just before we were about to get up, Daddy came to the door. "That Jewish lawyer called."

"What about?" Ellena asked. I knew she was nervous because she didn't correct Daddy and tell him to call Mr. Weinberg by his name. I could hear the fear in her voice. I clasped her hand in mine, trying to calm her nerves and mine.

"They dropped the case," Daddy said, the emotion strong in his voice. "Said they weren't going to pursue any legal action against you or the others."

"But," Ellena sputtered, "I don't understand. What do we have to do for them to drop the charges? I am not going to promise them—"

"No conditions. They said they didn't have sufficient evidence to prosecute."

I wrapped my arms around Ellena and we hugged so tight. "It's over," I whispered. "It's over."

I could feel the wetness of Ellena's tears against my face. "This won't ever be over. Not as long as these hateful folks are alive."

The day went by uneventfully. I helped Daddy at the store, and Ellena and the twins went to their summer jobs. When we all got home from work, we gathered around the television. Daddy turned on Walter Cronkite, who was showing footage from earlier in the day when the governor of the state of Alabama was forced to move out of the doorway of the University of Alabama so that two young Negroes, Vivian Malone and James Hood, could enter as students. Daddy, Mama, Ellena, and I were sitting together in the living room watching it. Mama and I were shelling peas, and Ellena was reading one of her schoolbooks for the fall. But when the story about the two students came on, she put her book on the floor beside her.

It was like something out of a dream hearing that racist little man say he would not move away from the entry to the university, and all of those white men with guns saying otherwise. The United States attorney general himself ordered that white man to step aside. After a bit of back and forth, he did, and those two Negro students walked into that university just as boldly as they pleased. I think we all sat up a little straighter. Alabama wasn't our state, but any advances made by a Negro was an advance for all of us.

"Well, will you look at that," Daddy said, leaning back in his recliner with a smile on his face. "You wouldn't be able to convince me this happened if Cronkite wasn't telling us about it. Ellena, between the charges being dropped for you and these young folks getting to go to that white school, well, it's like I said, we just have to wait and be patient."

"About time," Ellena said with a haughty sniff from her seat on the floor. "I'm shocked the University of Georgia integrated before Alabama."

"Governor Vandiver wasn't the greatest governor," Daddy said. "But he did his part, and he didn't make a fool of himself trying to stop . . . What were the names of those kids who integrated the University of Georgia?"

"Hamilton Holmes and Charlayne Hunter," Ellena said, sounding proud, like she knew them or something.

"That's right. Like I was saying, at least Governor Vandiver didn't try to block them from entering the university after the government said they could attend," Daddy said. "Ellena, go get me a glass of sweet tea. I'm parched as all get-out."

All the window fans were on, but it was still hot inside, even this late in the evening. I had taken a bath as soon as I got home from the store, but I was still sweating. It seemed like the summers just got hotter and hotter. I didn't remember it being this hot when we were children. Back then, all of us would be outside this time of day playing baseball or some other game. Now, all any of us wanted to do was stay up under the fans or try to catch a breeze on the porch.

"Yes, sir." Ellena hopped up from the floor. "Mama and Rose, would y'all like some sweet tea?"

We both said yes as she hurried toward the kitchen. Before she got out of the room good, Walter Cronkite announced that at 8:00 p.m., President Kennedy would deliver an address to the nation.

"What did he say?" she called back out to us.

"The president is going to address the nation," I said loudly. I was debating whether I was going to stay and listen. I wasn't into politics like the rest of my family, but I didn't want to leave Mama shelling those peas alone, so I kept my seat.

"What do you think he's going to talk about?" Mama

asked, picking up the pan of peas again and continuing to shell them.

"He needs to be talking about lowering these gas prices. Whoever heard of thirty cents per gallon?" Daddy grumbled. "When I was courting y'all's mama, gas was only nineteen cents per gallon. I need Kennedy to tell us how he's going to keep our boys out of this war and lower the price of gas. We don't need no fancy speeches about anything else."

"Oh, honey," Mama said laughing. "You can't expect gas to cost the same as it did nearly thirty years ago, and President Kennedy isn't a warmonger. If he can keep more boys from having to go over there and fight, he will."

Before Daddy could answer, Lawrence came in the front door with the triplets rushing around him to get inside first, their sweet giggles filling the house.

"Y'all watching the news?" Lawrence asked. He sat beside Mama on the couch. The triplets hurried over to Daddy, each trying to get onto his lap first.

"Sure are," Mama said, patting his cheek. "Where's Naomi?"

"She has a headache. Probably this heat. I told her the boys and I would come over here and watch the president's speech while she rested."

"Let me go help Ellena with the drinks," I said, getting up from the floor where I had been sitting too. Seemed like it was cooler down there. When I got to the kitchen, Ellena was mixing up a pitcher of Kool-Aid for the boys.

"I heard those loud ruffians," she said. "I'm glad we had some cherry Kool-Aid on hand since that's all they want to drink."

"That's good," I said, going over to the cookie jar. Mama always kept some cookies available just in case the boys came over. Today there were chocolate chip. Their favorite. I took three cookies out of the jar and put them on a plate.

"How are you doing, Sissy?" Ellena asked as I went to the cabinet and took out some small plastic cups for the boys to drink out of.

"I'm fine." I touched my face. The bruise was almost completely healed.

"For real?"

"Yes." I looked at her curiously. "What are you getting at? Do I not seem fine to you?"

"Well, I have noticed that you and a certain young SNCC leader seem very interested in each other," she said in a teasing voice. "Every time y'all are together, y'all seem very close."

"Don't say that," I snapped, turning around to make sure no one had entered the room. I would have been mortified if Mama or Daddy had heard her talking that way. "I've only seen him a handful of times, and neither he nor I have acted any way but appropriately. He talks kind to me, and I do the same to him."

"What about all those letters y'all exchanged with each other?"

"The letters were just friendly letters," I insisted, feeling my face get hot. "I am forever in love with Jasper, and for you to insinuate anything else is blasphemous."

Ellena put down the spoon she was using to stir the Kool-Aid and looked at me intently. "'The lady doth protest too much, methinks,'" she said. "I was just joking."

"Well, your joke is not funny. I am still a married woman, and I am not interested in anyone else but my husband, Jasper."

I felt hot tears beginning to fall down my face. I swiped at them quickly, but Ellena saw them and came to me, putting her hands on my shoulders.

"Sissy, I was just teasing. I didn't mean to imply anything untoward was going on between you and Isaac," she insisted.

"I'm sorry. I overreacted," I said softly. "These last few months have been so difficult, and my emotions are all over the place. I didn't mean to snap at you or anything."

"You stay here and let me take these drinks out to everyone. I'll be right back."

Ellena put the drinks on a large rolling cart and pushed them out to the front room. I sat down at the kitchen table. I heard the triplets squeal and Mama ordering them to be careful. I wiped my tears and tried to calm myself. I knew Ellena didn't mean any harm. I had been so careful not to have any emotions bubble up inside me toward Isaac that weren't sisterly in nature. I thought I had done a good job. Now I was wondering, *Have I failed?* When Ellena came back to the kitchen, she joined me, handing me a glass of cold iced tea.

"Tell me what's going on, Sissy." She reached for my hands. "I know you are hurting over the baby and Jasper, but there seems to be more than that going on. Talk to me. Like we used to."

I felt the tears begin to fall once more. I didn't want my sister to think bad about me.

"I don't want to feel anything for any man ever again," I said. "I owe it to Jasper to always be true to him. I did wrong by my husband and maybe this is God's punishment."

"Oh, honey." She rubbed my arm. "Now you know I'm not as religious as everyone else. I love the Lord, don't get me wrong, but I just don't think he's that into us."

I looked at her with shock. I didn't even know what that meant. "What are you saying?"

She sighed. "I just look at all of the things that happen in this world—things that, if I were God, I would immediately bring in check. Racism. Hatred. War. If I were God, I would fix those things with a quickness. So I finally came to the conclusion that God gave us everything we needed to fix this world and ourselves, and after that, he was like, 'Y'all got it. I'm going to fix my mind on other things.'"

I was speechless. I had never heard such things before. It made sense, but it was scary because we had all been raised to believe in God the exact same way. The idea of Ellena or anyone, for that matter, coming up with their own idea of what God was thinking was very unnerving to me.

"I know what I just said is a bit much, but Rose, when Jasper died and Olivia Rose died, I had to find meaning in their deaths. I knew God was not punishing you. I just knew it. So this made sense to me. It helped me not to be angry at God every day that I got up and every night that I went to bed," she said, tears flowing down her face now too.

"I didn't know you were feeling this way." I felt awful that my sister was battling with her faith over what happened to me.

"You didn't need to carry my pain along with yours,

Rose." She pulled me into a hug and we stayed there for a time. Then she sat back and lightly touched my face. "May I say one more thing?" she asked. I nodded. "I don't know when it is a good time to feel again, Sissy. But from the little bit I learned about your husband, Jasper, I can almost promise you that he would not want you to pine after him for long. He would want you to carry on with your life and live."

"I don't think I could ever feel right thinking about another . . ." I couldn't finish the sentence.

"Girls," Mama called out from the living room. "The president is about to start his address."

"We're coming," Ellena called back to her. "Come on. Let's go hear that beautifully handsome president of ours speak," she said, causing me to laugh. "You know he is cute as all get-out. Mrs. Jackie Kennedy is one blessed woman. Am I right?"

"You are right," I said, standing and linking my arm with hers. "And thank you for . . . for everything."

"Always and forever," she said as we walked out front and sat on the floor beside Mama.

The triplets were stretched out on the floor lying on a pallet. They would be asleep soon. Mama reached down and patted us both on our heads like she used to do when we were girls. I picked up the pan of peas I was shelling, and Ellena, much to my surprise, started helping. I knew she was still feeling bad for making me cry, even though it was my own guilt that got me to crying, not her words.

There was no time to think about anything else because the president started talking.

"Good evening, my fellow citizens. This afternoon, following a series of threats and defiant statements, the presence of Alabama National Guardsmen was required at the University of Alabama to carry out the final and unequivocal order of the United States District Court of the Northern District of Alabama," President Kennedy said from his chair in the oval office.

I was shocked that this was what he was going to talk about. I sat up a little straighter and put down the pan of peas so that I could listen. His words were beyond memorable. They were like no other words I had ever heard a white person utter before, especially one as powerful as President Kennedy. He was talking to white America, telling them they should treat us as equals. Oh, of course, he tasked us to be good people, too, but this was him speaking to his people directly and there was no way anyone could not understand what he meant. It made everything that had happened last week make even more sense. The work Dr. King, SNCC, and all of us were doing was working. President Kennedy was listening to us. I looked around the room to see if everyone else was feeling the same as me, and clearly, from the looks on their faces, they were.

"I can't believe this," Ellena said. Everyone shushed her, not wanting to miss a word of what President Kennedy was saying.

"This is one country. It has become one country because all of us and all the people who came here had an equal chance to develop their talents," he said, looking deeply into the camera. It was like he could see into everyone's souls. Then he paused before continuing with his inspiring words.

"We cannot say to ten percent of the population that you can't have that right; that your children cannot have the chance to develop whatever talents they have; that the only way that they are going to get their rights is to go into the streets and demonstrate. I think we owe them, and we owe ourselves a better country than that."

"My God," Daddy said, slapping his knee like he was in church. "My God from Zion. I have never heard such an inspiring speech from a president. Not Roosevelt. Not Truman. Not Eisenhower. None of them."

I turned around and looked at Mama. Tears were rolling down her face. Lawrence stood up, beaming like the rest of us. "Naomi is going to hate she missed this. I think we just turned a corner, y'all. I think this country just got its wake-up call."

I looked at Ellena, who had become quiet. I grinned at her. "Well, what do you think? Wasn't that a wonderful speech?"

"It was," she said softly. "I pray nothing happens to him. Good men like that are easy targets for people filled with hatred."

"Then we will pray for President Kennedy and all of our leaders who are trying to do right by us," Mama said firmly.

We all gathered while Daddy said a prayer for President Kennedy, his family, and all of the leaders in our country. As soon as we said "Amen," the phone rang. I figured it was one of the aunts or uncles calling for Mama and Daddy to talk about the president's speech. Ellena hurried to the kitchen to answer it. When she came back, everyone looked at her expectantly.

"It's for you, Rose," she said quietly, but not quietly

enough. Everyone still heard her. One thing about our family, there were very few secrets. I was about the only one who had been able to keep a secret for any length of time.

"Who is it?" I asked. I couldn't imagine it was Katie Bell calling this late. Normally, she went to sleep when L.J. dozed off. Now that she was pregnant again, she definitely went to sleep early. Naomi would have been the other possibility, but since she wasn't feeling well, I didn't imagine it was her either. Those were the only two people who ever called me on the phone.

"It's Isaac."

I knew everyone was looking at me. I couldn't meet anyone's eyes. I felt like I wanted to melt into the floor. I felt shame and I hadn't even done anything. Mama touched my arm.

"Go see what he wants," she said. "Unless you want your sister to tell him you can't come to the phone."

I looked up at Mama and she smiled at me real tender-like. I hoped she didn't think I had led Isaac on in any way. I wanted so desperately to be a good widow, and part of that meant presenting good to my family. I wanted Jasper to be in heaven looking down at me with pride, but I also wanted my family to do the same. I wanted them to believe that I had changed and had become the woman Jasper deserved. I was torn. I didn't know what to do.

"She ain't got no reason to be talking on the phone this time of night with any man," Daddy said gruffly. "I'll go tell him that myself."

"Cedric," Mama chided. "Let the child decide what to do. We trust her to do what is right."

"I won't be on the phone for long," I said quickly. I knew they were both right. I should have asked Ellena to tell him I wasn't available to talk, but I did want to hear his voice and what he had to say. I prayed that didn't make me an awful person. "He probably was just excited about the speech tonight."

"I don't see why he would be calling you about that speech," Daddy grumbled. "Why can't he talk to some of those people he came here with and leave my daughter alone?"

"I'll go back in the kitchen with Rose," Ellena said. I looked at her and smiled. "Come on," she said, and we walked back into the kitchen together.

I picked up the phone gingerly, almost like it was a rattlesnake that could bite me if I wasn't careful. "Hello," I said. Ellena put her ear to the receiver so she could hear what Isaac was saying. I didn't mind. I was happy to have her close by.

"Oh, Rose," he said excitedly. "I apologize for calling so late, but did you hear President Kennedy's speech?"

I nodded and then realized he couldn't see me. "I did. We all gathered around the television to hear what President Kennedy had to say. It was amazing. None of us could believe it."

"I know," he said. I could imagine him smiling while he was talking. "I felt the same way. We all did . . . those of us from SNCC, I mean. It just feels like there is something in the air, Rose. It feels like this summer might be the summer when this country . . . when white America realizes we are their equals. Like President Kennedy said in his speech, we 'have a right to expect that the law will be fair' to us. That's all we want, Rose. Fairness."

I couldn't help but laugh. He sounded so youthful and hopeful all at the same time. It was funny. Isaac had to be a few years older than me, but even though I was only twenty-two years old, I felt like an old woman in comparison. I knew I needed to end the call.

"I have to go, Isaac," I said. "I'll see you tomorrow at the church for our training."

"Yes, I . . . I apologize for calling so late," he said again. "I was so excited by the president's words; you were the first person who came to my mind to call."

I didn't know what to say, so I remained quiet. The silence became awkward, and then we spoke at the same time.

"Well, I'll . . ." I started.

"I should just . . ." he said and then stopped.

"You go," I said.

He waited for a second and then he continued. "I'll talk to you tomorrow, Rose. I hope I didn't cause you any issues with your family. Please bid them all a good evening from me."

"You didn't cause me any issues," I said. "Thanks for calling. Good night."

I handed the phone to Ellena, and she gently hung it up.

"He likes you," she said, putting her arm around my waist. "And you like him."

"It doesn't matter." I shook my head. "It's too soon. My husband and child haven't even been dead a year. I can't think about any relationship beyond Jasper. He is my husband and I plan to remain true to him."

Ellena kissed my cheek. "Whatever you decide, you know I will back you up 100 percent. Love you, sis." She left the kitchen.

I decided I didn't want to go back to the living room where everyone would be expecting me to explain why Isaac called. So I went outside and sat on the back porch steps. It was dark out and the sky was filled with stars. I looked for the star that Mama said was Great-Grandma Birdie, but I couldn't find it. I hoped it didn't mean that she was disappointed in me to the degree that she refused to shine tonight. I needed to see her twinkling in the heavens to reassure me that I was still in her good graces, but more importantly, in the good graces of God.

I heard a few voices from porches down the street, but I didn't see anybody moving about. It was too hot to be doing anything but sitting outside, praying a breeze would come through. Each of the houses surrounding ours was filled with our kin and neighbors, many of whom had lived here since before I was born. I felt safe sitting out here alone with my thoughts. I knew all I would have to do was raise my voice and a whole host of people would come to see about me.

Daddy's dogs came out from underneath the house, where they slept, and each laid his head against my legs. I rubbed their heads. They were sniffing and licking my legs like old times.

"Hey, boys." I petted them like I used to when they were little puppies. Daddy had gotten them from a man from McDonough who had come all the way to Parsons to do business with the "Colored man who owned the grocery store," as he called it. Daddy had graciously taken both King and Jupiter as payment for the man's groceries. Daddy did things like that often. He said he always wanted to make sure he helped somebody keep their dignity while they fed their family. I came from such good parents. Mama would give her last nickel to help somebody, and all of my siblings were good people too.

"What's wrong with me?" I questioned as a sob escaped my lips.

"Nothing is wrong with you," I heard a voice say behind me. I turned; it was Mama. "Do you mind if I join you?" she asked from the door.

"No, ma'am," I said tearfully.

She walked out onto the porch and then put her hand on my shoulder so she could ease down onto the step beside me.

"That Isaac seems like a nice young man," she said once she got settled. I could feel her eyes on me. I was happy that it was getting dark, and I couldn't see real good the look on her face. I didn't want it to be anger or disappointment. I could handle a lot of things when it came to Mama and Daddy, but those two things always left me feeling awful. Right now, I felt awful enough.

"He seems to be," I said, trying to be careful as I picked my words, but then my feelings began to bubble over. I couldn't help but to say everything I was feeling. "Mama, am I awful? Jasper ain't been dead no time, and here I am talking to another man. We even exchanged letters. Nothing untoward was said, but somehow, I feel guilty. What is wrong with me?"

"Oh, honey." Mama put her arm around me. "There

ain't nothing wrong with you. Not one little thing. You are twenty-two years old. You were far too young to be married and having a baby. It's natural for young women your age to be attracted to young men Isaac's age. Being attracted to someone isn't the same as being in a relationship with him."

I laid my head against Mama's shoulder. "I love Jasper."

"I know you do," she said, kissing the top of my head.

"And I miss him, Mama," I whispered as the tears began to fall. "So very much."

"And you always will. And someday, when you are ready to give your heart to someone else, you will find a way to make room for new love while still holding on to the old. Jasper was your first love. You will never lose your connection to him. I promise."

For a time, Mama and I just sat in silence. King and Jupiter finally made their way back underneath the house. For the first time in a long time, my soul began to release some of the turmoil and heartbreak I had been carrying. I wasn't at peace, but I was in a better place, and that meant everything to me.

CHAPTER 23

I WOKE WITH A START THE NEXT MORNING. I HAD BEEN DREAM-
ing all night, but for some reason, the second I opened my
eyes, the dream evaporated like early morning dew. I think
I was dreaming about Jasper, but it also felt like Isaac was
there too. As peaceful as I had felt the night before, I woke
up feeling out of sorts again. I lay there, tossing and turning, until finally I decided to get up and start my day. I
looked up at the clock; it said five-thirty. I looked over at
the other bed. Ellena was still asleep, of course. I heard some
bumping around out in the kitchen. I figured it was Mama,
so I put on my robe and went into the kitchen. Sure enough,
she was up. Mama had on a yellow housedress and a summer hat on her head.

"Where are you going, Mama?"

She turned around, startled. "Oh, Rose. I'm sorry, honey.
I didn't see you. Aunt Shimmy, Lucille, and I are going to
pick some peaches so we can make some preserves. I also
thought I would make a peach cobbler or two for tonight.

I figure everyone would love something sweet after all that studying we're going to be doing."

"Do you mind if I go with y'all?" It had been a while since I had picked peaches with the family. I had missed that so much when I lived in Mississippi. It wasn't necessarily the work that I missed but the togetherness with my family, primarily the women.

Mama put her arm around my waist and squeezed. "I always love having my Rose with me. Go get dressed. We want to get out there and back before it gets too hot."

"I won't be long." I hurried to the bedroom. I made sure I was quiet and didn't wake up Ellena. She shifted a bit in her bed, but she didn't wake up. I put on a pair of shorts, a pale-blue linen dress, and some tennis shoes in case I ended up climbing a tree. When I got back to the kitchen, Mama had a hat for me to wear. I put it on, and then we headed out the door. Once we got outside, Aunt Shimmy and Aunt Lucille were coming up the road. They waved. When they got close, they hugged me and Mama.

"You doing okay, baby girl?" Aunt Shimmy asked, looking me up and down as if she were making sure nothing was out of place.

"Yes, ma'am. I'm doing just fine."

She stared at me for a few more seconds, then kissed my forehead. Aunt Lucille came over and linked her arm with mine as we walked toward the peach orchard. The closer we got to the orchard, the headier the scent became. It was like walking into the best part of heaven. I imagined that the garden of Eden smelled like this: fresh and pure and good. I thought about Jasper and Olivia Rose. I prayed they had peaches like this in heaven and that Jasper would feed them to our baby girl. The thought was so beautiful it almost pained me to have to focus on what was happening here.

"Looks like we're going to have a good harvest," Aunt Shimmy said, picking one of the peaches and smelling it. "Y'all, I say we stick to the low-hanging fruit and let the boys and men come and tackle the rest."

"That sounds good to me, Mama," Aunt Lucille said. "It's already hot out here and we haven't even gotten started. Let's get going so we can get back to the house."

Everyone started picking in silence. It was getting too warm to do much else. I felt a slow trickle of sweat down the front of my dress. It wasn't even seven o'clock yet. Once we had picked enough peaches to make several jars of preserves for everyone, the twins showed up to help us carry our bags and baskets filled with peaches back to the house.

"How did y'all know we were out here?" I asked Micah, who ran up beside me, giving me a squeeze. Mitchell came up on the other side of me and did the same. I hadn't seen much of them. They were all over the county helping the white doctor take care of Negro patients who didn't necessarily feel comfortable with him. I was proud of them for the work they were doing and they weren't even full doctors yet.

"Mama told us last night y'all would be picking peaches. We figured you would need the help," Mitchell said.

It didn't take long to get back to the house, but when we did, I was soaking wet with sweat. Ellena was up making pancakes and sausage, and Daddy was sitting at the table already, reading his newspaper. I excused myself and hurried to the bathroom to take a quick shower. Then I slipped on a pale-blue sundress and tied my hair back with a matching scarf. By the time I got back out to the kitchen, there was so much activity going on. Daddy and the twins were eating breakfast in the dining room, and Mama, Aunt Shimmy, Aunt Lucille, and Ellena were sitting at the kitchen table peeling and pitting the peaches.

Mama had taught all of us, the boys and the girls, how to make Great-Grandma Birdie's peach jam as well as other food items. She said she didn't want to die taking a single recipe with her. So even though I wasn't much of a cook, I could make Great-Grandma Birdie's jam. We all could. But today, I was here to do what I was told.

"Rose," Mama said from her seat at the kitchen table, "go over to the stove and start sterilizing the canning jars."

"And don't burn the water," Ellena called out, teasing.

"Well, I'll make sure I don't 'burn the water' if you make sure you don't cut away more peach than you should," I said with a grin. Ellena threw a dish towel at me, and I ducked just in time for it to hit the floor. I swooped it back up and tossed it back to her. "You never could throw worth a flip."

Everybody laughed. It was nice having laughter in the house.

"I sure do love having you girls here this summer," Mama said with a smile. "It's like old times again."

Daddy walked into the kitchen carrying his plate. "That was a good breakfast, Ellena. You getting to be a fine cook. Just like your mama."

"Thanks, Daddy," she said sassily, looking over at me with a huge grin.

"Pudd'n, if you want to stay here and help your mama and everybody with these peaches, you can," he said. "Things have slowed down over at Lawrence's farm, so I imagine he could spare Jemison to help me today."

"No, Daddy," I said. "I like helping you. Give me just a minute and I'll be ready to go."

"You don't have to," he said, but there was a huge smile on his face. I knew Daddy liked having me at the store with him about as much as I liked being there.

"I know, but I want to go with you." I turned to Mama. "You don't need me, do you?"

She smiled and waved me away. "You go on, Daddy's baby. There's plenty of hands here to help. By the time y'all get home, the house will be smelling delicious."

"It already does." Daddy kissed Mama on her cheek, then he turned back around and looked at me. "I think we'll take the car today, Rose. It's a bit too hot to be walking to work." Then he turned back to Mama. "And y'all don't get too hot in here yourselves."

"We won't," Mama promised.

I hurried to the bedroom and quickly put on a nicer dress. Another Mama creation—a pink dress with blue flowers. The skirt flared out and the neck had a Peter Pan collar. I then strapped on a pair of white sandals. When I walked back out, Daddy had already gone to the car.

"See everyone later." I hurried out. Daddy opened the car door for me.

"All right, sweetie. Let's get ourselves off to the store so we can open up."

"Yes, sir." I got comfortable in the seat.

After Daddy had eased the car out of the driveway, we started down the road.

"Rose, I want to talk to you about last night. I wasn't pleased with you carrying on a conversation with that young man on the telephone," he said in his quiet but stern voice.

I kept looking straight ahead. I had forgotten about Isaac calling the night before, but clearly Daddy had not.

"Daddy, there's nothing going on. He just called to talk about the speech President Kennedy gave. That's all." I felt like I was six years old instead of twenty-two.

"Your husband hasn't been long dead."

"I know." I didn't need Daddy to remind me of that. Every day I woke up realizing I had no husband and no little girl. It hurt me that Daddy thought I had forgotten about Jasper. But considering my previous behavior, I could see why he might not have faith in me anymore.

"I don't want to see you do anything to sully Jasper's good name or yours."

I knew he meant "again." I had already done the worst thing a woman could do to a man. I had no intentions of doing something equally awful by starting a relationship with another man, but I also would be lying if I didn't admit that I enjoyed the letters and the brief conversations with Isaac.

"You are young, and I understand that, Rose," Daddy said. "And maybe your mama and I should have tried harder to get you to wait before you married Jasper, but—"

"I had made up my mind, Daddy," I said quickly. "Wasn't nothing you or Mama could have said. It wasn't y'all's fault. It was all me. I did a bad thing and God not only punished me for it, he punished Jasper and the baby too."

Daddy pulled the car over to the side of the road and turned to face me. He had a stern look on his face. "You are not being punished, Rose. Jasper and the baby didn't die because God was angry with you. That's just not how God works. Every man, woman, and child have an appointed time to be born, an appointed time to live, and sweetheart, we all have an appointed time to die. God wasn't punishing you, and if that's what you've been carrying, let that go."

"Yes, sir." I brushed away a tear, but it was hard for me to believe Daddy's words. I thought about all of those Bible verses where God punished folks, starting with Adam and Eve. But I didn't argue because I knew Daddy knew the Bible much better than me. I would try to let go of some of my guilty feelings, but I knew it wouldn't be easy. They subsided, and then they came back like a rushing wind.

Before Daddy could pull the car back onto the road, we heard a siren behind us. We both turned and looked. It was a police car. I felt my stomach begin to twist. I prayed the car kept going, but it slowed to a stop behind us. Daddy reached over and patted my leg.

"It's all right, Rose. It's all right. Just let me do the talking."

I was so scared I couldn't even say anything. I gripped the bottom of my seat and started silently praying.

"Hand me the registration papers in the glove box and then put your hands on the dash where he can see them," Daddy said. "Hurry."

I fumbled with the door of the glove compartment until

finally I was able to get it opened. I pulled out the paperwork and handed it to Daddy right before the policeman reached his window. I made sure my hands were flat palmed on the dash of the car. I felt the tears begin to lap underneath my chin, but I didn't dare wipe them away.

"What y'all doing out here?"

My heart felt like it was going to jump out of my chest. I knew that voice. It was the policeman who had hurt me. I felt like screaming and running, but I knew if I did any of those things, it would not end well. I just sat there with my head bowed, tears dropping like huge raindrops.

"On our way to work, suh," Daddy said in a voice that didn't sound like him. He sounded like Stepin Fetchit or Amos 'n' Andy. When we were kids, he wouldn't let us listen to or watch any of those shows. He said being a Negro was hard enough. We didn't need those negative stereotypes haunting us. But here we were, Daddy having to do the very thing he hated: sound ignorant so white folks would feel better about us and not hurt us. "I had just pulled over to talk to my daughter."

"You don't know how to drive and talk at the same time?" he asked. "Hey, gal. What was you and your daddy talking about?"

"She a bit on the shy side, suh," Daddy said. "I have my registration and driver's license if you be wantin' to see them."

He snatched the license and paperwork out of Daddy's hands.

"How a nigger like you get a car this nice? I don't even have a car this nice," he said, his voice sounding angry. "Get out the car." He opened the door, ripping it open so hard I expected the door to come off the hinges.

"Daddy," I cried. "Don't—"

"It's okay," Daddy said in a soothing voice. "Everything is going to be okay. Yes, suh. I'm getting out now. Ain't wanting no trouble."

"Put your hands up where I can see them!" the policeman yelled.

Daddy raised his one good arm so the officer could see it as he exited the car.

"I said your hands. Raise both of them," he barked and slapped Daddy across the back of his head.

"Stop it!" I screamed. "Stop it! Stop it!"

"Shut up in there, gal!" the officer yelled.

"I'm okay, baby," Daddy called back to me. "I'm all right. Suh, I only got one arm. I lost the other one."

"One arm. Wait a minute. Are you that nigger store owner? Is that why you dressed like you 'bout to go preach a funeral?" the policeman asked. "You own a store, and you think you better than everybody."

"No, suh. Not at all, suh."

I watched as the policeman struck Daddy again. Daddy's knees buckled, and he fell to the ground. I screamed. I couldn't hold it back. I just knew this awful man was going to kill my daddy.

"Stay in the car, baby," Daddy called out. "Don't look. Just stay in the car."

Out of nowhere, I heard another car pull up. I was too scared to turn around. I prayed it wasn't another policeman.

"Please help us, God," I prayed.

"What's going on here?" I heard a female voice say angrily. "What is the meaning of this?"

I thought I recognized the voice. I turned a bit and to my relief, it was Miss Jainey from Powell's Fabric Store. Ellena was in the car with her. Miss Jainey must have picked her up for work. I prayed Ellena didn't get out. I didn't want this policeman hurting her too.

"Please don't get out," I said underneath my breath. "Please don't get out the car."

Thankfully, Ellena didn't move.

"I said what is the meaning of this? Why do you have Cedric Perkins on the ground like some farm animal? Get up, Cedric," she ordered. Daddy didn't move.

"Ma'am, you are interfering with police business," he said in a gruff voice. "I would advise you to—"

"What is your name?" she asked as if she had not heard a word he said.

"Officer Rufus W. DeWitt, ma'am," he said. "And I am—"

"Well, Officer DeWitt, my name is Miss Jainey Powell. I own the fabric store as well as the controlling shares in First National Bank. Along with the Parsons family, my family were also founding members of this town. I do not appreciate you harassing this good man. So unless you want me to go have a conversation with your superior, Chief Burnett, I would suggest you get yourself back into that car and hightail it out of here. Am I making myself clear?"

"Yes, ma'am." He spun around and marched back to his police car. Nothing was said until he was gone.

"Cedric, are you all right? Do you need me to help—"

Before she could finish talking, Ellena and I had both rushed to Daddy's side. We fell to the ground beside him, hugging him tightly.

"I'm okay, girls. I'm okay. Let me get up."

We moved aside. We knew he wouldn't want help even if he needed it. We grabbed each other's hands and watched as Daddy got up from the ground, brushing the dirt off his suit as best he could. Ellena helped brush off the dirt from behind, but his suit needed more than mere brushing.

"Thank you, Miss Jainey," Daddy said. His voice sounded hoarse. He didn't shed any tears, but I knew this incident had hurt his spirit because mine had been hurt by the same awful man. "I appreciate you stopping."

Miss Jainey waved her hand as if it was nothing. Maybe to her it was nothing, but to us, it meant we got to live another day. "You are a good man, Cedric. You and Opal are good people. You've raised some wonderful children."

"Thank you, ma'am," he said. "We do the best we can."

"Well, I tell you what . . . I don't know what has gotten into the minds of these local policemen. This kind of behavior might fly in Birmingham, but we will not stand for this foolishness here in Parsons, Georgia. That Bull Connor has got all of these policemen thinking they are bigger than the law. I'll stop by the station and have a good ole talk with Chief Burnett. He needs to know his officers have gone rogue."

"Thank you, Miss Jainey, but I would rather you didn't," Daddy said. "It might just make things worse. Nobody got hurt. It was just a . . . misunderstanding."

"Cedric, that man had you on the ground like you had just robbed a bank," Miss Jainey snapped. "Something must be done. I hope this is a message that you all need to stop with this protesting and voting mess. It's just stirring up unnecessary emotions."

I immediately looked at Ellena and shook my head. I didn't want her to say something to make things worse. She nodded back at me, but she grimaced and rolled her eyes. Thankfully, Miss Jainey didn't see her.

"Miss Jainey, I understand your intentions are good. And I agree we all have to be careful," Daddy said. "But what that policeman did to me is evidence that we have to fight for our rights. I didn't think so before, but things have happened over the last couple of weeks that let me know that we have got to press on. I don't want my grandchildren to have to live like this."

"Live like what, for God's sake?" she insisted. "You and your family are doing fine for yourselves. Y'all are doing better than most white folks in these parts. Why can't that be enough?"

"My family is doing okay. But what about all the other families?" Daddy asked. "If one of us suffers, we all suffer."

Miss Jainey shook her head. "Well, I suppose you know best, Cedric. But I can't promise to be around every time something like this happens. Then what? Y'all demanding all of these rights, but what good will it do you if you are dead?"

Suddenly, I remembered the words of a poem I had read in school years ago. "'If we must die, let it not be like hogs,'" I said, raising my voice so that she would hear me.

She turned and looked at me curiously. "What did you say, Rose? Hogs?"

Ellena looked at me and smiled. "My sister said,

'If we must die, let it not be like hogs
Hunted and penned in an inglorious spot,
While round us bark the mad and
      hungry dogs,
Making their mock at our accursèd lot.'"

Daddy looked from Ellena to me and then back at Miss Jainey. "I don't exactly know what my daughters are talking about, but this much I do know. We appreciate the help you gave us just then, but my family will not lay down and die without a fight."

Miss Jainey shook her head. "Well, Cedric. I won't argue. I've business to attend to. Ellena, are you ready?"

"I don't think so, Miss Jainey. I should be with my family," she said. Without another word she got into the back seat of Daddy's car.

"Bye, Miss Jainey," I said and got into the front seat. I turned around to see Ellena smiling broadly. "What are you smiling about?"

"Two things. One, my sister, who always hated literature but especially poetry, actually quoted lines from a Claude McKay poem."

I smiled back at her. "What's the second thing?"

"Our daddy finally gets it," she said. "Daddy finally gets what I've been talking about for the longest."

I understood what she meant. Daddy wasn't quite a hothead, but he definitely showed us that he was willing to fight and not be content with the crumbs white folks were offering us. That made me feel as proud as any daughter could feel. He did what he had to do to stay alive in that moment, but he also made it clear to Miss Jainey that we were not going to back down. Not now, not ever.

After Miss Jainey drove off, Daddy got into the car.

"You girls all right?"

"Yes, sir," we said in unison.

"Good," he said. "Let's go home so I can change."

"Yes, sir," we repeated.

Daddy turned the car around and headed back home.

CHAPTER 24

I COULDN'T BELIEVE HOW QUICKLY THE WORKDAY AT THE STORE came to a close. It seemed like one minute we arrived, and the next minute it was time to go to the voter registration class. Daddy and I had been busy all day. It seemed like every Negro in Parsons, Georgia, had shopping to do, and every single one of them had questions. *Which cut of meat was the freshest? When would we be getting more canned peas? Did we offer credit? Were we out of castor oil?* We were so busy, we didn't even get a chance to talk about what had happened earlier. Part of me was happy that we didn't, mainly because I didn't want to have to tell Daddy about that policeman.

I thought about telling him that the officer who stopped us was the same officer who hurt me, but I was afraid. I had previously said I was willing to identify him, but when it was decided that we wouldn't, I had put that awful man's identity behind me. But now he was front and center in my thoughts again, and the idea of confessing to Daddy or anyone that it was Officer DeWitt who beat me was more than I could

311

handle. So every time a car stopped outside the store, I was spooked. I knew that man knew where Daddy and I were, so if he had wanted to come by and pick up where he left off, he could. But thankfully, the day went by without any incident.

After Daddy and I closed the store, we headed straight over to St. Luke's Missionary Baptist Church, where the voter registration classes were meeting. When we got there, the parking lot was virtually empty except for Lawrence's car, the car I remembered Isaac and the group from SNCC arriving in, and another car I didn't recognize.

"Wonder where everybody is," Daddy said as he pulled his car up beside Lawrence's. "We didn't get our days mixed up, did we?"

"It's still early," I said. "Maybe folks are still trying to get here. They'll come."

Daddy got out and opened my door. He put his arm around me, and we walked into the church together. When we got inside, there was only Reverend Hamilton, Mama, Ellena, and Lawrence talking in hushed tones. It was clear that something bad had happened.

"What's wrong?" Daddy asked as Ellena ran toward us, tears streaming down her face.

"Oh, Daddy," she said, bursting into tears. "They killed Medgar Evers."

"Who?"

"Medgar Evers, Daddy. He was doing the same kind of work we're trying to do here in Mississippi. They murdered him in front of his wife and three children," Ellena said.

Mama and Lawrence came over to us. Mama put her arms around Daddy, laying her head against him.

"He was just thirty-seven years old," Mama said through her sobs. "His youngest child isn't much older than the triplets. I just can't understand that level of hatred."

"Once everyone heard about what happened, they all went home," Lawrence said. "We wanted to wait for you. The SNCC teachers are in the back having a meeting."

"We're not going anywhere," Daddy said in a firm voice. "We came here to prepare to register to vote and that is what we're going to do. If nobody else shows up, then we will carry the mantle ourselves."

"Are you sure, Cedric?" Mama asked. "I think everyone is worried that what happened in Mississippi might happen here. Folks took to the streets down there in Jackson and the police started beating them with clubs. They say over a hundred people got arrested. After what happened this morning, we might be better off just going home."

We all looked at Daddy to see what he was going to decide, because whatever he said was what we would do. I watched as emotions played out on his face. He took being the leader of this family seriously. I knew that whatever decision he made, it wouldn't be easy. If anything happened to any of us, he would never forgive himself.

"We're not going anywhere," Daddy repeated. "The best way to honor that young man and everyone else fighting for what's right is for us to study and get ourselves ready to take that voting test. So y'all go find your study books and let's get busy."

To say I was proud of Daddy would be an understatement. I knew how much it took for him to say what he did. I, for one, planned on making him proud. Somehow, with

God's help and the help of our teachers, I was going to pass that unfair voting test, no matter what it took.

"Let's go," I said to Ellena. It was just going to be her, Lawrence, and me. Naomi was still not feeling well, according to Lawrence. When we got there, Isaac and Clifford were consoling a crying Deirdre. She looked up when we walked into the room.

"We will reconvene on Friday night," she said in a hoarse voice, wiping her eyes with a handkerchief.

Isaac looked equally stunned and saddened. "We're sorry we didn't get word to you all earlier. We just got the call a little while ago about Medgar. It's hard to believe. I just saw him a couple of months ago."

"We are sorry for the loss of your friend," Lawrence said. "And we understand if you don't feel up to teaching tonight. But my family and I have all decided to stay and take advantage of the study materials you provided us with last week. We want to honor your friend by continuing to do the work."

Isaac looked at Deirdre and Clifford, then back at us. "If you all are willing to work tonight, then we will do everything we can to help support you. Thank you for reminding us that the work doesn't stop. No matter what."

Deirdre cleared her throat. "Please, give me just a minute or so and I'll be ready." She left the room.

"I'll go take care of the other class," Clifford said as he left too.

Isaac looked a bit scattered, but he walked to the front of the room and grabbed the study guides we were using. He gave each of us one but told us to keep them closed.

"Let's see what you retained from last week." He began firing questions at us. "What are the names of the three branches of the United States government?"

I raised my hand. "Legislative, executive, and . . . and . . ."

"Judicial," Ellena said softly. I looked at her and smiled.

"Correct," Isaac said. "What does the Constitution of Georgia prescribe as the qualifications of representatives in the Georgia House of Representatives?"

"They must be a citizen of the United States, twenty-one years of age, a citizen of Georgia for two years, and . . ." Lawrence stopped. "I can't remember the last qualification."

I knew this answer, so I raised my hand. "They must also be a resident of the county from which they are elected for one year."

"Excellent," Isaac said, the smile on his face finally meeting his eyes. "You all are doing great. Let's keep going."

So Isaac and then Deirdre, once she returned to the room, asked us question after question. When we had answered all of the questions from our last meeting, we started studying the new material.

"One thing all of these county registrars have in common is their need to confuse and confound," Deirdre said. "As soon as they realize we have copies of their tests, they change them up or they ask the question differently from how you studied, so we have to be several steps ahead of them."

"Like playing chess," I said with a smile.

"Exactly," Isaac said. "Perfect analogy." He looked very pleased with my response. I ducked my head in embarrassment.

"So let's divide you into pairs so that you can work on the flash cards," Deirdre said. "Ellena, why don't you and your brother work together. Isaac, would you mind quizzing Rose?"

"Not at all," he said.

Before I could protest, Isaac was leading me to the far corner of the room. Once we got settled, he immediately started going over the cards with me. There wasn't an ounce of flirtation going on. It made me feel good that we could just focus on the material I needed to learn.

"Let's start with the United States Constitution." He sounded like a teacher, which allowed me to relax even more. Clearly, Isaac took his job seriously, and I was grateful to have his help. "I want you to be able to commit to memory as much of the first five articles as you can."

I looked at the printed material. "Oh my. That's a lot."

"Don't worry," he reassured me. "We'll take it one step at a time."

An hour and a half later, he said I was ready to show what I had learned. I wasn't so sure about that. He had shown me several memorization techniques, but I was afraid everything was getting jumbled in my head.

"What does Article V of the United States Constitution say?"

"Uh." I was drawing a blank. "I don't remember."

I felt deflated. I didn't see how I would ever get all of this information.

"It has to do with amendments," he said.

"Oh, okay." I closed my eyes and tried to let the words flow through me. "The Congress, whenever two-thirds of both houses shall deem it necessary, shall propose amendments to the Constitution . . ."

I stumbled over parts, but I remembered the majority of it. Isaac continued to quiz me for about another thirty minutes until it was time to go.

"You did good, Rose. I mean really good. I'm proud of the work you have accomplished. In just a few weeks, you will be ready to take that test, if not sooner."

I shook my head. "No way. I'm not even close to being ready."

"Name the last five governors of Georgia, including the present one," he said quickly.

"Carl Sanders, Ernest Vandiver, Marvin Griffin, Herman Talmadge, and Melvin E. Thompson," I rattled off.

"Who is the current chief justice of the Georgia Supreme Court?"

"William Henry Duckworth." I was shocked at myself. Somehow, I had figured out how to organize all this information inside my head and pull it out when I needed to. Maybe I would be ready for that test sooner than I thought. For the first time in a long time, I felt proud of myself. I had been a marginal student in school, but I realized now that I could have done better. I wasn't slow or behind my siblings. I just hadn't found something I was passionate about, and this—*this* I was passionate about.

"You're going to be just fine, Rose," he said. "Just keep studying and try not to stress over it. The very worst that can happen is you have to take the test over again."

"It's not the worst that can happen," I said softly. I was thinking about Medgar Evers and his poor wife and children. They were experiencing the very worst that could happen, and as much as we might not want to believe it, it could happen here too. My family experienced that type of hatred firsthand years ago. The death of Great-Grandma Birdie and Daddy's loss of an arm were proof positive that bad things could happen anywhere—including Parsons, Georgia. This morning could have been our end just because someone couldn't look at us and see people whose lives mattered as much as his.

"You're right," Isaac said. "I'm sorry. Tonight isn't the time for idle words or sweeping generalizations. I appreciate the correction."

Ellena walked over to us and put her hand on my shoulder. "How did you do?"

"Good," I replied. "Well, I guess I will see you tomorrow," I said to Isaac as I stood up. I wanted to make a hasty exit. I didn't want any alone time with Isaac beyond studying.

"Thank you all for coming tonight, and thank you for pushing forward," he said to us both, but he was looking directly at me.

"You're welcome, Brother Isaac," Ellena said. "Come on, Rose."

I didn't say anything. I just followed Ellena out of the classroom and back into the auditorium where Mama and Daddy were talking with Reverend Hamilton. When we got close to them, they turned and looked at us.

"How did you all do tonight?" Mama asked. I could still hear the sadness in her voice.

"We did fine." I reached out for her hand. She squeezed

mine slightly, but she continued to hold on to it. These last few days had been one awful thing after another, but at least we were all alive and well.

"Your daughter was exceptional," I heard Isaac say as he came up behind us. "I'm thinking she will be ready to register to vote in the next week or two. Her memory is as sharp as a tack."

I felt my cheeks grown warm. I hoped no one noticed any changes in my demeanor.

"Well," Mama said. "That's nice to hear. Thank you for helping her study."

"Time to go," Daddy said, interrupting. I was happy he did. I wanted very much to escape from this awkward situation.

"Brother Isaac, you, Sister Deirdre, and Brother Clifford should come over to the house next Sunday after church. We'll be celebrating Mama's birthday and there will be plenty of food and people to talk to about registering to vote," Ellena said, causing all of us to give her harsh looks. She didn't pay us any attention, but I could see a slight spark in her eye. If I could have discreetly pinched her, I would have.

"Oh, that sounds like a family event," Isaac said quickly. "We wouldn't want to intrude."

I could see Daddy was not excited by Ellena's invitation, but he and Mama exchanged glances before she said in a firm voice, "You wouldn't be intruding. You all must come and break bread with us. My family always makes a huge deal about my birthday. There will be more food than one body can eat. Do come."

I turned away like I wasn't paying attention to the con-versation. If running was an option, I would already be half-way home.

"Well, if you think it's okay for us to drop by, I will mention it to the others," I heard Isaac say.

"Then it's settled," Ellena said. "We'll see you Friday for class and again on Sunday."

I couldn't meet anyone's eyes. I know Ellena was just trying to help, but creating more situations where Isaac and I had to interact with each other was not helpful at all.

"Thank you, Ellena . . . everyone," Isaac said, sound-ing a bit awkward. I wondered if he was feeling some of the same emotions I was experiencing. "You all travel home safely."

He turned and walked away. We all seemed at a loss for words. Daddy cleared his throat and said we needed to go. As we were exiting the church, we noticed a police officer out in the parking lot. He was writing down something in a notebook as he went from Daddy's car to Lawrence's. I worried that it was that same man from earlier, but once I got a good look at his face, I knew he wasn't Officer DeWitt.

"Be calm," Daddy said. "Everything is going to be all right. You womenfolk get behind me and Lawrence."

I prayed Daddy's words would end up being true as Mama, Ellena, and I stepped back so that Daddy and Lawrence were in the front. The policeman stopped what he was doing when he saw us standing near the doors of the church.

"These y'all's cars?" he called out.

"Yes, suh," Daddy said, returning to that voice he had used earlier with the other policeman.

"What y'all doing here so late on a Wednesday night?" He took out a billy club.

"The church was just having a meeting and we were here fellowshipping with them," Daddy said, his voice sounding calm. I didn't know how he did it. I was struggling to keep myself from sinking to the ground. I felt light-headed, but I was determined not to make the situation worse. I grasped Mama's and Ellena's hands. We all held on to one another for dear life.

"I see," the officer said. "So y'all wouldn't be working with those out-of-towners on voting and other such nonsense."

"We are not breaking any laws, suh," Daddy said, raising his voice slightly. "We'd like to head on home if it's all right with you."

"That would be fine and dandy except you all have a busted taillight," he said. "I'm afraid if you left the premises, I would have to ticket you. Maybe even get your car towed. Maybe even take you down to the station."

"Beggin' your pardon, suh," Daddy said, "but our taillights are not—"

Before Daddy could finish his sentence, the man began striking the taillights on Daddy's car, then Lawrence's, then the other two cars. Reverend Hamilton, Isaac, Clifford, and Deirdre ran outside. Evidently, they heard all the commotion.

"What is the meaning of this?" Reverend Hamilton exclaimed. "You have no right to—"

"I'm the law," the officer said, spitting onto the ground. "I have all the rights. I suggest you fine people get your taillights fixed before attempting to drive them off these premises. I also might have to cite y'all for unlawful assembly."

"Sir, we have done nothing wrong," Reverend Hamilton said. "I will be calling the mayor."

"You do that. And while you're at it, tell Mayor Cunningham that Officer Scott Aiken said hello. Y'all take care." He tipped his hat and walked back to his car.

"They just never quit," Ellena said as he drove away. "No matter what, they are always lurking around, seeking whom they can devour."

"It's okay," Daddy said. "Let's go back into the church. We'll get some of the family to come get us. Everything will be fine."

"It's not okay, Daddy. We need to do something about this," Lawrence said hotly. "He had no right to do what he did. None of them have the right to continue harassing us like this. Surely there is something we can do or someone we can call."

"I will be making a call to the NAACP and John Lewis. My father is still staying at the hotel. I'm sure he will have some ideas too," Isaac said. "In the meantime, we should probably go back inside the church where it will be safe."

We all turned and walked silently back into the building. I wondered, was there really a place in this world where it was safe to be a Negro? The more time went by, the less I believed that such a place existed. If it did, I had no clear idea of how to get there.

CHAPTER 25

EVERYWHERE WE TURNED FOR THE NEXT FEW DAYS, WE WERE being followed by the Parsons Police Department. It didn't matter where we went; the police were never far away. They didn't say anything to any of us; they just sat in their cars or they would get out and lean against their cars, looking at us like they hated us. This was all new to me. I was not used to being the object of anyone's hate. Mama and Daddy had done a good job of sheltering us children. Maybe too good of a job, because none of us quite knew what to do. Lawrence just stayed angry, which was so out of character for him. The twins and Ellena were ready to rush out and register every Negro in Henry County to vote. Katie Bell didn't say much. She was pregnant and focused on L.J. and her new baby-to-be as well as her husband, Luther. She said this wasn't her fight, and as much as it frustrated Ellena, I understood. Fighting for freedom, I was learning, could be both loud and quiet. We all didn't have to be on the front lines.

Reverend Hamilton called Daddy and told him he had spoken to the mayor and Senator Ketchums. Reverend Hamilton said neither man seemed to want to get involved. According to him, the mayor said he would "look into things," and Senator Ketchums said we should all calm ourselves and stop with the voting and the picketing—that if we did that, the actions of the police would change. We were at the grocery store when Daddy got that call, and he slammed a jar of pickles onto the floor, causing it to break into large shards. He apologized but hurried out of the store "to get some air." I cleaned up the mess. Fortunately, no one was in the store when Daddy's outburst happened. When he came back in, he immediately apologized.

"I'm sorry, Pudd'n. I shouldn't have done that. Thank you for cleaning up your daddy's mess."

It was hard seeing Daddy so angry and frustrated. It made me wonder how all of this would end. Would positive change happen, or would our community become so broken that nothing could heal it? I didn't know the answers, but I prayed constantly. For us. For Negroes all over the South. For the entire world. It seemed like I was constantly bombarding heaven with my pleas. I prayed somebody up there was listening. I prayed that Ellena's view of God not being that into us wasn't true. I prayed that God still paid attention to his children, especially those of us who were Black and brown. Even if just a little bit.

Before we had class Friday evening, when everyone was done with work, Daddy and the other men in the family met and discussed what needed to be done to keep us all safe. The first mandate was we couldn't go anywhere alone.

We always had to travel in small groups. Daddy also said he didn't want us young folks helping SNCC recruit voters.

"Y'all are doing enough," he said in a firm voice. "We are not going to poke the bear any more than we have to."

Of course Ellena was beside herself with anger. Usually, I could calm her down, but she was not willing to bend.

"I'm nineteen years old!" she exclaimed in our bedroom. "It's not fair for the men in this family to dictate what we all do. Where is the democracy?"

I shook my head and allowed her the space to vent. Better she do it with me than with Daddy or some of the others.

I was wishing the meeting would get canceled, but when it was time to go, we all loaded up into Daddy's car and headed to the Baptist church. Other than our family, no one else was present, unless you counted those three police cars in the parking lot. The policemen didn't get out of the cars; they sat and watched.

"Don't y'all dawdle," Daddy said as he opened the door and helped us out of the car. He then put us in front of him and we walked hurriedly toward the door of the church.

"It's shameful that the others are not here," Ellena grumbled just low enough for me to hear as we made our way into the building. "Why can't people understand that tucking tail and running is exactly what they want us to do?"

I understood her disappointment, but I also understood the fears others must have been feeling. If it had just been me and I had seen those policemen in the parking lot, I would have kept going.

"Folks are doing the best they can," I whispered to

Ellena as we went into the main auditorium of the church and sat down beside Mama and Grandma Perkins. We both gave Grandma Perkins kisses. She patted me on my leg.

"Good to see you, Grandma," I said.

"Good to be seen, baby," she said with a smile. "I decided this gout was going to hurt me whether I was here or at home, so I decided to bring these feeble bones to the training. Before I die, I want to vote for somebody. Preferably a good candidate like President Kennedy, but if not him, then at least a halfway decent one."

"Welcome, everyone, and thank you for coming out today," Reverend Hamilton said. "And thank you to my dear wife and children for being here as well."

I noticed Isaac sitting in the front pew with his father and the other members of SNCC. The other lawyer who had come by our house, Joel Shannon, was also sitting with them.

"Before we get started, I would like to ask Brother Tobias Weinberg to come and lead us in a prayer," Reverend Hamilton said. "Everyone, please stand."

We all rose to our feet. To say I was surprised that Reverend Hamilton asked Isaac's father to pray would be an understatement. It wasn't that I thought something was wrong about what he would pray; it just seemed strange. I mean, it was strange enough for us—Methodists—to come and worship with Baptists. I just didn't think a Jewish person would want to pray in a Baptist church. I watched as Isaac's father went to the front of the congregation.

"I would like to thank Reverend Hamilton for giving me this opportunity to say a prayer that often brings comfort to my community," he said. "Times like these, we must all celebrate our similarities, not our differences. I hope that you will find peace as I pray the Shehecheyanu Blessing. I will sing it first, and then I will share the English translation.

"'Baruch atah, Adonai Eloheinu, Melech ha-olam, she-hecheyanu, v-kiy'manu, v-higiyanu laz'man hazeh,'" he began to sing. I didn't know what he was saying, of course, but it sounded so beautiful. I found listening to him say those foreign words to be so comforting. It felt like what I imagined angels would sound like. When he came to the end, I didn't want him to stop. I felt tears fall down my face. I was embarrassed until I looked at Grandma Perkins, Mama, and Ellena. They were crying too. Grandma Perkins reached for my hand.

"That is how our Lord would have sounded," she said softly, her face washed with tears. "We mustn't forget that."

"The English translation is this: 'Blessed are You, Adonai, our God, Sovereign of all, who has kept us alive, sustained us, and brought us to this season.' And to that I will add this: Bless everyone within the sound of my voice. Bless each and every person who wanted to be here but couldn't. May what is spoken here tonight help someone to help another."

We all said amen and sat as Reverend Hamilton stood again, wiping away his own tears.

"Thank you for sharing with us your religion and your faith. We are especially grateful that you chose to spend part of your Friday with us. We know that for those in the Jewish faith, Shabbat is an important observance, so we do not take it lightly that you are, in essence, sharing part of your Sabbath with us," Reverend Hamilton said. "Now, back to the business at hand. Unless anyone has more to say, please adjourn to the classrooms."

Like before, Ellena, Lawrence, and I went to the back of the church, and as before, Isaac and Deirdre quizzed us. This time, I didn't miss a single question. I had really been taking this seriously—more seriously than anything I'd ever tried before. I discovered that I actually liked learning. Every chance I got, I looked over the materials they gave us to study, sometimes during a break at the store and other times when I was in bed and everyone else in the house was asleep. Partly because I wanted to prove to myself that I could learn all of this material. If I were to admit it, I also wanted to impress Isaac. I didn't want him to think I was dumb. After I answered several questions in a row, Isaac stopped and looked at me with a huge grin on his face.

"What?" I asked.

"You're ready, Rose," he said. "You're ready for the test."

"No." I shook my head, feeling near panic rise in my chest. "It's too soon. You said a couple of weeks."

He continued to grin at me. "I thought that before, but Rose, you have answered questions that we haven't even covered yet. You're ready."

I wasn't sure how I felt about this. It was one thing to answer questions in the safety of the church with friends and family surrounding me, but it would be something altogether different when I was trying to take the test in front of a bunch of hostile white people. The very thought made my heart drop.

"What's wrong?" he asked, looking at me intently.

"I'm afraid," I finally admitted.

"I understand." He nodded. "I wish I could say you have nothing to worry about, but I can't. I can say this: You are ready, and we won't send you in there alone. I'll go in there with you myself if you like."

"You would do that?" I looked around the room. Lawrence and Ellena were busy with their own studies.

"I would do anything to . . ." He stopped. "Yes. I would do that if it would make you feel less afraid."

"Thank you." I was beginning to feel uncomfortable again. I looked around the room once more, but Ellena and Lawrence were still hard at work studying.

"Rose, I would like to talk to you about something, if that is okay?"

"I should probably go out front where Daddy and Mama are." I felt like I was twelve instead of a grown woman. I felt like I knew what he wanted to talk about, and I knew without a doubt I was not ready for that conversation.

"Please, Rose. It won't take long."

I counted to three silently in my head before answering. "Okay then. Tell me what you want to tell me."

"You are a very nice woman," he said. "And I cherish the friendship—well, I hope it is friendship—that is blossoming between us. But I don't want to ever do anything to disrespect you or your deceased husband. My Jewish faith calls for at least a year of mourning. Of course some people take more time, but no matter what, we give one another the time and space to grieve, and I would like to do the same for you."

"That sounds wonderful," I said, feeling relieved. Almost immediately, the awkwardness seeped away.

"I just wanted you to know that. I also want you to know that when the right amount of time has passed, and you will know when that time is, I would like for us to continue to get to know each other."

I nodded. "That sounds wonderful." I could have kicked myself for sounding like a parrot.

Lawrence and Ellena walked over to where we were standing.

"You two seem to be in deep conversation." Lawrence had a look of suspicion on his face.

"We were discussing the fact that Rose is ready to take the test to become a registered voter," Isaac said with a smile. I was grateful that he was saying the truth. "I believe, if she is willing, she can take the test on Monday. I told her that I and the other SNCC members would be happy to be there to support her."

"She has family for that," Lawrence snapped. "Come on, Rose. We should be going. Thank you for the lessons, Isaac. We appreciate it."

I knew Lawrence was just being protective, but I didn't like his tone. "You go on," I said boldly. "I'll be right behind you."

Lawrence looked at me with surprise. Ellena shot me an encouraging smile. She linked her arm through Lawrence's.

"Let's go, brother," she said. "Big sis is fine. Take care, Brother Isaac. See you on Sunday."

Lawrence looked like he wanted to protest, but he allowed himself to be led out of the room. I looked around and saw Deirdre was busy collecting books, pens, and papers.

"Thank you for understanding, Isaac," I said. "I am new

to being a widow. Everything happened so fast. It's not easy because I feel alone so much. I miss my husband and right now I can't see my way out of this grief, even though I want to be done with it. I want to be happy again, but for now, I just need to focus on him and my baby girl."

"I admire you, Rose," he said. "It's easy to love someone when they are right there in your face. It's not so easy when that person is gone. You try to remember things about them, but with each passing day it becomes more and more difficult. I lost someone I loved too. We weren't married, but she was my first love. Unfortunately, she developed leukemia, and within a few months she was gone. So I do relate."

I felt tears begin to flow down my face. Isaac reached into his pocket and handed me a handkerchief.

"It's going to be okay," he said as I dabbed at my eyes. "I know statements like 'this too shall pass' don't always feel true, but I do believe, as time goes on, your grief will diminish. Not your memories . . . just the grief."

I couldn't believe how wise Isaac was at such a young age.

"What are you going to do once you are done here?" I asked.

"I don't know. My father wants me to continue my studies at Morehouse, but my heart tells me The Movement is important and I need to continue to do this work in communities like Parsons, Georgia. What about you, Rose? What do you want to do with the rest of your life?"

"Nursing school, eventually. And once you all are gone, I want to continue the work that was started here. It can't stop with us."

Isaac smiled. "That sounds wonderful, Rose. You should

do it if you want to. The sky truly is the limit, and you learn so quickly. I just know you would make a great nurse, and I definitely know you will be a great leader in The Movement here in your hometown. Are you going to enroll this fall?"

"Oh my." I suddenly felt overwhelmed. "I don't know if I could be ready to go to school this fall. It's almost here. Ellena is already reading the books for some of her fall classes. I just don't know if I can do it."

Isaac placed his hand on mine. "You don't have to be afraid, Rose. You are a smart woman, and you can do anything you want. I believe in you."

"Thank you," I said, not quite able to meet his eyes.

"No matter what you do, I know it will turn out fine."

Deirdre came over to us. It was clear she had given us time and space to talk. I felt my cheeks grow warm. We were just talking, but I could only imagine what she must have been thinking.

"Good work tonight, Sister Rose," Deirdre said.

"I'm thinking Rose will be ready to go take her test on Monday," he said, then looked at me. "That is, if she wants to."

Deirdre clapped her hands. "That is wonderful news, Rose. I think your brother and sister are just about ready to take the test themselves. You all taking the test and passing it will boost the morale of so many of your neighbors and family members."

"Thank you both for your help." I tried to smile even though taking that test on Monday felt scary. "I should go. I know my family is probably waiting."

"See you on Sunday," Isaac said.

"See you Sunday." I hurried out of the room. When I got to the main auditorium, Ellena and Lawrence were waiting. "I'm sorry I took so long. We were just talking about the test." I knew later I would share everything with Ellena, but I didn't want to upset Lawrence any more than he already was.

"It's okay," Ellena said. "Mama and Daddy left with Grandma Perkins. Lawrence and I decided to stay back and give you a ride home."

"That sounds good," I said. I could tell by the look in Ellena's eyes that she was hoping I would say more, but for now, I needed to process everything that had happened without my sister's input, especially in front of our brother. "Let's go home."

Ellena linked her arm with mine and whispered in my ear, "I expect all of the details later."

I just patted her hand and smiled.

When we walked outside, mercifully, the police cars were gone. I hoped this meant they would leave us alone and allow us the freedom to live. That was my solemn prayer.

CHAPTER 26

ALL OF THE GIRLS WERE IN THE KITCHEN COOKING ON SATURDAY in preparation for Mama's birthday celebration after church the next day. Or maybe I should revise that and say Katie Bell, our leader, and Ellena were doing most of the cooking. Naomi and I were cutting up vegetables and washing dishes. I was getting better with my cooking skills, but Mama's birthday was too important of a day for me to do much more than what I was told. Katie Bell and Naomi's boys were with Mama and Daddy.

As was our custom every year, Mama and Daddy went over to Grandma Perkins' house while we made all of the food. We didn't even let Grandma Perkins help. Aunt Shimmy was going to fry the chicken tomorrow, and Aunt Lucille was making two pound cakes, Mama's favorite dessert. Uncle Little Bud, Uncle Michael, and Lawrence were taking care of the grilling. Before Mr. Tote died, he taught Lawrence everything he knew about seasoning and barbecuing a goat, so Lawrence was taking care of the goat while the uncles cooked the ribs and chicken. If you walked out into the yard, the smell of the meat filled the air. Inside, the smells were equally mouthwatering.

"I'm ready to put the collard greens on," Katie Bell said, resting her hands on her swollen belly. "Are you done washing them, Naomi?"

"Almost," she said from the sink, dunking the greens for what seemed like the hundredth time in the water. "I don't want to accidentally leave a bug in them and have you tell me off."

We all laughed. Last year, Naomi had been in charge of cleaning the greens, but she didn't understand what all that involved. When Katie Bell looked through them, she found a bug and pretty much told Naomi she was not ever going to be put in charge again of something so serious as washing the greens. Naomi had begged her this morning to give her one more chance to prove she could do the job properly.

I was busy peeling the potatoes for the potato salad. Ellena was making Mama's favorite—turkey dressing.

"Girl, you thought I was bad," Katie Bell said to Naomi as she wiped her hands on her apron. "If Mama had bit into that little green worm you left behind last year, you would have thought your name was mud. I remember one time I didn't clean the chitlins good enough and Mama swore she would never let me in her kitchen again."

I wrinkled my nose. I couldn't stand the sight, smell, or taste of chitlins. I was so happy when Mama's doctor said she couldn't eat them anymore due to her high blood pressure. Those awful things would stink up an entire house for days.

"I'm done with the potatoes," I said, taking them over to the stove. "What next?"

"That basket of corn needs shucking," Ellena said. "Soon as I'm done mixing up this dressing, I can get to work on the corn casserole. Naomi, we're going to have to take a lot of this over to your house."

Naomi pulled the greens out of the water and put them into a pan that she took over to Katie Bell. I sat down at the table and started working on shucking the corn.

"I dare you to find bugs this year, missy," Naomi said with a huge grin. "That's fine, Ellena. Whatever you need. Rose, I'll help you with the corn, unless there's something else I need to be doing."

"Before you help with the corn, would you mind peeling those peaches?" Katie Bell asked Naomi. "I'm going to go ahead and make a couple of cobblers and Grandma Perkins's upside-down peach cake. Everybody loves it."

"Yes, ma'am." Naomi took a knife from the kitchen drawer. Once we were all settled again with our various tasks, Ellena broke the silence.

"So, sister," she said, looking at me with a sly grin. "Are you going to tell us about the conversation you and Brother Isaac were having last night?"

I rolled my eyes at her. I had been able to fend off her questions last night, saying I was just too tired to talk, but there was no escaping her curiosity and my other sister's and sister-in-law's.

"Who's Isaac?" Katie Bell asked, looking from one of us to the other.

"He's one of the leaders from SNCC," Ellena said, looking over at me with a huge grin on her face. "And he is very clearly smitten with our dear sister, Rose."

"Rose's husband hasn't even been dead for a year," Katie Bell said with a disapproving look on her face. "It's too soon for her to be thinking about seeing another man. And now I remember him. Isn't he Jewish?"

I started to respond, but Ellena jumped in first.

"Why do we continue to live by these archaic rules?" Ellena demanded. "Brother Isaac is a good man, and he would make any woman a good mate. Why does Sissy have to wait for a year or two or however long the 'rules' state if she finds someone who is interested in her and she shares those same feelings?"

Once again, I tried to say something, but Naomi piped in.

"But he's Jewish," Naomi said. "I can see a Methodist and a Baptist making it work, but a Jewish person and a Methodist? I can't wrap my brain around that."

I had to confess that I couldn't see it either. I didn't know a lot about the Jewish religion, but I knew they didn't believe that Jesus was God's son, or at least I thought that was the case. How would two people with such different religious beliefs make a marriage work? Thankfully, I didn't have to worry about that now, if ever. I was only focused on continuing my journey as Jasper's widow. There was no room for anyone else—Jewish, Methodist, or any other religion.

"Just because Isaac is Jewish shouldn't discount him as a possible love interest," Ellena said in a firm voice.

"Oh yes, it should," Katie Bell said as she turned and faced us with her hands on her hips, looking just like Grandma Perkins. "What kind of relationship would it be with someone who doesn't even believe in the basic tenets of the Christian faith? How in the world would they raise children? Just let them go wherever they please? Sounds like a bunch of confused children to me."

"Everybody, I—"

"Interfaith couples make it work all the time," Ellena snapped, once again interrupting me midsentence. This was how conversations often went in this house. Among all of us children, Ellena and Katie Bell had the strongest personalities, and often the two of them were at odds with each other, which made it almost impossible for the rest of us to get a word in edgewise. "And anyway, Brother Isaac was raised Jewish, but he doesn't strike me as the closed-minded type. They would be able to figure it out."

"I can't believe—" Katie Bell started.

"Stop it," I said, raising my voice. "Stop talking about me like I'm not sitting here."

They all turned and looked at me with various degrees of surprise. They were not used to being interrupted during one of their lively debates, but this time, I didn't want to be their form of entertainment for the day.

"There is nothing to debate or argue about," I said firmly. "If you all must know, Isaac was very kind and he told me he respected me and my feelings for my husband. I am not ready for another relationship. Yes, I am lonely and I miss Jasper with everything inside me, but I am not going to allow that to cause me to jump into another relationship too soon. I made mistakes before with my relationship with Jasper. I don't want to make those same mistakes again."

"Good," Katie Bell said decisively, turning back to the pot of collard greens. "We can let this subject go."

I was happy to have the conversation end, but I could tell by the look on Ellena's face that she was not satisfied, so I decided to change the topic to a subject I knew would cause her joy.

"I think I might want to go to nursing school," I blurted out.

Ellena knew I wanted to go to nursing school, but I hadn't shared it with Katie Bell or Naomi.

"Nursing?" Katie Bell exclaimed as her face split into a wide smile. "Oh, Sissy. That's wonderful. You will make a phenomenal nurse."

"She sure will, and she can go to school in Atlanta at the Grady Memorial Hospital School of Nursing. I know a lot of women who graduated from there," Ellena said.

"When did you decide this?" Katie Bell asked. "I don't recall you talking about wanting to go to school before now. And nursing? I think it's wonderful, but I am surprised."

Naomi got up from her chair to give me a hug. "You will be a fantastic nurse."

"I didn't mean to imply you wouldn't be a good nurse, Sissy," Katie Bell said. "I'm just surprised. This one," she said, pointing toward Ellena, "has always talked about law school or teaching or medical school. You've never been one to indicate you wanted to do more schooling."

"I know. I first mentioned it to Jasper before . . . well, before he died. He encouraged me to do it. Only here of late have I given it serious thought. I never wanted to go to college before because I was afraid I would fail."

"Have you told Mama and Daddy yet?" Ellena asked.

I nodded. "They know."

"Are you going to start this fall?" Ellena asked, excitement all over her face.

"I'm not sure. I'm still figuring it all out in my head. I just don't want to start it and not finish. I think I can do it, but I'm nervous."

"Don't be nervous," Katie Bell said. "Your faith is strong and your will to succeed is equally as strong. You will be just fine."

I appreciated the faith my sisters and sister-in-law had in me. Now that I had said I was thinking about attending nursing school out loud, I couldn't stop thinking about it. I found myself getting excited at the prospect. But right now, there was so much left to do for Mama's party that I threw myself into whatever Katie Bell or Ellena needed doing.

By six o'clock that evening, most everything was done. We were all sitting outside on the porch as Lawrence finished up the barbecuing. Katie Bell and the uncles had all gone home, so it was just me, Ellena, Naomi, and Lawrence. Just as Lawrence was taking the last of the meat off the grill, we heard a fire truck siren in the distance.

"I wonder what that's all about?" Ellena said, getting up from the swing. She walked out into the yard and glanced toward the direction of the siren. "Looks like smoke in the distance."

She came and sat back down beside me on the swing. Not too long afterward, we heard more sirens. Almost at the same time, the phone rang in the house. Ellena ran inside. It wasn't long before I heard her cry out. Just as I hopped up to run and see what was wrong, she came flying out the front door.

"That was Daddy on the phone. Somebody bombed St. Luke's!" she yelled. "The church is on fire."

"Was anybody hurt?" I asked, trying not to let my mind think the worst. *Please, God*, I said silently. *Let everyone be all right. Please.*

"Daddy didn't know." Tears streamed down her face. "He's bringing Mama, Grandma Perkins, and the triplets here. He said for none of us to try to go to the church. Not until we know more. Oh my God. How could anyone bomb a church? What kind of evil people would do such a thing?"

"We already know who would do something that evil," Lawrence said angrily. "This has got to stop. We cannot continue to let this kind of behavior go unpunished. It has got to stop."

"All this because we want to vote?" Naomi cried. "They hate us this much that they would bomb our churches. Over voting? Over eating at a lunch counter?"

Naomi got up from her seat and wrapped her arms around Lawrence's waist. He stood rigid for a moment, and then he pulled her into a hug. It wasn't long before the uncles, aunts, and cousins started to come into the yard. They had all heard the same news, and as always, Great-Grandma Birdie's old home was the meeting ground for the family. The women stood on the porch talking in hushed tones while the men huddled together in the yard.

"Do we know where everybody is? Where are Micah

and Mitchell?" Aunt Lucille asked. She was sitting in the rocking chair that used to belong to Grandma Birdie. As soon as she asked, I felt panic like I had never felt before.

"Micah and Mitchell," I whispered. Then I said their names louder. "The twins. Where are Micah and Mitchell? They should be home by now or they should have called."

I felt so much panic right then I didn't know what to do. I wanted to take off running, looking for my brothers, but I didn't even know where to start. They could be anywhere—delivering babies; taking care of some poor, sick person out in the country. There was no telling where they were, but something in my spirit said they were at the church. I just knew it.

"I'll go call Doc Russell's office," Ellena said. She ran into the house again. This time I ran after her, praying aloud that they were okay and hadn't gone to the church. I closed my eyes as Ellena dialed the operator. It took another few minutes for her to be connected and Doc Russell's wife to answer the phone. "Mrs. Russell, are my brothers there? This is Ellena Perkins." Ellena didn't say anything for a few seconds, and I thought I might jump out of my skin.

"What is she saying?" I asked, gripping Ellena's arm.

"Okay, ma'am," Ellena said. "Thank you." She hung up the phone and looked at me with wild eyes. "They and Doc Russell went to the church. They got a call that there might be some injuries. Along with the fire, there were also reports of gunshots. Oh God. Oh God," she cried, and I started crying right along with her. Lawrence came rushing into the house.

"What's going on?" he asked. "Where are Micah and Mitchell?"

"They went to the church with Doc Russell to see if anyone there needed help. She also said there were some gunshots," Ellena managed to choke out.

"I'm going," Lawrence said and hurried out before we could stop him. When we got to the front porch, he was already sprinting across the street to where his car was parked. Uncle Lem, Uncle Little Bud, and Uncle Michael followed and hopped in the car too.

Just as Lawrence pulled out with a loud squeal of his tires, Daddy, Mama, Grandma Perkins, and the triplets drove into the yard. We ran to the car and told him about the twins and Lawrence going to see about them.

"I'll go see what's going on," Daddy said. "Opal, you and Mama go inside and wait. I won't be long."

"Be careful," Mama said. She kissed Daddy on his cheek. "Bring yourself and my boys back home."

"Be careful, son," Grandma Perkins said.

The triplets were all asleep in the back. I reached in and got David and Demetrius and Naomi got Daniel. Mama and Grandma Perkins walked together toward the porch, holding on to each other. I could tell by the way they walked, they were scared. Naomi and I carried the sleeping boys inside the house and laid them on a pallet on the floor in the living room. Then we went back outside and waited.

Time moved like it was at a standstill. Every time we would hear a car, we would jump but each time, it wasn't them. Finally, about two hours later, Daddy's car pulled into the yard with Lawrence's car behind it. When Daddy and the twins got out, I took off running to them. They both wrapped their arms around me.

"Oh my God," I whispered, hugging them as tightly as I could. "Thank you, God. Thank you." I leaned back so I could get a good look at them. "Are y'all all right?"

"We're okay," Micah said.

Ellena must have been right behind me because she started questioning them too. "Was anyone hurt? How are Reverend Hamilton and his family and the volunteers from SNCC? We heard there were gunshots."

I braced myself for the answer.

"No one was hurt," Mitchell said. "The church was empty when it happened. As far as we know, there were no guns involved. Probably the electricity popping from the fire or maybe a car backfired."

I felt my legs almost buckle. Mitchell kept me from falling.

"Come on. Let's get you on the porch," he said. "Everything is going to be fine. No one was injured. Unfortunately, the church can't be salvaged. It was burned to the ground."

We all walked back to the porch where the rest of the family sat waiting. Mama made her way over to Daddy. He pulled her tight and held on to her like they hadn't seen each other in weeks. I loved how much my parents loved each other.

"I spoke with Reverend Hamilton," Daddy said, with his good arm wrapped around Mama's waist. "He is heartbroken over what happened, but his spirit is strong. Reverend Shipman and some of the other deacons from both churches met and decided that tomorrow, we will all hold service together at our church. There will be a lot of people, so maybe we can load up all this food and take it there to feed folks. If you don't mind," he said, looking at Mama.

Mama kissed Daddy's cheek. "I wouldn't have it any other way."

The next day, just as Daddy had predicted, the church was packed, but even with it overflowing with people, I spotted Isaac immediately. He and his father were sitting toward the back. I didn't see Deirdre or Clifford. When he saw me looking, he waved, but there was a sadness about his posture that I could spot all the way in the front of the church. The service was a mixture of sadness and joy. Sadness for the loss of St. Luke's building but joy that no one was hurt.

"Saints," our pastor, Reverend Shipman, said after the combined choir finished singing, "we have a lot to be joyous about, but we also have a lot to be angry about too. The Bible says in Ephesians 4:26, 'Be ye angry, and sin not.' Well, I'm angry today. I'm angry that the devil would be so bold as to burn down a church. I have been one of the main ones to say we should wait and allow God to move in his time. But then I am reminded of the words of Dr. King in his 'Letter from a Birmingham Jail' where he states that 'freedom is never voluntarily given by the oppressor; it must be demanded by the oppressed.' It is high time for us to demand our freedom and our safety. It is, in fact, past time."

The church erupted with applause and amens, but Reverend Shipman continued.

"I also owe our dear Brother Hamilton, his family,

and the congregants at St. Luke's an apology," Reverend Shipman said. "You all were leading the way and I was resisting because of fear, even though 'fear not' is the most repeated command in the Bible. Three hundred and sixty-five times, to be exact. If our God took the time to tell us not to fear 365 times—one 'fear not' for every day of the year—then we as his chosen people have the obligation, the moral obligation, to act in a fearless way when faced with the deeds of the enemy."

The church was loud with the emotions everyone was feeling. That was the thing about the Negro church, regardless of the denomination. We showed our emotions through our praise, and everyone, it seemed, was feeling the weight of Reverend Shipman's words.

"Starting today, saints," Reverend Shipman nearly shouted from the pulpit, "we let our fear go, and we join forces with our brothers and sisters from St. Luke's. Today, the enemy will find out that we are one voice, one people, serving the one mighty God."

Everyone rose to their feet. People were hugging and crying, but there was a new resolve that I had never witnessed before. It was like the burning of St. Luke's was just what we all needed to recognize that we were the ones who had to put a stop to all of the hatred. Not by making the white people love us, or even like us. No, our task was to make them respect us. It was going to be a long and arduous road, but together, we could do it. I looked at my family and from their faces alone, I knew they were feeling the same emotions.

The choir stood and began to sing "Lift Every Voice and Sing." We all joined in with them.

Lift every voice and sing
Till earth and heaven ring,
Ring with the harmonies of Liberty;
Let our rejoicing rise
High as the listening skies,
Let it resound loud as the rolling sea.
Sing a song full of the faith that the dark past has taught us,
Sing a song full of the hope that the present has brought us.
Facing the rising sun of our new day begun,
Let us march on till victory is won.

When service was over, I went outside to get some air. I walked out to the cemetery and sat down on the bench by Jasper and Olivia Rose's grave. I wanted to tell them so much, but I decided to start with my plans for tomorrow.

"I'm going to go register to vote," I told them. "I'm afraid, but I'm not going to let my fear get the best of me. I pray I can make you proud."

The sounds in the graveyard were the sounds of summer. I heard bullfrogs croaking in the little stream that ran beside the thicket near the back of the cemetery. The birds were singing particularly loud as well. Eastern bluebirds. Northern mockingbirds. American robins. If nature had a choir, it was as if all of God's noisiest creatures were harmonizing as one. It was warm outside but not as hot as it normally was. If we didn't know that St. Luke's had burned down, today would be the best day ever, what with both of our congregations coming together as one.

"It is peaceful out here," I heard a voice behind me say. I turned around and saw that it was Isaac. It was strange having him so close to the graves of my husband and daughter, but at the same time, it felt right. I smiled at him.

"It is peaceful," I said. "I come here regularly. Well, not as regular as I used to, but I try to come by at least once a week and clean up their graves. I was telling them that I am going to register to vote tomorrow."

"Are you sure? The police are trying to say what happened at the church was faulty wires. Things could get even worse. I couldn't bear . . . I couldn't bear it if something happened to you."

I felt a tear trickle down my face, but I smiled as I wiped it away with my fingertip. "'The Lord is my strength and my shield.' Psalm 28:7. I will be fine."

Neither of us said anything for a time.

Finally, Isaac spoke. "I was supposed to be at the church when it got bombed."

I looked at him with surprise. "You were? What caused you to not be there?"

"*Hashgacha pratit,*" he said simply. "It means divine providence. Some Jewish people are torn when it comes to the interference of the Almighty. Today, I have no other answer for why I wasn't there besides him. I guess luck, but that doesn't seem a sufficient answer. Every time I got ready to leave, something would happen. I couldn't find my shoes. The car had a flat tire. The battery wouldn't turn over. You name it, and it happened. I was never so frustrated, but then we heard the explosion as we were driving toward the church. By the time we got there, the church was engulfed in flames."

"Thank God you all didn't make it there," I said. "And God sounds like a good answer to me."

"I'm going to go now," Isaac said abruptly. "I will be at the registrar's office tomorrow when you go to take your test. Don't worry about it. You are ready. No matter what they try to throw at you."

"Thank you. See you tomorrow."

I watched as he walked away, and then I turned back to the grave. I wondered what Jasper would think about Isaac.

"You don't have anything to worry about," I said out loud. "My heart is still yours, Jasper Bourdon. Always and forever."

I continued to sit there until Ellena came out for me.

"You okay?" she asked as we walked back toward the dining hall of the church.

"Yes," I said, linking my arm with hers. "Tomorrow is going to be a big day." I shared with her my plans to go through with registering to vote.

"Are you sure?"

"Yes." And I was. I knew that I had to let go of my fear just like Reverend Shipman had said. We had the right to fight for our rights, and I was determined, no matter what, that tomorrow I would exercise that freedom.

CHAPTER 27

I COULDN'T DECIDE WHAT TO WEAR. I HAD STOOD IN FRONT OF my closet for what seemed like hours trying to pick out just the right dress. I wasn't sure why I thought that what I was wearing would matter, but in my mind, it did. The night before, I had painstakingly rolled and rerolled my hair so that the curls would be perfect. I didn't want to give anyone any reason to say no to my ability to become a registered voter in Henry County. Somehow, this moment had come to mean a lot to me. I wasn't just doing this for myself. It was for everybody in my family, at church, and any Negroes anywhere who were being denied the right to vote. I didn't have a clue who I'd vote for come the next election. I knew when President Kennedy ran again, I would proudly select his name on the ballot. As for everyone else, I guessed I'd figure that out when the time came.

"You haven't picked out something to wear yet?" Ellena asked, walking into the room. "You've been standing there for at least an hour. Just pick something. It's almost time to go."

The entire family had decided they would go with me

to the courthouse in McDonough where I had to go to register. The only ones not going were Grandma Perkins, the twins, Katie Bell, and her family. The twins had to work and Katie Bell was still skittish about all of this marching and protesting.

"You know I love you and I will be praying the entire time you are there," she said to me on the phone this morning. I could hear the tears in her voice. I reassured her that I didn't hold it against her for not going. How could I? I had just gotten used to the idea of all this myself. One thing I had learned is we had to meet folks where they were. I knew this because someone did the same for me.

I looked over at Ellena and smiled. She was wearing a pretty pink dress she and Mama had just finished making a week ago.

"I can't think what to wear," I said. "Pick something for me."

She went to our closet and looked inside for a few seconds. She pulled out a blue sheath dress with a high, round, neck bodice and a fitted skirt. Then she reached up on the shelf and took down a blue pillbox hat with a veil that Grandma had given me for Christmas last year.

"You will look just like Jackie Kennedy," she said decisively. "Classy and elegant."

"I don't know about that," I said, but I put on the dress. Ellena helped me with my hair and makeup. Mama didn't like it if we wore too much face paint, as she called it, but Ellena was able to make mine look tasteful. By the time I was ready, I felt I at least looked like I knew what I was doing.

"I wish I was taking that stupid test with you," Ellena grumbled. "I'm afraid I haven't been as diligent with my studies this summer as you have, and my memorization skills are not nearly as good as yours."

Hearing Ellena say that made me feel better, if the truth be known. It wasn't often that anyone, but especially me, outdid Ellena when it came to learning.

"We should go," she said. "Daddy was pacing. Not a good sign."

I followed Ellena outside and sure enough, he was wearing a path in the living room floor. Daddy was handsome as always in a light-blue seersucker suit. When he saw us, he came up to me and kissed me on the cheek. He had tears in his eyes.

"I am so proud of you, Pudd'n," he said. "So very proud."

"Thank you, Daddy."

Mama was sitting in the rocker wearing a bright-yellow shift with buttons down the front. She smiled at me. "You look beautiful, Rose. Absolutely beautiful. You are so very brave, my love. No matter what, just know your family believes in you."

Daddy led us in prayer before we got into the car and made the twenty-minute drive to McDonough. When we arrived, several cars were already there, most of them my family. They were all standing outside in their Sunday clothes too. There was Lawrence and Naomi—the triplets were staying with Grandma Perkins—and there was my uncles, aunts, and cousins. But there were also some Negroes I didn't know.

"Who are all of these people?" I asked down-low to Daddy.

"They're here for you, sweetheart," Daddy said, turning around in the seat to face me. "Word got around that a young Negro woman would be the first to try to register to vote. So they all wanted to come witness it for themselves, I reckon."

Immediately I felt my stomach begin to do flip-flops. I had no idea anyone other than our family would show up like this. What if I failed? I almost didn't want to get out of the car. Mama turned around in her seat.

"They just want to give you support," Mama said. "Don't worry."

Mama always knew my thoughts even before they were formed good in my mind. We were just about to get out of the car when Miss Jainey walked up. I was surprised to see her. Daddy rolled down his window.

"Good morning, everyone," she said. "Rose, I hear it's a big day for you today."

We all looked at Ellena. She shrugged. "I may have mentioned to Miss Jainey that Rose was registering to vote today, and her support would be appreciated."

Daddy gave Ellena a look but turned and smiled at Miss Jainey. "We appreciate you being here, but we don't want you to feel obligated to get involved."

"Cedric, I have loved your family and Opal's family for as long as I can remember," she said. "I will confess, I thought this desire to vote and integrate was a whole lot of nonsense at first, but I realized, thanks to your youngest back there, that you all have a right to fight for your rights.

And I have an obligation as a citizen of this town, but more importantly, as a Christian woman, to support your efforts. So here I am. I'll do whatever you want me to do, including stay out of the way."

I looked at Ellena. She had a huge smile. I couldn't believe she was able to educate Miss Jainey in such a short period of time. I couldn't even imagine when she could have had a conversation with her.

"We thank you, Miss Jainey," Daddy said. "Having you here means a lot. For now, I believe we know what has to be done."

"I understand," she said. "I'll just go stand over there with Senator Ketchums and his wife, Lori Beth."

"Who?" Mama asked, a look of shock on her face. "Did you say Senator Ketchums and his wife?"

"Yes. They're here. So are the white pastors of the local Baptist and Methodist churches in Parsons. Y'all are not in this alone," Miss Jainey said and walked back toward the courthouse where, sure enough, Senator Ketchums stood with a white woman and two white men wearing clergy collars.

"Well now," Daddy said, shaking his head. "I never would have believed I would see something like this."

"Me neither," Mama said. She turned around and reached for my hand. "You don't have to do this, Rose. I don't care who all is standing out there. If you decide right now that you want to turn around and go back home, no one will think any less of you."

I was scared. More scared than I had ever been in my life, but I wasn't going to back out now. This meant too much to too many people. This meant too much to me.

We got out of the car, and everyone was standing there like a protective web. Each one hugged me and whispered prayers or words of encouragement. People from the community I had grown up seeing in church and in the store all came up to me to say they were already proud of me. Lawrence came and took my hand, which made me feel better, as we approached the doors of the courthouse. No matter what happened inside, a whole bunch of folks cared about me and about what we were trying to do.

"Are you ready?" a voice to my left said. I turned and smiled. It was Isaac. Like normal, he was dressed in a black suit with a matching yarmulke.

"I think so," I said. "I'm just—"

"You people need to disperse!" a voice over a megaphone yelled, causing me to jump. Lawrence pulled me closer, and Isaac stepped in front of me to shield me from whoever was yelling at us.

I peered around Isaac and saw ten police officers all in a row, one of which was the officer who jumped on me and treated Daddy so rude. He was the one with the megaphone and the rest of them were carrying billy clubs, swinging them like they were going to come after us.

"That's it," Daddy said. "We're going home. Lawrence, get your mother and sisters to the car."

But before we could turn around, Senator Ketchums, his wife, Miss Jainey, and the two white preachers all came and stood in front of us. Senator Ketchums stepped forward and put up his hand to stop them from coming any farther.

"That's enough!" Senator Ketchums yelled at them. "Don't you take another step. I am Senator Jimmy Earl

Ketchums of the state of Georgia, and I hereby demand that you let this young woman through."

The officer with the megaphone handed it to the man beside him and came toward us, motioning for the others to stay still. When he was standing in front of all of us, he stopped. "Senator, you have no jurisdiction here. These people are guilty of unlawful assembly, and if they do not disperse, we will arrest each and every one of them."

"They are not hurting anyone, and they are not breaking any laws," Senator Ketchums said, stepping closer to the officer. He wasn't bothered by their megaphone or their billy clubs. I couldn't imagine ever feeling so safe that I could go up against the police like that. It must be very special being a white person. They just didn't know fear the way we did. I stood in awe as he continued to speak. "They are law-abiding, taxpaying citizens. They are not chanting or marching or impeding anyone's ability to enter the courthouse, so your accusation that they are unlawfully assembling is simply false. If you plan on arresting them, then you will have to arrest me, my wife, Miss Jainey, Reverend Stewart, and Reverend Smith. Is that what you want to be on the front pages of every newspaper in Georgia and beyond? Is that what you want the national news to talk about? Are you sure your mayor would want this type of publicity?"

It was clear that the policeman was not happy. Every emotion known to mankind played out on his face, but then he moved aside and motioned for his men to do the same. Senator Ketchums turned around and looked at Mama and Daddy.

"I would be honored to escort your daughter into the courthouse," he said. "I will stand there with her and make sure the test is administered as fairly as it can be."

Mama looked at Daddy, and he nodded. Mama looked at me. "Are you sure you still want to do this?"

"Yes, ma'am."

"Then yes, Jimmy Earl," she said with a tight smile. "We appreciate your support."

He nodded, then reached his hand out for mine. I looked at my family and then at Isaac. He smiled at me and gave me the thumbs-up. I nodded and looked up at Senator Ketchums.

"I'm ready to go, sir." I allowed him to tuck my hand into the crook of his arm.

"Don't you let nothing happen to my daughter," Daddy said, his voice hoarse with emotion.

"I will guard her with my life," Senator Ketchums said, looking at Daddy and then Mama. Then we walked up the stairs of the courthouse and into the building. Once we were inside, Senator Ketchums walked with me to the back of the building where the registrar's office was located. He stood back as I went to the desk. There was no one inside waiting for service. There were only the three women behind the desk. They stood there without uttering a word at first, but then Senator Ketchums cleared his throat. Finally, one of them spoke.

"May I help you?" she asked, but the tone of her voice wasn't that of someone wanting to help. I looked back at the senator, and he gave me an encouraging smile. The woman who had spoken looked red in the face, like my very presence was stealing the air she was trying to breathe. I tried to ignore all of that and just do what I was taught. *Smile. Don't ask unnecessary questions. State my purpose for being here. Don't argue. Retreat if it appears it is going to get violent.*

"Good morning, ma'am," I said, trying to sound as pleasant as possible. "I'm here to—"

"To what?" she snapped before I could finish, tapping her fingernails on the counter like I was holding up a long line of people. I was determined not to get flustered, so I continued to smile.

"I'm here to register to vote," I said, trying not to shake or stutter, which was almost impossible with that awful lady glaring at me so.

"We're not registering voters today," she said and turned back around to the other ladies, who started laughing. "Come back tomorrow. Or maybe the day after."

"Ladies, my name is Senator Jimmy Earl Ketchums," he said, his voice stern like a teacher. "You are required to register this woman to vote. Your stated hours say you are registering voters today. Please do your job or I will have to speak to your supervisor."

When she heard him say who he was, her entire demeanor changed.

"Yes sir, Senator," she said. "We do have the discretion to change our days and times of operation, but we will go ahead and test this woman if you like." She then asked for identification and all of the questions about where I lived and what I did that Isaac and the others had prepared us to answer. Then she asked me if I could read or write.

"Yes, ma'am. I can do both."

"Well, before you begin the test," she said, her voice sounding bored with the whole process, "you will need to read to me the Georgia Constitution. Start reading page one and stop when I tell you to stop. If you miss a word or mispronounce a word, you automatically fail. Understand?"

"Yes, ma'am." I had just practiced reading it out loud to Daddy this morning before breakfast. I knew I could do it. I read each word carefully and slowly and I made sure I read it loud enough that she and everyone in that office could hear me. It wasn't long before she stopped me.

"Fine, fine," she snapped, slapping a pencil and the written test on the desk. "Go over there and take this test. You have to get twenty-nine out of thirty questions correct. You've got an hour."

"An hour?" Senator Ketchums asked, raising his voice. "Since when is there a time limit attached to the test?"

"We close voter registration in an hour," she said. "That's the law. If you don't like it, then you will have to take it up with my supervisor, who happens to be out today."

"It's okay," I said hurriedly. "I won't need longer than an hour. Thank you, ma'am." I hurried over to the table in the corner. She stopped me as I started to sit down.

"You can't sit. That's the rules. You can stand."

"Yes, ma'am." I began looking through the test. The questions were difficult, but I knew the answers. It was awkward trying to stand while writing, but I put the test on the back of my purse and began writing with a fury.

How many electoral votes does Georgia have in the electoral college? Twelve.

What is treason against the State of Georgia? Levying war against her; adhering to her enemies; giving them aid and comfort.

What does the Constitution of the United States provide regarding the right of citizens to vote? The right of citizens of the United States to vote shall not be denied or abridged by the United States or by any state on account of race, color, previous condition of servitude or sex, so sayeth the Fifteenth and Nineteenth Amendments to the United States Constitution. Code Sections 1–820 and 1–827.

My hand was flying, but I was very careful to make sure my printing was neat and easy to read. Isaac had encouraged us to print instead of using cursive because he said they will use any reason to say no. I made it to the final question, and it was one I had just answered the other day when we were studying. It said: *How does the Constitution of the United States provide that it may be amended?* As I wrote the answer, I felt tears welling up in my eyes. I knew I passed. I looked up at the clock when I was finished. I had five minutes to spare. I went up to the desk and laid it down. I went back and stood next to Senator Ketchums.

"What do you think?" he asked.

The tears did fall, but I didn't try to stop them. "I passed, sir. I knew the answer to every question."

He patted me on my back. "Good girl. You're smart. Just like your mother. She never thought she was smart, but she was. Still is, I imagine."

"Here's your voter registration card," the woman said, placing it on the table.

I walked over and picked it up. I couldn't stop the smile

on my face. "Thank you, ma'am," I said. "You ladies have a blessed and wonderful day." I turned and walked to the door, where Senator Ketchums was standing. He nodded at the ladies and then we walked out. Once we made it outside, I saw everyone looking toward me expectantly. I waved the card in the air, and the parking lot erupted into applause and screams. My family rushed up to me and Daddy pulled me into an embrace, crushing me with his one good arm.

"I knew you could do it," he said. "I just knew it!"

Everyone came up to congratulate me. It felt good for us to win. It felt good to know they didn't get one over on us. As the crowd began to disperse, Isaac came to me. He awkwardly patted my shoulder.

"I told you that you would pass," he said. "You were such a quick learner. Quicker than anyone I have ever met. You digested in a week or so what takes a lot of people years to memorize. Congratulations."

"Thank you," I said. "I . . . I mean . . . I couldn't have done it without you. What next?"

Isaac cleared his throat. "Next, I go to Jackson, Mississippi."

"You're leaving?" I asked softly. "But there's so much left to do. How can you leave us now?"

"You and the others are ready to take this on yourselves, but Sister Deirdre and Brother Clifford will be here until the beginning of August. You all don't need me. I'll be helping with the work Brother Medgar started when he was in Jackson."

I was terrified at the thought of him going to the same place Medgar Evers was brutally murdered. What if it happened to him? The thought of one more person I cared about dying was almost too much.

"Can't you wait and go later when things have cooled down a bit there?" I asked, my voice sounding tentative.

"If the truth be known, I agreed to go because I need to give you space, Rose, and I am fighting my emotions when it comes to you," he said plainly. "I care strongly for you, but now is not the time for that. So I need to go far, far away until the time is right for you to perhaps consider a relationship with me."

I was stunned. I didn't know what to say.

"It's okay," he said softly. "You don't have to say anything. Is it okay for me to write you?"

"Yes," I finally said.

"Will you write me back?"

"Yes," I said again.

He smiled. "Then expect a letter from me at least once per week. Just to stay in touch, not to pressure you. If you are willing to take a chance on me after sufficient time has passed, then I will come back and we can start a true courtship. I am willing to wait for you, Rose. However long it takes."

I nodded. I couldn't speak. I didn't have any words. I wasn't sure what to say, but as always, Ellena walked up to us and linked her arms in mine and Isaac's.

"You kids look awful serious," she said with a grin on her face. "Anything I should know about?"

"Isaac is leaving," I said hoarsely. "He was just saying goodbye."

"No," he said with a smile. "Not goodbye. Just see you later."

With that, he walked away. I looked at my sister. "I doubt I'll hear from him again."

She kissed my cheek. "If that were a bet, my sister, I am afraid you would lose."

Daddy began rounding us up and before I knew it, we were heading home. I was celebrating the win at the registrar's office, but truly, my mind was focused on Isaac's words. Right now, I couldn't imagine opening my heart to another. Isaac was a good friend, and for now, that was enough.

CHAPTER 28

THE DAYS AFTER I FINISHED MY TEST WERE BOTH HAPPY AND sad. Happy that so many people wanted to study for the test themselves, and sad that Isaac was leaving. I knew his leaving was for the best. I needed more time to process my thoughts about life after Jasper. And I knew I wasn't ready for anything other than friendship. Isaac stopped by the store before leaving. Daddy came and shook his hand.

"Thank you for everything you have done in our community, son," Daddy said. "We'll keep up the work. And you take care of yourself."

"Thank you, sir," Isaac said. "I appreciate your kind words and I will do everything I can to be safe."

"Well, I will be over there putting some cans on the shelf." Daddy walked to the other side of the store, but he kept his eyes on us. I was happy he was there. I wanted him to see there was nothing inappropriate going on between Isaac and me.

"I'll write you regularly," Isaac said in a solemn voice.

"And I will pray for your continued healing from your losses."

"Thank you, Isaac. You will be missed."

"I've grown to love your Parsons, Georgia," he said with a smile. "There are some very good people here. I am happy to know you will continue with the work. Oh, I brought you something."

I felt my cheeks grow warm. "That wouldn't be appropriate, Isaac."

He pulled a book out of his bag and handed it to me. "It's the main sacred text Jewish people use to govern every part of our lives. It's called the Tanakh. I wanted you to have it. Just so you could see the similarities and differences between our two religions."

"Thank you, Isaac." I held it close. "I will read it. I promise."

"I should go," he said. "Take care, Rose." I watched as he turned and left the store. I felt like crying. I was going to miss having him around, especially at the study sessions that we were doing at our church since the Baptist church was bombed. The police insisted that it was faulty wiring, so as far as they were concerned, the case was closed.

The days after Isaac left moved at a snail's pace, but it helped to have the classes. It was strange. I went from being a student to helping people who were my age and the age of Grandma Perkins. Our numbers increased by dozens. So many wanted to get the right to vote. We had people from

DeKalb County, Gwinnett, and Rockdale all coming to our classes.

My mornings and my evenings were filled with those study sessions. We also had people like Miss Jainey accompanying folks when they went to take the test here in Henry County. One thing about Miss Jainey, she didn't take any back talk from the people at the voting registration office. She even started teaching integrated sewing classes. When I didn't have to work or teach voting registration classes, I would drop in for one of her classes. Staying busy kept my mind occupied, and I needed that. It wasn't long afterward that I received my first letter from Isaac.

I was happy to hear from him. It took a few weeks for his first letter to reach me. But I decided, before I opened his letter, I needed to read my husband's final letters to me first. I had kept them in a drawer in my bedroom. I would take them out and hold them, but I never read them. It all felt so final. Somehow, in my mind, reading those letters would signify something final about Jasper's death.

So I took all of Jasper's letters out of the dresser and walked down to the cemetery. I sat down to read them by Jasper and Olivia Rose's grave. The first two letters from Jasper were short. They didn't say much. It was clear he was in a hurry when he wrote them. He quickly told me about arriving at Wolters Air Force Base and what the conditions were like—mainly, it was hotter even than the worst days in Mississippi. He mentioned that he had spoken to his commanding officer about becoming a pilot, but he hadn't heard any more about it. By the end of the second letter, tears rolled down my face as I read his words aloud:

"I can't believe how much I miss you, Rose. Every day I wake up thinking about you and that baby in your belly, and every night I pretend like you are lying beside me. I promise you, I'm gonna do all I can to get back home to you alive. Whatever I have to do, I will do it, because I don't want anything more in this life but to be with you and our little girl."

When I finished reading, I almost thought my heart would break. I wished so desperately he could have fulfilled his promise to come home to me. I wasn't angry with him though. I knew if there was a way that he could have come back to me, he would have.

"You needed to go take care of our Olivia Rose," I whispered, stroking his name on the headstone. "She needed you more than I did, my love."

I wanted to run back to the house and fold up all of the letters and stuff them back down in the bottom of my dresser, but I knew I couldn't read another word from Isaac unless I read my husband's final words to me. I owed Jasper that much, no matter how much it might hurt. I looked at the third letter. I knew it was the one with Olivia Rose's name in it. I was slow to open it, but I made myself read it anyway, despite my sadness.

My dearest Rose,

I know we kept going back and forth on a name for our baby, but I hope you will consider this: Olivia Rose. My grandmother's name was Olivia. I always thought it was a beautiful name. Grandma Olivia was a kind-hearted woman. She was born a slave, not long before the

Civil War ended, and she worked herself to death picking cotton and tending to white families. Her entire life was about being in service to others. I never heard her utter a negative word about anyone. I think her name would be a good name for our baby. And, of course, I think she should carry your name too. I pray that you like this name. Already, in my dreams, she is Olivia Rose. I hope she can be the same in yours.

I dabbed at the tears falling down my face. I hadn't known the whole story about the name, but I was thankful that I had listened to my husband's request. Olivia Rose was the perfect name for our baby.

"Thank you for this name," I whispered, my tears baptizing the ground. I rubbed my fingers over Olivia Rose's name on the headstone, wishing like always that I could hold her once more. I still had the pictures Daddy took on the day she was born, but I couldn't look at them yet. These letters were hard enough. Seeing her lifeless body and the pain and sorrow on my face would be too much. I couldn't imagine a day when I would feel strong enough to look at those pictures.

Finally, I opened the last letter Jasper ever sent to me. I closed my eyes and prayed to God for strength. I needed to hear the words, so I read this letter out loud.

My dearest, darling Rose,

I miss you. I miss touching your belly, knowing that we made that baby from our love. I miss our lovemaking.

You made me feel like the most powerful man on earth. I thank you, my wife, for allowing me to be your husband. I need to say something to you before I fly off across the big water. I will move heaven and earth to come back to you whole, my love, but if for some reason the good Lord decides to take me home to live with him in Glory, I ask that you do three things for me, Rose. Live. Love. And laugh. Don't spend all your days pining for me. Fall in love and be happy. That is all I have ever wanted for you.

I absolutely plan to get back into your arms, but if I don't, I wanted you to know where I stood. You are my best friend and the love of my life. I pray for you every day and when I see you again, either on this side of life or the other, I will never let you go.

Eternally yours,

Jasper

I lay down on the grave and I cried. I cried bitter tears and, finally, tears of release. I knew, in that moment, if I ever wanted to heal, I had to properly say my goodbyes to Jasper and Olivia Rose and start the hard process of living again. In the words of Grandma Perkins, I had to rejoin the land of the living and recognize that both of them were nestled in the bosom of Abraham—free of pain and sorrow.

I kissed the headstone, pulled myself up, and started the walk home. When I reached the house, I went to the back porch and sat down in the swing. I hesitated only for a moment, and then I ripped open the letter from Isaac.

Dear Rose,

There is something surreal about being back in Mississippi. I had vowed never to return to this place, but the death of Medgar has created a hunger in the belly of so many people down here to vote and be counted. The authorities just arrested Byron De La Beckwith Jr. for Medgar's murder. I don't hold a lot of hope that he will be convicted, but I am hopeful that this case will bring attention to the cause and maybe prevent another such death from occurring. I have been hearing such great things about the work you all are continuing to do there in Parsons. Keep it up. This work we do truly is the work of the Almighty, I believe.

Best always,

Isaac

I went inside and grabbed an ink pen and some paper off the desk in my room.

Dear Isaac,

It's good hearing from you. I am so happy that the work is going well there. We have been following the news and it is alarming how much unrest is in this country, but especially in places like Mississippi, Alabama, and here. Just the other day, several SNCC field secretaries were arrested in Albany, Georgia, for attempting to enter Tift Park. Each day, some new atrocity occurs, but then something amazing will happen that makes us all stand in awe.

Every eligible voter in my immediate family is now

registered to vote, including Katie Bell and her husband. We all are excited about the next election, knowing for the first time that we will be able to cast our votes. These are such exciting times. Please, take care of yourself.

Sincerely,
Rose

PS: I have been reading the Tanakh. I'm currently reading Numbers. I've already made it through Genesis, Exodus, and Leviticus. I'm noticing the similarities in language as well as some of the differences. I look forward to discussing it with you when I see you next.

Ellena came into the room one day and found me reading the Tanakh.

"Are you converting?" she asked in a teasing voice.

I looked up and smiled. "No. Just learning."

"Learning is good. We can never learn too much."

I agreed. I was very interested in finding out how Jewish people and Christians became so different in their beliefs, especially since their Bibles were so similar. As I read, I would jot down questions in a notebook to ask Isaac the next time I saw him. *Why is the Tanakh broken up into sections? Why are there fewer books in the Tanakh than the Old Testament? Why are the books in the Tanakh organized differently than the books in the Old Testament?* It wasn't long before my notebook was filled to the brim with questions. Ellena started bringing me books to read about the Jewish religion, and from them, I had more questions.

Mama came into the room once while I was studying.

"Are you changing your mind about being a Christian?" she asked.

I looked at her face to see if she was angry or disappointed, but I didn't see anything but curiosity and concern.

"No, ma'am," I said. "I'm not converting to Judaism. I'm just curious, that's all."

"Nothing wrong with that," she said and left me to my books.

I was looking forward to the time when I could ask Isaac all my questions in person. He never called, which I think was a good thing. The letters were easier. I didn't have to worry about saying or doing something wrong. Sometimes, there were long stretches between letters. I tried not to pine for them. I tried to tell myself that it was just two friends swapping letters to update each other on what they were doing, but I knew in my heart it was more than that. At the end of July, I received another letter. I was in the kitchen washing dishes when Daddy walked in with it. He handed it to me, kissed me on my cheek, and walked out of the room. That was probably the closest Daddy would come to saying he was okay with me and Isaac writing each other. I ripped it open and began to read it slowly.

Dear Rose,

I apologize for taking so long to write you. I have missed you every single day. I think about you often. I write with exciting news. You may have already heard about it.

There will be a march taking place in Washington, DC, on August 28 of this year. I spoke to John Lewis on the phone, and he said he was helping to plan the event with A. Philip Randolph, Whitney Young, James Farmer, Martin Luther King Jr., and Roy Wilkins. Rose, I don't know how much you know about this historic event, but this is going to be revolutionary. I plan on being there if possible. I wondered if you and your family planned on attending?

Best always,

Isaac

I already knew what Daddy would say about us going, so I didn't even bring it up. Of course, Ellena begged and begged, but Daddy wouldn't budge. She pouted like she always did, but by the day of the march, she got over her saltiness and watched the march with the family. We saw many of the SNCC leaders, and when John Lewis spoke, I looked at Ellena beaming proudly at every word he uttered. Her crush on the young leader was evident to everyone. My brothers teased her until Mama told them to stop.

I paid close attention to Rabbi Uri Miller, who offered the prayer, and Rabbi Joachim Prinz, who spoke right before Dr. King gave his speech. I didn't see Isaac in the crowd, but I knew he had to be elated to see people from the Jewish community taking part in the event. When Dr. King spoke, you could have heard a pin drop in our house. Everyone was there, crowded into our living room. I looked at Grandma Perkins and she was in tears before Dr. King said his first word.

When he got to the "I have a dream" part of his speech,

there was not a dry eye in the room. From Lawrence to Daddy to all of the uncles, everyone was full of pride and emotion. We had never witnessed anything on television like that march.

"I've got to hand it to King," Daddy said, looking around the room, smiling at everyone. "He can speak like no other leader I have heard. We just might be looking at a future president of the United States."

Grandma Perkins laughed. "Now you must have bumped your head, Cedric. No way these white folks are gonna let a Negro be the president. I don't care how well he speaks."

"Grandma, the world is changing," Ellena said excitedly. "There is every reason for us to believe a Negro will be president someday. Mark my words: it will happen, and I think Dr. King would be perfect for the job."

"I'm not doubting his capabilities," Grandma Perkins said as she worked on some embroidery. "I'm just saying these white folks won't stand for it. Maybe a local mayor or city councilman. Not the president."

I decided to include this discussion in my next letter to Isaac. I wondered what he thought about it since he got to hear the speech firsthand.

Dear Isaac,

My family has been discussing the possibility of a Negro president someday. Daddy even thinks it could be Dr. King. It sounds phenomenal, but I can't imagine it ever happening. What do you think?

Sincerely,
Rose

Dear Rose,

Just a few short weeks ago, I would have said I doubt it, but after seeing Dr. King command the crowd in Washington, I have hope that one day we will see him raise his hand and take the oath of office, surrounded by Coretta and their children. That would definitely be a sight to see, and you must definitely go to Washington when it happens.

Best always,
Isaac

I held on to those words, but then, not even a month after the march, Addie Mae Collins, Cynthia Wesley, Carole Robertson, and Carol Denise McNair were brutally murdered in a bombing at 16th Street Baptist Church in Birmingham, Alabama. We were at church when someone called and told our church secretary what happened. She came out to the main sanctuary stunned, tears streaming down her face. The rest of that day felt like a funeral. I worried that we would never feel safe at church again. As grateful as we were that no one was injured when the Baptist church here in Parsons was bombed, the weight of it never lifted off us. Every Sunday I would sit and wonder, *Will it happen today? Will the evil seep into our midst this Sunday?*

Then, just a little over two months later, President John F. Kennedy was assassinated. Mama was inconsolable as she sat with all of us watching the funeral. Most of the time she wept with her head pressed against Daddy's chest. It was hard to believe that President Kennedy was gone. We had never had a president like him before. We'd never had a First Lady like Jackie before. They brought something to the presidency we had never seen and doubted we would ever see again. I wrote Isaac on the same day of Kennedy's funeral, but I didn't hear from him until mid-December, and most of his letter was questions.

How can they hate us so, Rose? How can they kill four innocent children? How do we survive losing the greatest leader this nation has ever known? How do we keep fighting when their hate for us is so strong?

I wanted desperately to have some words of comfort, but I had none.

> This world does not make sense to me, Isaac. The hatred is everywhere. I'm not sure how we can ever recover from the trauma of losing our leader in such a horrendous way. I try to pray for everyone, including the ones who do terrible things, but it is so hard. All I want to do is wish bad things on them, but then that will mean I am no better. I pray for you to find peace.
>
> Sincerely,
> Rose

After I sent that letter, I did not hear from Isaac again. At first I was afraid something had happened to him, but Ellena checked with John and he said Isaac was still working in Mississippi. As much as it saddened me not to hear from him again, I decided that I was not going to allow myself to wallow in sadness. Instead, I got about the business of applying to the nursing school in Atlanta.

The process for getting into school was extensive. I had

to complete an admissions exam and an in-person interview with the admissions office at Spelman. When I finally got that letter inviting me to attend Grady Memorial Hospital School of Nursing, I cried like a baby. I kept saying to myself I didn't care if it happened, but when it did, I was the happiest I had been in a mighty long time. My first year of studies would all take place at Spelman; in my second year I'd begin doing my clinical work in the medical and surgical wards at Grady Memorial Hospital.

Daddy bragged that he had two girls attending Spelman. Mama was quieter. I knew she was going to miss having me around, but I could tell she was proud too. My siblings teased me about being a late bloomer, but they all chipped in and bought me my very own stethoscope. The twins said we would open up the Birdie Pruitt Medical Clinic in Parsons once we finished. When Mama heard them say that, I thought she would never stop crying and laughing all at the same time.

That night when I sat on the back porch looking up at the stars, Great-Grandma Birdie's star shined brighter than I had ever seen it shine before, and I imagined that somewhere in the heavens she was smiling, pleased with how her family had turned out.

CHAPTER 29

"HEY, ROSE," A GIRL FROM MY INTRODUCTION TO THE ART OF Nursing course called out to me as I was walking across the Spelman campus. "We're all getting together later to study. Do you want to join us?"

"I can't," I said with a smile, swinging my book bag over my shoulder. "I'm meeting up with Ellena shortly. Maybe tomorrow?"

"Sure," she said. "Have fun."

I watched as the girl—I think her name was Kimberly—ran off to join some of the others in our class. I still had to pinch myself at the idea of me being a nursing student at Spelman.

I looked across the schoolyard and saw Ellena waving at me. I hurried toward her and as always, we hugged like we hadn't just seen each other that morning. I was wearing a Columbia blue skirt and a white, high-necked ruffled shirt. I thought it quite nice that Spelman's school colors were blue and white. It felt like yet another sign that I was doing the right thing by being in college. I could just hear Jasper say how nice I looked in blue. Thinking about him didn't cause sadness for me like before. I was able to manage my emotions and think about him and Olivia Rose with joy that I had been so fortunate to have them in my life even for such a brief period of time.

"Hey, Sissy," Ellena said. "How were classes?"

"Complicated," I said wryly. "Our teacher goes out of her way to teach things in a convoluted manner. Thank God I have a good memory for details, or I would be woefully behind. How was your day, and why were you so gung ho about meeting for lunch?"

She linked her arm with mine. "Because I never see my big sister anymore. I miss you, so I figured I would make an appointment."

I laughed. "We see each other every day and we sleep in the same bedroom at Cousin Florence and Cousin Hiram's house. If we saw each other any more than we do, we would be joined at the hip. What are you up to?"

"Nothing," she said. "Let's go."

"Okay then." I gave her a sideways look. She and I looked more like each other since she had grown her hair back out again from the short pixie cut she had worn for the last year. "Is Larry going to join us?"

I watched as she blushed. She had finally given up her crush on John Lewis. He never saw her as more than a close friend. He even introduced her to Larry, a recent graduate of Morehouse and an assistant pastor at Friendship Baptist Church. I had thought Mama and Daddy would have an issue with her dating a Baptist preacher, but when they came to visit a few weeks ago and got the chance to meet him, they had nothing but good things to say.

"No, ma'am," she said. "Larry is not going to have lunch with us. This is a sister's lunch only. And we're going to Paschal's."

I should have known she would pick one of the most well-attended restaurants by those in The Movement. But if it meant having lunch with my sister and eating some of their world-famous fried chicken, well, I was game. I followed her to the car Daddy had bought for the two of us to share. Cousin Hiram and Cousin Florence had graciously allowed us to use one of their cars, but Daddy said his girls needed their own vehicle. We were now the proud owners of a green 1960 Chevrolet Corvair. Ellena did most of the driving, but I was learning. I hopped in the passenger side and Ellena started the short drive to Paschal's. Normally, she was bending my ear with some SNCC news or the latest updates about her and Larry, but this time, she was quiet. I didn't question it. I was tired from a late night of studying, so I welcomed the silence. When we got out at the restaurant, she was hanging behind. I turned to look at her.

"What are you dawdling for, Ellena? I thought you were hungry."

"Umm, I am, but I need to get something. Why don't you go inside and save us a seat? I need to get something out of the trunk."

"I can wait. There's no need for me leaving you here on the street. Just hurry up and get whatever it is."

"No," she said decisively. "You go. I'll be right behind you."

"You sure are acting funny." I didn't feel like arguing with her. It was hot outside, and all I wanted to do was get somewhere cool. I went inside and looked around for an empty table. As I scanned the room, my eyes fell on Isaac walking toward me. I couldn't breathe. Seeing him after all this time and so unexpectedly left me speechless. He stepped closer and pulled me into an embrace. It was the first time he and I had ever hugged. I should have felt embarrassed, but I didn't. I should have felt guilty, but I didn't. I had made peace with Jasper. I would always love him, but I was ready to see what the next chapter of my life was going to look like. As I looked at Isaac standing before me, I prayed it would involve him.

"You stopped writing me," I whispered. "I thought you changed your mind."

"There's no way I could change my mind about you, Rose," he said, brushing a lock of hair out of my face. "I've been a mess, and I didn't want to just keep writing you sad, depressing letters. I spent the summer back in New York with my family, trying to figure out what I want to do with my life, but the one thing I did know without a doubt is I wanted to see you, be with you, love you, Rose. Nothing has changed for me. What about with you?"

I looked up at him and smiled. "I'm glad you are here. I've missed you."

"Do you think you could have feelings for me, too, some-day?" he asked tentatively. It was strange hearing Isaac, the most confident person I had ever met, sound so indecisive and unsure of himself. It endeared him to me even more.

"Yes, I already do have feelings for you, Isaac. It just

took me time to heal from losing my first love. I will always love Jasper, but there is room for you, if you don't mind him always having a special place in my heart."

"I don't mind," he said. "From all that you have shared with me about Jasper, he was a very good man and one who is worthy to be loved as long as you have breath. Are you hungry?"

I shook my head. "Not really."

He took me by the hand. "Then let's go. I want to go somewhere where I can kiss you properly."

I felt myself blush, but I was just as eager as he was to share a kiss. Our first kiss. There was still a lot that we had to work through—our religious differences, my desire to be a nurse, and his desire to work in The Movement—but one thing I knew for sure was we would figure it all out. Together.

AUTHOR'S NOTE

Dear Reader,

THERE IS NO TIME IN HISTORY THAT WE NEED TO REVISIT AND learn about the past more than now. When I started writing *Homeward*, I wasn't doing the math that my novel would come out around the 60th anniversary of so many historical events like the assassination of Medgar Evers; the March on Washington; the bombing of the Sixteenth Street Baptist church killing four little girls (Addie May Collins, Carol Denise McNair, Cynthia Wesley, Carole Robertson); and the assassination of President John F. Kennedy. Because I am a lover of history, but especially 20th century American history, those historical events live in my mind constantly. But I realized, from the interactions I was having with my students as a college professor, that the historical details I wrote about in this book and other books, are fading from the collective memory, especially because so many in this country want us to pretend like United States history is pristine and free of all things contentious.

I am happy that this book will remind some and enlighten others about this time in our not-so-distant past. I am happy that people will get to read about people they know of like Dr. Martin Luther King, Jr. and John Lewis, but that they will also encounter people they might not know like Ralph D. Abernathy, Sr., Charlayne Hunter, Joseph Lowery, and Judy Richardson. Because my daddy was determined that I knew my history, these people felt like older aunties and uncles in my head, but when I would mention them to my students, they would look at me with blank expressions on their faces. I am grateful that this book will bring some of these historical figures back to the forefront of the minds of those who pick up this book.

My research for writing this book was extensive. I am grateful to all of the old newspapers and magazines from that era, and I am also grateful to the following books: *Freedom Riders* by Raymond Arsenault, *In Struggle: SNCC and the Black Awakening of the 1960s* by Clayborne Carson, *Parting the Waters: America in the King Years, 1954-1963*, by Tylor Branch, *Lighting the Fires of Freedom: African American women in the Civil Rights Movement* by Janet Dewart Bell, *Lovesong: Becoming a Jew* by Julius Lester, *Becoming Jewish: A Handbook for Conversion* by Rabbi Ronald H. Isaacs, *The African American Experience in Vietnam: Brothers in Arms* by James E. Westheider.

I would also like to thank my late uncle, M.J. McCall, for all the stories he used to tell me about his time as a Marine during the Vietnam War. His stories were difficult to listen to, but my understanding of that time would not have been complete without the many narratives he shared.

Also, thank you to Paw Paw Joel for remembering and sharing. I know that time in your life was difficult. I appreciate you going there with me through memory anyway.

This book includes many factual events, but it also includes some fictional ones, such as the sermon by Dr. King. I did not want to use an actual sermon, so I studied *I Have a Dream: Writings and Speeches That Changed the World* by Martin Luther King, Jr. Obviously, I am no Dr. King, but I did my best to approximate his ideas in my purely fabricated sermon.

I hope this book sparks dialogue on this 60th anniversary of so many amazing, historical events. My one hope is that sixty years from this date we will have become the people Dr. King and others dreamed about.

ACKNOWLEDGMENTS

TODAY, I WRITE THIS ACKNOWLEDGEMENT ON THE SIXTH ANNI-versary of my mother's passing. Mom is always with me, but especially today. Six days from now, I will be remembering my dad, M.C. Jackson, who passed away on May 3, 2004. Even though the two of them never met (figure out that puzzle, why don't you), they have been so influential in all that I do. Their spirits are always hovering close by, keeping watchful eyes on me.

I would like to thank my best friend and husband, Robert L. Brown, for always supporting me with his quiet presence. Without his support, I would not be able to be Angela Jackson-Brown. He freely releases me to the fictional universes I create, and he never makes me feel guilty for the time I spend there. I love you, honey. You always make this free spirit feel even freer.

I also want to thank my son, Justin. You are your mama's heartbeat . . . a constant source of pride. I love you even more than I did the day I looked into your eyes and saw my eyes looking back at me. You are an amazing son. Thank you for being you.

Acknowledgments

Thank you to my beta readers and friends, Lauren, Libby, and Elaine. Your opinions mean everything to me because I know you three love books as much as I do. I appreciate you so very much.

This book would not have happened without my phenomenal agent, Alice Speilburg. You always know the right things to say to calm me and keep me focused on the work before me. I value you as a business partner and a friend. I can't wait to see where this writing takes us next.

Finally, thank you to the amazing team at Harper Muse. You all are an author's dream, starting with my dynamic editor, Kimberly. Your support and encouragement keep me going, and I appreciate you for loving these characters and helping me to tell their stories the best way possible. I would also like to thank the rest of the editorial, sales, and marketing team but especially Amanda, Becky, Jodi, Savannah, Kerri, Nekasha, Patrick, Margaret, and Taylor.

DISCUSSION QUESTIONS

1. *Homeward* begins with controversy. In what ways does the initial news Rose has to share with her family affect your opinion of her?
2. Discuss the mourning practices illustrated in *Homeward*. Do they feel familiar or different from the ways you or people from your community mourn death?
3. In James Baldwin's 1963 book, *The Fire Next Time*, he addresses what he views as "the detriment of Christianity to the Black community." In comparison, how would you describe this author's depiction of the Black church in *Homeward*?
4. Depictions of the Civil Rights Movement are often misleading, such as the level of support from members of the Black community. Evidence shows that many members of the Black community were hesitant to support Dr. King and members of the Student Nonviolent Coordinating Committee

(SNCC). When you saw that Rose's family was hesitant to get involved, what were your thoughts and how did their hesitancy measure up with what you knew or didn't know about that time in history?

5. Opal and Cedric were teenagers in *When Stars Rain Down*. How has their love evolved over time, and how has that love affected the relationships their children have with their spouses, specifically Rose?

6. Often, the women of the Civil Rights Movement are omitted or downplayed. In what ways did the author highlight those women in *Homeward*?

7. Discuss how historical events like the assassination of Medgar Evers affected the civil rights efforts taking place in Parsons, Georgia.

8. Rose finds herself falling in love with a nice Jewish boy. Although their relationship is not explored fully in this book, what are your thoughts about their relationship? Do you think they will still be together twenty years into the future?

9. HBCUs were integral to the Civil Rights Movement. What are your thoughts about the depiction of these young movers and shakers? Were you surprised by their involvement, or did this novel confirm what you already knew?

10. The Vietnam War was still in its infancy in this novel. What did this story reveal to you about the role poverty played in the enlistment of men in the military both then and even now?

ABOUT THE AUTHOR

Ankh Productions LLC—Photography by Chandra Lynch

ANGELA JACKSON-BROWN IS AN AWARD-WINNING WRITER, poet, and playwright who is an Associate Professor in Creative Writing at Indiana University in Bloomington, IN and a member of the graduate faculty of the Naslund-Mann Graduate School of Writing at Spalding University in Louisville, KY.

Angela is a graduate of Troy University, Auburn University, and the Spalding low-residency MFA program in creative writing. She has published her short fiction, creative nonfiction, and poetry in journals like the Louisville *Courier Journal* and *Appalachian Review*. She is the author of *Drinking from a Bitter Cup*, *House Repairs*, *When Stars Rain Down*, and *The Light Always Breaks*.

angelajacksonbrown.com
Instagram: @angelajacksonbrownauthor
Twitter: @adjackson68